# THE CYCLE OF THE
# RED MOON

# THE CYCLE OF THE
# RED MOON

## BOOK TWO:
## THE CHILDREN OF
# DARKNESS

## José Antonio Cotrina

DARK HORSE BOOKS
Milwaukie, OR

Book design by Sarah Terry
Cover painting by Fiona Hsieh
Translation by Katie LaBarbera with Gabriella Campbell

Special thanks to Gabriella Campbell, Ervin Rustemagić,
Jemiah Jefferson, Annie Gullion, Adam Pruett, and Patrick Satterfield.

Published by Dark Horse Books
A division of Dark Horse Comics LLC
10956 SE Main Street
Milwaukie, OR 97222

DarkHorse.com
SAFComics.com

First edition: February 2021
ISBN 978-1-50671-944-3
Printed in the United States of America

1   3   5   7   9   10   8   6   4   2

Library of Congress Cataloging-in-Publication Data

Names: Cotrina, José Antonio, 1972- writer. | LaBarbera, Katie,
    translator.
Title: The cycle of the red moon / written by José Antonio Cotrina ;
    translated by Kate LaBarbera.
Other titles: Ciclo de la luna roja. English
Description: Milwaukie, OR : Dark Horse Books, 2021. | Volume 1: The
    harvest of Samhein -- Volume 2: The children of darkness -- Volume 3:
    The shadow of the moon | Audience: Ages 12+ | Audience: Grades 10-12 |
    Summary: Twelve teenagers from Earth fall under the spell of a demigod
    and are transported to a dangerous and mystical realm where they must
    survive until the Red Moon returns.
Identifiers: LCCN 2020030658 | ISBN 9781506716800 (v. 1 ; paperback) | ISBN
    9781506719443 (v. 2 ; paperback)
Subjects: CYAC: Fantasy.
Classification: LCC PZ7.1.C67475 Cy 2021 | DDC [Fic]--dc23
LC record available at https://lccn.loc.gov/2020030658

# TABLE OF CONTENTS

This one's still for my sister.

And soon there will be nothing left but the abyss.

—*Mirror in the Mirror*, Michael Ende

# PROLOGUE
# THE STORY SO FAR

Every year, on the night of Samhein, the portal that connects Earth with Rocavarancolia opens, allowing Denestor Tul to cross into the human world in search of select individuals useful to the kingdom. On this occasion he returns with twelve teenagers, the most promising harvest of recent times. One of the chosen, Hector, exhibits great potential, and is said by Old Belisarius to embody "the essence of kings."

Against the kingdom's decree, two members of the Royal Council interfere in the harvest's arrival in Rocavarancolia. They know better than to leave everything in the hands of fate—if not a single teenager survives when the Red Moon comes out, the kingdom will perish. Lady Scar casts a spell on Hector, granting him the ability to detect the city's danger zones, thereby avoiding them. Mistral, the shapeshifter, is more discreet: he assassinates one of the boys and infiltrates the group in order to help them from inside. If either of the two is discovered, all will be lost. The harvest will be considered tainted and every one of them will be killed. And that will be the end of Rocavarancolia.

Most of the teenagers join as a group to face the risks they might encounter in the city. Only one decides to go alone, a young boy from São Paulo whose essence, according to the analysis, is the second strongest of the harvest, after Hector's.

Soon the mysteries that surround the city and their place within it take form. Why are they needed in Rocavarancolia? What's special about them? They're just a handful of normal, ordinary teenagers—or so it would seem, on the surface. There's much more to them than meets the eye. Hector learns that Natalia, a Russian girl, sees beings that the others cannot. And there's something strange about Marina, another of the harvested: the stories that she wrote on Earth resemble Rocavarancolia to an eerie degree. And what about Bruno, the Italian, who's as cold and expressionless as a robot?

The group manage to survive their first day in the ruined city and take refuge in the Margalar Tower, a well-protected structure. Of course, it was Mistral who led them there.

The days go by. The mood is tense, and if it weren't for Alexander, an Australian boy with a sense of humor and a striking personality, the situation would be even more distressing. Even so, Adrian, the group's youngest member, is so terrified that he refuses to leave the tower. He has his reasons. The day he finally works up the nerve to join the others in search of food, they have a confrontation with a solitary boy, who without provocation attacks Adrian with a sword. They carry him, severely wounded, back to the Margalar Tower. Shortly after, Natalia's life is jeopardized when she is poisoned by one of the many creatures that wander the ruins.

Mistral watches as everything falls apart. He hasn't been able to keep Rocavarancolia from slaughtering them. If he does nothing, the wounded will die, and the others will follow. So he makes a decision: to secure the group's chances of survival, he sacrifices Alexander. He leads the boy to one of the city's enchanted towers, where a fatal spell cast upon the entrance engulfs him. His friends are powerless to save him and can do nothing but accompany him in his final moments. But his death is not in vain: once aware of the spell's existence, Bruno is able to neutralize it with the help of Rachel, a girl impervious to magic.

That same night, the group enters the tower. Rocavarancolia is a cruel city that has already shown its willingness to do everything to destroy them. If they want to survive, they're going to need a miracle. And that's what they believe the tower possesses: magic.

Alex isn't the only one to die in the city that day. In the castle atop the mountains, Old Belisarius's corpse is discovered. Does his death have anything to do with the plots of Lady Scar and Esmael, Lord of Assassins of Rocavarancolia, who both scheme to gain the position of regent? Denestor Tul visits Lady Dream, an ancient sorceress, who shows him a terrible vision:

*You can't hear it, can you? Roaring, death, battle. Blood, fire, and dragons. Don't you hear them? Oh, my marvelous demiurge. You still don't know what you've brought us from the human realm . . .*

*You've brought us the end.*

# FIVE WEEKS LATER

The hyena snapped its jaws barely an inch from his arm. The bite resounded like an enormous trap closing shut. Hector rolled on the ground to escape the attack, gathered momentum, and sprung forward, sword in hand. His counterattack wasn't precise or elegant, but the weapon's flat blade delivered a splendid blow to the hyena's snout. It retreated, snarling, with long threads of drool hanging from its twisted fangs.

A second hyena attacked him from the left. Marco intervened and stopped it with such a violent blow from his shield that it was sent flying several feet away. The German boy snorted and looked at him, panting.

"Everything okay?" he asked.

Hector nodded and leapt toward the first hyena just as it charged a second time. The sword sank into the animal's right side. It wasn't a very deep cut, but it was enough that the beast turned and fled with a long strip of Hector's shirt in its jaws. Hector gasped at the sight, then looked down and confirmed that his shirt had been torn up to his stomach. It must have happened in that last attack. He'd been so ready to fight that he'd let down his defenses. He was lucky to have gotten away with nothing more than a torn shirt.

He looked around, prepared to repel another attack, although at the moment he seemed to be out of danger. Ricardo, Marco, and Natalia suffered the brunt of the attack a few yards ahead, at the gates to the corral where most of the hyenas dwelled. The three of them seemed able to contain the animals for now. Natalia and Ricardo had improved greatly in the last few weeks; the Russian girl's elegant maneuvering with the halberd was impressive, and Ricardo was not far behind with his sword. But Marco exceeded them all by far. His movements were so fluid and agile that the others appeared frozen in comparison. With each of his blows, an animal fell. And very few of them got back up.

They were fighting in the cellars of a small amphitheater located halfway between the Margalar Tower and the cliffs to the east. They'd spent a week exploring the area, and not a single day had gone by without the hyenas pestering them. They'd attacked in small groups, and truthfully, the teenagers hadn't had problems fighting them off, but the persistence of the attacks prompted the kids to go after the animals. But they didn't expect to encounter so many—the amphitheater was infested with them. Hector wasn't surprised by the thick black mist that surrounded the area.

Marina was now at their back. She turned slowly from side to side, trying to cover them from all angles. On the ground lay five animals shot down by her arrows. Suddenly, another hyena emerged from behind a block of stone dislodged from the wall. It was heading straight for them with its head down, growling viciously. The girl had to shoot twice to stop it. The first arrow went high, but the second struck clean in the throat. The animal fell on its side midleap and, after skidding several feet across the ground, was motionless. Marina nocked another arrow on her bow and stepped back to climb up the base of a short column.

A little further behind were Bruno, Rachel, and Lizbeth. Lizbeth averted her gaze every few minutes, horrified by the fight; Rachel, on the other hand, only laughed and cheered on her companions. Hector knew that if she could have, she would have readily joined the fight. Bruno was a step ahead of them. In his right hand he brandished a staff of green wood topped with a small birdcage of sorts, while he kept his left hand inside the bundle that hung from his side; the Italian must have used up the energy from all of the pendants and rings that he wore, so he had to resort to the amulets he kept in reserve. There were seven paralyzed hyenas on the path between them and the gate, all covered in a fine, viscous film. One was frozen midjump; it floated in the air with its jaws open and its left paw stretched forward.

Bruno panted and Hector knew he was at his limit. He signaled to Marina to move closer to the group at the rear, which needed the most protection.

At that moment they heard a piercing whistle from the cellar. The hyenas raised their heads in unison and retreated. The whistle blew a second time. And a third. Then they heard a frenzied voice that seemed to come from underground.

"No! No! Have mercy! Please! No!" A trapdoor opened between two corrals and a scrawny man emerged with long blond hair and a tangled beard, waving his arms frantically above his head. He was dressed in a long black fur jacket and pants made from hide. A wooden whistle hung from a chain around his neck. "Stop! Stop! No! No more harm! No! Please! No!"

Marina aimed her bow at the stranger.

"Stop!" Marco exclaimed. A large group of hyenas had moved between them and the newcomer.

The man knelt down at the foot of a dead hyena and cried in desperation. It was impossible to guess his age.

"Murderers! Murderers!" he shouted. He took the creature's broken face and cradled it in his hands, which were covered with scars and poorly healed bites. "Cruel and murderous children! Monsters!"

"Are they yours? These creatures are yours?" Ricardo asked. He approached the stranger, brandishing his sword in a threatening manner. Hector could see that one of his friend's sleeves was torn and covered with blood. He was wounded, but either he didn't realize it or he didn't care.

The man opened his eyes wide as he watched him approach. The hyenas held firm around him, growling and snapping at the air, ready to attack if Ricardo took one step closer. Mistral rushed in to stop him. He took him by the arm and pulled him back unceremoniously. The shapeshifter knew the little man sobbing with the dead hyena in his arms and didn't want them to hurt him. It was Caleb, the son of the amphitheater's deceased caretaker. He'd been born shortly after the war's end and had always been crazy. Those creatures were everything to him.

"Easy, Ricardo," he said. "The guy seems harmless."

"What?" he looked at him, perplexed. "Harmless? Didn't you see him? Those things obey him! He must have ordered them to attack us!"

"So what are you going to do? Kill him?"

Ricardo's expression grew even more perplexed. He lowered his eyes to the bloody sword that he wielded and shook his head.

"No! Caleb no order! Not attack!" reassured the prostrate man. He looked at Marco with tears in his eyes, almost begging. "The young ones leave, hunt, and come back . . . Not attack! They play outside! They only play!" He let the lifeless body fall so that he could embrace the bristled back of one of the creatures protecting him.

Hector shuddered. It was true that most of the hyenas that had attacked them weren't as big as the ones taking a stand in the cellar. Maybe they'd made a mistake?

"Can you control them?" Marco asked. "Can you stop them from attacking us?"

Caleb nodded like one possessed. His enormous blue eyes were the only part of his face that remained visible through the chaotic tangle that formed his beard and hair.

"If they go, I will go with them. Caleb promises and swears. No more attacks," he assured. "Caleb will be very careful. Caleb will be careful. Please, please . . . Don't kill Caleb . . . Don't kill his children . . ."

"Let me talk to him," Bruno said.

"He's just an idiot," Ricardo warned. "You won't get anything out of him."

The hyenas' growls increased as the Italian approached Caleb. They were everywhere. Close to fifty of them were scattered throughout the area. Bruno leaned in close to the little man, who still hadn't stopped crying. The hyenas growled only inches away from his face, but he didn't bat an eye.

"Do you know who we are?" he asked. Caleb nodded. His lower lip trembled.

"The harvest, the kids of Samhein. Good kids, good kids . . . Don't kill Caleb. Don't hurt his children. Have mercy. Please. Mercy . . ."

"If you don't answer my questions, we will kill every last one of your little monsters. We won't spare a single one. Do you understand?" Bruno's lack of expression made his threat all the more imposing. "Do you understand?"

Caleb's terrified face was enough of a response.

"Do you know why we've been brought here?" the Italian asked.

"Caleb doesn't know anything," he whimpered. "Caleb just takes care of his children. Nobody talks to Caleb, and Caleb doesn't talk to anybody."

"If you're lying to me . . ."

"It's not a lie! Caleb's telling the truth! I swear and promise! The kids of Samhein come and die quickly. We hardly ever see them. We don't know what they do, or what they want! We just want them to leave us alone and not hurt us . . ." He returned his gaze to Marco, desperate. "Don't hurt us . . . Please . . . Don't hurt us."

"What happens when the Red Moon comes out?"

The celestial body had become an obsession for them. As if watching the ten-pointed star advance day by day toward the red point of the sphere didn't make them anxious enough, throughout their time in Rocavarancolia they hadn't been able to avoid running into representations of the moon. They found it in engravings and tapestries, on coats of arms, embroidered in rugs . . . The Red Moon was everywhere. One painting in particular found in a ramshackle mansion made Hector's hair stand on end: it depicted a multitude of strange creatures kneeling in a barren wasteland, worshiping an immense scarlet moon which rose over a city that could only be Rocavarancolia.

Caleb shook his head, still sobbing.

"I don't know. I don't know. I don't know . . . I hide when the big moon comes out. I go down to the catacombs and lock myself in for days. The big moon isn't good. It's no good. The city trembles. The animals scream. And I scream with them, and I'm so afraid . . ."

"It's no use, Bruno," Marina said. "Leave him alone. He doesn't know anything. All you're doing is scaring him."

The Italian nodded, turned, and took a step back.

"Lock them up," he ordered Caleb.

The man stumbled to his feet, nodding over and over. He brought the whistle to his lips and blew it several times. The hyenas started going into the corral, without taking their eyes off the group.

The odor of dampness and huddled beasts was suffocating. Three corrals took up the interior curve of the cellar, all with wooden gates of varying height and thickness, and an endless number of cages were piled up against the walls. Between the columns were glimpses of what looked to be the remains of primitive elevators and trapdoors, identical to the one that Caleb had used. The walls were covered with mosaics. Most of the pieces were in ruins, but one of them was in better condition than the others; it showed an impressive warrior in dark armor, escorted by several armored hyenas with spiked helmets. The warrior grasped a scimitar in his left hand and held a set of chains fastened to the beasts.

"Is everyone okay?" Marco asked, once the hyenas were shut in the corrals.

They all nodded except for Ricardo, who stepped forward, raising a hand to his wounded arm without touching it.

"One of them gave me a good swipe. I didn't see it coming."

Little remained in Ricardo of his earlier confidence. After Alexander's death, he had washed his hands completely of the group's leadership, leaving it entirely to Marco. Although he hadn't spoken openly about it, Hector knew that he felt responsible for what happened.

Bruno made Ricardo sit down and crouched next to him, with his backpack open at his feet. He carefully removed the torn sleeve to uncover the wound. It was quite dramatic, a deep gash that stretched from his shoulder to his elbow. Ricardo gasped and looked away, his face ashen.

"Do you want me to do it?" Natalia asked Bruno, leaning on her halberd.

The Italian shook his head and rummaged through the bag until he retrieved a charged talisman. He took out a lion figurine, carved out of brass and hung on a long iron chain. He enclosed it in his fist, threw his head back, and began to softly sing a chant that Hector was starting to know very well.

He hadn't forgotten the chill he'd felt the first time he saw Bruno cast that spell. Adrian lay immobile in bed, more dead than alive, his eyes half-closed and that awful wound exposed. He was hardly breathing. The Italian had gathered all of the charged magic crystals they had and, holding them in his left hand, had begun to hum the same incantation that he now sang, continuously waving his right hand. The spell took effect on the third try. An amber light bathed Bruno's hands before he extended them over the wounded boy's body. They all watched, astonished by how the stomach wound closed little by little, and how the purple and blackened skin around it became pink by the minute. That process lasted a few instants, until Adrian sat up in bed with a force and speed that frightened them. His eyes bulged from their sockets.

"The horses! Get the horses! Can't you hear them? Can't you see them? They're on fire! They're burning!" he yelled. Immediately afterward he collapsed again, and the light that surrounded him dissipated.

Curing Adrian exhausted Bruno considerably. The young man breathed with difficulty and was drenched in sweat. When he stood up they had to support him so he wouldn't fall. Marina and Ricardo tried to cast the same spell on Natalia, but despite following the book's precise instructions, they were unsuccessful. Then it was Hector's turn. He intoned the magic chant as best he could while he performed the appropriate movements, one eye on the book and the other on Natalia. Halfway through the spell he noticed something coming to a boil inside of him, an inexplicable current that tried to reach his fingertips. It didn't work; the fire was weak and diffused halfway.

Finally they had no choice but to wait for Bruno to recover. After he cast the spell, with that amber haze bathing Natalia's entire body, the Italian passed out. It took so long for him to wake up that they worried something had gone wrong. Only later did it become clear that extreme weakness was a side effect from using magic. Sorcery turned out to be more demanding and exhausting than they'd imagined. They learned over the following days that for most of them, it was out of reach. Of all who tried a spell, only Natalia was successful.

Ricardo's wound also began healing before their eyes. In a few moments, the only trace that remained was the blood on his clothing. Bruno panted and stood up, weak but calm.

"Are you okay?" Natalia asked him.

"A few minutes, give me a few minutes to catch my breath . . ." He let the amulet drop from his hand into the sack.

"Good kids of Samhein. Good kids." Caleb had knelt down next to a paralyzed hyena. He patted its side and looked at Hector imploringly. "You no leave them like this, right?"

"Don't worry, they'll recover in time," he said. The little man remained devastated. "They attacked us, right? They've been doing it for days, you can't blame us for defending ourselves."

Caleb shrugged his shoulders and looked at the ground.

"Can I cure the ones that are wounded?" Natalia asked Marco. She looked at a hyena who whimpered at the gates of a corral, its hindquarters soaked with blood.

"Oh!" Caleb's face lit up. "Good girl! Precious girl! Big heart and soul!" He got up halfway and approached Natalia almost on his knees. He took her hand and brought it to his cheek. The Russian girl made a face and pulled it away before he could kiss it.

"You make sure that they don't bite me," she warned.

"Just a few minutes . . ." Bruno murmured, sitting on the ground, still out of breath. "Just a few minutes and I'll help you."

"It's all right," Marco agreed. "But only cure the most gravely injured. We can't risk you wearing yourselves out. Tomorrow we can come back to cure the others."

"Blessed kids!" Caleb dragged himself toward Marco, who stepped back to avoid being touched. "Good, holy kids!"

"If any of them bite me . . ." Natalia said as she shook her halberd before her.

"No, Caleb promises and swears, no, no . . ." he insisted. "They won't bite, no, no . . ."

Hector looked with a furrowed brow at the bizarre little man who kept kneeling before them. He wasn't the first inhabitant that they'd run into on their expeditions. Only a few days before, they'd crossed paths with a scrawny man with straight blond hair who carried a pair of harpoons across his back and a good-sized barrel in his arms; he had observed them with limited curiosity before he continued on his way. It was obvious that Rocavarancolia wasn't as uninhabited as it had first seemed.

Natalia was able to cure two hyenas before exhausting the energy of the talismans as well as her own. Four wounded animals remained, only one seriously injured, with a considerable gash on its stomach. Bruno tended to it once he recovered. Meanwhile, the rest took to wandering the cellars, taking care to keep away from the corrals and their occupants.

"Hey," Marina called. She stood next to the line of cages and pointed to them. "This one's full of junk. Come take a look."

"They're my things," Caleb said quickly, coming toward them hurriedly. "Things that I find and keep. Nothing valuable. Nothing that would interest the kids of Samhein, I'm sure. They're silly things."

The group neared the cages. There were twelve of them, all filled with the most diverse objects: pieces of armor, bits of multicolored furniture, small sculptures, frames from paintings and windows, fragments of stained glass . . . They even saw a silver harp with broken strings. The only quality these objects had in common was their abundance in color. The predominant tone of Rocavarancolia was stone gray, but this proved there had been light and color in the city's past.

"How pretty," Marina said, stroking the neck of a marbled jade swan through the bars.

"Pretty? No! Stupid shiny things, that's all," assured Caleb, as he anxiously wrung his hands. "That's all. Silly things for silly Caleb. Nothing to interest the good kids of Samhein . . ."

"We're not going to take them from you," Hector said. He'd grabbed a hand mirror with a gold frame and now he studied it, bewildered. The glass had been shattered and his reflection was fragmented and multiplied. There were no mirrors in the Margalar Tower, and it had been weeks since he'd seen his face. He was surprised to see that it wasn't as round as he remembered. In addition, his hair had grown a fair amount and, to his surprise, there was the shadow of an almost imperceptible mustache above his upper lip, more fuzz than actual hair.

*And who the hell are you?* he asked the stranger in the mirror. *I don't know you. Who are you?*

"What's this?" he heard Ricardo ask.

He had removed two long cylindrical objects from the cages that vaguely resembled telescopes. They were tubes of multicolored wood about three feet in length, with golden caps screwed on the ends. Ricardo unscrewed one of them, and immediately several scrolls slid out partway. Once he saw them, Bruno rushed over, eager to add any document or book to his growing library of magic.

Ricardo tried to unfurl one of the enormous sheets in front of him, but it was so unmanageable he could only hold the top section open. The parchment was divided into three columns, with characters in red ink and various illustrations scattered throughout the document. One of them depicted several men on horseback in front of the ramparts of a black-walled city. In another, a group of demonic beings seemed to be throwing themselves off a cliff, and the smiles on their faces suggested they were happy to do it. The pictures weren't very reassuring.

"It's not written in the language that we know," Ricardo said. "Wait . . . Yes . . ." He squinted. "It's similar, very similar. I know some words, but there are plenty I don't."

"It's some kind of related dialect, or maybe a primitive form of the same language," Bruno said, another curling parchment in his hands. "In the sorcery tower, I found several books written in this language, and for at least one of them I also found a copy written in the language that we learned at the fountain. If I remember correctly, I brought both copies to the tower."

"If so, I can try to translate," Ricardo commented. "The issue is whether it's worth it to try."

Marina and Natalia had opened the other tube and pulled out several scrolls. One of them, a dismal red color, was so striking that they'd begun to unroll it together. Most of the group gathered around them as it unfurled.

At the top of the parchment was the Red Moon, with its broken and cracked equator, drawn with the same level of detail they'd seen on so many occasions. A spectacular drawing of the rust-colored cathedral filled the rest of the scroll. Its prickly pinnacles and buttresses rose up off the scroll like a nightmarish vision leaping from the page. The entire structure seemed to emit a strange shine, a radiance mixed from blood and fire. But what was most frightening about the drawing wasn't the cathedral; the most dreadful part was what emerged from it.

From the walls and high towers appeared countless dark silhouettes. They were indistinguishable, ghostly forms that seeped through the walls, anxious to be free. Very few were alike. From the cathedral surged hunchbacked specters that twisted horrifically as they squeezed through the stone, leeches made out of darkness, shapeless monsters, and winged horrors. A grotesque creature was depicted escaping from one of the main towers, with a gigantic head and hairy arms that extended to its long claws. Hector had no trouble recognizing the ghoulish horror—it had left quite an impression on him in the square of the petrified battle.

All of the creatures that emerged from the cathedral raised their arms to the heavens in a reverential gesture as the moon floated above them.

"Is that what happens when the Red Moon comes out?" Natalia asked. "The cathedral starts spitting out monsters? Is that what's going to happen?"

No one answered.



They decided to return to the Margalar Tower as soon as they left the amphitheater, despite the fact that they still had a couple of hours of light left. The fight against the hyenas, Caleb's appearance, and the discovery of the scrolls had been enough for one day's exploration. Besides, Bruno was exhausted and seemed incapable of casting another spell. He was so exhausted that he did what he'd never done before: he handed his staff and the bundle of reserve talismans to Natalia.

They set off for the tower using the same path they took to get there. Hector, with one of the big rolls of parchment under his arms, looked at the Rocavarancolian sky, almost white and cloudless. Each time it became harder to remember what Earth's sky was like, and what pained him more was how it became more difficult to remember his family members' faces. Only his sister, Sarah, remained unfaded in his memory; the rest were being erased, little by little. Hector feared that all of his memories in life before that fateful Halloween night were going to disappear.

They'd been in Rocavarancolia for a month and a half, and they'd spent the last ten days finally exploring the city. It was Bruno who ultimately convinced them to do it. He kept repeating that it was absurd to stay locked up in the tower when they should be trying to unravel the mysteries of Rocavarancolia as soon as possible.

Their survival, he insisted, could depend on it. Hector had no choice but to admit he was right. With each passing day he became more convinced that the tower provided a false sense of security.

They headed east, toward the cliffs and the sea, choosing clear roads and avoiding winding passages. Their progress was slow—every day they meticulously searched two or three buildings inside and out. They chose the locations they entered very carefully, ignoring unassuming shacks as well as dilapidated buildings where even placing one foot inside was risky; what interested them were small palaces and great mansions, fortified towers and unique structures. When the light began to fade, they returned to the Margalar Tower.

Rachel always walked in front. The girl was such an integral part of exploring the city that they waited for her ankle to heal completely before they could begin. She was always the first to cross thresholds and open doors, closets, or the few chests that they found along the way. Without her immunity to magic, exploring Rocavarancolia would have been too dangerous. They'd already lost count of the times that their friend had felt the intense itching that indicated the presence of magic; most often they found it in the entryways to buildings or the doors to rooms, but sometimes it awaited in the most unexpected of places, such as the middle of the street, a step on a stairway, or the peephole of a door. When the girl detected the presence of a spell, Bruno searched for a way to nullify it, although he was rarely successful.

And if Rachel was imperative to the group, the same could be said for the Italian and for Natalia. Knowing that they had someone capable of healing their wounds almost immediately gave them confidence. Natalia couldn't cast more than four or five spells without exhausting herself, but Bruno was already able to use at least a dozen before he showed any signs of fatigue.

"At any rate, remember that there are wounds that can't be healed," Marco warned them time and time again. "If something cuts your head off, I don't think there's any magic able to attach it back onto your neck. Don't be any less cautious just because Bruno and Natalia can cure us, okay?"

Rachel walked right in front of Hector. She brushed her hair from her eyes with one hand, realized that he was looking at her, and smiled.

"You did good in there. Good hits, quick and strong."

"But I was distracted." Hector shrugged his shoulders, then grabbed the tattered lower half of his shirt and made it flap in the air. "One of those creatures almost disemboweled me."

"You'll learn. We're all learning."

What was surprising was how quickly she'd learned the language of Rocavarancolia. Ricardo had shown himself to be a capable professor with endless patience. Every night they separated from the group to teach each other their respective languages. Marina joined them for the initial lessons. Since Rachel spoke French, Marina thought it would be beneficial to try to restore her ability to speak her native language. But shortly after, she declined—it was disheartening to relearn the language that had once been hers.

While Ricardo and Rachel dedicated themselves to learning languages, Bruno and Natalia delved deeper into the mysteries of magic. They'd almost emptied the sorcery tower, at least the three floors that they'd been able to enter. They hadn't found a way of accessing the fourth and last floor, which was different from the rest. There wasn't a door, stairway, or hallway that led to it. Bruno had spent entire afternoons examining the ceiling and exploring the tower for any clue that might reveal how to get to that last floor, but it was futile. The Italian suspected that the only way to manage it was through magic.

Hector remembered all too well the first time they'd entered the tower whose door had killed Alexander. Rachel went first and they all followed, stricken with fright, clumsily wielding their weapons and torches. The first thing they found was a terrifying wolf-like creature with leather plates covering its back and the top of its oversized head, watching them from the center of the room with bulging eyes. It turned out to be a dead animal that had been stuffed, but it took them a while to recover from the shock of such an encounter. There were several rooms on the tower's first floor: carpeted halls full of tapestries, bookshelves, tables, and trunks, with eternal torches scattered throughout.

They remained huddled together behind Rachel as she slowly advanced across the ground floor, alert to any possible spells. She ran into several throughout the area; the most potent was between two impressive silver and gold suits of armor, located at either side of a hallway that led to a green carpeted room, which they, of course, didn't attempt to enter. It was Rachel who guided them. Nobody touched anything without her touching it first, nor took a step that she hadn't taken. They didn't stay very long during that first visit to the tower. It had only been a few minutes before Marco discovered a book on a crowded bookshelf—on the spine, written in a language they recognized, was the eloquent title *Healing Magic and Immediate Restoration: Spells and Teaching.*

Most of the books, amulets, and talismans that they found in the sorcery tower were now spread out among the rooms of the Margalar Tower. The majority of the books were written in foreign languages, but many of them were easy to understand. None of them spoke of Rocavarancolia. They didn't find a single mention of the city, but they did find information about various types of magic and their spells to keep them occupied for months. From time to time, Bruno and Natalia got the others up to speed regarding their discoveries, or demonstrated the few spells that they'd managed to learn. Most of them were unfeasible: either they required a power that they lacked—even when resorting to magical charges—or they were so exhausting that they ran the risk of fainting when they attempted to cast them.

But they had to admit that the few spells they mastered were quite useful. One night, the Italian seeped through the walls of the tower like a ghost, scaring the life out of everyone. For over half an hour he was completely intangible. It was impressive to see him pass through the tower walls, but when he decided to prove that he could cross through a human body, it disturbed Hector to feel the cold viscosity of Bruno's hand passing through his own. On another occasion, while they trained in the courtyard, Natalia got sick of Ricardo forcing her backward repeatedly, and she cast an immobilization spell on him. He was left frozen for some time, to his distress and her delight.

The more they practiced magic, the easier it got.

"It's like we've started using muscles that we've never used before. It's normal that they're weak at first, but with practice they grow stronger," Bruno explained.

"Is that why we can't cast even a single spell?" Hector asked. He was disappointed by his obvious ineptitude when it came to magic. "Is our muscle more atrophied than yours or what?"

"No. Those muscles, that ability to do magic, are in each and every one of us. At least, that's what the books say. What's missing is your energy flow, your power . . . And don't think that ours is a lot better. Natalia and I have enough for low-level spells and not much else, and that's only if we rely on the help of talismans."

*Then why did they bring us here?* Hector often asked himself. *And what makes me so special?* From what he'd been led to believe by Denestor's words, as well as those of Lady Serena, his potential was enormous. Greater than any other's in the group, the phantom had assured him. But potential for what? It was clear that it wasn't for magic. He couldn't perform a single spell, no matter how small, neither with the help of talismans nor without. Every time he tried, he felt a strange force humming inside him. He first noticed it when he tried to cure Natalia; it was a whirlwind of shapeless energy that boiled and bubbled until it simply dissipated.

What they could all do, except Rachel, was charge talismans. In this case, Hector could feel how that unsettling energy was put to good use; he felt it bounding through his fingertips and transmitting into the amulet he was charging. It had become a daily routine to see any of them with such an object in their hands. Luckily, most of the talismans didn't need blood to charge; mere contact with their skin was enough. Most of the magic batteries had small capacities, but others, like Bruno's staff, were able to store so much energy that one could spend hours charging them without ever filling them up.

On the way back to the Margalar Tower they passed another sorcery tower, the second one they'd discovered in the city. It was at the end of a curved street and was composed of cylindrical edifices with differing heights that made it look like a gigantic cathedral organ that shot up from the rocky ground. Rachel had detected a powerful curse on the tower's doorstep, but it had proved impossible to deactivate. It didn't seem to be the same kind of curse that had killed Alexander and, from the itchiness that Rachel felt, it must have been even more potent. Naturally, they didn't risk entering the building. Rachel offered to proceed alone, and although Bruno was tempted by the idea, it was obvious that it wasn't a wise decision. If something happened inside, they wouldn't be able to help her.

Mistral stopped in the middle of the street with the tubular structures. A brilliant flapping of wings had caught his attention. Lady Scar's bird flew among the overhangs, the repulsive eye of the guardian of the Royal Pantheon in its beak. The woman was still keeping a close eye on them. He lost sight of the bird in a quick array of metallic flashes, and for a few moments he stared at the spot where the bird had been. Lady Scar's behavior wasn't normal, but what could he say about strange behavior? Every day he spent with the harvest was a bigger risk, for him as well as for them. He was surprised that they still hadn't exposed him.

"Is something wrong?" Hector asked.

The shapeshifter shook his head and continued walking, with his hands resting on the hilts of the two swords equipped on his belt, one on each side. He had to leave, that was the logical choice—he had to resign them to their fate, once and for all.

What more could he do for them?

They knew enough about weapons to defend themselves from the vermin of Rocavarancolia, and besides, now they had magic. His presence was no longer necessary; he had done what he came to do. But something kept him from leaving: the promise he made to Alexander to protect his sister went far beyond a sense of duty. That promise uttered almost instinctively in front of the Serpent Tower obliged him to remain at the Margalar Tower, despite what common sense and Denestor Tul insisted.

The promontory and tower rose up in the distance. The stream flowed through the cracked land like a sparkling blue ribbon, turning with the elevation as if trying to strangle the earth, then vanished into the moat.

On the tower clock, the ten-pointed star had reached the height of four minutes to six.

Madeleine lowered the drawbridge, but as usual, she didn't come out to meet them. They found her sitting at the table furthest from the main gate, with her legs stretched out and her bare feet propped against the table's edge. She was working on charging talismans and was placing them in a basket once they were ready. They greeted her as they came in and she responded to each with a slight nod, keeping her eyes on the medallion she was charging: a necklace in the shape of a wolf's head. From her chair hung the green sword that Alexander had barely used; she always kept it close, even while she slept.

Adrian wasn't on the ground floor. Hector figured that he was outside in the courtyard, where he spent his hours obsessively training with his sword. Only when night fell and the flaming bats arrived did he sheathe his weapon and go back inside. But he no longer seemed to do it out of fear; rather it was as if he took the appearance of those creatures to be a convenient sign to end his obsession for the day.

Lizbeth and Rachel approached Madeleine while the others laid Caleb's parchments on the main table. Ricardo unfurled one, placing glasses and jars at the ends to keep it from rolling shut, and studied it with care. He asked Bruno about the books that he'd mentioned in the cellar of the amphitheater, and the Italian went to look for them.

Hector sat in a worn leather armchair and tore off his boots. His relief was so intense that he let out a loud sigh. For the past ten days they hadn't stopped for a moment: in the mornings they trained in the courtyard under Marco's supervision, in the afternoons they went out looking for provisions, and after that they explored the city. It was no wonder that by nightfall Hector was always exhausted.

Someone passed behind him on the way to the courtyard and tousled his hair tenderly. He didn't turn around to see who it was. Maybe Natalia, or perhaps Marina. All of his attention was now focused on Maddie. The young girl was talking with her two friends, or rather she listened with little enthusiasm to what the others had to say. Rachel and Lizbeth didn't seem bothered by her apathy. They recounted the afternoon's events as if she were as excited as they were.

Madeleine was still lovely; neither the sadness reflected in her features nor the fact that she was always disheveled had marred her beauty. On the contrary, she'd gained an air of wild abandon that made her even more attractive.

It was impossible for Hector to have any idea what Madeleine was going through. No one close to him had died in his entire life. And the mere idea that something bad could happen to Sarah or to his parents completely disarmed him. But what he couldn't understand was Adrian's behavior. He had withdrawn himself to such an extent that he was even more out of reach than Madeleine. For Adrian, the world seemed to be reduced to his eternal fights in the courtyard. Not even the books of magic had gained his attention. Hector often wondered what he was fighting against out there. Maybe his cowardice? Maybe some strange feeling of guilt over Alex's death?

Natalia believed that Bruno's healing spell had come too late for Adrian. The Italian had managed to save his body but not his spirit. At least, not entirely.

"It's like a part of him died before Bruno could save him," she'd told them the night before. "That boy isn't Adrian, at least not the same Adrian that we knew."

They were sitting at the table in the courtyard, all of them except Madeleine, who'd already gone to bed, and Adrian himself, who'd just gone back into the tower after the first trace of flames in the air.

"They give me chills. It's like they're ghosts." Marina sighed, leaning on the table, her face turned to the side as she rested her head on her crossed arms. "How long are they going to be like this?"

It was Ricardo who answered.

"There's no set time." His eyes shone. Hector knew he was thinking of his mother, who'd died two years before. "You simply get better without realizing it. One day it hurts less, all of a sudden . . . But there's no timeline, no dates . . . It's . . ." He swallowed. "It's the absence. And that terrible coldness every time you wake up and remember that your world has been shattered."

"That sounds horrible," Lizbeth said.

"It is horrible. But it passes. Everything passes," he continued. "You get used to the new world. You have no choice if you want to keep moving forward."

"But what if they don't want to keep moving forward?" Marina asked. "What happens then?"

Natalia's voice brought Hector back to the present. She handed him a lump of stewed meat wrapped in a grease-stained cloth.

"Aren't you hungry?" she asked him.

"I'm always hungry."

He took the meat, trying not to get grease on his hands or on the seat. Natalia sat on the arm of the old sofa with her legs crossed and a piece of fruit in her hand. She took out a chunk of crusty bread from one of the pockets of her skirt and dropped it into Hector's lap. Then she started to eat the fruit. Natalia was the only one who had gained weight since they'd been in Rocavarancolia, and it suited her. Her once harsh features had softened, giving her face a sweetness that it lacked before. And just like a mirror image, her character had sweetened too, although not to the same degree: most of the time she was as curt and bitter as she had been.

She still insisted on not talking to the others about the shadows that stalked them. Her view on the subject hadn't changed, despite the fact that one of the creatures had protected her.

"You can't see them, you don't know what they're like," she'd told him a few days prior, when he brought the subject up for the thousandth time. "You can't see their hatred when they look at us. Do you know why I think that shadow helped me? Because it couldn't stand the idea of something else getting to kill me."

"But what if you're wrong?"

"Are you stupid? Are you not listening? I'm not wrong! They're evil! Do you want me to tell you what they're doing right now?" She leaned in quickly to whisper in his ear. "There are two behind you." Hector resisted the impulse to turn around. And not because he knew the gesture would be useless, but because he feared that maybe for once it wouldn't be. "They're writhing over one another and stretching their claws out toward us, as if they wanted to catch us or tear us open or . . ." She snorted and moved away from him. "They're monsters, you hear me? Monsters! And they hate us."

That had been the last conversation they'd had about Natalia's shadows. Even so, the fact that she avoided speaking to the rest of the group about the creatures didn't stop them from realizing that something odd was going on. More than once they found Natalia staring into space with an uneasy expression, sometimes even a frightened one. Hector knew what she was looking at on those occasions, but the only thing the others could see was that Natalia would suddenly become upset for no apparent reason.

Hector started in on his meat and bread, making small talk with her. When he finished, he was no longer hungry, but he wasn't fully satisfied either. He could have easily eaten more. That sensation, of not being completely satiated, was as familiar to him as the evening exhaustion. After Alex's death, they'd decided not to divide the group unless they really needed to. This meant that they only collected provisions from one of the drop-off points. They opted for the spooky plaza overrun with petrified creatures, mainly due to its close proximity to the tower. With the supplies cut in half, they could no longer allow for indulgence, and they had no choice but to ration out their food.

Bruno finally came down with the two books in hand. The Italian was still nervous; in the weeks that they'd been in Rocavarancolia nothing had changed with regard to his behavior and personality. He remained cold. Only when he was involved with his books or performing magic could they get a glimpse of any emotion in his eyes—it was a faded, sickly gleam that Hector found unsettling. The Italian descended the stairs like a robot, and handed the books to Ricardo with the same affectation. They were two medium-sized volumes, although fairly thick. Natalia and Hector got up from the sofa and approached the table where Ricardo examined the books and parchments under Bruno's expressionless gaze.

"How does it look?" Hector asked as he glanced at the messy pile of unrolled scrolls covering the table. To him they appeared to be written in incomprehensible gibberish, although now and then he would recognize a word amid the nonsense.

"I can translate them," Ricardo assured them. "It won't be one hundred percent accurate, but it should be enough to know what they're about." He rapped his fist on the horrible drawing of the red cathedral. "And there are answers here. I know it. From what I've seen, most of the texts are about the history of Rocavarancolia, and two of the scrolls are dedicated exclusively to the Red Moon and the monstrous building on the outskirts of town. I'll translate those first."

"How long will it take?"

"I don't know, a couple of days, I suppose. Although if everything goes well, I'll have answers before then."

They decided that it would be best for Ricardo to focus on the translation of the scrolls while the others rested in the tower. They didn't want to risk exploring the city without one of their main offensive pillars, and besides, Hector wasn't the only one who was exhausted. The long week of adventures in the city had taken its toll on everyone. Rachel was the only one disappointed by the news: she enjoyed the outings and, above all, having everyone depend on her.

After chatting with Ricardo and Natalia, Hector looked with both horror and fascination at the terrifying hordes that flowed out of the walls of the red cathedral, and decided to go out to the courtyard. That drawing distressed him greatly; he'd questioned Natalia with a subtle gesture to find out if those dark silhouettes resembled her shadows, but she shook her head.

Outside, the wind began to blow fiercely. The weather in Rocavarancolia was always the same; day after day it followed the same pattern. The wind kicked up as the temperature dropped. There had never been the slightest variation in this routine, save for the intense storm that shook the city the night of their arrival, which Hector still remembered vividly.

Adrian was in the middle of the courtyard, his bare torso drenched in sweat. He paid no attention to Hector when he came out. He thrust his sword at the air and then retreated a step, parried an imaginary attack that came at him from the left, and then counterattacked with devastating speed. His hair had grown more than the others' and now his disheveled blond mane fell around his shoulders. Lizbeth had offered to cut it, but he refused. He'd cut his bangs himself with the sword so they wouldn't obstruct his view when he was fighting.

Hector watched him for a while. The young boy seemed more skilled, though it was difficult to judge without an actual opponent. Adrian jumped to the side, dodged a blow in one direction, and charged in the opposite. The constant exercise had strengthened the teenager; it had hardened him. Adrian seemed more alive than ever. Even so, Hector couldn't help but recall Natalia saying that Bruno's spell came too late and that a part of his spirit hadn't been saved.

Marina was also in the courtyard; she leaned against the well, with a listless hand draped over the mouth of the bucket. She gazed out beyond the wall. She hadn't noticed his presence either. Hector approached the girl, still surprised at how his heart sped up as he got closer. It seemed incredible to him that even now his feelings hadn't diminished in the least. Every time he looked at her he felt revived; every time she touched him he felt complete.

Marina continued looking out beyond the wall. Her fingers stroked the bucket's mouth, slipping dreamily along the edge of the wood.

When he was only a few steps away, Hector diverted his gaze from his friend to figure out what she was staring at with such interest.

The young boy who had wounded Adrian was on the peak of one of the rooftops beyond the wall, also immersed in imaginary combat. He leapt from one side to the other, jabbing his sword to the left and right and deflecting invisible thrusts. Hector was greatly surprised to see him. But what surprised him even more was that Marina was so entranced with spying on the kid that she still hadn't realized Hector was there.

"What . . . ?" he managed. He was too bewildered to say anything else.

The girl turned around, startled, and her elbow hit the bucket, which then dropped noisily to the bottom of the well. Hector looked at her in disbelief, shook his head, and turned to the tower, ready to warn the group of the boy's presence. Marina grabbed his wrist and pulled him toward her. Hector felt an electric current all over his body. Something twisted his insides, a new and bitter feeling.

"It's not what you think," she whispered.

And what did she think he was thinking? And why was she blushing like that?

"He comes every afternoon, he has for some time." Marina talked very quickly. She kept her hand around his wrist, and for the first time, her touch didn't make him feel complete, but rather the opposite. He felt like it was robbing him of something. With every second they remained in contact, a terrible coldness took over the warmth that she'd always awoken in him. He forcefully pulled his hand away.

"And you knew about it and didn't say anything? What were you thinking?"

"Well, what do you want to do? Go over there and kill him? Or would you rather we lock him up in the dungeons?" She gestured with her head upward and then toward Adrian. "Look at them. Look closely at the two of them."

Hector did as Marina asked. It only took a second to realize what she meant. No, it wasn't what he'd thought. He wasn't looking at two separate fights: it was just the one. Adrian responded to the attacks from the boy on the rooftop, just as the boy deflected the blows that Adrian made in the courtyard. Despite the distance between them, they fought with the same fury and concentration as if they were face to face, their lives on the line with every lunge.

Hector watched them from this new perspective. He saw how Adrian deflected a lethal attack from his adversary, turned after jumping out of his reach, and then swung with a dizzying speed from the right. The other didn't hesitate; he parried the blow and counterattacked with such ferocity that Adrian stumbled as he avoided the slash to his stomach.

"I can't believe it," Hector whispered. The battle between them was one of unusual fierceness. There was no mercy, no respite.

Finally, the boy on the rooftop found a flaw in Adrian's defense. He sprung forward and thrust his sword in a brutal strike that, had it reached Adrian in reality, would have split him in two. The blond lost his balance, as if he'd actually suffered that mortal blow. He dropped his sword and cursed.

Hector looked up at the rooftop just in time to see Adrian's adversary take off running. The dark-haired boy jumped from one rooftop to another until he was lost in the twilight. In the courtyard, Adrian picked up his sword and returned the attack. There was no longer any trace of technique or control in his movements; he was just delivering sword blows to the air with increasing power and rage until, limp and breathless, he fell to his knees on the cobblestones. Marina and Hector ran to him and helped him up.

"How long is this going to last?" Hector asked. "Are you just going to keep at it till you burst?"

Adrian looked at him, panting. His eyes burned with fury and determination bordering on madness. Sweat dotted his forehead and ran down his face.

"Soon . . ." he murmured, haltingly, his eyes fixed on the rooftops far beyond the wall. "Very soon."

# ROCAVARAGALAGO

It was midnight, and the council of Rocavarancolia was meeting in the room that held the Sacred Throne. The tentacles that protected the throne projected shadows of gigantic proportions against the wall. Next to the door stood one of the imposing castle guards in an austere pose, wearing a dragon mask and holding a red-tipped halberd.

The regent, still on his never-ending deathbed, was absent from the meeting. Mistral, whose whereabouts were unknown, and Lady Dream, submerged in lethargy, were also missing. The rest of the council were seated around the table, laden with untouched food and jugs of wine.

Old Belisarius's place had been taken by Solberinus, the castaway. He was a sinewy man with matted blond hair. He leaned into the table as if gathering momentum to leap on top of it and take off running. Solberinus felt out of place within the castle—he felt this way any time he was on dry land. He lived among the boats shipwrecked on the reef, and finding himself so far from the water and its shifting tides unsettled him beyond words.

Lady Serena, who occupied the seat that had previously belonged by right of seniority to the assassinated elder, was in charge of initiating the meeting.

"As you all know, today we laid the noble Belisarius to rest at the Royal Pantheon," the specter announced. She floated before the table in her eternal evening gown of emerald green, as beautiful, radiant, and cold as ever. "For several weeks we have tried to find a way to communicate with his spirit or with that of the murdered servant," she said, "but it has all been in vain. There is no magic art or spell able to achieve it."

Lady Scar spoke next.

"Belisarius and his servant are not just dead. Whoever murdered them eliminated them completely." The horrible woman kept one eye focused on what was occurring at the table while the other, in the beak of Denestor's bird, flew over the Margalar Tower. "They didn't just kill their bodies, they annihilated their souls," she pointed out. "It's as if they've been erased."

"Oh. What awful cruelty," murmured Enoch, bringing his hands to his face.

The vampire sat next to one of the Lexel brothers. Enoch was as hungry and desperate as ever, but he took comfort and satisfaction in having not given in to his impulses back at the Margalar Tower and allowing the blond boy to live. He almost believed himself to be a hero—a tragic hero, but a hero nonetheless. Soon the grimace of dismay that played across his face transformed into an immense and ridiculous smile of absurd self-gratification.

"I gave Belisarius the poison of the accuser's resurrection," said the invisible alchemist. It was obvious by the way he held his cup and slurred his words that Rorcual was drunk. "If everything had gone well, the corpse should have shouted the name of his assassin seven times."

"And if he hadn't already been dead, you surely would have killed him with your useless concoctions," muttered Esmael.

The alchemist slammed his glass down on the table. Lady Serena felt him shaking furiously at the Lord of Assassin's words. The ghost shook her head. Esmael was right. Rorcual's elixir not only hadn't done what it was supposed to, but once it touched Belisarius's lips, it dyed his skin an unpleasant shade of brownish gray. For decades the alchemist had been unable to get a single one of his potions to work. Along with his visibility, he'd lost the magic touch that had propelled him to first alchemist in the kingdom. This task now fell to Lady Spider, who could not officially occupy the post. After the bloody dominion of the spider kings, those beings were forbidden from accepting prominent positions in Rocavarancolia. In fact, their role became that of mere servants.

"Maybe our fearless black angel knows of something better," Rorcual spat out. "Some spell he could share with the council that could bring the dead from their graves so they can reveal their secrets."

Esmael cast a quick glance at Lady Serena. The ghost didn't even flinch from the alchemist's comment. Lady Scar, on the other hand, had an amused smile.

"I'll admit that I know ways of contacting the kingdom of the dead," he answered Rorcual with a voice so calm that it was chilling. "And I have tried to, although it's hardly my obligation. But I must say that I have failed, just like our dear colleagues here."

It was true. The Brief Resurrection spell from Hurza the Eye-Eater's grimoire was the same enchantment he'd used to revive Lady Serena's king, and had proven completely useless. That spell hadn't worked with Belisarius or with the servant. The mere thought of the book and Lady Serena infuriated him. He still raged over the humiliation he'd suffered at the phantom's hands. What pained him the most, even more than the dire setback of his aspirations, was that the mistake of not checking the existing literature regarding Hurza's book had been his own. He should have known that specific information would be recorded in the compendia—that only whoever occupied the position of Lord of Assassins could read the book. Ultimately, he was the one who'd exposed himself to humiliation. And that affected him much more than the humiliation itself.

"Nor have I found any way of contacting their souls or finding out what happened in Belisarius's study that night," declared Denestor Tul, bringing a hand to his forehead.

The demiurge was tired and haggard. It had been some time since he had a full night's rest. As soon as he closed his eyes, he saw Lady Dream's visions of the night Belisarius was murdered. He kept seeing that strange and hazy battle that she had foretold, but Lady Dream hadn't only prophesied a war, she'd also prophesied his own death:

*Poor Denestor!* she'd said. *We wish we could take you with us! We wish we could save you!*

"It's not normal, it's just not normal." Enoch rubbed his hands with affectation. He was anxious to participate in solving this mystery. "Oh. Something terrible is happening in Rocavarancolia. I tell you. I tell you. Dark times are drawing near. Just like Lady Dream predicted when she spoke to our demiurge."

Denestor had thought it necessary to share the old woman's visions with the rest of the council. During the day he regretted having done so, but at night he felt more at ease knowing that the others were acquainted with his delirious dreams.

"Armies fighting in Rocavarancolia?" Ujthan the Warrior raised his head and sighed. His enormous weight warped the chair's legs to the point that it was surprising they didn't break. "My eyes won't get to see that." He still remembered the last war with nostalgia. He'd never been so happy. Ujthan had been born for battle; fighting was everything to him, it was the only thing worth living for. For Ujthan there was nothing better than the sound of steel clashing against steel and the cries of armies in the fray. He couldn't conceive of life without the brutality of combat, the smell of freshly spilled blood, and the uncertainty of not knowing if your next enemy would be your last, the one that removed you once and for all from the battlefield.

"Who knows?" Esmael stretched his arms. "Maybe you'll have a last war to fight after all, old friend." He looked at Lady Scar. The tattered woman watched him with a mocking scowl, which angered him. But he refused to give her the satisfaction of making his rage known. "Tell us, dear Commander: have you lost one of the kingdom's armies that you watch over so zealously? Has some legion of horrors gone missing that someone could use against us?"

"Don't turn this into a sideshow, Esmael," Denestor reprimanded. "And let's continue the meeting. Ujthan, you were designated as principal investigator in Belisarius's death. Do you have your final report ready?"

"It's ready and I can sum it up in a single word: nothing. The servants have searched Belisarius's study a thousand times. They haven't found anything to be missing, nor have they found anything that didn't belong there. Except for the servant's head, of course; that's still missing. Denestor's creatures haven't detected any magic in the area besides the fortress's protection spells, and my own inquiries throughout the city have been unsuccessful. There is nothing. Absolutely nothing."

"Someone covered their tracks very well," murmured the Lexel twin with the black mask as he turned his head to look at his brother, seated opposite him.

"Without a doubt, someone went to a lot of trouble to avoid being discovered," he responded. "Where were you that night, Brother? You weren't in our chambers . . ."

"I was searching for you in the castle, Brother," he replied. "Because you never leave our rooms if I'm there, and last night you did."

They both looked at each other through their masks with such overwhelming hatred that it made the space between them vibrate.

"And Mistral?" Esmael asked next, leaning in to grab a cup of wine. The brothers' madness and paranoia held little interest for him. "Where is the shapeshifter?" he asked. "It's been so long since we've heard from him that I'm beginning to worry."

"Do you suspect that he could be involved in Belisarius's murder?" Denestor asked.

"No. Mistral is spineless, he wouldn't murder someone who was defenseless even if his own life depended on it." And he was truly convinced of this. "It's uncertainty and worry, nothing more, nothing less. It's been so long since we've seen him that I'm afraid something might have happened to him."

"You want Mistral declared dead so that another of your followers can take his place on the council?" Rorcual blurted out. "Is that what you're hoping for?"

"Don't worry about the shapeshifter, Esmael," Denestor intervened. "I spoke with him myself less than a week ago. He's fine, and you'll see him again soon, I'm sure."

It was hard for Lady Scar to keep her emotions from showing on her face. She studied the demiurge carefully. She knew very well where Mistral was hiding. She'd found him on the day that the redhead died; he had taken on the German boy's appearance. She'd been so amazed to see him among the other kids that she'd almost exposed him, which would have thrown all hope for Rocavarancolia out the window. That discovery had been as surprising as now hearing Denestor say that he'd spoken to Mistral recently.

*So you know, you sly old fox.* This turn of events had caught her off guard. Two members of the council helping the harvest was strange enough; now, as it turned out, there was a third party involved, even if all they did was keep a complicit silence. But she should have known.

Denestor was the one who'd brought the kid from the human world and would have immediately picked up on Mistral's move. Or maybe they'd been conspiring since before the night of Samhein? She'd have to think about it.

She had been more subtle than Mistral. She'd limited herself to helping only one of the children, the one that she considered most vital to the preservation of the kingdom; on the other side, the shape-shifter wasn't beating around the bush: he'd infiltrated the group to help them from within. What Lady Scar couldn't stop wondering was how long he planned to stay with them. With every passing moment, the risk of exposure grew. Maybe Denestor knew of the shapeshifter's intentions; she had to find a way to approach him to uncover how much he knew and to what extent he was involved.

Lady Scar smiled to herself. She had to admit that events had taken a truly interesting turn.

During the next two days they barely saw Ricardo. He remained secluded in a room on the first floor, submerged in documents, books, and papers. He even slept there, if he actually slept. The second day, Hector ran into him on the way to the bathrooms in the courtyard. Not only did he not speak to him; Ricardo did all he could to avoid his gaze. Something about his face disturbed him much more than his behavior: a vague shadow had darkened his features and made one faint of heart just looking at him. Whatever it was he was finding in the documents, it wasn't good.

As the day progressed, the ambience in the Margalar Tower grew increasingly sullen. Only Madeleine and Adrian seemed removed from the growing tension. The boy trained without respite in the courtyard, peering from time to time at the rooftops furthest from the wall, while the redhead simply sat on the ground floor, letting time go by.

The others sensed bad news on the horizon. They could almost feel it mounting word by word atop their heads. The door to the room where Ricardo worked had always been partway open, but by mid-afternoon they found it closed. This darkened their spirits even more.

Mistral was the most melancholy of them all. He knew what Ricardo was going to find, and he couldn't help but wonder how they were going to react once they learned of it. The scrolls contained a copy of *An Illustrated Historiography*, by the warrior, poet, historian, and painter Blatto Zenzé. It was fairly old, but that hardly mattered. Those documents detailed much of Rocavarancolia's origin, as well as its traditions, legends, and most noteworthy peculiarities. And, as expected, among them was the most crucial one: the Red Moon.

It was shortly after nightfall. The group was chatting in the courtyard under the light of two torches as bats fluttered overhead when Ricardo finally appeared. His demeanor was terribly grave. All conversation stopped. The wind and the sporadic howls coming from the mountains couldn't penetrate the unnerving silence that weighed upon them. He avoided eye contact and tensely bit his lower lip. His anxiety infected everyone there. Marco stared at him, hardly blinking. Ricardo waited for Madeleine and Adrian to leave the tower and join the group before he began.

The first thing he did was toss a handful of rhomboid crystals on the table, the same that they'd lit with their own blood the first night in the tower. His hand shook as he did it. He dropped into a chair and pointed to the crystals with a tired gesture.

"That is what we are. That's why they brought us. Only for that."

"What do you mean?" Hector asked.

"They brought us to be magic charges. That's what we're good for. Batteries. Talismans in human form. However you want to call it . . . We are what will activate the cathedral when the Red Moon comes out. Remember the drawing? All those monsters coming out of the walls of the red building? That's what's going to happen. And it will be thanks to us."

"Would you mind explaining yourself?" Lizbeth asked. "Because right now I feel very lost."

"That cathedral . . ." Ricardo snorted and ran a hand through his curly hair. "It's the heart of the city, the heart of the kingdom, really . . . Only it's not a cathedral. It's not even an actual building, at least not completely. It's a spell. It's called Rocavaragalago." He struggled to pronounce the word.

"And when the Red Moon comes out, it will spit out monsters like in the drawing, is that right?" Natalia asked. "And you're saying it will be our fault?"

"I'm still not entirely sure how it happens. The author of the scrolls explains everything in the form of poems. Some of them are very difficult to translate." He gestured toward the tower to his back. "I must . . . I must keep working on them. But yes, it will be our fault. Of that much I'm certain. Rocavaragalago needs two elements to be activated. The first is the Red Moon in the sky; the second, energy to run on, like Natalia and Bruno use the talismans. That energy, in addition, has to be new and from the outside. 'Untainted essence never lit up by the Sacred Red Moon,' says the scroll . . . Now do you understand why they brought us? They need our energy to activate Rocavaragalago. That's the potential that Denestor Tul wouldn't stop talking about. The cathedral is the door, the Red Moon is the key, and we're the ones who turn it."

"But how?" Bruno asked. He had his grandfather's watch in his hand and opened and closed it, over and over. "Is it a spell that creates monsters? I don't understand it."

"I think it has to do with the nature of this world," Ricardo answered. "Or maybe it's just in this city, I'm not sure. It's hard to explain . . . There are still a lot of scrolls to translate, but . . ." He looked directly at Bruno. "Remember the sphere that you invoked shortly after we came here?"

The Italian nodded.

"You created a door between worlds. It only remained open for an instant, the time it took for you to invoke that thing." He got more comfortable in his chair. "Rocavarancolia is an intermediate kingdom, a world situated in a crossroads between dimensions or something like that . . . Whatever it is, wherever it is, it's very easy to open doors to other worlds here. Like the one that Denestor used to go to Earth and bring us back. I think that Rocavaragalago is one of those doors, and it leads to a diabolic world populated with freaks and monsters. Our energy and the Red Moon will open it and . . . they'll pass to this side."

Lizbeth brought a hand to her chest.

Hector thought of the thousands of skeletons piled in the Scar of Arax. Bones that belonged to humans, but also to all kinds of strange beings. He remembered the dozens of tapestries and paintings that they'd discovered in their explorations throughout Rocavarancolia. Plenty of them showed true armies of horrors.

"How many?" Natalia asked. "How many monsters will come out of this Rocalo-whatever?"

"That will depend on the amount of energy that we possess. From what I've read, there has been record of thousands of creatures emerging from the cathedral when the Red Moon came out." On seeing the expressions on several of his companions' faces, he hurried to add: "But there wouldn't be that many this time, no, that's impossible . . . They used the energy of hundreds of children brought from an endless number of different worlds. Now there's only eleven of us."

"For now," Marina pointed out.

"Monsters . . ." Lizbeth shook her head. "But what kind of monsters are we talking about? This city is infested with repulsive creatures."

"No. Those are vermin, scavenger beasts who live in the ruins. The creatures of Rocavaragalago are of a different kind, they're the ones you saw in the drawing on the scroll. Trolls, vampires, demons, the living dead . . . Giants, werewolves . . . Maybe even dragons."

"And then what will happen to us?" Marina asked.

"What do you think?" Natalia groaned and let her head fall on the table. "The city will be full of monsters. And they'll probably be starving to death."

"We must assume that once we've served as batteries for Rocavaragalago, we will no longer be of use." Bruno took off his glasses and rubbed his eyes. "Our lives have never been worth anything in this city. After the Red Moon they'll be worth even less."

"They told us that they'd give us the chance to return to Earth after a year!" Lizbeth exclaimed. Her large eyes shone with rage and fear. "And Denestor Tul couldn't lie to us!"

"He didn't lie to us about that either." Hector sighed. His head was starting to hurt. "In a year they'll give us the opportunity to return home . . . but it's likely that we won't be alive to accept it."

"That's very cruel." Marina shook her head. "They can't be so cruel."

"Cruelty is inherent to this city," Bruno pronounced. "I don't think it matters much to them to sacrifice a few kids to get what they want."

Adrian's voice, coming from the far end of the table, took them by surprise.

"Kids? You're wrong. We're not kids anymore," he declared. He had been sitting back in his chair. When he began to speak, he slowly sat up, until he was leaning his forearms on the edge of the table. "So what are you saying is going to happen? Monsters in the city?" His lips twisted in a strange grimace that somewhat resembled a smile. "Let them come. As many as they wish." A flaming bat passed over their heads and Adrian didn't flinch. He looked at Bruno, with the fire from the wings of the creatures still shining in his eyes. "How long until this moon shows up?"

"According to the calculations I've made using the movement of the star from the clock on the front of the building, I estimate that the Red Moon will come out one hundred and sixty-six days from tomorrow."

"That's an eternity!" Adrian exclaimed. "Look at how far we've come in the weeks that we've been here. And just think how much we could learn before the moon comes out . . ." They hadn't heard him talk this much in a long time. His voice was deeper than Hector remembered. "Let the monsters come, as many as they wish. We'll be ready when it happens. We'll send them straight back to hell."

Hector didn't know what to think. Adrian's passionate outburst had left him stunned.

"Marco . . ." He turned toward the German. "What's your take on this? You've been very quiet."

Instead of responding, Marco turned his attention to Ricardo.

"Don't take this the wrong way, but is there any chance that you've gotten the translation wrong? Maybe that's not exactly what will happen when the Red Moon comes out?"

Ricardo shook his head.

"I'm going to keep working on the scrolls, of course, but I think that for the most part I'm correct."

Mistral nodded slowly, without taking his eyes off Ricardo. The shapeshifter knew very well that his friend was wrong. That wasn't what would happen when the Red Moon appeared: the truth was even worse. What he couldn't help wondering was whether Ricardo had misinterpreted the scrolls or if he was hiding what he'd discovered on purpose: the truth about the Red Moon was so terrible that Mistral would understand if he preferred to keep it to himself.

Despite what Adrian had said, nothing they could do would prepare them for what would happen when that monstrous red celestial body ascended from the east. Absolutely nothing.

★★★

In Rocavarancolia, even on the darkest nights there was room for light, even when it was sickly and evil. To the south, the neighborhood in flames stood out in the darkness like a large motionless rip in the landscape; one couldn't hear the crackling of the fire but only the screams of those who burned interminably, never falling to ashes. To the west, the walls of Rocavaragalago radiated with the incandescent reflection from the lava pit that surrounded them. The quivering luminosity of the Scar of Arax crossed the city from east to west, zigzagging and broken; and from time to time over the cliffs flashed the light of the lighthouse that tried in vain to lure ships to the reefs.

There was also light in the cemetery. Among the tombs flickered torches of eternal flame, and in the doors of the mausoleums hung oil lamps that spilled their gloomy light onto the marble, the rock, and the moss. In the ponds between the paths floated will-o'-the-wisps, and on occasion, a flaming bat left a blazing trail in the sky above the graveyard.

Underground, two thousand dead chatted incessantly. Their conversation was nonsensical; the choppy monologues interrupted one another with no rhyme or reason, just excuses to hear the sound of their voices. They were so consumed by their own chatter that not a single one noticed when one of the doors to the Royal Pantheon opened.

A figure wrapped in torn bandages emerged from the darkness. It was Old Belisarius, and by his clumsy movements it would appear that he'd never walked a day in his life. He fell to the ground after several steps. He got up with difficulty and looked to his left and right. He stumbled again as he tried to walk, and only the fortuitous support of the pantheon's wall kept him from falling again. His mouth opened from time to time, but in a peculiar way, as if it were not at all operated by the will of its owner.

Belisarius's body took another couple of jerky steps forward while the mind that now occupied it tried to take control of those awkward extremities. He was so disoriented that it was hard to distinguish where his body ended and the rest of reality began. After leaving the niche where that grotesque woman had buried him, he had concluded that he must have inhabited the body of a tentacled creature, and the jumble of bandages that surrounded him were his own extremities.

He reached a hand up to his face: it was old, incredibly old, and human. Its color, however, a brownish gray tone, wasn't quite right. He started to walk among the tombs. He heard voices, but he paid them no heed. His eyes were so terrifying that even the dead in the cemetery would scream if they could see him. It took him a few moments to realize that he was walking with his mouth open. He shoved his lower jaw upward until it met with the upper one. Then he turned to look in all directions. An unrelenting itch had reached his left wrist. He tried to scratch it but was unable to. His right hand swept right by it, completely without coordination.

He groaned. Resurrection was traumatic; he knew that, he accepted it. It was intrinsic to that complicated spell, but he loathed the extremely weakened state in which he found himself. At the moment he was so fragile that a bad fall could mean the end of him.

He murmured a levitation spell and immediately lifted into the air; at least the body in which he'd awoken had strength enough for that.

He rose up in the night like a sinister, ragged projectile, allowing himself to be carried by magic. As he ascended, he realized that the city was nothing like the one he remembered. It was much larger and by the ruined state it was in, it was evident that it had fallen on hard times. Was he in Rocavarancolia, or had they resurrected him elsewhere? He had forbidden the spell to be cast outside the city, but who knew what may have occurred since his death; maybe his followers had no choice but to bring him back to life in another linked world.

He looked to the west and saw the red brilliance of the walls of Rocavaragalago. And further out, embracing the city, the mountains that he knew so well were dark as the night of a massacre. His smile grew so wide that it ripped the corners of lips that were not his. Yes, he had returned. He was in Rocavarancolia.

The itching in his wrist persisted. He could now coordinate his movements, and he scratched so furiously to free himself of the terrible sensation that he tore his skin open. He frowned. There was something buried in his flesh. He squinted his eyes and brought his hand up to examine the object embedded in his skin. A tiny spine stuck out, covered in blood. The itching came from that spot, insidious and constant. And magical, evidently. He grabbed the spine between his thumb and index finger and yanked. As soon as it exited his wrist, the spine changed consistency and unfurled into a grayish parchment.

The creature who now occupied Belisarius's body held the sheet before his eyes. It was written in an ancient dialect of Nazara, the first linked world: the language that he'd made his disciples learn. The lettering was crude, the hand of a child who's just learning to write or that of an old man who'd lost control in his movements. Floating miles high in the air, with the city beneath him converted into an obscure pool of shadows between the mountains and the sea, he read what was written on the parchment:

*My name is Belisarius Donócate and I am the last of my line, the last of your followers, My Lord. For centuries I have been the last. I have spent centuries prolonging my life to allow you the opportunity to return, though I can only offer a container as fragile and worn out as this damned body of mine, so unworthy of becoming a vehicle for your essence.*

*And if this body is not worthy to serve you, the same can be said for the Rocavarancolia that you will find upon your return. Nothing remains of our glory. The linked worlds united against us and destroyed that which by right of conquest belonged to us. But I don't have the time nor the patience necessary to relate the history of Rocavarancolia here. Soon you will find out on your own, I have seen to that personally.*

*Now I must apologize, not for the body that I leave you, or for the ruined state of this kingdom which was once grand. I must ask pardon because we have failed you. From the first of your followers to the last, which is myself, I ask pardon in the name of all those who have adored at one time your Majestic Name and the Name of your Sacred Brother. We have failed you: we lost your book, My Lord . . . It was stolen from us. There remains no trace of it, not in this world nor in the linked worlds. We searched for it endlessly, but—forgive us, My Lord—we could not find it.*

*Now your book is in Rocavarancolia, although I do not know its exact whereabouts. The magic that lies within its pages awoke the night following the harvest. And in that harvest, My Lord, arrived one recipient suitable for your plans: a child whose power surpasses by far everything that my eyes have ever seen. And I know that coincidences do not exist. I know that if your book and this child appeared in Rocavarancolia at the same time, it's for a reason: the time has come.*

The entity that floated in the void used its voice for the first time. It sounded as if a slow rumble of thunder rose from its throat:

"A child . . ." He looked up at the darkness that hung above the world, searching for something that wasn't there.

He began to fly upward. The lines of the horizon curved down as he ascended. The perspective changed; the world far below his feet became spherical and grew smaller by the minute. Sheets of ice formed over Belisarius's body as he sped up, leaving the planet's troposphere behind and penetrating the highest layers of the atmosphere like a blade. He whispered a spell of protection, and an energy field surrounded his body. The night's darkness gave way to the deep black of space. He turned his head with difficulty. The outer layer of the magic mist that separated him from the void had frozen over. He raised its temperature so he could look around. The ice broke apart immediately.

The Red Moon was still far from the planet. It floated in space thousands of miles away, enveloped in that intense scarlet fog brought on by the perpetual storms of its northern hemisphere. He smiled at the sight of it, as if looking at an old friend.

There was still a significant amount of time before the influence of that celestial body would be noticed on the planet. He had time to prepare, to recover his strength and plot a course of action.

The hand that once belonged to Belisarius reached again for the parchment. He continued reading. His last follower didn't disclose much more in his letter. He only pointed out that there was one creature in Rocavarancolia who knew the whereabouts of the lost book. Curiously, it was the Lord of Assassins of the kingdom, a black angel named Esmael. The creature floating in the void frowned. He wasn't prepared to confront such a being. At least not yet.

*My time is short, My Lord,* continued the parchment, *and my brain is not as quick and sharp as it once was. But I was able to prepare a present that I'm sure will be to your liking. It's hidden in the last line of this letter, along with the tool that I used to obtain it. I know that both will be useful to you. And now I must go. There are no words to express the honor that it is to give my life for your Cause. There are no words in this or in any language to express what I am feeling right now. The only thing I regret is that I will not be present to see your Plan fulfilled.*

The being that occupied Belisarius's body focused on the last line of the letter. There was a dash and a dot, written in the same ink as the rest of the letter, but somehow different. They seemed to float lightly above the paper. He smiled again. He took the dash between his index finger and thumb and easily removed it. Once in his hand, the black line transformed into a short sword covered in blood. The blade and hilt were made of crystal, and inside he saw hundreds of tiny silhouettes. There were souls trapped inside the sword, so many that the weapon appeared to be full of smoke. The trapped spirits rotated, moving in a line, howling desperately at the sword's keeper; among them was the spirit of the servant murdered by Belisarius. What he now wielded was a sword of Kalora, which seized the souls of those it slayed, imprisoning them for all eternity.

Next he extracted the black dot from the parchment. It didn't surprise him to see it transform into a human head.

Hurza the Eye-Eater honored his nickname before tossing the decapitated head. As soon as it left the protective field, it was frozen in ice. There it remained, turning in space like a large diamond flecked with red. The first Lord of Assassins sheathed the sword containing the voices of the condemned souls in his bandages. Then he set course for Rocavarancolia.

# TALES OF DELIRIUM

At the foot of the cliff were the remains of dozens of amassed ships, some run aground on the reefs, others sunk completely. These were ships of all types and designs, from primitive fishing boats to gigantic war galleys. So many there were that it seemed to the teenagers that they were entering a city constructed from decks, keels, and rigging. Masts jutted up here and there like hundred-year-old trees. Some retained the sails tangled around their trunks; others had broken and fallen on the bridge, their decks at an angle. Algae painted the hulls green, and several sinister gray birds flew around the wreckage, searching for fish and crustaceans. The mass of rotted wood, sails, cords, and steel rocked slowly, in sync with the motion of the sea. Every ship was covered in the black warning mist. Further out extended the ocean, full of ripples and reflections.

The lighthouse was located two hundred yards to the north, rising majestically from an overhang in the cliffs. The platform was enormous, but so narrow that it would have been impossible for it to support the bulk of the structure without the aid of magic. The lighthouse measured more than 150 feet tall and was carved from a single piece of white stone, pitted with holes from erosion and saltpeter.

"It lures them to the rocks and leads them to wreck," Marina whispered. She stared at the chaos of ships, horrified, as if the disaster were her fault. "It's my story . . ." She shook her head incredulously. "It's my story. The story of the lighthouse keeper and the castaway: 'The Light That Guides Me.'"

Hector remembered the story. Marina had told them shortly after they'd arrived in Rocavarancolia. It was another tale of tragic love that took place in Delirium, the city she'd invented; it was about the strange relationship that arose between the keeper of a lighthouse and the last survivor of one of the shipwrecks it caused. The man held on as best he could among the remains of the ships, eating fish and algae, fighting tooth and nail with the carnivorous mermaids that lurked underwater. She spent her days and nights at the top of the lighthouse, keeping watch so that the light never went out.

"Something's moving in between the ships," Natalia pointed out. She was closest to the edge of the cliff, so close that Hector avoided looking at her so he wouldn't feel the shudder of vertigo. "They look like huge fish." She looked at Marina out of the corner of her eye before she added in a malicious tone, "Or mermaids."

Hector dared to take a step forward so that he could see more clearly. It was still early for the wind of Rocavarancolia to start picking up, but the ocean breeze was enough to brush the hair from his forehead and fill his lungs with the smell of salt and seaweed. Natalia was right. Several shadows slid rapidly between the sunken ships. One of them emerged only to dive quickly below, but there was no mistaking what they saw. It had a humanoid form, so skeletal that even from a distance they were able to see the outline of its ribs; its bullet-shaped head was completely bald, and below its waist sprouted a long fish tail, ash gray and scaly. It also had a large, sharp-looking dorsal fin. Two other creatures became visible shortly after, identical to the first; they swam casually through the sunken remains. When he saw them, Hector thought they looked more like marine predators than fairy-tale creatures.

"It's my story . . ." Marina repeated. "My story . . ."

Bruno approached the edge of the cliff.

The Italian no longer wore glasses. Several days ago he'd discovered a spell to treat vision ailments and he'd used it to cure his myopia. His eyes looked bigger without the lenses, but still lacked any expression.

"Those ships don't belong to one single civilization," he remarked. "There are too many differences in terms of form and technology for that to be true. I'd go so far as to say that they don't belong to the same world."

"The Sea of Delirium is enchanted," Marina said. Her voice trembled as she spoke. Hector felt the impulse to embrace her, but he didn't move from where he stood. "The underwater currents flow through different dimensions, to different lands. All ships that lose their way in the other worlds end up in Delirium."

Mistral looked at the dark-haired girl. On occasion, the world destined for the children of Rocavarancolia had manifested itself within them far before their arrival, as if the interdimensional variation were so traumatic that it affected them prematurely. It was rare, but it was possible. The currents that she referred to were the famous Uncidas that circulated through more than twenty worlds, leading hundreds of ships astray throughout the centuries.

"Some ships seem to have been here for an eternity," Natalia said. "Look at that one, the one closest to the reef that looks like a crab . . . You can hardly see it. It's like a huge mountain of coral."

"Maybe we'll find something useful on the vessels," Bruno ventured. He couldn't pass up an opportunity to increase his magic supplies.

"Forget it. We're not going down there," Marco warned. "Don't even think—"

"You don't have to come with me," the Italian interrupted. "I'm perfectly fine going by myself."

He took a step off the cliff as he whispered the spell that allowed him to defy the laws of gravity and walk on air. The pendants and amulets that he wore gleamed for an instant as their energy bonded with his own to keep him floating.

"Bruno!" Marco also moved toward the edge of the cliff. For a second he seemed ready to walk after him in the air. "You can't go down there alone! Have you lost your mind? Come back this minute!"

The Italian turned slowly to look at him. A shiver ran down Hector's spine to see him there, floating over the void, with the breeze fluttering his shirttails. It wasn't just about his fear of heights. Hector remembered all too well what had happened in the sorcery tower the week prior, when Bruno tried to climb up to the top floor of the building, the one that they still hadn't managed to access. It was the day after Ricardo told them what he'd learned from Caleb's scrolls, as if knowing what awaited them when the Red Moon came out had motivated Bruno to try to get to the top floor for the thousandth time. As he approached one of the tower's windows, the levitation spell suddenly wore off, and the Italian dropped like lead to the pavement below. If it hadn't been for the speed with which Natalia cast a healing spell, Bruno would have died only inches from where Alexander met his end.

And now he seemed ready to undertake another solo flight. But if he fell this time, there would be no one below to reconstruct his broken bones.

"I only want to take a look," he assured them. "If I sense the slightest danger, I'll come back up."

"You're not going down there," Marco insisted.

For a few seconds the Italian remained floating in the air, his cold glare fixated on Marco. Finally, he nodded his head and in two strides returned to the safety of the cliff.

"You're in charge" was all he said.

By now they'd lost count of the number of spells that Bruno could cast. He was able to invoke clouds, make small objects levitate, and induce sleep in someone just by stroking their forehead. He could sculpt the flames of candles and torches, light up a room with a clap, record his voice on rocks or project it from a distance . . . And with each passing day he learned a new enchantment. But despite all of those wonders, Bruno swore that he was still short of practicing actual magic. All that he'd learned, he said, were no more than low-level spells, incantations for beginners. True magic was as far from his reach as the top floor of the sorcery tower.

Natalia was considerably behind the Italian. She couldn't keep pace with him. While to Bruno each spell he learned seemed simpler than the last, the opposite was true for the Russian girl: each new spell required more effort. That frustrated her to the point that she'd started to talk about giving up on magic.

"Well, it looks like I can't do much more than I'm doing now," she told them grouchily one day, after spending hours trying to learn a spell that Bruno had picked up in only a few minutes.

After looking at the chaos of reefs and overlapping ships for some time, they decided to investigate the lighthouse. The seven teenagers moved from the edge of the cliff and began the slight ascent to the rocky platform. As always, Rachel led the way, with Marco and Ricardo not far behind. The girl amused herself with a stick she used to cast rocks over the edge of the cliff. The mermaids didn't seem bothered; Hector supposed they must have been quite used to landslides. After the two boys and Rachel came Natalia and Marina, and at the rear, Bruno and himself. Lizbeth had stayed in the tower taking care of Madeleine, who'd had stomach problems for the last couple of days. The redhead refused to have Bruno or Natalia help her with magic; after what happened to Alexander she didn't want anything to do with it.

The only sign of deterioration on the lighthouse was the door. It was detached from its upper hinge and hung at an angle to the right like a mocking grin. Rachel crossed the threshold while the rest waited at the foot of the stairs which led to the entrance. Once the girl announced that all was clear, they entered the lighthouse.

It was a sturdy and simple building, dark without being dismal. A large wooden staircase wound around itself on the way up to the dome, with a rusty handrail to the right that inspired very little confidence. In the lower part of the lighthouse they found a trapdoor leading to a cellar full of ropes, tools, and barrels. There were also several curious rolls of thin, rough paper piled up on the ground. Each roll measured about six feet, and the ends were fitted with metallic washers.

As they climbed the stairs, Hector remembered Marina's story and its tragic protagonists: a lighthouse keeper and a shipwreck's sole survivor. At first, they had communicated through flashes: she used the light of the lighthouse by night, and he used mirrors by day. Until the lighthouse keeper, weary of this slow and tiresome dialogue, launched a cable from the lighthouse platform and lowered a small barrel for him. Inside was food, parchment, pen, ink, and the first of the hundreds of letters that over the course of seven years would be exchanged up and down along the wall of the cliff. During that time they spoke of everything under the sun; they told of their lives and dreams, their nightmares, their desires; and as might be expected, they fell in love. He asked her a thousand times to keep the rope lowered so he could climb up to her, but the lighthouse keeper always said no—frightened, she said, that they would be discovered and put to death. One night during the seventh year, the castaway, tired of the loneliness and waiting, decided to climb up the cliff himself. He almost fell countless times, but he persisted and ascended the nearly one thousand feet that separated him from the platform. Without stopping to catch his breath, he entered the lighthouse, anxious to find his beloved, shouting her name as he rushed up the stairs.

A frightening creature came out to meet him in the building's dome. Marina had described it as a hybrid of human and octopus, with a torso covered in tentacles, the head of a giant squid, and a cluster of trembling pseudopods for legs. Without thinking twice, the castaway ran his harpoon through the horror. Then he resumed his search for his love. It wasn't long before he realized that the being he'd killed was in fact the woman he searched for. The revelation drove him mad, and in his pain and sorrow, he threw himself from the top of the cliff into the abyss.

Hector found the harpoon sticking out of the wall to the left of the hallway that led to the dome of the lighthouse and its lamp. What truly shocked him was that no one was surprised to see it. He understood that they had all been waiting for definitive proof that Marina's story was true. In fact, they would have been disappointed if they hadn't found it.

"Rocavarancolia is Delirium," Marina said, looking with wide-open eyes at the harpoon and the old, damp stain which it penetrated. She didn't blink. "It's the city from my stories." She reached her hand back, grabbed Hector by the waist, and pulled him toward her without even looking at him. "How can it be? How can I have written something that actually happened?"

Hector put his arm around her shoulders, and she turned to bury her face in his chest. She trembled. He felt so uncomfortable holding her in front of everyone that he shifted his gaze out of the hallway toward the lamp in the dome, an enormous contraption hung from the ceiling with one of those thick scrolls of parchment inserted inside. He still managed to glimpse Natalia's grim and somber face. He ignored it. He ignored everything that wasn't Marina's embrace and the vision of the sea out beyond the lighthouse dome.

The young girl stopped trembling and said something that no one understood. She separated from Hector and repeated herself.

"We have to find the cemetery in Rocavarancolia," she said, determined. Her voice no longer shook. She nodded forcefully, as if she were convincing herself of the idea. "We must find it."

"The cemetery?" Mistral raised an eyebrow. He didn't like the idea of approaching Lady Scar's territory. "It's one of the forbidden places, remember? Why do you want to go there?"

"We just need to get close to it. I want to check something, okay? That's all . . ."

"It has to do with the stories you haven't told us, right?" Ricardo asked. "The one that's half finished or the one you haven't even started yet."

Marina nodded. She stroked her right arm as she looked back at the harpoon sticking out of the wall.

"I only had a few things written in a notebook and a couple of finished pages. 'The Voices of the Dead,' I was going to call it." She looked away from the harpoon. "The story was . . . It was about . . ." She huffed and furrowed her brow before continuing. "In the cemetery in Delirium there lived a monster, a horrible being that terrified everyone in the city and had forbidden anyone to enter. He declared the cemetery to be his dominion, and he'd kill anyone who dared pass through its gates." She swallowed. For some reason it was hard for her to explain herself, as if emotion were clouding her thoughts. "Then . . . in my story, someone died in the city, someone important to the main character, a kid our age. And despite the monster, despite his forbidding it and how dangerous it was, he decided to bring the body to the cemetery. Because that was the place where it should be." She shook her head. "I'd only written a couple of pages, I told you . . . But some things were very clear to me. The cemetery's dead, for example, never stopped talking for even a moment, that's where the title came from. And at the end, the protagonist, although I still hadn't decided how, was able to bury the corpse there. Plus, the tomb would be incredible, a tomb unlike any other in the whole cemetery." She was silent for a few moments. "That's what I want to see. I want to see if that tomb exists. If it does, I'll recognize it. I'm sure of it."

"But why?" Rachel asked.

It was Bruno who answered.

"It seems obvious that Marina believes that, as with the tale of the lighthouse keeper, the story she is now telling us is also true. Or rather, it will be. She suspects that the protagonist of the story is one of us. And therefore the body that's brought to the cemetery must inevitably belong to another member of the group. Am I wrong?"

"No, you're not wrong."

"You couldn't have come up with a happier story, huh . . ." murmured Natalia in a bitter tone. "Why do you always have to be so sinister?"

"It was just a story," she explained. "At least, that's all I thought it was." She looked at Marco. "I have to see that cemetery," she insisted. "If I recognize the tomb from my story, then it belongs to the past as well, just like the one with the lighthouse. But if that's not the case . . ." She left the sentence unfinished. She returned her gaze once more to the harpoon embedded in the wall.


Dario discovered a flaw in his rival's defense and immediately took advantage of it; moving with astonishing swiftness, he swung a horizontal blow with his sword, which would have decapitated Adrian had he been in front of him, and not many yards away, in the tower courtyard. The Brazilian saw him throw his sword to the ground in a rage and walk quickly to the gate, without even throwing him a glance. Dario sighed, sheathed his weapon, and wiped the sweat from his forehead with the edge of his cloak. Each day it became harder to beat Adrian. Today he thought he'd lost more than once, but his adversary hadn't known how to take the upper hand. Adrian only needed an ounce more of malice and cunning to defeat him.

He waited a few minutes before he climbed down the front of the building. He did it with a spectacular agility, with an innate skill that had saved his life many times in Rocavarancolia as well as during his days as a thief in São Paolo. When he was just ten feet shy of the ground, he let himself fall. He landed in a squat. He made sure that his belt and sword were still in place before he got up and began running alongside the wall. He reviewed the details of the fight that had just taken place, as if the result were truly of importance, and not just a ridiculous pantomime that he took part in without entirely understanding why.

In São Paolo he'd been involved in numerous fights, although none with a sword: sticks and knives at most, usually just fistfights. He looked at his sword's blue hilt. The guard was fine and slim, with two precious stones embedded at the ends which seemed to watch him like restless eyes. Dario didn't know much about swords, but one of the few things he was certain of was that they didn't act on their own, that it was the will of the person wielding it in control, not the other way around. However, it wasn't that way with the weapon that he wore on his belt. There were times, like that day on the staircase, when the sword acted of its own accord. He hadn't wanted to hurt that dumb kid, he only wanted to be left alone, that was all; his only desire had been to get out of the way. But the weapon had wanted blood, and as it leapt forward, he couldn't stop it.

He'd found it in the fissure that divided the city in two. Dario went down there as soon as he saw the number of weapons scattered among the skeletons. He grabbed the first one in his reach, and managed to avoid setting foot in that bloodcurdling ossuary. A skeletal arm, with bits of cloth still attached, reached through a mountain of remains close to the wall, with the sword grasped tightly in its bony hand; it almost seemed to be offering it to him. As soon as he took it, a mighty clattering shook the chasm and several waves of bone headed in his direction. Dario climbed the wall at top speed but stopped halfway, knowing that he couldn't get to safety in time. He had a fleeting glimpse of a mouth full of knives that leapt toward him in a cloud of splinters. It was the first time the sword acted on its own. The boy felt it pull from his arm in a violent downward arc. The blow split the beast's head in two with startling ease; the creature shivered in the air and fell back into the ossuary from whence it emerged. The other waves fell upon the corpse of their companion, completely oblivious to Dario.

That had been the first of many tests that Rocavarancolia had submitted him to. The patched-together woman had assured him that it mattered little whether he sought his destiny in a group or on his own, that the difficulties for an individual would be the same as those for a group, but Dario had found that this wasn't true. There were creatures that wouldn't have dared to confront a group as well nourished as the one from the tower, but they had no qualms about going after him. Without his peculiar sword, he would have died his first week in Rocavarancolia, he was sure of it. The magic weapon and his own skill had kept him alive. That, and the fact that he learned quickly that it was safer to travel by rooftop and terrace than on the ground.

He climbed the ruined wall of a three-story red brick building with slender pillars. He'd hidden his sack among the covey of gargoyles gathered in the façade's center, all with open jaws and mismatched faces looking down with pure rage.

The Brazilian looked around. The wind ruffled his black hair, which flapped about his head like a restless cloud. The ruined city extended in all directions, a chaos of damaged buildings, destroyed streets, and rubble.

Denestor Tul had assured him that he was bringing him to the place where he belonged, and Dario couldn't agree more. He even felt that all of his years in São Paolo had been nothing more than preparation for what awaited in Rocavarancolia, for a life of frenzy, being chased, and constant fear. He'd lost count of all of the creatures that had attacked him in the time he'd been there. He'd managed to evade most of them, but in some cases he'd had no choice but to confront them.

His back was still sore from the blows of a crazed, ape-like creature that had jumped on top of him from the rooftop of a broken temple. The ape was dressed in a dirty, tattered tunic, and as it hit him again and again, it shouted: *Tell me your name! Your name! Tell me! Tell me!*

The sword had taken care of that.

But the monsters that roamed the ruined city weren't his major concern. Those creatures had flesh that could be cut, and he had a sword eager to do it. What scared him was that which he couldn't confront with steel: the houses that whispered, the strange presences that he felt some nights, or the voices that came from nowhere. He didn't know how to confront those.

For a while, a ghost had pursued him through the city. It had appeared suddenly. It was a pale woman with tangled black hair full of spiders, flies, and beetles, and all she did was point to him with her long fingers as she spoke in an incomprehensible language. It didn't matter how far he ran; she always glided through the air to follow him, speeding up when he did or stopping if he himself stopped, gesturing and speaking all the while. Dario hadn't been able to sleep during that time. As soon as his eyes began to close from exhaustion, that horrible woman woke him up, shouting and bringing her hands to her head. Two days after he first saw her, the woman vanished.

At any rate, he'd managed to stay alive, showing himself worthy of the monstrous place. He'd passed, one by one, all of the tests that were set before him, growing stronger in the process. And he hadn't needed any more help than what he got from the magic sword. He didn't need anything else. Nor did he need anyone else.

He began moving from roof to roof, at a good pace without running, always heading southeast. Terraces, rooftops, and pinnacles of the city passed under his feet, in quick succession. He knew very well which areas to avoid and which rooftops, though they appeared in good shape, were no more than treacherous traps. The riotous birds flew overhead every so often, flapping erratically. A feathered serpent that slept curled up in a chimney hissed furiously as Dario passed, awakening the creature, but it did not attempt to go after him. On more than one occasion he had to climb down to bypass a hazardous area or to cross the street.

It was when he was climbing up to the rooftops along a wall of cracked pottery that he saw the rest of the group from the tower. They walked down the middle of the road, with the skinny girl in front. His eyes settled immediately on Marina, walking as if in a daze between Hector and the tall teenager who served as the group's leader. It was difficult for him to look away from her. He clenched his teeth with force, cursed his own stupidity, and, careful not to be seen, continued maneuvering through the tiles and gargoyles, repeating over and over that he didn't need anyone. Absolutely no one. And definitely not that dull girl with her listless airs.

He came down from the rooftops when he reached a street that had been completely demolished. The majority of the buildings were no more than ruins, huge mountains of rubble that roughly marked the edges of the avenue. There were areas where the ground seemed to have liquefied, only to solidify again almost immediately, giving way to curious rocky whirlwind formations that rose up several yards. At some points of the terrain he saw, sunken firmly in the stone, tracks left by gigantic claws. At first he suspected dragons, although the place seemed more like the aftermath of a bombing than of fire. He headed to an alleyway located between two of the few surviving structures.

It was a damp, dark side street, one of the few places in Rocavarancolia where the ground was soil instead of rock. The walls of the buildings that formed the passage were covered in a reddish, foul-smelling mildew. Water flowed from the eaves and windowsills, a constant dripping that turned the ground into a filthy quagmire. Dario looked up as he entered the alley. Two gargoyles watched him from above. One of them had its claws clasped against its cheeks in an expression of absolute horror, as if the sight of the young boy had filled it with dread.

The alleyway ended at a brick wall. The lower part opened into an archway two feet tall and six feet wide, with thick bars of black iron. He hadn't taken a single step into the alley before a gigantic arm shot out from between the bars. A grotesque hand with seven long, hefty fingers scratched anxiously at the muddy ground.

Dario stopped a few feet from the hand that stretched out toward him, ever more frantic, more full of rage. The fingers opened and closed desperately in the air, as if the imprisoned creature sensed how close he was. Each finger had four joints and ended in a broken nail.

The Brazilian crouched down a few inches from the desperate hand. It gave off a strong odor of rot. The hand and its forearm were covered in black scales edged with brown bristles. Through the gated archway he could hear labored breathing. The same hand always appeared through the opening, in an unnatural posture. Dario supposed the being was chained to the wall, but he didn't dare get close enough to find out.

The hand had almost grabbed him over a month ago, when he was seeking refuge in the alleyway after hearing footsteps running in his direction from the other side of the avenue. That danger had never manifested—the footsteps turned north and disappeared—but a dark claw had rushed at him, closing scarcely an inch from his right ankle.

Dario let his sack drop at his feet. He opened it and took out several scraps of raw meat. He threw one close to the hand, which scrabbled in the mud to find it, grabbed the meat, and disappeared hastily through the bars. It wasn't long until he heard the sound of eager chewing. Shortly after, the hand emerged again from the darkness, with the palm facing up. It almost seemed to be begging. He threw another piece, and the claw grabbed it and retreated again behind the wall.

Dario listened to the imprisoned monster chewing. He found the noise oddly comforting. He didn't understand why, just like he didn't understand the reason he was drawn to the Margalar Tower day after day to duel with the little blond boy, or to spy on the others' daily activities. He brushed the hair from his forehead. When the dark claw crept from the shadows and felt around the muddy ground for more food, he almost smiled.

★★★

Lizbeth realized at once that something had occurred during the day's outing.

"Hey, what happened?" she asked, with her hands on her hips. The question was directed to all of them, but she never took her large eyes off Marina. Hector was surprised by the way Lizbeth had gotten to know all of them in the almost two months they'd been in Rocavarancolia. She could pinpoint their moods from a mere gesture or a tone of voice, whether they were feeling homesick, annoyed, or anything else.

"Little Miss Tragedy says that one of us is going to die," Natalia answered. "That's what happened."

Adrian was sitting with his feet on the table, using a knife to carve a piece of wood. From the sulky look on his face it was clear that he'd already received a visit from the rooftop kid, and the result of their fight had been the usual.

"You don't have to be very bright to know that," he growled.

Marina stepped in to explain. When she was telling them about the harpoon they'd found at the top of the lighthouse, Madeleine appeared on the spiral staircase, dismal and disheveled as usual. She stayed to listen to the rest of the story, remaining still, with one hand on the wall and the other on her stomach. Hector looked at her out of the corner of his eye while their friend continued speaking. Her eyes gleamed in a strange way as she listened. The hand on her stomach twitched from time to time. Hector didn't know if it was from pain or because Marina's tale made such an impression on her.

"And does anyone have any idea where we can find the cemetery in question?" Lizbeth asked.

Bruno nodded.

"I don't know the exact whereabouts, but I can point out approximately where it is. In the map from the atlas that we found shortly after we got here, there was a large cemetery in the northeast part of Rocavarancolia. That's where we should head."

Hector paid no attention to the Italian's words. Madeleine was growing paler by the minute. The trembling in her hand had transferred to her whole body. He approached her, worried.

"Are you okay?" he asked.

The redhead was startled. She looked him straight in the eye.

"We didn't bury him," she said. Her expression was one of absolute bewilderment, and it didn't change even as tears began to run down her cheeks. "There was nothing left to bury. Nothing. He turned to ash."

"Maddie?" Lizbeth started walking toward her.

"My brother, my brother, my brother . . ." She looked around. She seemed crazed, lost. Her knees gave out, and she had to sit on the stairs. "Alex is dead," she said, as if she'd just received the news that very second. She repeated it over and over again, incredulous, without taking her eyes off Hector, who crouched before her. "He's dead."

Mistral slid from his bed, trying not to make a sound. Darkness spread throughout the top floor of the Margalar Tower, like an extension of midnight that reached in through the embrasures. There were a dozen candles lit, but the light was not enough to dispel the darkness. The only thing he heard was the desolate howl of the wind among the ruins and the tranquil breathing of the sleeping teenagers.

The shapeshifter moved slowly toward the stairs. They still all slept together, although the common room had been free of its original chaotic state for some time. The beds, mattresses, and blankets were now in good condition; there were dressers and chairs placed here and there, and even two large wardrobes that he and Ricardo had moved piece by piece from a nearby room. In the beginning, the space had resembled an improvised campsite, but now it was, without a doubt, a home.

Someone turned in their sleep. Mistral supposed it was Adrian, who stubbornly fought his fears and phantoms even in slumber, sometimes with such violence that he ended up on the floor. When he reached the staircase he realized he was wrong: for once it wasn't Adrian who stirred nervously in bed, but Madeleine. The girl shook her head from left to right in constant denial, with trembling lips and a furrowed brow. Her red hair shook on the pillow like a choppy sea. The shapeshifter leaned over and stroked her forehead tenderly. She calmed down at once. He watched her for a few moments. Her crying fit that afternoon had gone on for so long that Bruno offered to put her to sleep with a spell, a suggestion that they all rejected, scandalized.

*Sometimes,* Mistral thought, *you have to hit bottom in order to gain the momentum to return to the surface.*

He was convinced that from that moment on, Maddie would start to recover. It had taken weeks for her to come to terms with the tragedy, anesthetized by her own pain. Now the bubble had burst, and everything should be, if not better, at least a little easier.

Mistral moved away from the red-haired girl's bed and went down the stairs. When he got to the second floor he saw light coming through the half-open door to one of the rooms. Ricardo was still working on the translation of the scrolls that they'd found at the amphitheater.

He knocked on the door before entering.

The Spaniard was sitting at the table, surrounded by candles and candelabras. He had a pen in hand and ink stains on each of his fingers. He smiled as Mistral walked in.

"You're not planning on sleeping tonight?" Mistral asked. "Your eyes will melt if you keep this up."

One of the beasts from the pack in the mountains howled, but neither of them flinched.

"I want to finish this part I'm working on before I go to bed," Ricardo said. "It won't take long."

In the week since they'd found the scrolls, Mistral still hadn't figured out if the teenager was lying or if he really believed that he'd translated them accurately. And he had even more doubts after he'd secretly read the texts of Blatto Zenzé. He had to admit that the poems that spoke of Rocavaragalago and the Red Moon comprised such complicated lyricism and metaphors that it was likely to misinterpret them.

"And have you found anything that could be useful?" he asked.

Ricardo shrugged his shoulders.

"That depends on what you consider useful. Obviously nothing that we found here will lead us back home, forget about that . . . But at least we'll know more about this place and its history, and that can be helpful to us." He sat back in his chair and rubbed his eyes. He looked exhausted. "I'm finishing up the poems that talk about the founding of the kingdom. It's no wonder this city is such a horror, considering who founded it."

Ricardo was referring to Harex, the first king of Rocavarancolia, and to his cruel brother Hurza the Eye-Eater. He'd already told the group about them, unaware that Marco knew more of those sinister characters than anything the scrolls of Blatto Zenzé could teach him.

The two brothers had arrived adrift in a badly damaged schooner, first of the hundreds of ships that the Uncidas, the cursed currents, would bring to their world.

The damaged ship ran aground close to a small fishing village. Despite the fear inspired by the impressive vessel, a hundred times larger than the biggest of their barges, the locals rushed to help the crew before the boat sank. They found dozens of corpses on deck. They were beings almost identical to themselves, although much paler and with curious grayish horns on their foreheads. The corpses showed no sign of a struggle, only the effects of thirst, hunger, and prolonged misery. To their misfortune, the locals made the ill-fated discovery of two emaciated survivors in the forecastle: Harex and Hurza. They brought them into the village and made the grave mistake of saving their lives. As repayment, the brothers murdered half the population and enslaved the rest. That was the beginning of Rocavarancolia.

And what could they expect from a kingdom founded on murder and terror? A land created by monsters could only produce monsters. And he was one of them, although sometimes his ability to change form was so spontaneous that he'd forget. But he couldn't deceive himself for long. His hands would never forget the pressure they'd exerted around the neck of the sleeping child he'd strangled. In his dreams he still heard Alexander's screams as he fell under the spell of the gate that Mistral himself had encouraged him to pass through. As long as he lived, he'd never stop hearing it. That scream had become part of his being.

Mistral chatted with Ricardo for a few more minutes before excusing himself and going on his way. He went silently down the stairs, attentive to the sounds that came from above. He walked out into the courtyard with a torch, more for appearances than out of real necessity. His eyes were able to see in the darkness as well as they could during the light of day.

He went into the bathroom located right in front of the main tower gate. He closed the door behind him and left the torch on an overhang while he searched for Denestor Tul. He found him fluttering around the ceiling, his consciousness once again projected into the usual blue butterfly. It was the first time that Mistral used the system designed by the demiurge to contact him. It wasn't very complicated. One of the spiders in the tower was a creation of Denestor's, and required only a touch for it to send a message to Highlowtower. It was even easier for the demiurge; anytime he wanted to talk to him, he simply sent his butterfly flying about the patio.

"Give me some good news: tell me you called me because you're going to leave the tower once and for all," the butterfly whispered, flying around his head.

"It's still not the right time," he growled. He was starting to get tired of that same old story. "No, it's not . . . And I didn't come for you to bother me about that again. Listen: tomorrow we're going to the cemetery, and I don't want to run into Lady Scar. I thought it would be good if you could distract her somehow. Send for her to talk about some council nonsense. We'll go after we've eaten, as usual."

"You must leave," the butterfly insisted. "You've already done everything that you could for them. The only thing you're doing now is putting us in danger. The children, you, me, and the entire kingdom."

"All the more reason to keep Lady Scar out of my way."

"I knew you were stubborn, but it surprises me to find out to what extent."

"Will you do it?"

"Do I have a choice?" the butterfly asked.

In the mountains, in Highlowtower, Denestor Tul furrowed his brow. He had no alternative but to give in to Mistral, and he knew it. The demiurge felt the weight of destiny on his chest, the inescapable fate that approached, quickly and ravenously. *You've brought us the end*, Lady Dream had predicted. And in those moments, unable to stop the shapeshifter's madness, he couldn't help but think that he was right on the edge of the abyss, with nothing he could do or say to change his course in the slightest from that fatal trajectory.

# VOICES OF THE DEAD

Shortly after waking up, Bruno informed them in his usual dispassionate tone that it was Christmas Day. Of all of them, he was the only one who made an effort to keep up with Earth's calendar. The others had given in to the unremarkable passing of time on Rocavarancolia.

"Christmas. What joy," crooned Natalia, looking with a bleak expression at the meager meal that had been laid out on the table for breakfast. "Should we have a party to celebrate it?"

"We can hang ornaments from the spider in the courtyard," Rachel said, after stifling a yawn with the back of her hand. Ricardo mussed up her hair. She dropped down at the table, laid her face on her crossed arms, and pretended to sleep.

"Christmas," Hector grumbled, and he felt like the word left a bitter taste in his mouth. It seemed impossible that in some part of the universe someone could be having a party. He leaned back in his chair, a piece of moldy cheese in one hand. He sighed as he began to scrape the greenish film off the cheese with a knife. Back at home, they would spend days putting up Christmas decorations, and it was their tradition for his sister to light up the tree. His mother served what had come to be known as her Christmas delicacies: a wide selection of hors d'oeuvres that kept Sarah and Hector enthralled for hours, first watching their mother prepare them and then enjoying them at the table. They rarely touched the main course simply because they were too full from canapés. Last year, he and his sister had organized a competition to see who could eat more appetizers. He'd won, of course.

But that was in another life.

When they talked about Earth and their families—and all of the many things they missed—it was mostly at night, right before they went to bed. These conversations weren't very frequent; realizing what they'd lost made them sad. Memories provided no solace, knowing that they would probably never be able to return to their world. And the fact that no one on the other side remembered them just made it worse.

"I miss so many things . . ." Marina said during one of their chats. "Music, flowers, sunset on the Seine. The light from the stars . . ." She sighed. "That's something I don't understand. There should be stars, right? The universe is full of them, isn't it? So why don't we see any from here?"

"I'm dying for a good meal," Rachel piped up. She had the largest appetite out of all of them, which was unusual, given her scrawny appearance. "Real food. A good roast, with little potatoes and bread with dipping sauce . . ."

"A glass of chocolate milk," Lizbeth said. "And biscuits . . . I'd be good with that. And muffins. Okay, and maybe something chocolatey . . . with toffee sauce on top."

"And what I wouldn't give to have my books here," Ricardo added. "My father gave me one every week."

"A television," Rachel whispered. "To spend hours watching cartoons and horror movies. Can you conjure a TV for me, Bruno?"

"I doubt that there's a TV-conjuring spell," the Italian answered. "But even if there were and I could, I think we'd have a seriously hard time tuning it. I don't know what signal we'd be able to get here—"

"Bruno, Bruno," Hector interrupted. "It's a joke, just a joke. Don't waste any more time thinking about it, please."

"Oh."

"I miss my parents most of all," Natalia said. "And that's surprising, because on Earth I couldn't stand them, they were always on my back, always controlling me . . . But now I miss them." She seemed taken aback. "And I also miss the rain. I could spend hours listening to the rain."

Hector knew that Natalia missed something else from Earth: her elves, those creatures that only she could see, nothing like the ones that stalked them in Rocavarancolia.

"I don't miss anything," Bruno stated. "Although that's probably because my life on Earth was so far from what you'd consider a normal life."

"And because you're strange," Natalia told him.

"You'd be strange too if you spent years without even leaving the house, with no one to give you a kind or caring word," Marina said in his defense. "You're pretty weird yourself."

"Look who's talking!" said Natalia.

"I miss silence most of all." Adrian sighed. "Yes. Silence at nighttime. I miss getting into bed and sleeping without hearing anyone talk nonsense."

"Well, go sleep downstairs," Natalia said. "You have a whole tower to yourself."

"And leave you guys alone and helpless?" he asked. "What kind of heartless creature do you take me for?"

It wasn't hard for Hector to decide what he missed most about Earth: he knew very well. It was his sister's laugh. Sarah had an explosive way of laughing, one of those contagious laughs that were impossible to resist. There was one afternoon in particular, when they went with their parents to the annual end-of-school show. He'd whispered something in her ear while they watched the boring play that closed the event. He couldn't recall what he said, but the girl suffered one of the greatest bursts of laughter that he could remember, which spread little by little to all of the audience members, traveling through the rows of seats like a swell of thunderous guffaws. The terrible actors had no choice but to stop midscene and wait for the laughter to die down before they continued the play. As they were leaving, everyone agreed that Sarah's laugh had been the highlight of the performance.

"What about you, Marco, what do you miss the most?" Hector asked, after telling the theater story.

The shapeshifter rolled over in bed face up, with his eyes fixed on the ceiling of the Margalar Tower. How could he answer that? *I miss the time when Rocavarancolia was great and feared,* he could say. *The time when the city was beautiful and walking through the streets was a pleasure, a delight; when you didn't know what miracle or marvel you might find around the next corner. I miss the singing shadow of the Incredible Tower, destroyed by giants from the world of Kalamadara. I miss the songs of the bards in the Devil's Jawbone Square, the brilliance of the open vortices sparkling at twilight,*

*the fierce flapping of dragon wings in the Dragon Towers and the furious roaring*
*as they slept . . . I miss so many things and I'm afraid to look back and realize*
*the price that I've had to pay for them.*

"Everything. I miss absolutely everything," he said. His voice broke
in his throat in such a way that the conversation ended then and there.


Hector thought of how paradoxical it was that the place most splendid
and full of life that they'd encountered in Rocavarancolia was the
cemetery. It was an hour's walk from the tower, in a hollow beyond
the Scar of Arax. Its beauty took their breath away—the burial ground
was in perfect condition, without the slightest trace of ruin or neglect.
The battle that had reduced most of the city to rubble had spared it.

The group had congregated at the top of one of the eight ramps that
led down to the great complex of tombs. A black pantheon of startling
grandeur rose up in the middle. It consisted of a huge pentagonal
building, topped with a black dome, and four impressive pyramids.
The main entryway of the pentagon featured a large double-leaf gate
with intricate gold-and-silver arabesque engravings.

The other tombs were spread out around the gigantic pantheon.
There were tombs of every type, size, and design: some were little
more than packed earth with no distinctive markers, others were mausoleums so elaborate that there was always a new archivolt or feature to
discover—a previously hidden detail, or another tiny creature sculpted
in the stone—no matter how long one looked at them. Not only
tombs abounded, also obelisks covered with inscriptions, wooden
signposts, commemorative columns, fountains, and statues.

However, the most striking feature was the lush vegetation that
flourished throughout the cemetery, which they found much more surprising than the revelation that the dead buried there never ceased their
chatter. Marina's story had prepared them for the voices from beyond
the grave, but nobody had told them that after weeks living among
rock, stone, and granite, they'd finally run into nature again.
Everywhere they looked they saw gardens, ponds, trees of every kind—
most of the species were unfamiliar, but they did recognize cypresses,
pines, and willow trees. The greenery of the gardens, the ivy, and the
moss spilled out onto the paths and climbed up tombs and mausoleums.

Hector was so absorbed in the beautiful sight that for a while he forgot about the dead. Most of them talked about nonsense, at least to the group's ears; others chatted in barely audible whispers, and only a few made mention of them.

"Live children with hot blood in their veins," crooned a voice coming from a white stone tomb situated at the foot of the ramp where they stood. "How long has it been since the living visited us?"

"Decades!"

"You're wrong. Yesterday afternoon I had a lovely visit," said another with an affected elegance, from beneath a gray slab covered halfway with moss. "A girl dressed as an angel who hummed a song as she danced around me, don't you remember her?"

"That was two hundred and twenty-three years ago, you smelly fool," the neighbor replied. "And she wasn't singing, she was screaming because a troll was after her. She ended up devoured, if I remember correctly."

"How disgusting."

Natalia looked at Marina with unease.

"Is your tomb here or not?" she asked brusquely. The dark-haired girl shook her head. If Natalia's tone had bothered her, she didn't let it show.

"No, it's not here. I'll recognize it if I see it. I think."

"So can we go already? This place gives me the creeps."

"The creeps?" Rachel looked at her, surprised. "What do you mean? It's a lovely place."

"I don't like cemeteries, okay? They're spooky."

"They're not spooky, this one least of all," Marina said. "They're not places of death, although many people think so. They're places to honor those who've lived and remember them as they once were."

"You like cemeteries because you're creepy."

"You're so annoying!" Marina glared at Natalia. Then she huffed and looked at Marco. "We should go down and take a look. Maybe we can't see the tomb from here."

The shapeshifter nodded and gestured for Rachel to lead the group. He knew that there was no evil magic in the cemetery, but it was better to keep up appearances. Ricardo followed behind her. Hector stepped back to bring up the rear. There was no trace of the warning mist in the area. Natalia, growing more vexed by the minute, sank her halberd violently into the muddy ground.

"What about the monster?" she asked. "Marina said there was a monster, remember?"

Marco unsheathed his sword and waved it dramatically in the air.

"Let him come out if he wants!" he shouted. He felt a rush of euphoria with his childish posturing. "We'll let him have it!"

He knew that the monster from Marina's story was Lady Scar, and thanks to Denestor Tul they wouldn't have to worry about her. Besides, the woman hadn't been completely honest during her welcome speech when she spoke of the cemetery being forbidden. What was actually prohibited by law was the harvest entering the Royal Pantheon; if Lady Scar had extended the ban to the rest of the cemetery, it was for the simple reason that she didn't want the kids running around her territory.

"Come down, come down!" a voice from a tomb covered with petrified crowns of roses called to them. "I, the deceased Count of Bratalante, victor of the siege of Masquerade, officially invite you into our holy place of repose! You are welcome!"

"And I, Duke of Malvaraburn, retract the invitation this instant! Take your poisonous breath and filthy heartbeats elsewhere!"

"Please! Come, come!" some shouted.

"No! Leave here with your cursed life and your cursed heat! Get out! Get out!" howled others.

They descended the slope and began walking through the cemetery's gardens, captivated by the tombs and mausoleums. Natalia followed them at a distance, dragging her halberd behind her, with an air of disgust at everything and everyone. The dead never stopped talking:

"I was surprised to see her in the castle, I assure you, my good friend. We'd separated on such unfriendly terms that . . ."

"You bore me. You bore me so much."

"I died in the battle of Muddywater, the fifth day of the fifth month of the year of the first spider . . . I led a company of dead giant lancers on horseback. We didn't see them coming, no, we didn't see them. Suddenly the wings of the dragons of the Effigy Kingdom darkened the sky, their flames finished us off to the very last . . ."

"I used to love cheese smeared with honey. And the crunch of corn in my mouth, although I've forgotten its flavor. But the last strawberries of the season are what I remember best. Oh. It gives me the shivers . . ."

Bruno tried to communicate with them, but all of his efforts were in vain. Either they ignored him, or their responses had nothing to do with what he asked. They soon got used to the constant murmur of their chatter. The voices of the dead weren't the only sounds in the cemetery. The late afternoon wind rustled the leaves on the trees. They also heard the songs of several gray and green birds that flew above like little feathery bolts of lightning.

The roads and paths made their way among the tombs, following a spiral pattern that led downward to the black pantheon at the bottom of the hollow. There were endless statues: warriors standing guard in front of the pantheon doors; poets seated on white stone pedestals, writing on their parchments; musicians who played their stone instruments over the tombstones; angels and demons, and other unidentifiable beings. Some were as beautiful as others were horrifying.

They reached a landscaped park in the shape of a half moon, with a small pond full of water lilies in a corner, and they decided to take a break. Atop a colonnade next to the pond rose a silver-and-bronze statue of a woman warrior, garbed in chain mail and armed with a gigantic lance; she looked to the sky with an alert expression, as if expecting something to pounce on her.

Lizbeth, as always, had brought meat, bread, and fruit in her back-pack, snacks that she handed out to the group. Some sat to eat on the scattered banks around the pond, while others wandered through the park. Bruno approached a tomb and studied its inscriptions with fascination, ignoring the voice that arose from the grave that begged him, if it weren't too much trouble, to move away, because he was blocking the light.

Marina stood still in front of the barred door of a mausoleum that appeared to be made of ice and crystal. The bars of the gate were hollow glass and inside flowed long strands of water that entwined with one another as they trickled down. The effect was hypnotic. An amphibious gargoyle, also made of glass, crouched over the structure's pyramidal arcade; the expression on its face was one of striking severity.

"That's strange . . ." the girl said.

"What is it?" Hector approached her. The polished crystal door of the pantheon reflected their silhouettes, but in a ghostly way: they were reduced to simple shifting shadows with no identifying features.

"This cemetery is warm and friendly, and it doesn't make sense." Marina gestured all around her. "Okay, the dead talk, and that's weird, I admit, but the rest . . . It's so beautiful." She lowered her voice. "My father says that to know a city well, you have to visit its cemetery, because that site in particular says a lot about it, about its soul. In big cities they tend to be cold and anonymous. Instead of burying the dead it seems like they're warehousing them. This one, on the other hand . . ." She exhaled. "It's going to sound strange, but . . . this is the cemetery of a place with a good heart."

"If this city has a good heart, it's because it tore it out of someone," said Hector.

Marina smiled. She turned toward him and straightened his shirt collar, which was crooked.

"It just doesn't fit," she said. "That's it . . . It doesn't fit that a place so horrible would honor its dead this way." She shrugged her shoulders. She fixed her gaze on Lizbeth, who'd plucked some yellow flowers from a hedgerow and was placing them in Rachel's hair. "It doesn't mesh with what I thought about this city."

"So just in case, you don't trust it."

"No, I don't. Not for a second. How could I? I know we're not going to find the tomb from my story here. I know it. And I know that someone's going to die, and that one of us will bring them here. Does that seem terrible to you?"

"Very. And it scares me. But it could be that your story doesn't happen, it could be just that: a story. Or who knows? Maybe it already happened, and so long ago that you can't recognize the tomb . . . It's—"

"Can I ask you something?" she interrupted.

"Anything," he quickly answered.

"It's silly, but . . . If something happens to me, bury me here, okay? And not because of my story. This place is beautiful. I'd like to be—"

"You're right." It was his turn to interrupt. He tried to keep his voice from wavering. "It's silly. That's not going to happen because you're not going to die." He hurried to add, afraid that she might think that her life was more important to him than the others', "No one's going to die." As soon as he said it, a cold shiver of doom ran through his body. The certainty that he was wrong was so powerful that it was hard for him to keep his anguish hidden.

Marina took his hand, gave it a hard squeeze, and smiled. Hector returned the smile. He looked around. The unease that he felt was so intense that he rushed to make sure everyone was okay. He saw Natalia sitting on a bank next to the pond, listlessly eating a piece of bread and pretending not to look at them. Ricardo had joined Bruno in studying the inscriptions on the tablets, and they conversed in hushed tones. Rachel and Lizbeth chatted next to a hedgerow, with their hands entwined and their hair full of flowers. Marco stood further away, looking vacantly at the black pantheon.

And under their feet, the dead kept talking:

"I didn't see it coming. Can you believe it? Poison in the food! I expected something more creative from someone living under my very roof! As if murder weren't bad enough . . . the betrayal felt worse!"

"I thought I was going to live forever. How naive, how stupid I was. I thought I had all the time in the world . . ."

"Children with hot blood and fresh breath. Lost children, stolen children . . . Avoid the darkness, do you hear me? Be careful with the shadows, you'd never guess what's waiting for you there. Do you hear me? Never."

Through the eye carried by the metallic bird, Lady Scar saw the children nearing the cemetery, and finally understood the reason Denestor Tul had summoned her with such urgency. It took all she had not to break out in laughter as she continued to listen to the empty excuses that the demiurge had been giving her. He'd mentioned the fate of the kingdom, talking all the while about nothing in particular; he offered endless lists of developments, from the complete demolition of the peripheral area of Rocavarancolia to the extermination of the vermin that swarmed the city, which were nothing more than old propositions rejected by the council.

Lady Scar, already tired of the whole charade, didn't hesitate to interrupt the demiurge midsentence.

"I know that you have no intention of revealing Mistral's whereabouts to me," she said in such an innocent tone that the demiurge's eyes narrowed immediately, "although it would be good if you could get a message to him on my behalf: tell him that he's always welcome at the Royal Pantheon." Lady Scar smiled; the scars that surrounded her lips seemed to curve in unison, giving her face an even more monstrous appearance. "And warn him of one other thing, please: as you well know, I spend a good part of my time in the cemetery, but please emphasize that he should let me know in advance if he's visiting. Everyone knows that an inconvenient and pointless distraction could get me to leave."

The glance she shot at Denestor was revealing. The little gray man's cheeks turned a violent red. The demiurge quickly regained his composure, looked around with a frown, and proceeded to tap on the table where they sat. Almost instantly, a lamp with long velvet wings and the feet of a tortoise at its base glided over to them and alighted on the table. Denestor reached out his hand and pulled a silvery beaded cord to turn it on. A soft, diffuse light enveloped their bodies. Silence surrounded them, a magical, impenetrable silence that emerged from the same lamp that illuminated them. Below that light, their words were heard only by each other.

"So you know."

Lady Scar nodded with amused solemnity. He leaned toward her, his eyes squinting so tight that they were barely visible in the web of wrinkles that was his face. "I don't think I need to tell you of the consequences that this could lead to, it's—"

"Denestor, Denestor . . . I'm guilty of the same crimes that you've committed," said the guardian of the Royal Pantheon. "There's something I should tell you: I've also been bad, my dear demiurge. Very bad . . ."

Crouched in the castle's battlement, Esmael watched over Highlowtower with growing concern. He didn't know what matters Denestor Tul and Lady Scar were dealing with, but they couldn't be of any interest to him. If the demiurge decided to support the guardian of the Royal Pantheon as regent, there was nothing he could do. The thought of Lady Scar taking the reins of the kingdom, which became more of a possibility by the minute, made him shudder. The woman disgusted him; she was a brainless hypocrite, a bland and pitiful creature incapable of understanding that cruelty was a necessary tool for the good government of Rocavarancolia, and not a defect that should be condemned.

He thought he saw her peer out from one of the tower's embrasures, but it was nothing more than one of Denestor's pieces of junk sticking out, a paper kite full of antennae and colored ribbons that climbed up the façade of Highlowtower before taking off in flight. The whole building was a hive for the demiurge's creations; bands of multicolored birds, tiny ships, and insects of all kinds fluttered around its walls like bees around a honeycomb. Even he wouldn't be able to approach undetected, so he had no choice but to spy on them from the castle, growing increasingly tense and ill humored.

Sick of waiting, he took flight, sliding like a shadow through the mountain passes on his way to the city, beating his wings energetically, as if doing so could rid him of his rage and frustration. But there was only one way of letting loose the fury that seized him: he had to kill.

Twilight settled on the mountains with its red and violet splendor. In the castle courtyard, the pack roamed back and forth, conscious that nightfall was near. As they saw Esmael pass by, one of the creatures, a large gray male, bristled his fur, bared his rows of fangs, and growled, as if he were aware of the black angel's thirst for blood and was warning that he wouldn't be easy prey.

Esmael soon left Rocavaragalago behind. The red cathedral seemed to breathe as restlessly as he did above the pit of magma that surrounded it. He entered the ruined city. In the distance, he could see Denestor's kids crossing the Scar of Arax on the way back to the tower. He looked over. Dario was battling with Adrian—one on a nearby rooftop on a hill, the other in the courtyard of the tower. Esmael could almost hear the sound of weapons clashing.

Despite the distance between them, the combat was so intense that the Lord of Assassins couldn't help but be amazed. The kids' enthusiasm was that of two warriors confronting each other on the battlefield, not just with their lives on the line, but with the fate of kingdoms hanging from the edge of their swords.

He watched the extravagant duel until a movement at the base of the building where the Brazilian stood caught his eye: a grotesque creature, all arms, claws, and membranes, climbed silently up the façade. Its two heads swung from the end of a single long, sinuous neck. Dario was too engrossed in his duel with Adrian to notice the danger sneaking up on him.

Esmael flew at top speed between buildings and alleyways, toward the Margalar Tower and the climbing creature. Just before crashing into it, he sank one hand into its stomach and another in its neck, shredding its throat. The beast's scream was a slight, barely audible whimper. Without slowing the momentum of his flight, the black angel violently grabbed the monster in a frightening silence. The monster's two pairs of eyes shifted frantically in an attempt to see who had snatched it so brutally.

The black angel headed like a sigh into a street lined with tall buildings, oblivious to the creature's desperate blows. He gained height, dropped the monster, and before gravity could reclaim it, hardened the edge of his wings and used them to cut it to pieces. A violent rain of flesh and blood descended onto the alleyway.

Esmael, Lord of Assassins, panted in the sky above. He felt better already.

Night had poured its cargo of shadows and darkness on the sea of Rocavarancolia.

Solberinus, the castaway, walked on the wobbly planks that secured the ship where he dwelled, a small sailboat stuck on top of a reef in the shape of a fang, with a raft he used to lay out his fishing gear. He was so accustomed to the constant motion of the sea that he didn't even notice the swinging of the planks as he moved across them.

He stopped halfway. He raised his eyes to the cliff only seconds before the light from the lighthouse flashed, sudden and blinding. The light blinked three times and after a prolonged pause, a fourth. It was of a flawless brilliance, as luminous as it could be. Solberinus calculated that two weeks remained before he'd have to change the bulb. The irony was not lost on him that it was he, the last living victim of that lighthouse, who maintained it in good working order. But someone had to do it. Even though in thirty years not a single ship had run aground there, someone had to keep that light alive.

Solberinus checked the lures one by one. He hadn't needed to fish to survive for some time, but a fresh catch was a dish that he couldn't live without; other foods seemed tasteless in comparison. Maybe it was because fishing was the only thing that had kept him alive during his early days in Rocavarancolia. He was disappointed to find only one on the hook, and not even a whole one: it was the head of an enormous spotted trout. The rest of the body had vanished. Was this the work of mermaids? He threw the remains back into the sea.

It seemed strange to him that the mermaids would steal his catches; those aggravating creatures were voracious, but they preferred live prey to carrion. And that wasn't the only odd thing that Solberinus had noticed about them recently. For days now he'd often seen them perched on the rocks, swimming aimlessly among the shipwrecked boats or climbing them. It was unusual to see them for so long and to see so many of them on the surface; they usually preferred the seabed, where sunlight hardly reached and darkness always reigned. Only the brutal tides caused by the Red Moon changed them in that regard, but weeks remained before the celestial body's influence would be felt in Rocavarancolia.

Solberinus returned again to the sailboat stuck on the reef, looking out of the corner of his eye at the oily black shadows of the restless mermaids. He couldn't resist the impulse to look to the east to confirm that, indeed, the Red Moon had not come out early. And no, it hadn't. There was nothing, just the quiet darkness of night and the shifting dark of the sea, joining one another at the line of the horizon.

Hurza the Eye-Eater, the first living creature brought by the Uncidas to Rocavarancolia, was dreaming among rotting pieces of timber, not far from the sailboat of Solberinus, the lighthouse's last victim. He was wrapped in a cocoon of pulsating light, clinging to the corner of a dilapidated shack, grazing on seaweed and crabs. The room was slanted to the right, and a third of it was full of water. Sometimes the sea's waves completely submerged the chrysalis, but this didn't affect Hurza in the least. In his lethargic state, he wasn't even breathing.

A sudden nostalgic impulse prompted him to look for the remains of the schooner that had brought him and his brother Harex to

Rocavarancolia so long ago, but he was unable to find it. If he hadn't felt so tired, he would have continued the search, but as his body succumbed to fatigue, he had no choice but to look for another hideout. He'd snuck in through a waterway that had shipwrecked a freighter and curled up into a ball in the first compartment he could find.

He spent a week inside that iridescent shell, strengthening himself, preparing for what awaited when he revealed himself to the world. If there was a single virtue in Hurza the Eye-Eater's species, it was patience: waiting was of no hindrance, and time was no more than an insubstantial trifle. More than two thousand years had passed since his murder, but that span was insignificant to him. Only a parenthesis, a rest before continuing with the plan that he and his brother had put into motion so long ago, when they realized the mistake they'd made by underestimating the creatures that surrounded them.

For the moment everything was going according to plan. Perhaps better, since Hurza hadn't expected to find a dying Rocavarancolia upon his return. Belisarius may have expressed his regret for the sad legacy that he'd find on his return, but not even in his wildest dreams had he dared to imagine a scenario so favorable to his objectives. He preferred a broken and dying Rocavarancolia to a strong Rocavarancolia as it would take much less effort to bend it to his will. What truly bothered him was the extreme weakness that had befallen the body he was forced to inhabit. Before taking his next step he should strengthen it, turn it into a vehicle worthy of his essence, or he would be destroyed at his first confrontation.

Meanwhile, Hurza learned. And watched. Even with his eyes closed within the cocoon, he could see. His gaze peered out from the eyes of the twenty-four servants that toiled at the castle of Rocavarancolia, and his mind shared their thoughts, even when they were ignorant of his presence.

Many believed that his custom of devouring his victims' eyes was just another example of the cruelty he was known for, but it wasn't so: Through consuming the victims' eyes, Hurza took on their magic essence, their memory, and their abilities. The first Lord of Assassins wasn't content with taking their lives—he snatched away all that they were and all that they were capable of. The essence of the servant assassinated by Belisarius had joined with that of the old man, but it was such a puny, feeble essence that he didn't suppose it provided any benefit. However, what he found to be most useful was that thanks to this victim, he had access to the hive mind formed by the servants of the castle and everything that went with it: he saw what they saw, he read their thoughts as if they were an open book, and—this was even better—he could access all of their memories. With that, he could reconstruct most of the kingdom's recent history.

Among all the memories he'd been able to access, there was one in particular that Hurza liked to evoke in the solitude of his chrysalis. It was of the moment when Denestor Tul, at the famous council meeting after the night of Samhein, activated the sphere he'd just retrieved from his sleeve and the light from inside spilled out into the throne room. He already knew the name of the boy who possessed that tremendous force. He was called Hector. And although he had no visual reference of him, since not a single servant had seen him, he was never very far from his thoughts. That child was a fundamental part of his plans.

Hurza brought that memory stolen from the collective mind of the castle servants to the front of his brain. On this occasion he watched the council members, surprised by the impressive bubble of energy that bathed their faces in light. Thanks to the servants' memories, he now knew them all. And not just the ones who were there; Hurza the Eye-Eater knew most of the beings who inhabited the city.

There were only two he was afraid to encounter. One of them was Denestor Tul, the demiurge of the kingdom. That gray little man may have seemed fragile and frail, but Hurza knew very well that the power of a life-giving sorcerer was always considerable. The second creature was, of course, Esmael, the black angel who occupied the position that he had held so long ago. There were few beings as terrible as those angels; they were lethal, magnificent with magic, and in battle, fierce and dreaded. And if Hurza knew anything, it was that a confrontation with each of them was practically inevitable.

If he had any intention of winning, he needed to recover his grimoire. That should be his first goal after he finished remodeling Belisarius's body. Grimoires weren't just simply books of magic: their creators inserted a good part of their essence in their pages. When performing a spell from a grimoire, one wasn't just using the sorcerer's knowledge, one was using the power of the spell itself. That was why they were such sought-after objects. Hurza the Eye-Eater had placed most of his vital energy inside that book, and to possess it would mean recovering that energy. Although he didn't know its whereabouts, he knew that the book was in Esmael's possession. It was highly likely that another creature, the black angel's closest follower, shared this knowledge.

And right then, Hurza could see this follower through the eyes of a servant in the north tower of the castle.

Enoch walked down the hallway, crouched almost at floor level, with his nose barely a palm's length away from the ground. He walked in complete silence, unaware of the servant approaching at his back. A rat peered through a hole in the wall, discovered Enoch lying in wait, and tried to return to the safety of the wall. The vampire was quicker: he jumped forward and trapped it. The animal writhed in his claws. Enoch let out a childish burst of laughter. He looked like he was about to start dancing. All of a sudden he came to a halt, aware that he wasn't alone in the hallway. He turned around and saw the servant.

"What are you looking at? Huh? Huh?" hissed the vampire, half-crouched in the shadows with the rat shaking and squealing in his hands. "What are you looking at?"

The servant lowered his head in a gesture of apology and went down the hallway to the right. The last thing that the creature who occupied Belisarius's body saw was how that pathetic vampire sank his fangs in the animal. Hurza took his mind off the servants and let drowsiness overcome him. Before he fell once more into his revitalizing sleep, he guessed at the taste of Enoch's eyes. *Do they taste dry? Bitter? Like dust and misery? What did hunger and desperation taste like?*

He would soon find out.

# THE GARDENS OF MEMORY

It was always autumn in Rocavarancolia, a dusty, dry autumn that persisted with no sign of coming to an end. In the three months they'd spent there, the climate hadn't varied in the least; each day was a carbon copy of the last. Their todays, yesterdays, and tomorrows melded into one another so that they were almost indistinguishable. Hector hadn't forgotten the storm that woke him up his first night in Rocavarancolia, though he suspected that phenomenon wasn't natural, but a consequence of their arrival.

And those identical days went by faster and faster. He noticed time speeding up in his very bones; it was a kind of invisible current that dragged him through that endless autumn, with nothing he could do to stop it. Bruno assured him over and over that it was only a subjective feeling with no basis in reality. The Italian had used hourglasses, water clocks, and even a rudimentary sundial that he built himself to measure the passing of time and prove his point. The days hadn't gotten shorter, the wind kept appearing at midafternoon, and dusk and dawn invariably arrived at the same time each day. Even so, despite the cold, hard proof that Bruno offered him, Hector felt the passing of time in a way that he never had before. He had only to look at the clock on the tower wall to feel the future and the Red Moon—both swift and horrifying—rushing to meet him.

"Your time and his are different, that's all," Marco told him as he walked back to the tower, the baskets of food on his shoulder. "Each one of us carries their own time and their own way of perceiving it."

"Is that also something you learned in your father's gymnasium?" Natalia asked.

"No," Marco answered. "I learned that in Rocavarancolia." He shrugged his shoulders. "Sometimes I have the feeling that I've been here for centuries."

Hector looked at his friend out of the corner of his eye. Something in his words made him shudder. He didn't think much about it; they'd arrived at the tower and, as always, the sight of the clock made him momentarily forget about everything and everyone. The ten-pointed star had already passed the six-thirty mark. According to their calculations, scarcely four months remained before the coming of the Red Moon and before Rocavaragalago, that terrifying cathedral on the outskirts of town, began to vomit horrors.

"We don't have to be here when that happens," Lizbeth had said during one of the many afternoons they spent talking about the matter. "There are passes through the mountains that lead to the desert, right? That's what that awful woman from the square told us. We could leave the city before the moon comes out. We'd have to plan carefully and take enough provisions to hold up for as long as we need."

"It's risky," Ricardo began.

"Riskier than staying here to see what happens?" Natalia asked. "Besides, it seems like this thing will only happen if we're nearby. So let's get far away! Let's escape! That old sack lady told us the desert was dangerous, but we don't have to stay there long. We only have to wait for the moon to go back down, then we can return to the city!"

"That old sack lady also said that fleeing to the desert would mean certain death," Mistral intervened. He couldn't tell them the truth. He couldn't tell them that there was no way of escaping the Red Moon and Rocavaragalago.

"Run away? Is that what you want to do?" Adrian piped up. His tone of voice made it clear what he thought of that plan. "What kind of idea is that?"

"Why do you ask? Do you have a problem with it?" Natalia lashed out. Adrian leaned back in his chair, his blue eyes wide open. Natalia brought her hands to her chest in a gesture of feigned innocence. "Oh, I'm sorry. You're right. To escape the city you'd first have to leave your beloved tower, and how would you ever do that? That's crazy!"

"I'll leave when the time is right," Adrian answered icily.

Natalia was about to respond, but a quick warning glance from Hector dissuaded her. The young girl shrugged her shoulders, as if it no longer concerned her. Adrian's isolation grew steadily. Although they lived under the same roof, he hadn't really been a part of the group for some time. He went for days on end without speaking to anyone, trapped in his sword-fighting routine or lost in his own thoughts.

Hector remembered one afternoon in particular when he found him in one of the rooms on the second floor. He was standing still, in complete silence, looking with an expression of astonishment at what seemed to be a blue-and-white cloth in his hands. It took Hector a few seconds to realize it was the pajamas that he'd worn when they arrived in Rocavarancolia, the ones with the little lambs. He waited motionless in the doorway, not knowing what to say. Suddenly, Adrian looked directly at him. Hector couldn't tell if his eyes shone with tears about to spill or contained rage.

"He promised to bring me home," he whispered. Then he rolled the pajamas up into a ball, threw them on the floor in disgust, and strode out of the room, without another glance.

Everyone now knew about his duels with the boy on the rooftops. Natalia had insisted on doing something, but to her disappointment they'd decided it was best to keep out of it. At least as long as the extravagant rivalry remained on the same terms as it had until now: with one of them on a rooftop and the other in the courtyard. On occasion Hector imagined them all as if they were planets orbiting one another: most of them were grouped together, orbiting in unison, sheltered by their own proximity. Bruno rotated in the distance, always the same, cold, distant, and unchanging, but accessible in his own way. Adrian had distanced himself further and further, until his orbit seemed to be closer to the boy who visited him every afternoon than to the group's orbit. Madeleine's trajectory was the most eccentric of all; after being so far off that they could barely make her out, she'd returned little by little, and rotated nearby.

The girl who'd returned to them hardly resembled the one from their first days in Rocavarancolia. Most of her arrogance and frivolity had vanished, although Hector thought that her personality was not softened but dormant. Sometimes he saw a trace of the old Madeleine in a gesture or a smile. She'd completely reentered the group dynamic, sharing in the daily tasks and setting off with the others to search for provisions or explore the city.

It was after the first of these expeditions that Madeleine left the green sword that her brother had liked so much in the armory. She placed it in a privileged spot, caressed its scabbard, and left.

"I was keeping it for him," she told them. "But now I know that he's not coming back for it."

Then she asked Lizbeth to cut her hair. The beautiful mane that she had on their arrival was now an untamable tangle that made her look like a restless wild animal. The kids couldn't help but watch as the Scottish girl gave her a haircut in the courtyard. The locks fell on the cobblestones and were swept away by the breeze. Long scarlet tresses flew through the air, held fast by the eddies of the Rocavarancolian wind.

"Is that better?" she asked, after she'd cut and modestly organized the chaos.

Madeleine shook her head.

"No. Cut it all off."

For an instant the locks of red hair swirling around them looked like the air had caught fire. Hector thought of Alexander, turned to ash in front of the tower of sorcery.

He wasn't the only one thinking of Madeleine's brother.

"She looks even more like him with short hair," Marco said, his arms crossed, leaning against the pedestal of the spider king. He was right. The girl's features were softer and rounder than her brother's, but with hardly any hair one could barely tell the difference. The few times that Maddie smiled, she was the spitting image of Alexander.


The redhead accompanied them when, after several weeks of stalling, they finally decided to explore the area west of the city. The geography of Rocavarancolia didn't vary much in that region; it was the same assortment of ruins and badly damaged buildings, but there the presence of Rocavaragalago hovered over the world like an infectious shadow. To Hector's eyes the place was even more terrible, since it was completely covered by the black warning mist.

In the distance, the red rock of Rocavaragalago seemed to pulse as if it were alive. Its rough, irregular walls jutted upward, surrounded by a pit of burning lava. An actual forest of sharp towers, pinnacles, abutments, and jagged minarets swarmed around the body of that grotesque cathedral, connected to it by narrow, asymmetrical flying buttresses. There was no sign of a door or window anywhere on the entire surface of the building. It was a mass of oxidized rock that shot up like a scream made of stone, between the edge of the city and the foothills of the mountains.

According to the scrolls, Rocavaragalago was the work of Harex, the more powerful of the two creatures who'd arrived in the drifting schooner. Everything involved in the story of its construction was so shocking that Hector was convinced they were all gross exaggerations.

Ricardo told them that, after taking control of the town where the magic currents had brought them, the two brothers started a campaign of conquest throughout the entire country. There was little that the towns in their path could do to resist: that world wasn't prepared to face creatures like Harex and Hurza. They were both magicians in a place where magic hadn't existed, and that made them practically invincible. There was nothing, and no one, that could stop them.

The leading force of their army was formed by their own victims, resuscitated by Hurza's necromancy. Terrifying spells preceded them on their way. Screaming specters would announce imminent destruction to the places that were about to be attacked, pointing toward the columns of fire that marked the advance of the army of corpses.

"Crops in their path were scorched, rivers dried up, and pregnant females gave birth to monsters," Ricardo read to them. "The world ended as they passed."

With these methods, they cut a path through the continent, taking control at a nauseating speed, the same speed with which their armada of slaves and living dead grew. Only the most immoral men were allowed to join them freely; and of these, only the most cruel and depraved were given command posts in the growing army.

Hurza and Harex's reputation spread quickly throughout the planet. Every last kingdom of that world formed an alliance with its neighbor, aware of the coming danger. Sworn enemies joined in common cause against the two brothers. All sent their armies to war, thousands upon thousands of men united under the same banner, in an attempt to put an end to Hurza, Harex, and their legion of the dead. The only thing they could do against the enemy's perverse magic was resist with the largest number of troops possible and pray that it would be enough. And maybe they would have succeeded, but days before the great battle was to take place, something occurred that completely altered the destiny of not just their own land but of dozens of worlds: as it did every year, the Red Moon came out. Suddenly and much to their surprise, with that heavenly body in the sky, the brothers' already overwhelming powers became greater than they ever could have imagined.

"According to the scroll, the Red Moon is made of pure, solid magic," Ricardo explained. "Maybe that's poetic license. I don't know . . . It doesn't matter. Either way, it amplifies magic and it just escalates. The brothers themselves effortlessly annihilated more than three hundred thousand men. And they did it in one single night."

When the Red Moon was gone, they'd already taken over the whole planet. They established the kingdom's capital in the fishing village that had the misfortune of taking them in and turned it into a city as monstrous as themselves. And once Harex was crowned, with his brother Hurza as his second in command, they devoted their time to waiting for the next coming of the Red Moon.

The following year, its arrival and the effects bestowed upon them didn't take them by surprise. They were prepared for what was going to happen. As soon as the moon loomed over the horizon, Harex flew toward it, landed on its surface, and ripped off a huge chunk with his bare hands. He then returned to the city with his cargo. The way the scroll described it, it was as if a gigantic red mountain descended from the heavens.

According to Blatto Zenzé's account, the effects of the appalling mutilation of the Red Moon were felt instantly on the planet. Earthquakes and eruptions broke out, as if the whole world shook, frightened by what happened in the sky. The planet's surface changed completely; tectonic plates collided to create new mountain ranges, oceans flooded the land, and coastlines were forever changed.

Unbothered by such chaos, Harex continued with his task: to erect Rocavaragalago. He built it with his own hands, using so much magic that the stone itself burned. Although the Red Moon had now vanished, his powers were magnified by the material that he manipulated.

In a way, Harex had taken the Red Moon down from the sky. As his building grew, the sorcerer cast complicated enchantments over its surface, linking his magic to the stone's. Some of those spells activated instantly; others required so much energy that they could only be triggered by the next coming of the Red Moon.

It took an entire year for the sorcerer king to finish his work, a hybrid between architecture and magic like none had ever seen. Just as the moon was about to emerge, everything fell into place: Rocavaragalago was set in motion for the first time; the doors to hell opened, and monsters reigned over Rocavarancolia.

Hector didn't know which parts of the story were real and which were mere legend; the only thing he knew was that just being close to that place made him want to scream. Walking near it suffocated him, robbed him of his breath. That was why, despite Bruno's insistence, they never got too close to it. They didn't dare walk along the esplanade that surrounded it, or enter the few buildings located nearby. Nevertheless, it was hard to ignore. Its presence weighed upon the soul, clawed at the mind insidiously, even when they weren't looking at it, as if it were claiming the attention it deserved. The few days that they spent exploring that area, they fell to exhaustion, from mental rather than physical fatigue.

"It's like it's absorbing your soul," Rachel said one day. And Hector couldn't help but agree. No one could have happy or positive thoughts when they were near that huge mass of rock.

Bruno was convinced that the Red Moon would amplify the group's powers just like it had for the two brothers, but for Hector the prospect of being able to cast spells when the moon came out didn't excite him at all.

"I'd like to do some experiments around Rocavaragalago," Bruno said as they returned to the Margalar Tower. After eight long days, they'd finally decided to put an end to exploring in that area, and the Italian hadn't taken the news well. "Nothing complicated or dangerous. I just want to see if our abilities are actually amplified close to that building. Perhaps one of you might be able to perform magic in its proximity. And there's the possibility that I could cast spells there that are usually beyond my capabilities."

"We've already talked about it," Marco told him. "No magic close to that thing, not if we can avoid it."

"It's not a nice place, Bruno," Lizbeth said. "Please forget about it." And with that the discussion ended.

They arrived back at the tower exhausted, with nightfall at their heels. Adrian, as always, didn't ask them how it went; he just lowered the drawbridge and snuck out to the courtyard without saying a word. The expression on his face wasn't his usual—he seemed worried about something, but of course no one asked him about it. Talking to him made Hector uncomfortable. Every time he did, he couldn't help remembering the lively, naive boy he'd known during their first days in Rocavarancolia.

The girls went up to the bathroom to clean themselves up, while the boys did the same in the stream that surrounded the promontory. The temperature of the water was pleasant, and the current wasn't too strong. They returned to the tower, half-dressed, shivering, wrapped in old towels. They spread out, waiting for the girls to come down.

The shadow of Rocavaragalago still weighed on them.

Hector went out to the courtyard, drying his hair with a scratchy towel. He needed air. He found Adrian sitting at the table by the entrance, with his chin in his hands and his gaze fixed on the rooftop. He immediately understood what was bothering him.

"He didn't come today?" he asked.

Adrian shook his head, not once lowering his eyes.


Dario still wondered what stupid impulse led him to try to touch the imprisoned monster's paw. He hadn't even brushed against it when it closed like a trap around his wrist, so forcefully that he couldn't suppress a scream. The next thing he knew he was flying against the wall. The impact was brutal. He fell to the ground, dazed, but didn't faint, and that was what saved his life. He stomped on the hand desperately, forcing it to let go when he squashed its knuckle under his heel. Dario then spun out of its reach, and a frenzied cry echoed from inside the building. He spent a long while on the ground, semiconscious, his gaze lost in what little sky he could see from the alleyway, cursing his stupidity. He heard the claw slapping and scratching frantically at the soil. He got up, still stunned, unsheathed his magic sword, and took a swipe at the hand that kept anxiously searching for him. He felt the hilt tugging away from him, as if the blade trembled eagerly to taste the blood of that treacherous monster. But finally he sheathed his weapon and left, limping out of the alley.

An hour later his head was still throbbing. He had a swollen and bruised cheek, his ear was raw, his left shoulder was completely numb, and his leg hurt. He limped through a part of the city where he'd never set foot: a labyrinth of narrow alleyways with tall stone buildings the color of slate. The light of day scarcely reached that chaos of twisted streets. He was aware of the risk he was taking, but it didn't matter to him in the least. He was furious. He almost wanted something to come at him so that he could kill it.

He walked up the gentle curve of the handrail of a granite bridge that stretched across a crack in the ground, a deep trench that split the street in two. When he reached the highest point, a voice spoke to him.

"Poor boy. Poor sad and lonely boy."

He immediately drew his sword and looked around, trying to locate the speaker. It was a dry, soulless voice, a voice that seemed so distant from the living that it was as if the silence itself had addressed him.

"Who's there?"

There was no one in sight, not in the windows of the buildings, in the doorways, or in the two alleys that opened to his right. And there was no one next to him on the bridge. The voice asked him:

"Aren't you tired of fighting against the impossible?" He heard a prolonged hiss. "Lonely boy, there's nothing here for you. Denestor tricked you. You don't belong in Rocavarancolia. You don't belong anywhere. You'd be better off ending it once and for all and jumping this minute."

"Where are you? I can't see you!" Dario turned around. His heart thumped in his chest.

"And what would happen if you saw me? Let me guess." The voice was silent for a moment. The wind howled in the depths of the abyss below the bridge. "You'd kill me, right? You'd stab me with that ridiculous sword of yours and then you'd blame the magic that enchants it. Is that a valid excuse in this world? It wasn't that way on Earth, was it? Was the knife that you used to stab that man also enchanted?"

Dario felt a frozen current in the back of his neck. Unease turned to fear. He bit his lower lip and slowly headed for the handrail on the left side of the bridge, made from twisted bars of blue metal. The voice came from the crack.

"How do you know that?" he asked. He switched the sword to his other hand to wipe the sweat that drenched his palm on his cape.

"I know everything, lost child. From here you can see the world much better. From the darkness, one's perspective is clearer." Once again he heard a long hiss. Dario had to resist the urge to take a step back. He'd never been so afraid in his entire life. But he wasn't about to succumb to it. "You stole his briefcase and he chased you. You didn't expect him to be so quick, right? My dear child, let me tell you a secret: there's always someone faster, stronger, and more terrible than you. You turned around in the alley when you saw you were trapped and you stabbed him in the stomach with your knife. Was it magic that guided your hand once again? Was it fear? Hunger? Rage?"

Dario looked down. The void was bottomless. He squinted, trying to find the source of that voice. After a few moments he realized the horrible truth: it was the void itself that spoke to him.

"Poor, lost child," whispered the nothingness. "Did you really think you had found a home in this damned city? So foolish, so pathetic . . . I'm sure that even you can see the humor in the situation. Besides, listen, I hope you don't mind what I'm going to tell you, but it just strikes me as so very funny . . ." The abyss let out a burst of laughter before continuing. "The hand that came out of the wall tried to kill you, kid, don't you think that's funny? The hand that came out of the wall! Your only friend in the city wanted to kill you!" He heard a guffaw, a cruel laugh that unfurled beneath the bridge like the wings of a gigantic bat in a cavern. "And it wouldn't even have been so bad, right?"

"Shut up." Dario took a step back. Every word painfully echoed inside of him, like a dagger plunged into his being that twisted in his soul.

"I'm sorry—that hurt you. I'm so sorry," said the abyss. "It's time now for you to open your eyes. It's a shame that you keep deceiving yourself and wanting what you can't have. That's what made you seek the company of the monster in the alley, don't you see? That's what drags you day after day toward the tower. That's why you spy on them, why you play that stupid game with the kid that you tried to kill . . ." He heard a sigh. The voice softened, but underneath that softness lurked extreme cruelty. "That's why you can't stop looking at her: so precious, so perfect, so sweet . . . You yearn for warmth, lost child, but warmth isn't for you. Let it go, let it go already. You're alone. You'll always be alone. Listen to me, Dario. We both know what's good for you. Jump this minute. Put an end to this. Here, in the darkness, you'll be happy."

The teenager shook his head. Part of him wanted an out, part of his being was pushing him to climb over the handrail and let himself fall. It would be so easy, so comforting . . . He managed to overcome that impulse and took another step back. He shook his head again and again, despite the fact that the pain in his cheek and his temples doubled with every movement.

"No," Dario whispered. He began walking backward down the bridge.

"Lost child, stupid child . . ." the bridge growled. "It's okay. Go. Go. But you'll be back, I promise. Sooner or later, you'll be back. We both know that the abyss is your destiny."

Dario leaned against the wall, clenching his teeth, his breathing ragged. He wondered how many would have jumped from that bridge to end their lives, spurred on by the words of the void.

"Dario . . ." the voice called, as he backed away, limping, as quickly as he could, his sword in hand.

He didn't stop. He didn't want to know what the void was trying to tell him, but when he tried to block his hearing with his hands, the pain from his skinned ear made him pull them away.

"If you ever feel lonely, please . . . Come talk to me, okay?" continued that hair-raising voice. "I'll be here, waiting for you. Who knows? Maybe we could be friends."

The abyss let out a grotesque peal of laughter that hurried Dario's pace, despite his intense pain. It took him a while to realize that he'd started running.


Mistral tried to guide them in their adventures through Rocavarancolia without making his influence too obvious. Because of this, he often let others choose which direction to take, but he was always the one who decided when they came to a crossroads where a bad choice could lead them to a troublesome area. The only person he sometimes trusted in these situations was Hector, and only since he'd found out that Lady Scar had cast a spell on him to make him aware of the city's dangers.

It had been quite a surprise to him to learn that the guardian of the Royal Pantheon was also breaking the sacred laws of Rocavarancolia. It seemed curious that what had started as one risky solitary venture had resulted in a full-blown conspiracy.

That afternoon Natalia chose their course. For days a conspicuous reddish wooden minaret southeast of the city had held her attention, and that was the direction she had them take. During the entire route, Mistral only had to steer them once, not so much to avoid a dangerous area, but rather to keep them away from something he didn't want them to see. It was the leprous tower, a building constructed from diseased flesh. It was a revolting place, inhabited in the past by ghouls and now scavenger territory. When the wind blew from its direction it carried a nauseating stench that was hard to stomach. Marina and Maddie wrinkled their noses, but they remained silent.

In the end, the minaret turned out to be a huge disappointment. The outside was beautiful, decorated with friezes and arabesques that entwined with one another, but the inside was in complete ruins. It looked like a powerful bomb had exploded. Everything was destroyed to such a degree that they couldn't help but wonder how the building was still standing. Mistral knew why. It had been the headquarters of the Brotherhood of the Workers of the Flame, sorcerers dedicated to the production of explosives. The walls of the minaret were reinforced with strong spells to ensure that an occasional accident didn't send the structure tumbling down onto the adjacent ones.

They walked aimlessly for over an hour under the white sky of Rocavarancolia as evening fell. The wind soon made an appearance and gained speed as the temperature dropped, whipping the shirttails of their tunics and blouses. Mistral looked to the left and right as they reached a crossroads. Apparently at random, he chose the large slope that descended to the east, by merely placing his hand on Rachel's back and guiding her softly toward it. There was something nearby that he did want them to see, something that might partially make up for the distressing days they'd spent exploring in the shadow of Rocavaragalago. Once they were headed in that direction, he no longer had to guide them. The walls that surrounded the Gardens of

Memory soon stood out among other buildings; they were tall walls made of tiny pale violet hexagonal bricks, with pointed arches on the north side.

They entered in silence, astonished, their eyes open wide. That walled garden was one of the largest enclosures they'd found until then: stretching as far as the grounds of the Margalar Tower and its courtyard. Several grandiose, magnificent statues were located throughout. For a moment, Hector thought they were creatures that had turned to stone, but in this case they were actual works of art, not the sinister atrocities from the square with the towers.

Mistral enjoyed the view from among the statues, watching out of the corner of his eye the awe that they instilled in the group. Some of the creations, carved out of weightless stone, hung motionless several feet above the ground. The shapeshifter wished they could have seen the place when it was one of the wonders of the kingdom and not another sign of its decline. Of the fifty sculptural ensembles that the garden contained, only ten were intact, while only fragments remained of a dozen others. Not a trace was left of the spectacular orchards that had adorned the place, some of which had floated over expansive layers of flying earth.

But even though they were a pale reflection of their former self, the Gardens of Memory were still impressive. The marvels of the old days still peeped out amid the desolation and ruins. And that was what the shapeshifter wanted to show them.

He smiled, pleased to see them spread out through the gardens, mouths agape. Seeing Marina and Rachel pointing excitedly to the blue stone statue of Lady Shiver filled him with joy—she was wrapped in her long shawl of silk and precious stones, kneeling as if begging for mercy. He watched Bruno floating next to the sorcerer Maronet as he faced the giant king of Esfronax with his staff and his double-bladed axe. The statue of the mage, sculpted from weightless stone, was suspended more than fifty feet high. Right before the monstrous giant's head, Maronet raised his staff in his left hand and his axe in his right, as he prepared to slash at his adversary's face, which already showed damage from the weapon's bite. The king of Esfronax, clad in armor that appeared to be made from huge turtle shells, held his arms out and seemed about ready to collapse.

The history of Rocavarancolia surrounded them, fragmented and incomplete. Every relevant historical event had left its footprint on the Gardens of Memory. Molor, the artist king, had given the order to build the site over a millennium ago. It was said that the king himself spent his last years more preoccupied with constructing that gigantic complex than with governing the kingdom.

Mistral felt an intense warmth spread through his body.

*This is Rocavarancolia,* he wished he could say to them. *Look at it, look closely. It's not terror and cruelty, it's grandeur and honor. It's achievement. The majesty of the impossible. Open your eyes, children. Don't let yourselves be blinded by the darkness, look at the light it contains. Don't focus on the shadows. Contemplate the miracle.*

The largest of the surviving statues was of Lady Irhina, the blood-thirsty queen, and her spectacular mount, the vampire dragon Balderlalosa. It was a hundred feet long and twenty-five feet tall. The black dragon was depicted in a low-flying position, its four wings extended. Its fangs, as big as scimitars, gleamed dark in the shadow of its half-open jaws. The first vampire queen of Rocavarancolia rode upon its back. The artist of such a wonder had made sure that the enormous mount didn't overshadow its rider. He'd sculpted Lady Irhina in such a way that she was the center of the piece. She had her left hand resting on the beast's back in a dynamic stance that seemed to say: "Don't be afraid of the dragon I ride. Fear me, for I am its master."

Ricardo reached out his hand and stroked the dragon's open jaws.

"I can't believe it" was all he could say. His voice trembled.

"Ricardo! You told us about this!" Rachel shouted. She stood next to Lizbeth in front of a grouping of statues located in the very center of the gardens. There, atop a pedestal in the shape of a crescent moon, a dozen hooded figures surrounded an emaciated man who raised a hand in an inviting gesture, while his face showed such contempt that it was hard to hold his gaze. He wore what at first appeared to be a large pearl necklace. It took a second glance to realize that it was a grisly necklace made of eyeballs. In the exact center of his forehead surged a sharp horn about eight inches long.

"It's Hurza," Ricardo said, and then added in a whisper, "the Eye-Eater."

The shapeshifter nodded. He didn't know who'd sculpted that crucial moment in Rocavarancolia's history, but they'd made Hurza look much more dangerous than the sorcerers who were sent to kill him.

"The execution of the first Lord of Assassins," Mistral said.

Facing the crescent moon where Hurza's scene unfolded, there had been another identical platform, depicting the death of the first king of Rocavarancolia. Harex had been killed in his sleep. Icaria, his lover, had been charged with pouring a trickle of Penuria, the most lethal poison known, into his ear. The poison was enchanted and broke through all of the king's magical protections as if they didn't exist. It had taken ten years to curse the small flask of liquid that they gave to Icaria—the exact amount of time she needed to gain the sovereign's trust—but the effort was worth it. Harex's death was instant.

With the construction of Rocavaragalago and the arrival of the Red Moon, Harex hadn't just infested the city with monsters; he also set in motion another, more turbulent, magic: one that tore through the fabric of reality itself and created portals to other worlds. These were hallways that opened at random in the most disparate parts of the city: in the sky, in the mountains, or submerged beneath the sea; some led to desolate planets, without any trace of life or even the possibility of supporting it, but others connected to flourishing lands populated by civilizations in varying stages of development. Those vortices between worlds never stayed open for very long; they all closed after a couple of hours. Harex couldn't control the magic that created them, but he was able to permanently open the passages that led to the most promising realms, linking them continually to the kingdom.

The inhabitants of Rocavarancolia were captivated by this new wonder. They were convinced that Hurza and Harex meant to conquer those territories for the greater glory of the kingdom. That assumption gathered force as over the coming years they set off on various expeditions to what they had discovered were linked worlds. These small groups explored and made maps of the terrain, took stock of the different civilizations that resided on those planets, and above all, tried to find out what technology they used and whether or not they were capable of performing magic. They undertook their missions with the utmost care, avoiding being discovered by the natives of the region they were studying. Every citizen of Rocavarancolia was certain that these ventures were a prelude to a long-awaited invasion, although neither Harex nor Hurza spoke openly about it.

They realized their mistake when Harex announced that expeditions to other worlds would cease, and from then on, he and his brother would be the only ones to cross the portals. The rest of the city's inhabitants were forbidden to use the vortices under threat of torture and death. The Royal Council, composed of the twelve most powerful sorcerers in the kingdom, tried to discern the reason for such a senseless law, but neither Hurza nor Harex explained their motives.

The two brothers spent long seasons in the linked realms. Most of the time they traveled together, leaving the council in charge of the kingdom, although it wasn't uncommon for one of them to go through a portal alone while the other stayed in Rocavarancolia. It was rare that the brothers returned from their trips empty handed. They brought items of all kinds, most of them magical. To the astonishment of the council and the entire kingdom, instead of making use of the objects, they immediately threw them into the lava pit that surrounded Rocavaragalago.

From time to time they also brought with them some terrified inhabitants of those other worlds, mostly children who were discarded and imprisoned in the city's dungeons. And on more than a few occasions they returned stinking of blood and slaughter, beaming like teenagers who'd just pulled off a magnificent prank. They explained their actions to no one, spoke not a single word of their deeds.

Throughout the years, it was common for the council of Rocavarancolia to try to persuade them of their madness: they had in their hands the tools necessary to take over an infinite number of worlds, but they limited themselves to using those lands as mere playgrounds where they could act out their senseless, bloody games. Neither Hurza nor Harex paid attention to their arguments.

Until, almost a century after the first portal opened, the Royal Council's patience finally wore out. The madness of the king of Rocavarancolia and the Lord of Assassins had become a burden on the kingdom. They decided to free themselves from them, once and for all. Everything was planned with extreme caution; they knew the brothers' power and knew that they'd only have one chance to put an end to them.

After anxious anticipation, they saw their chance when Hurza began working on his grimoire. The elaboration of such a book would significantly debilitate its maker, owing to the large amount of energy the book would require during the process. Hurza wouldn't take long to recover his power again, but for a short period of time he would be more vulnerable than usual. And it was then that the entire council of Rocavarancolia attacked the Lord of Assassins. Despite his extreme weakness, Hurza killed four of the twelve sorcerers before they could eliminate him. While the council slayed Hurza, Icaria poisoned Harex.

"Monsters murdering monsters," Lizbeth said as she looked at the grim statue of Hurza the Eye-Eater. "That's what happened. Deep down, nothing changed."

"Yes, things changed," Ricardo said. "But for the worse. When Harex governed, only he and his brother had access to the linked worlds. After his death, the monsters of Rocavarancolia had free rein through those lands."

"How awful," Marina whispered.

They kept meandering through the Gardens of Memory until the light from above indicated that nighttime was near. They began their return to the Margalar Tower. Mistral was the last to leave. He stayed a few moments under one of the arches and directed one last glance behind him before following the others. The warmth that he'd felt on seeing the children's astonished faces had already faded; now coldness, doubt, and anguish took hold of him.

It didn't take long for silence to overcome the Gardens of Memory once again. The sun's fading rays carved a mantle of darkness over the statues of men, monsters, and kings, turning them all into immense, voiceless shadows, lost in the black of night.

# IN THE DARKNESS

Bruno boarded the bathtub when it entered the square of the tower of sorcery. He walked toward it through the air, with his cape flapping behind him, and let himself drop inside without the scarecrow pilot noticing. Then, he lowered the food to those waiting below. Defying gravity was a demanding spell, and when he reunited with them he looked tired. They left the provisions in the tower with Lizbeth and headed for the other drop-off point, the one in the square with the battle frozen in stone.

They'd been stockpiling provisions for over a week, but they already had sufficient reserves; they wanted to be prepared for any situation, not just a possible excursion to the desert. Bruno had cast a spell on the dungeons, turning them into refrigerated rooms. Now frost completely covered the walls and the ground, and the frozen bars had taken on a look of brittle crystal that belied their true strength. Every day, they piled up the contents of one bathtub there. Their main goal had been to stockpile provisions from all three, but they finally decided that two were enough to cover their daily needs and also store food at a decent rate.

"And this way the punk from the rooftops won't go hungry," Rachel said while they discussed the matter in the tower.

"It's been so long since we've seen him that he's probably dead," Hector commented, without removing his gaze from Marina, interested in seeing how she reacted.

The young girl directed a strange look at him, difficult to inter-pret—something between guilt and distress—but said nothing. Adrian showed a more open reaction.

"He's not dead," he insisted vehemently. "He can't be dead. Not like that."

Since his adversary had missed their appointment, the boy's mood worsened more than ever. He spent his hours in the courtyard, train-ing listlessly and casting furtive glances beyond the wall.

Mistral knew that Dario was still alive. Denestor had told him the boy suffered a mishap that left him wounded, although his injuries didn't prove to be serious. According to Denestor, the Brazilian's potential was enormous, second only to Hector's, but even so it was surprising that he'd managed to survive all this time alone. He won-dered if someone hadn't helped him, in the same way that he and Lady Scar helped the others.

While they walked down one of the streets that led to the square of the three towers, Mistral saw the metallic bird that carried Lady Scar's eye. It was perched on a window frame, watching them pass with its head tilted. He was about to say hello when a voice at his back surprised him.

"That bird's been watching us for some time." It was Bruno who spoke. His curls had grown down to his neck; they were long black ringlets that lent him a look of Bohemian neglect. "It has something in its beak, have you noticed? It's too far away for me to tell exactly what it is, but I'd swear it looks like a human eye. What do you think?"

"I think that maybe I can tell from here." Marina notched an arrow to her bow and stepped to the side. She still hadn't finished raising her weapon when the bird flapped its wings and took off flying, carrying its creepy cargo with it.

"They have to be watching us from the castle somehow, right?" Natalia said. She'd pulled her hair back in a ponytail that fell against her left shoulder, but she hadn't brushed it at all, and there were messy stray locks everywhere.

"Remember the woman with the sack." Rachel shook her hands dramatically in front of her face, as if pretending to separate them from her wrists. "It could be her eye, or the eye of something like her . . ."

"That's disgusting." Marina feigned a shiver as she placed her bow on her shoulder and returned the arrow to its quiver.

For weeks they hadn't had a single mishap in the city. Nothing stalked them or came at them. The last thing out of the ordinary that Hector could remember was a group of velvety-looking ghosts that flew over the rooftops of a mansion and screamed countless insults as they passed. The façade of the building was covered with an intricate net of blue veins and arteries, and from inside they could hear the slow beating of an enormous heart. The entire area was surrounded by the black mist that Hector believed to be the work of Lady Serena's spell.

The bathtub with its bizarre pilot at the helm appeared between the wooden tower and the glass tower, reflected in the web of cracks that covered the building's framework. They hurried to meet it. Hector found himself walking once again among the petrified combatants scattered throughout the square. The sight still made an impression on him; it was a monument to the violence, senselessness, and cruelty of war. The monsters fought one another in a combat as fierce as it was motionless. Swords transformed into stone, split flesh turned into rock. Lances clashed with claws and spurs, fangs met with shields and armor. As a horrible complement to the spectacle, the wind carried with it the cries of those in the neighborhood who burned in flames. No, that square had nothing in common with the colossal statues that they'd discovered barely ten days ago.

They collected the food and returned to the tower. Lizbeth, with her usual diligence, had already prepared dinner and set the table. From the beginning the girl had taken on the responsibility of domestic chores, and she carried them out with astonishing speed and efficiency. Natalia had described her as "a hurricane in reverse." Instead of destroying everything in her path, she left it sparkling and organized.

After they ate they went out again to explore the city. Lizbeth joined them this time. Adrian was the only one left in the tower, thrusting at the air and keeping his eye on the line of rooftops beyond the wall.

On the clock face of the Margalar Tower, the ten-pointed star was just about to strike eight.


With a frown, Hector examined the street they'd taken; it was a zig-zagging avenue, not very wide, with destroyed buildings on both sides, all half-sunk into the pavement, as if their foundations could no longer support their weight or as if the earth itself was devouring them. There was no sign of the warning mist, but even so the place made his hair stand on end. He stopped at a mansion which was nothing but a rooftop, twisted and broken, and the upper part of the top floor; the arch of a large window on its façade opened level with the street, like a sad grimace, as if the house screamed as it sank into the sidewalk.

As he stopped, the others walked along without realizing, but Marco turned toward him.

"What is it?" he asked, worried.

"I don't like the looks of this place," Hector answered. "I think we should search for another route."

Marco agreed and ordered the others to go back. All conversation stopped instantly, and anxiety plunged them into a tense silence. Hector squinted his eyes and looked at the sunken house to his right as they backed away. Suddenly he saw it. There were two shades of darkness in the window: one was the darkness itself, natural for the place and time of day, but the other was a live silhouette, an unmoving silhouette that crouched, stalking them from the shadows. *It's going to attack us as soon as we turn our backs*, he realized. For a second, his eyes met the gaze of the crouching being. The thing in the window moved when it saw it was discovered. A dark claw came into the light and rested on the windowsill, ready to launch itself out.

Hector reached for his sword and sounded the alarm just as the creature spread its horrifying membranous wings and flew toward them. It uttered a deafening shriek that stabbed his brain like a red-hot knife.

It was a huge bat with cracked black wings, almost six feet tall. Its head was monstrous, swollen and deformed, with a thick jaw and snub nose that looked like it had been punched into its face. Its eyes were enormous and were covered by a film of whitish skin. From its furry torso sprouted three sets of long, skinny arms. *A vlakai, a demon of the deep*, Mistral said to himself as he saw it appear, one of the many freaks that inhabited the underground passageways and alleys beneath the city. He drew both his swords and stepped forward.

"Leave him to me!" he shouted. Luckily it was just the one; usually the vlakai attacked in packs, and if that had been the case, they would have been in trouble.

A strong stench of sweat and excrement enveloped them as the creature drew near. Its screech was piercing. Mistral leapt to meet it, and just as he was about to strike a blow, the vlakai gave a vigorous flap of its wings and changed direction. The shapeshifter's swords sliced through air, far from their target. He looked around in fury and tried to chase it, but Ricardo inadvertently got in his way and he lost several valuable seconds dodging him.

The monster hurled itself at Marina and wrapped her in its wings. Hector shouted and stopped midthrust for fear that he would pierce her as well. The vlakai opened its mouth, showed its blackened fangs, and took off flying once again, carrying Marina in its six arms.

"Bruno!" Hector howled, pointing to the fleeing creature with his sword.

The Italian rose up in the air, clutching his staff in both hands; the birdcage at the end glowed with a powerful cyan flash that grew brighter as Bruno recited his spell. At a critical point, he pointed the staff at the monster and shouted a single word, a short syllable that burst from his lips like an explosion. At that moment, a sphere of silver light shot out from the end of the birdcage. The blaze collided with the bat's back and it writhed in the air, howling with pain. When it seemed close to hitting the ground, it zigzagged above the pavement, composed itself, and flew at top speed toward the house it came from. Spirals of thick smoke surged from one of its wings. Hector took off running in the direction of the sinking house just as the monster and Marina disappeared through the window.

"No!" he shouted

"How disappointing," Bruno mumbled from the air before flying toward the window himself. "I was convinced that spell would take it down."

Hector and the Italian jumped onto the ledge of the large window almost at the same time, one from the ground and the other from the air. Bruno held his staff out, said two words, and the birdcage lit up. The light dispersed through the house's ruined interior. The floor, barely five feet from the window, was destroyed; a large crack had opened in the middle, marked by planks raised in the air, truncated beams, and rubble.

The two boys jumped from the windowsill inside the room and moved carefully toward the immense gap in the center. The birdcage illuminated the vast subterranean passageway that it led to. The ground beneath their feet creaked ominously, but the only sound that Hector was conscious of was Marina's screams, growing more distant by the minute.

"Come back here, both of you! Come back right now!" Marco ordered them from outside.

There was no response. Bruno repeated the magic words, added another, and the light from his staff tripled in intensity.

They weren't able to find the end of the passage, but they did see the monster that dragged Marina into the depths slowly flap its wings. It still seemed stunned by Bruno's shot, and its flight was unsteady. They had already gone halfway through the lit area and neared the darkness where the light from the staff didn't reach. Marina kicked her feet desperately in its arms.

"Can you stop it?" he asked Bruno.

The Italian shook his head.

"I'd risk hurting Marina," he said.

Hector understood that only one alternative remained. He leaned into the crack. It was about twelve feet to the floor of the passage, but the path toward it was littered with rubble and debris. Driven by instinct, he jumped to the closest stone, and then the next, which wobbled dangerously as he landed. Without waiting for the ground to settle beneath his feet, he jumped onto another pile of debris. Bruno followed him, walking through the air, as calm as if he were walking down a stairway. The light from his staff accompanied him.

"You can't go down there!" Mistral shouted to them from above. *If they do it, they'll die. If they go down into the darkness, they'll only meet with death.* Rocavarancolia was demanding another sacrifice, and resisting it would only end in a bloodbath. "You don't know what might be down there!"

But he knew. Hundreds of abominations prowled the city's entrails, some as unknown to him as the alien life forms that could have inhabited the farthest planet. There lurked the pale cadavers who fed upon the marrow of their victims, the wandering specters always on the hunt for bodies to possess . . . In the depths of Rocavarancolia it was still possible to find the descendants of the human beings in whom Eradianalavela had implanted the souls of beasts, or the vampires of

Radix, capable of sucking out the blood, guts, and bones of their victims with just a touch, and creatures far more horrific than words could describe. The dangers weren't limited to monsters: there were gases under the city that were the exhaust from murderous magic, turbulent clouds of venomous smoke that arose from the combustion of magic residue . . . To descend into the bowels of Rocavarancolia was to seek certain death.

But Mistral only needed to see the resolution with which Hector moved through the rubble to understand that nothing he could say would deter him. Hector would keep moving forward, even if every demon from every hell awaited him at the bottom of the mountain of debris.

"Marina is down there," Hector told him, and that was the ultimate argument: the phrase that could make him march to his death without a single moment's doubt. The monster and the girl were still in sight, although their silhouettes were fading in the darkness.

The shapeshifter grabbed the edges of the crack, desperate. Marina would soon be dead, and anyone who went after her would meet the same fate before long. Although it would be a shame to lose Hector, in whom he'd put so many of his hopes, it was still a loss that Mistral could accept. But not Bruno, not the only one who'd shown true value thus far. The best chance the group had to survive until the Red Moon would vanish with him. If he was able to convince the Italian not to go through with this madness, maybe they'd still have a chance.

"Bruno! Come back this minute! Going down there is suicide! You don't know what you'll find! You don't know what you'll run into!"

Bruno looked at him out of the corner of his eye, but the only answer that Mistral got to his plea came from the kids behind him.

"And we're not letting you go down there alone!" Natalia said, resting the palm of her hand on his shoulder. If the girl meant the gesture to encourage him, it didn't work. Mistral felt the pressure of her hand like a blow. But she was right. He couldn't let them go alone, by simple virtue of the fact that the others wouldn't allow it. And the group couldn't split up, either. They were too far from the tower, and it would be crazy to leave anyone behind, not after the commotion they'd caused. He had no choice but to make them all go down into that hell of darkness and horrors.

*Into the darkness, then,* the shapeshifter said to himself, and turned to those still behind him to plan their descent. He wondered how many of them would ever see the light of day again.


They sped through the passageway. It descended down an irregular slope, so steep at times that it was almost impossible not to slip. Soon the light from Bruno's staff could no longer reach the ceiling, and he had to augment it to avoid leaving the slightest shadow where the bat could hide.

The immense grotto was of natural origin, a damp place, full of echoes, that headed toward the west. The only visible sign of the inhabitants of Rocavarancolia were the columns that held up the ceiling. There were dozens of them, scattered apparently at random, squeezed together in packs or standing solitary, maintaining the integrity of the passageway. They were made of black stone and extraordinarily thin. They looked, without a doubt, like magic columns. Despite their number, they seemed too fragile to support the ceiling of the cavern and the weight of the buildings on top. It was hard to imagine that Rocavarancolia was still above their heads.

The ground was covered in puddles and they splashed as they ran, spraying one another. They didn't move as quickly as Hector would have liked. Madeleine and Lizbeth couldn't keep up with the rest, but they couldn't leave anyone behind, not in such a dismal place. His desperation was so great that he couldn't help passing Rachel now and again. He had to stop when the girl came to a halt as they reached an area of magic. They waited while she paced back and forth, scratching her forearms and neck endlessly, until she found a safe path between two columns. Then they resumed their journey.

As he ran, Hector kept remembering Marina in the cemetery, asking him to bury her there if something bad were to happen to her. And he couldn't forget her prophetic story. While he ran, he already saw himself carrying her in his arms to the cemetery. It was as if he could feel the weight and the cold of her body where it brushed against his, see her violet lips and the deathly pallor of her face. *You're not going to die,* he had promised her at the gates of the crystal mausoleum, and now that promise seemed so vain and foolish to him that it made him want to stop running and smash his head against the wall.

Bruno hovered above them with his staff stretched out before him; he seemed to be running rather than flying, as if the air were solid. Sinister shadows on the walls of the passageway scattered when the light from the birdcage hit them. They were barely visible: some scampered away, terrified; others scurried down the walls toward the darkness the group had left behind. With each step, Mistral's nervousness grew. They were running toward death. No one would get out of there alive, he was sure of it. The fate of the kingdom would rest in Adrian and Dario's hands. And they'd probably kill each other.

After ten minutes of running they found Marina's bow, broken on the ground. Mistral discovered it lying in a puddle.

"We have to leave, we have to get out of here," he said. He grabbed the broken bow and waved it in front of the group as if it were irrefutable proof of the senselessness of their adventure. "It's too late. It was too late as soon as that thing dragged her into the tunnel."

He felt a strange stinging in his eyes, a bitter, heavy dampness that he refused to give in to. "We've lost her, you hear me? We've lost her . . . And we'll all die if we don't leave here as soon—"

At that very moment, they heard the bat's piercing cry, not very far off. Hector looked at Mistral with all of the contempt in the world and took off running toward the sound. He passed Rachel, who had no choice but to grab him by the arm to stop him so that she could retake the lead.

"Back, back, back," she warned angrily as she hurried her pace. "Either you stay back or I tie you to a column."

"Listen to me, damn it!" Mistral howled. No one paid attention.

As they ran toward the shrieks they came to a fork in the passageway, a second path that joined the first one from the left. They didn't doubt for a second which one to take. They heard screams ahead of them, closer and closer, more and more frenzied. They were nothing like the noises the creature had made when it attacked them; they were of a very different nature, although they came from the same throat. These were full of pain, pain and anguish. They stopped abruptly. The next thing they heard was a soft, revolting noise: the sound of something crashing into the ground after falling from a great height.

Barely two minutes later, they found a shapeless mass in the dark, lying in the middle of the cavern. The light from the staff reached it, giving it a clearer, more defined outline. It was the bat, fallen on its side in a pool of dirty water. Hector gasped when he saw it. Standing in front of the corpse, visibly confused, was Marina. Her eyes were half-closed, dazzled by the light after being acclimated to the darkness.

"G . . . guys?" She took a hesitant step in their direction. Then she seemed to recognize them and ran toward them, her gait unsteady but quick.

Hector watched her approach, shocked and bewildered, unable to believe that girl was really Marina. She was drenched in blood, gripping a broken arrow in her hand.

The girl threw herself into his arms and he couldn't help but embrace her.

"Thank heavens you're here!" she said a few seconds later, separating from him after planting a loud kiss on his cheek. "I didn't think I'd make it! I was so scared!"

She leapt to hug Madeleine with all her might. Then she did the same with Lizbeth, who was panting from the run, out of breath.

"Breathe . . ." she managed to say. ". . . Have to breathe . . ."

"Scared?" Marco looked at the monster's corpse. It had multiple wounds on its chest and throat. Of all of the endings he could have imagined for Marina's rescue, this one seemed the least possible. "It doesn't show. From what it looks like, you did a fine job saving yourself."

"I was desperate. And I lost my bow," she explained, "so I had no choice but to stab it with the arrows." She took a breath. "When I jabbed the first one in, it wanted to drop me, but I wouldn't let it. I climbed on its back and . . . and . . ." She looked around her, as if she wanted to see where she was. "The tunnel was dark and when we fell I didn't know how high up we were. I grabbed on to that thing, and it cushioned the blow, but even so I must have lost consciousness, if only for a second . . . When I opened my eyes everything was complete darkness."

Bruno examined her by the light from his staff.

"At first glance you do not seem to have any injuries, but I would like to cast a general healing spell anyway."

"Wait, wait," she said, and twisted to free herself from the blood-stained tunic. "What a mess." She turned her head to look accusingly at the dead creature. "This is your fault, you hear me? If you'd left me alone, you wouldn't be dead, and I wouldn't be all sticky . . ."

She crouched down next to a puddle and thrust her hands in. Then she scrubbed them vigorously on her tunic, smearing the cloth as well as her skin.

"I have to get this blood off me, I have to get it off . . ." She bit her lower lip forcefully. She looked as if she were about to cry.

"We'd better get out of here as soon as possible," Marco said. They'd been lucky to find the girl alive, but to stay any longer would be to invite disaster.

"Yes, please, yes, yes," Lizbeth said. She had one hand on her chest and was still breathing heavily. "While we were running I saw things sliding down the walls . . . Horrible things . . ."

"We all saw them," Natalia pointed out. "And they seemed to be pretty afraid of us, that's for sure."

"They weren't fleeing from us, Natalia," Marco warned. "They were fleeing from the light."

"Given the environment that they live in, I am hardly surprised they are photophobic," Bruno said, "but now that we have what we came for, it is too risky to remain here." He looked at the dead monster. "Not all the creatures that live here fear the light."

Then he approached Marina, who still insisted on cleaning the blood off in the puddle of water, and he cast a quick healing spell. The girl didn't even flinch, just kept rubbing her hands and clothing, getting them dirtier rather than cleaner, while the amber aura healed her bruises.

Lizbeth helped her up from the ground.

"Come on, let's go," she said. "You heard Bruno, we must leave, dear. We have to get out of here. You can take a bath at home."

She nodded and let herself be led away.

The light from Bruno's staff reflected in slow waves on the water-logged ground. They began their return trip at a good pace. Hector couldn't stop looking at Marina, who walked next to him, rubbing her hands compulsively. Only then, with her safe, did he comprehend the magnitude of the crazy stunt he'd just performed. He'd dragged them all into danger. Then he shook his head. He hadn't dragged anyone. If it were just him, he would have gone into that tunnel alone. *And I'd probably be dead right now*, he told himself.

"Are you okay?" he asked Marina in a whisper. "Are you really okay?" She nodded.

"I am, yes. But I'll have nightmares for the rest of my life. Listen, everyone, thank you for coming for me," she said. She stretched out her hand to touch Marco's shoulder, who was walking in front of her.

"Thank us when we're out of here," he replied uneasily.

The darkness accompanied them on their return.

Bruno had lowered the birdcage. The circle of light was still wide enough that it surrounded them, but it didn't reach far enough to illuminate the walls or the ceiling. Outside the radius, in the semidarkness before it became pitch black, they saw creatures lurking. They stayed outside the light's reach, but not too far. Hector watched as an immense being fell from above right after they passed by: a hunched creature that appeared to walk on its knuckles; he saw a shadow of an exaggerated jaw and twisted fangs that shone like diamonds. He wondered what would happen if the light from the staff went out. He watched Bruno. The Italian had started taking out the reserve talismans from his pouch and was placing them around his neck and wrists. It wasn't a very reassuring gesture.

"Silence," Marco suddenly demanded. He raised a hand to make the group stop.

They heard a drum beating, coming from an unknown area ahead of them. They listened attentively. The beats were irregular and grew closer. It took them a minute to identify them as the sound of trotting. Something was coming. Something enormous. The sound of its swift gallop made concentric waves appear in the cavern's puddles.

"I don't like this one bit," Madeleine said, and stepped back.

They waited anxiously in the center of the light projected from the staff. Ricardo put a hand on Rachel's shoulder and stepped forward to take her place, his sword unsheathed and the shield he always carried at his back on his arm. Natalia stood to his left, her double-breasted halberd held in front of her, and Marco was on his right, his two swords ready.

Hector heard the Italian recite a spell. A milky cloud instantly covered Bruno's eyes. He remained staring straight into the darkness, and if he could tell what was coming, it didn't show on his face. The sound of galloping drew nearer. The echo resounded in the cave.

Suddenly, to everyone's surprise, Bruno leapt toward Rachel, grabbed her by the shoulders, and practically hurled her toward the nearest wall, the one to her left. There he shoved her against a crack in the rock, a gap about five feet wide and ten feet tall. She protested, but he completely ignored her and began building a stone wall in front of her. He picked up rocks from the ground, piled them one on top of another, and with a light sweep of his hand joined them together.

"What are you doing?" she cried. "What are you doing? Have you gone crazy?"

"I am attempting to save your life," he said. "Unfortunately, your immunity to magic will be of no help to us on this occasion."

Rachel tried to climb over the wall, but the Italian gave her a rough shove to keep her still. The thunderous noise came closer. They could now make out a huge shadow in the darkness, and its size took their breath away. They heard a roar in the tunnel and then a deafening sound: the noise that a giant would make as it blows on an immense horn.

*We're finished*, thought the shapeshifter. *Rocavarancolia is finished.*

"It's not afraid of the light," Ricardo said. "It's coming straight for it."

"Whatever it is, it's too big," Natalia muttered. The halberd shook in her hands. "We can't stop it."

"No, we can't," Bruno agreed. He moved toward them after he'd finished closing Rachel up in the wall and asked her to remain still and absolutely silent. His eyes were still surrounded by a thick white aura. "My magic is not prepared to take on what's coming at us," he warned them, displaying a sickening calm for the thousandth time. It made Hector want to hit him; the way he never lost his cool—even in a situation like this—was maddening. "And I doubt that your weapons will have the slightest chance against it. It's too big, and too strong. Everyone join hands." He stretched his toward Madeleine. "And I am asking you to do it now, because it's here, it's coming."

Hector squeezed Marina's hand—while someone took his other hand—at the very moment the monster broke into the circle of light with a roar like thunder. It was an enormous creature, more than twelve feet tall and almost fifty feet long, like a hairy crocodile. It was a dirty gray color with a long prehensile tail ending in a stinger. Mistral hadn't needed magic to see it coming toward them in the darkness of the tunnel. He recognized it immediately: it was a chimera, a being created by thaumaturges by magically joining the most disparate animals. The beast lunged at them with the force of a derailed train. It went after its closest target, Ricardo. Mistral saw the expression of horror on the boy's face an instant before the chimera's fangs closed over him. The passageway was filled with screams.

When the creature reared its head, Ricardo was still there, unharmed, pale, and bewildered. He backed up and fell to the ground, his lips trembling. Hector was panting. His hand still clutched Marina's and Natalia's, but he didn't feel the contact. Bruno had made them all intangible, he realized. The monster, furious, took another bite at the boy on the ground, and once more its fangs went through him without doing the slightest damage. Ricardo screamed all the same. The chimera roared furiously, unable to understand what was happening, unable to comprehend why its mouth wasn't full of its prey's flesh. It roared again before biting at another target, Bruno this time. The Italian didn't bat an eye. He just passed through the beast's jaws as they were beginning to open. He emerged between the fangs, impassive.

"Keep calm," he instructed them. For once he raised his voice to make himself heard over the monster's commotion. "We should move away from where I've hidden Rachel. We do not want the beast to harm her by accident."

They did what he asked, stumbling along the wet ground. Hector barely noticed the ground beneath his feet, and when he looked down, he saw how his boots went right through it up to the ankle; it was a strange sensation, like walking on a cloud. Lizbeth tripped and fell down, white as a sheet. Tears ran in torrents down her cheeks. Her body went right through the rocks. She didn't get up; she seemed to be knocked out where she fell, her eyes closed, shaking her head over and over.

"Bruno!" Natalia shouted, who was the farthest behind. "We're getting too far away! We're too far!" She pointed desperately with her halberd in the direction of where they'd left Rachel.

The area was shadowy, but between the monster's charges and futile bites they could see three creatures climbing rapidly down the wall toward their friend. They were some kind of moths with spiky heads that slithered toward the crack with skeletal arms, each ending in a single twisted nail. Their abdomens were grotesque segmented globes covered in a pulsing labyrinth of veins.

Bruno hung the staff on his shoulder, joined his hands, and cast another spell. An explosion of light extended through the entire passageway like a flood of unstoppable clarity. The creatures stalking Rachel instantly spread their wings and took off flying, shrieking as they went. They weren't the only ones to flee from the sudden radiance. Both ends of the tunnel swarmed with monstrosities: dismal, Dantesque creatures, tentacled beings with pale faces, insects the size of men, indescribable vermin with skeletons emerging from their bodies, foul half-reptile, half-plant freaks . . . They only saw them for a fleeting instant, the time it took them to dive back into the darkness. The burst of light was very brief, the brightness retracted, and soon the only glow that remained in the passageway was from the staff.

The Italian took a few steps back so that the light illuminated the spot where Rachel was hidden. They couldn't move any further away if they wanted to protect her, and this made the situation difficult. Being intangible as they were, they wouldn't have had problems escaping the tunnel, but if they did they'd be condemning Rachel. As Bruno had said, her immunity to magic now worked against her. Hector looked at the Italian. Sweat was beginning to bead up on his forehead and he was showing signs of fatigue. And if one thing was clear, it was that they depended on him to survive. If anything happened to him, if his magic ran out or the light from his staff went dark . . . Hector preferred not to think of it.

Marco gestured for them all to reunite around Lizbeth. But if it was difficult to think with that insane creature attacking them over and over again, it was even harder to speak. They formed a circle, put their heads together, and shouted so that they could be heard over the commotion of roaring and stamping hooves. Neither Lizbeth nor Madeleine participated in the conversation. The redhead tried to console her friend, who was on the ground, hysterical. At least they'd managed to stop her screaming.

"It can't hurt us," she told her. "Calm down, it can't touch us. Breathe, take deep breaths . . . It will be over soon, I promise, it will all be over soon . . ."

"How long will the spell last?" Ricardo asked Bruno.

"Five minutes, six at the most," he answered.

"And do you think you're strong enough to cast another one when this one runs out?"

Bruno nodded.

"I could do so, but there are complications that would make that course of action inviable—"

"Could you talk like a normal person for once, damn it!" Natalia burst out.

"I do not know how to talk any other way, Natalia. I am sorry, I'm truly sorry . . ." He looked back at Ricardo. "I could do it, like I said, but for a few moments we would all be unprotected . . . I need to have physical contact with the target of the spell for it to be effective and if you're tangible for me, you're tangible for that abomination, with all that entails. But there is another problem that notably exacerbates the situation. The spell will not wear off at the same time for everyone. It depends on the body mass of each of the subjects affected by the spell. We can assume that Marco, being the biggest, will be the first to solidify—"

He was interrupted. The chimera had jumped on them and for an instant the only thing they could see was the sinister darkness of the beast's interior. They heard the rapid beating of its heart, the blood boiling in its veins, and the elastic snapping of its muscles as it moved. A few seconds later, the monster moved away, roaring and out of its mind. They blinked, stunned by the light's return. Hector shook his head, the beast's heartbeat embedded in his temples.

"Go. Go now," Ricardo said. He was pale. "If you hurry, you might have time to escape before Bruno's spell wears off. I'll stay with Rachel, I'll protect her, and try to get out of—"

"Escape, in the dark?" Natalia asked him and pointed to the shadows and the creatures hiding within them. "And how are you supposed to get those things off your back? Have you gone crazy?!"

"We don't have a choice, or time to argue!"

"Then quit arguing!"

"What would happen if I became solid inside that thing?" Marco asked. Hector looked at him, shocked. The answer was obvious and he should know it.

"You will both die," the Italian said. "You cannot occupy the same location in the same interval of time, not if you are both solid. You would shatter into pieces."

Marco nodded. The expression on his face made it clear what he was thinking.

"No!" Marina shouted and tried to punch him in the shoulder. As was to be expected, her hand passed cleanly through it. "Don't even think about it! There has to be another way!"

"We're not leaving anyone behind," Hector said. His voice shook. Then he leaned in closer to the Italian to ask, "Can't you kill it some other way?"

Bruno shook his head.

"It is too big for me. As I have told you all on many occasions: real magic is out of my reach. And only real magic can kill that creature."

"And if you make, I don't know . . . a rock intangible, or Natalia's halberd, whatever . . . we could throw it, and it will become solid when it's inside. Wouldn't that kill the beast?"

"That could kill it, indeed. But I would need to be in contact with the item that I wanted to make solid. And to do that I would need to . . ." He stopped suddenly. There was no change in his face; he simply stood looking at the emptiness for a long moment. Then he nodded with his usual mechanical cadence before saying, "There is probably an easier way to do what you are asking."

And without another word he began walking through the air. The chimera tried to bite him, but its fangs passed through the Italian's ghostly body as he continued upward, unaffected by the attack. He stopped about ten feet in midair and waved his staff wildly from left to right as he cast a new spell. Then he went back toward the group.

"I just renewed the spell for the staff's light. It should keep shining for at least another hour, no matter what might happen to me."

"What are you going to do?" Hector asked.

The Italian disappeared through the chimera's fangs. He reappeared moments later.

"Oh. Right. Forgive me. Perhaps a brief explanation is called for before I put my plan into action," he said. "It is basically just Hector's idea, but with a few alterations: I shall make our annoying attacker immaterial. Given his size, it should not take much time before he reverts back to his natural, solid state, and it is highly likely that when that happens part of his body will be underground or within one of the walls of the cavern. That should kill him, or at least damage him greatly." He was silent for a few moments as he looked at them, one by one. He looked like a boring teacher giving the most tedious lecture in the world. "One final warning: what I have just told you is valid for you as well. Be careful when you notice that your density is beginning to normalize. Itching all over will be a forewarning that it is about to occur. Make sure to stay aboveground and do not stand too close to one another to avoid problems."

Then he turned around and continued his journey. The monster had focused all its attention on him. As the Italian ascended, the chimera stood up on its hind legs, biting at the air and roaring with rage. Bruno appeared small and fragile in the midst of that violent whirlwind of flesh. The creature supported its front legs on the wall and threw its giant head back, trying to devour him. Then its tail and stinger cracked in the air. At that moment, while the creature flexed its spine to flick its tail, Bruno jumped atop it, his staff across his back. The noise they heard as Bruno collided with the chimera told them he was solid once again. A second later they saw him pass through the monster's body and fall to the ground.

He got up, dazed, shook his head, and ran toward them. He hadn't gone two steps when the chimera's stinger sliced through his throat, again without harming him, but to their surprise he suddenly stumbled and fell face down. He didn't get up. Hector and Marco rushed to his aid, although there was little that they could do for him in his ghostly state. The chimera howled and galloped over them. The Italian lay on his side, pale as a corpse. They could barely tell if he was still breathing. It wasn't the first time that they'd seen him this way: Bruno was exhausted. By casting the spell on the chimera he'd reached his limit. And he succeeded. The enraged creature was now as immaterial as they were. If it wasn't enough to see the stinger pass right through the Italian, they had further proof as its claws plunged completely into the ground with each stride.

They drew it to the middle of the passageway, far from Bruno and from Rachel's hiding place. Madeleine stayed next to Lizbeth, who still wasn't moving. The others taunted the monster, getting within its reach, shouting to incense it even further. When it charged at them, a good part of its stomach disappeared between the stones on the floor. On one of its jumps, it slipped and fell flat on its face, still roaring and biting. Its tail passed through the cavern's wall, and one of the thin columns stood in the middle of its body. The monster prepared for a new attack, its claws sunk inches into the ground, its huge body tense, the column sticking out from its back. Suddenly it became still. Throughout the passageway they heard a tremendous creaking, a repulsive liquid sound. The chimera didn't scream as it died, and that silence, that sudden and brutal passing from life to death, made the scene even more frightening. The monster's yellow eyes went out, just like that.

The beast collapsed, its feet cut off, its tail mutilated, and its body sliced through by the column. They looked at each other nervously, unable to believe that they'd survived. Hector was panting as if he'd just run a marathon.

Mistral was the first to regain form, just as he expected and just as Bruno had predicted. Little by little, the others followed suit. In just over a minute they'd all recovered their usual density. Hector was careful to move away from the others and make sure that his feet were above the terrain and not sunken into it when he noticed an intense tingling in his arms and legs. Madeleine and Marina took charge of Lizbeth, still in a state of shock. They lifted her up and placed her in a safe location.

"Get me out of here right now!" Rachel pleaded. "It's disgusting in here! I can't breathe! I hope Bruno's dead or I'm going to kill him myself for leaving me here!"

Ricardo and Hector had started walking over when a sudden vibration in the cavern made them pause.

"What was that?" Lizbeth asked, horrified.

"From above," Marina said. "It's coming from up above."

The column that had killed the chimera vibrated. Suddenly it was covered in cracks. They all appeared at once, as if an elaborate spiderweb had covered it. A second later, the column shattered to pieces. It practically disintegrated before their eyes. The rain of splinters fell on the dead chimera. The fragments were so small that they didn't make a noise. After a moment of dead calm they heard a spine-chilling creak from up above. They all looked up in time to see a huge fracture opening in the ceiling. The purple light of dusk filtered through from above. For a second, Hector was frozen stiff as he watched the strip of twilight seep in above their heads. Then someone screamed. The world took that scream as an agreed-upon sign to go mad. A huge section came crashing down, and another, even larger, part followed. The boy looked around him, but he could only make out shadows and falling rubble. The ceiling pulled the ruined buildings that it was supporting down with it. Hector made out a brick wall crashing down. It was as if the whole city were collapsing in on them.

The light from Bruno's staff flashed on and off. Everything was chaos and confusion, a sea of shadows tinted by the moving light of the birdcage and the purple gleam of twilight. Someone shouted, and their cry—like the light—came and went in the midst of the rumbling of falling rocks. He heard Marco calling to them, ordering them to retreat and find a safe place. But it was too late, there was nowhere to run. For a moment, Hector saw Marina in front of him, with her hair and shoulders covered in white dust, but when he took off running toward her part of a wall collapsed between them. He stepped back and a rafter fell to his side, sticking fast in the ground like a colossal spear. A shard of rock hit him in the forehead and he fell backward.

He didn't lose consciousness, but for a moment dizziness and disorientation got the better of him. When he recovered, the noise had diminished and all was utter darkness. He couldn't see a thing. He raised a hand and waved it in front of his eyes, sensing the movement more as a vibration than as something real. He never imagined that there could be such thick and total darkness. He touched his forehead and drew his hand back immediately, letting out a painful moan. He had a gash above his eyebrow, and it was bleeding copiously.

He rolled on the ground until he was sitting up. Apart from his forehead, his right hip and knee also hurt. He felt his leg and when he got to the kneecap he had to choke back another cry. He managed to bend his left leg, but didn't dare try with his right. He blinked several times. The blood ran down his face and into his eyes. He wiped at the cut with his shirtsleeve, biting his lower lip to keep from screaming.

Someone said his name. But it sounded so far away, and was muffled by something more than just distance. He tried to move, but an explosion of pain from his knee forced him to stop. He felt the ground with one hand and touched only rubble. He heard his name again, but didn't dare answer, not in this darkness from beyond the grave. Then he heard a second voice, closer, yet at the same time much weaker. Someone called for Ricardo, a girl's voice, although he couldn't tell who it was. They'd been separated from one another by the collapse, he realized. He still heard the clatter of falling rocks. He listened carefully. Those weren't the only sounds he heard. Something was slithering toward him from a vague point in the thick darkness. Then he heard a low, bestial growl, followed by running footsteps. Hector remembered the creatures that had been stalking them as they walked through the passageway. He drew his sword.

There was no longer any light to contain them. Darkness consumed the space. And darkness overflowed with death.

The echo of the footsteps drew closer. It was an uneven trot trailed by a rustling, dragging sound, like something was sniffing around in the dark. Another growl, sharper than the first. More footsteps, this time like hooves. And then there was a flapping around his head accompanied by a loud buzzing. Suddenly a damp claw seized his calf.

He stabbed at the darkness. The sword sank into soft flesh. It let out a howl and scurried away, whimpering with sobs that sounded almost human. Hector, in a state of fight-or-flight, started swinging his sword from left to right, frantically, ignoring the pain in his knee as he moved. The pitch-black void was full of hissing, scratching, and footsteps, of growls and screeches. As he kept slashing blindly with his sword he brought his free hand to his shirt pockets. He went from one to another and then to his pants pockets, sure that he would find what he was looking for in one of them.

A slimy body fell onto him, suffocating him with its weight. He heard rapid clucking and a frenzied cracking sound. Hector launched himself toward it, thrust his sword into whatever was on top of him, and then viciously twisted the weapon inside of it, screaming all the while. The clucking came to an abrupt halt. But more were coming.

He could hear them moving closer to him in the darkness. He took a deep breath and resumed searching his pockets, still swinging his sword from side to side.

His hand found the crystal among the jumble of tangled amulets that were in his back pocket. His heart sped up as he felt the surface of the rhomboid glass against his skin. Like the others, he had gotten into the habit of carrying talismans to charge in his spare moments, and when he grabbed handfuls of the amulets off the shelves there was often one of the crystals that they'd used to light their way the first night in the tower. He yanked the crystal from his pocket, bringing with it a long chain from which hung a silver charm. He plunged it into the palm of his left hand, forgetting he already had blood coming from his forehead. The flash of the charging talisman immediately lit up the passageway.

The first thing he saw was the monstrous head of a gray being with two muddy eyes hanging from stems protruding from its head. The creature covered its face with a semitransparent arm and slinked away, hissing.

More than twenty monsters retreated when the light hit them. Hector, panting from pain and fear, saw them running away. There were so many, and they were in such a hurry to escape that it was hard to distinguish between them; it looked like a gigantic hybrid beast withdrawing into the darkness. The gleam of the talisman was more red than he remembered, but he quickly realized that was because the crystal was covered in blood. In his haste for light, he'd sliced open the palm of his hand. He didn't stop to check his wounds. An enormous serpent with olive skin wasn't daunted by the light and slithered toward him through the rubble, its mouth opening and closing. When it got within reach, Hector cut off its head with a single blow.

Then, clutching the crystal in his right hand, he began bandaging his left with a strip of his shirt. Only then did he look around him. He was stranded by the rubble, in a closed-off area of the passageway. To his right rose up a sheer wall of debris; to his left the passage led into the darkness, where scarcely a few yards away the monsters awaited him. And between himself and the vermin lay Ricardo, still buried under the wreckage. His pale face was turned toward him, showing no sign of life.

"No," Hector whispered in a broken voice. "No, no, no . . ." He began dragging himself over there, sword in hand, ignoring the pain in his right leg, holding the crystal tight. "Ricardo!"

His friend opened his eyes all of a sudden and coughed forcefully. The relief Hector felt to see him alive was indescribable. Ricardo tried to talk, but the coughing kept him from saying a word. His lips were purple and his face was covered with dust. A shadow moved away from the brightness. The light reflected off a segmented tail, covered in spines.

"Hector . . ." the boy murmured when his friend was within reach. He stretched out his only free arm toward him. "Everything collapsed," he said, visibly shaken. "The world shattered to pieces and collapsed . . ."

"Shhh . . . don't talk," he told him. His knee seethed with pain. He placed his sword on the ground and began removing the debris that covered his friend. He was covered in bruises. He managed to free his torso, but there wasn't much he could do about his legs: they were trapped under a thick slab that seemed fused to the ground.

"Everything's in pieces . . ." Ricardo reached his hand toward the crystal that Hector held. "Light. I thought I'd never see it again. It's so beautiful. And so fragile."

"I need your help," he pleaded with him. "I need you to help me lift the slab . . ."

The boy shook his head.

"I can't move," he said. He coughed again. He seemed more lucid than a few moments before. "My back is broken and I can't move. This is the end for me . . . I can't take any more. I'm exhausted and I just want to rest . . . Close my eyes and never open them again. You'd better go. Look for an exit and escape."

"Even if I wanted to I wouldn't get very far, not with my knee like this." He gave up on the slab, feeling hopeless, and lay back on the ground. Everything hurt. "This isn't the end for anyone, silly. Bruno will get us out of this. You'll see."

Bruno lay unconscious on a flat rock, his staff next to him. Luckily, it was still shining even though the Italian was passed out. The anchoring spell had worked perfectly. And although some light came in through the wrecked ceiling, Mistral doubted that it would be enough to hold the underground creatures back if the birdcage went out. The shapeshifter checked Bruno's pulse for the thousandth time and tried to wake him up again. They needed his magic. And they needed it as soon as possible if they wanted to rescue the two others.

"Ricardo! Hector! Do you hear me?" Marina shouted desperately at the wall of rubble, cradling her wounded arm in her hand. "Are you there?! Can you hear me?!"

Just like before, she got no answer.

"Heeeeeeeeeeector!" she repeated. She hung her head and bit her lower lip. She looked like she was about to start punching the rocks.

Marina was the only one who'd gotten injured in the collapse. The others on this side of the tunnel were safe and sound. Mistral had worked hard to keep them all alive. He'd quickened his movements and multiplied his reflexes, trusting that in those chaotic moments no one would notice that he seemed to be in several places at the same time. He'd dissolved rubble with abrasive magic; constructed force fields around Rachel, still hidden in the wall, and around Bruno's unconscious body; and, in one quick moment, he'd had no other option but to transport Lizbeth three feet away from where she stood to keep her from being crushed by a rock. It had been so long since he used such a constant stream of magic that he felt strange, distant from himself.

But he hadn't been able to save them all. He'd lost track of Hector right after the collapse, and Ricardo had disappeared shortly after. The shapeshifter glanced at the wall of debris that blocked the passageway. He knew the two boys were on the other side and the situation was precarious. He could hear them whispering in the feeble light of the talisman that Hector was charging. When it was fully charged, their time was up.

Bruno remained motionless, submerged in a profound unconsciousness brought on by his last spell. That kid had killed a chimera and had almost died because of it. Mistral felt something similar to pride. He stroked the boy's tangled hair. Throughout his whole life, Bruno had known nothing but loneliness—not a kind word for him, not a caress, nor a gesture. Nothing. He wasn't normal, he never had been, and not just because he didn't know how to relate to others or because he had issues with empathy. Rocavarancolia had marked him, and that mark, that stigma, had been with him since the moment of his birth. Rocavarancolia had claimed him as its own well before Denestor Tul came into his life, just like all those who ended up in the city.

"Wake up, Bruno," he whispered. "You have to keep saving lives. Wake up, kid."

Mistral could have transferred part of his own energy to wake him, but he was convinced that the Italian would notice something wasn't right. He had no choice but to let him recover on his own.

"Hector!" howled Natalia, who had relieved Marina of her screaming duties. The Russian girl was smudged with dust and grime, and paced from one end to the other of the mountain of rubble, never leaving the circle of light projected by the staff. Mistral had had to stop her when she started obsessively tearing rocks away. That wall could come down any instant. "Ricaaardo! You can't be dead! Say something! Say something right now!" she demanded. The girl listened carefully and then turned in the blink of an eye toward those waiting next to Bruno. "I can hear them! I think I can hear them! They're calling! They're calling us!"

"Keep quiet," Marina ordered, suddenly somber and alert.

"What's your problem now?" Natalia asked the girl. "I'm telling you, I can hear them! Hector! Ricardo! We're going to save you! Don't worry!"

Marina gripped her arm tightly, put her index finger to her lips in a plea for silence, and looked at the tunnel behind them.

They all followed her gaze. From the darkness came a distant rustling, a growing murmur. The point where they'd entered the tunnel was still visible in the distance, no more than a shining speck ablaze in the shadows. That minuscule strand of light was eclipsed for an instant. Something had obscured it as it passed through the tunnel, something that was heading toward them.

"No, please, no more . . ." Lizbeth murmured.

The sound grew by the second. It went from a whisper to an actual uproar, a clamor of approaching wings and shrieks that seemed to trample one another.

Mistral cursed loudly, got up, and drew his swords. Natalia moved away from the rubble and picked up the halberd that she'd left on the ground. The commotion was coming from the tunnel. Madeleine took the staff and raised it up. Instantly, the circle of light surrounding them quivered and the refocused blaze lit up the inside of the cavern. The body of the dead chimera, half-buried in the wreckage, seemed to emerge from the shadows. More than thirty winged horrors—identical to the one that took off with Marina—were approaching from the other end of the corridor. They shrieked as their wings cracked in the air like whips.

"It can't be," Madeleine whispered. The staff trembled in her hands. "It can't be . . . There are too many, they're going to destroy us."

Lizbeth whimpered, terrified. Rachel put an arm around her shoulders and drew her closer. She unsheathed the dagger that she wore at her waist and watched as the horde of terrors grew near.

"I won't let them hurt you," she promised.

Mistral took a deep breath as he looked at the vlakai. Light wouldn't work against them. What could he do? Betray his identity in front of the children and all of Rocavarancolia to save their lives? What sense would that make if the Royal Council ordered his execution as soon as they realized what had happened? The bats were almost upon them, emitting terrible screams. Mistral shook his head and made his decision. He began walking. He needed more muscle, more power. And it was clear that he'd have to resort to magic if he wanted to get out alive. If all was lost, at least the children would die in the light of day and not in that gloomy cave. He'd live out his days in the desert, and maybe that was what he deserved. When he was about to cast the first spell, the horde of frightening creatures veered off and landed atop the dead chimera. They fell upon the giant creature and began devouring it.

His relief made him lose his balance. He quickly reversed all of the changes that were taking place in his body and retreated once again, swords still raised. He looked at the teenagers out of the corner of his eye. None of them realized what had just happened. They were too busy staring at the monsters to notice that he'd begun to change. They watched them still, nauseated by their repulsive noises.

"They prefer carrion," he said.

"At least for the moment," Natalia groaned.

One of the vlakai raised its grotesque head and fixed its beady eyes on them. Blood dripped down its jaw. Mistral looked right back at it, perhaps hoping that his defiance would convince the creature that it was better off sticking to dead flesh. The monster went back to tearing a chunk of meat from the chimera, but it kept its eyes on them as it chewed. *Wake up, Bruno, wake up already.*

Minute after minute went by, and no one came to rescue them. He'd been calling out to the others, and although he thought he'd heard a response, he couldn't make out a word of what was said, nor could he tell where the voices were coming from. The echoes down there were deceiving. He stopped calling for help, because every time he did the monsters got agitated. They responded to his cries with a litany of growls and whimpers, hissing and shrieking.

The light from the talisman seemed to be growing weaker by the second; he knew that couldn't be true and that its intensity was the same as when he'd activated it, but he couldn't help thinking it. Maybe it was his mood that grew darker and dwindled, his mood and his hope. He'd emptied every last pocket but he didn't have any other crystals, only normal amulets that didn't help in the least. He lay back on the ground and watched the area with the shadows. He couldn't see them, but the monsters were still there. And there were more every minute. Sometimes he could make them out: gloomy silhouettes in opaque colors, albino creatures with cracked skin and shining eyes crouching in the space between darkness and light. He saw a gigantic white slug around which crowded dozens of red lobsters and for a fleeting moment he could see the purple face of a revived corpse embedded in the dark. It wore a helmet in the shape of a lion's head and had a horrible scar that split its face in two. At least those monsters weren't smart enough to think of any other plan besides waiting for the light to diminish. Hector didn't even want to think what would happen if one of those beings started to throw rocks at them, for instance.

He couldn't remember how long it took to charge a talisman, but when it was finished, when the light went out, those creatures would annihilate them.

*No one's burying us in the cemetery,* he told himself. *There won't be a single piece of us left to take.* Then he looked at the mountain of rubble that closed off the passageway. He wondered what was holding up the others, then he remembered that the last time he saw Bruno he was passed out on the ground. He went back to studying the crystal in his hand. The radiance was fragile, Ricardo had just said as much, and maybe it was the truth. But the glow from the crystal was also beautiful, even though it was tinged with blood.

"I always wanted to be a hero," Ricardo said suddenly. "I always dreamed of being one . . . Since I was little . . ."

"We all do that when we're kids." He felt strange saying that, as if centuries had passed since he had imagined himself as the star of glorious adventures.

"I know, I know . . . But I . . ." He sighed. "I was so great in my dreams. I lived the most exciting experiences that you could imagine. There wasn't a single night that I didn't save the world, where my sword wasn't the most terrifying or my bullet the most true. A hero. Always a hero . . . Cheered for, loved, adored. Until the dream became reality, until Denestor came to offer me a real mission." He went silent, his gaze lost in the void. The monsters stirred out of sight. "I thought that this was my story, that the reason for my existence was here, in this cursed city. That here I could be a hero. I was so stupid! Reality has nothing to do with dreams. In real life I'm just useless, a burden. People like me can only be heroes in their imagination."

"You're an idiot, that's what you are. Where is this coming from?"

"I'm giving up, for once. I admit my defeat. At least I have the courage to do that. Hey, world, I admit it!" he exclaimed. "I admit it before you and the legion of horrors that want to devour us. Listen up, everyone! I surrender! I'm not a hero and I never will be! I tried, I swear, but I can't do anything but fail, over and over again . . ."

"If it hadn't been for you, we wouldn't have lasted two days."

"You're wrong. You don't know how wrong you are. Marco was the one who guided us from the beginning. He made the real decisions, the ones that mattered. I . . . I was just wrong time and time again . . ." He grabbed him by the hand. "I should never have let us split up . . ."

The light had returned to his eyes, a feverish, intermittent light. "On that day, I shouldn't have divided the group. We shouldn't have gone after that crazy kid. The door hit me in the face, remember? I was out of the game before we even started playing. Some hero I am . . ."

Several monsters broke out in a rough dispute in the darkness. The brawl was frantic for a few seconds, then they heard a deafening shriek followed by the sound of a body being dragged.

"And then? What happened next? A monster attacked us when we tried to leave those stupid notes in the bathtubs . . . Again I was out of it, right from the beginning. And that thing hurt Natalia. I couldn't do anything to stop it, nothing . . . Just watch, half passed out on the ground. I failed. I always fail. Did you see me up there earlier? When the bat attacked? All I did was get in the way."

"The hyenas . . ." he began.

"The hyenas! They were harmless, Hector! We were the ones who chased them home! And even so, one managed to hurt me, remember?" He brought a hand to his forehead. Hector noticed that blood was now flowing from his cracked lips. Even worse: his eyes glazed over at times, barely reflecting the blaze from the crystal. "I was the only one they wounded. The only one . . . I was so furious, so enraged, that I almost killed that ridiculous little man." He turned his head halfway toward him. His voice was a hoarse whisper. Hector remembered Alexander, dying in front of the sorcery tower, and he wondered if Ricardo, too, would disintegrate before his eyes. "What kind of hero am I, Hector? Can you tell me?"

"A real hero. One who matters. One who's afraid, who makes mistakes and keeps going anyway."

"But I don't want to keep going. I refuse. Let the . . . let the darkness take me . . ."

"You'll learn. We all will," he said, remembering the words that Rachel had used on the day Ricardo was referring to.

"A hero . . ." he whispered. His eyes closed. "In my dreams I was a hero . . . I was a . . ."

Everything went silent, a devastating silence. Hector, terrified, felt his friend's neck for his pulse. He found it and breathed a sigh of relief. There was still life in that damaged body.

He was alone with the darkness, and all it contained. He looked again at the glow of the crystal, stained with his blood. He watched it with renewed astonishment, almost reverence, as if it were a mystery that he'd never noticed before. Time slowed back down in the ruined cavern. He lost all sense of it, abandoned in the land of monsters, holding the hand of his dying friend.

An eternity later, there was a flash of light. Two ghostly figures, outlined with a bright radiance, came stumbling toward him. For a moment, he thought it was two of the creatures stalking them and he gripped his sword tightly. Then one of the figures became Natalia and he smiled, on the verge of tears. The girl was dirty and exhausted, with scruffy hair and torn clothes, but she'd never looked so beautiful. Bruno, pale, walked behind her. One of his hands was raised and a brilliant glow illuminated it from within. It made him look like he was wearing a gauntlet of pure light.

Natalia threw herself at him, ignoring his complaints. She hugged him so tightly that for a few seconds he couldn't breathe. She cried in his arms.

"I thought you were dead, I thought you were dead," she repeated endlessly, her arms around his neck. Hector couldn't even speak. He wanted to ask them to cure Ricardo, to bring him back from the dark, but the girl's weight upon him took his breath away and, at the same time, comforted him. Natalia kissed him on the cheek, one, two, three times; then her lips strayed and she left a sweet, warm kiss on the corner of his own. In the midst of his delirium he returned it, consumed with relief over being alive and the heat of her body pressed against his. The crystal dropped from his hand and was immediately extinguished. But it no longer mattered. Now there was more than enough light.


The shapeshifter was the first to reach the surface. He moved through the air with insulting elegance, as if he'd spent his whole life defying gravity. He carried Rachel in his arms: the girl looked at everything with eyes wide open and a smile from ear to ear. Marco had to scold her so that she'd stop moving in her attempts to see better.

"Be still!" he told her. "You're going to fall if you don't stop moving!"

"Quiet, party pooper, and go higher!" she replied. "Higher! I want to see the city from the sky! From up above!"

"No way! Haven't you had enough for one day?"

"No!"

Hector's movements, on the other hand, revealed not a bit of smoothness or elegance; he stumbled through the air, and with every slip his heart rose up into his throat. His vertigo didn't help in the least. But even so, that weightless walking was almost pleasant compared to what he'd just lived through.

Bruno and Natalia hadn't completely cured the two wounded kids; they'd only healed their most serious injuries before bringing them to the others and beginning the ascent to the surface.

Night was falling over Rocavarancolia, and they knew they couldn't risk the long trek back, given their current state. Hector's broken knee had been fixed, but the cut on his forehead and hand and the countless bruises all over his body still hurt. He breathed deeply. Marina dropped to the sidewalk and gave him a tired smile, right as he managed to land on the ground, clumsily waving his arms.

"You look like a duck," the girl told him.

"I wouldn't mind it, ducks can fly," he answered. He felt a jab of remorse for having kissed Natalia, but it hadn't meant anything, it had been an impulse triggered by tension and fear. It hadn't even been a real kiss. He glanced at the Russian girl, who'd just landed next to Madeleine. She wasn't even looking at him. *No*, Hector told himself, *it didn't mean anything. I bet she's forgotten about it.*

Ricardo carried Lizbeth in his arms; they were the last to reach solid ground. She was the one most affected by what had happened. She was pale and trembling. Madeleine approached her and took her hand. Rachel came over soon after, her desire of having Marco take her for a stroll in the sky unfulfilled. She kissed her friend on the forehead. They started out quickly on their journey. The horrendous bats were still feasting on the dead chimera, but the more distance they put between themselves and those animals, the calmer they'd be.

"It all worked out," Marco said, walking next to Rachel. He seemed surprised. He turned to the others and shook his head. "I still don't understand how, but it all worked out."

"Man of little faith," Rachel said. "When will you learn that over here we're all more than we seem?"

"Is that how it's going to be when the Red Moon comes out?" Lizbeth asked. She clung to Marina's waist as she walked. Her face had regained some of its color, but she was still visibly shaken. "Will it be

like that from here on out, like it was down there? Defending ourselves tooth and nail from whatever comes out of Rocavaragalago?
Please tell me it's not, please . . . I couldn't take it."

Bruno answered.

"We know very little about what will happen when the Red Moon
comes out, so I cannot give you a yes or no in that regard. None of us
can. Time will answer that question. The only thing I can assure you
is that I shall do everything in my power to protect you."

"I'm sure that you will," Madeleine said. "What you did down there
was impressive." She put her hand on his shoulder and the Italian came
to a halt, as if the girl had activated his stop button. He looked straight
at her without blinking. He had the air of a shocked bird. "We'd all be
dead right now if it weren't for you. You saved our lives." She leaned
toward him and kissed him on the cheek. "Thanks, Bruno."

"And you have saved mine," he answered. He spoke faster than usual.
"That is what this is about, correct me if I'm wrong. Keeping one
another alive. That is the plan. We do not have a choice. Helping each
other. Staying alive." He stopped and blinked twice, slowly, before
adding: "I apologize, I think I am repeating myself."

Hector smiled. Neither the underground monsters nor anything else
they'd encountered in Rocavarancolia had unnerved the Italian, but
because of the redhead's kiss, for the first time, Bruno showed signs of
being human.

"I'm not going to kiss you," he heard Ricardo tell him, walking by his
side. He was the one in the worst shape after their underground journey,
and it still showed. At least the emergency healing had fixed his broken
back. "But thank you for earlier. It's nice to chat with a friend."

"Don't mention it," he told him. "We had to kill time somehow
before they came to rescue us. And listening to your nonsense was
much more entertaining than listening to the monsters growl."

"Thank you, Hector," Ricardo repeated, and gave him a huge slap
on the shoulder before walking in front of him. He hadn't taken two
steps before he turned around halfway and winked. "One more thing:
I will learn, I promise you. However long it takes, I'll learn."

# DAMNED SOULS

Hector thought that if there were ever a place that deserved the name *desert*, it was what lay before them. Before him stretched a cruel and monotonous emptiness, a swirling blanket of white and sparkles that extended in all directions, as far as the eye could see. There was no sign of life, no color whatsoever. Only white sand everywhere, the furious glimmer of the sun reflected in its dunes, and whirlwinds of sand stealing through the plains like angry ghosts.

"This place is horrible," Natalia mumbled.

Everyone agreed. The prospect of setting foot in that wasteland made their hair stand on end. The mountain behind them seemed to push them toward the unending white desert, encouraging them to leave its shelter and lose themselves in the desert's immensity.

"Do we have to go very far to be safe from the cathedral?" Marina asked.

Marco shrugged his shoulders.

"Fairly far, I guess . . ." Ricardo responded.

They were at the mouth of the narrow gorge that had led them to where they now stood. After a week of seclusion in the Margalar Tower, recovering from their experiences underground, they'd finally decided to take a look at the desert. They'd spent two days finding the mountain passes which Lady Scar had spoken of and another day preparing for their trek. They'd left at dawn, entering

the cold gloom of the hidden trails. Although it wasn't truly necessary, Bruno had lit the birdcage on his staff to dispel any shadows
that might cross their path, to everyone's relief. They'd been moving
for hours through the narrow passageways that opened up through
the rock, impressed by the grandeur of the mountains that surrounded Rocavarancolia.

The hardest part of the trip had been the last. First they faced the
sand: white grains, almost transparent, that quickly and completely
covered the ground, making their progress difficult and signaling
unequivocally that the end of their journey was near. Then came the
wind, terrible gusts that howled through the gorge, carrying whirlwinds of sand that made it almost impossible to see. For half an hour,
they advanced against the devastating wind and the sand that scratched
their skin, and invaded their mouths and eyes.

The wind calmed briefly when they discovered the exit, as if wanting to give them a chance to contemplate the Malyadar Desert in all of
its unholy magnitude. They weren't ready for it. Nothing could have
prepared them for that tremendous stretch of nothingness.

*There's no hope for you here*, the wind howled, raising tornadoes of
sand the size of buildings. *There's nothing here but death and agony. This
is where hunger and thirst reign, where the gods themselves come to die.*

They didn't stay to watch such desolation for long. Disheartened by
the discovery, they promptly began their return voyage, each of them
lost in thought. The vision of the Malyadar Desert had been a crushing blow to their hopes.

"Now you've seen it," Marco mumbled as they were walking back
through the ruined city. Rocavaragalago, red and monstrous, was left
behind once again. "Bad idea to go into that desert. Very, very bad idea."

"But it's still our only chance," Ricardo said.

"There's another alternative," Bruno pointed out. "The most obvious and natural option: we stay here and confront whatever should
emerge from Rocavaragalago. Do not reject the idea so hastily. That
desert would be our ruin, without a doubt."

"Bruno's right," Natalia said. "We won't survive a day in that
inferno. Not with all the magic in the world on our side."

"You think that's an inferno?" Lizbeth asked. She still had nightmares about the events underground from the week before. "Look at

where we are right now. What's happening to you? Are you so used to this place that you can't see what it's like? If it were up to me, I'd walk straight into that desert right now, I wouldn't wait a minute more."

"We'll have time to discuss it." Rachel approached the girl and put her arm around her shoulders. "We don't have to decide now, right?"

They arrived at the Margalar Tower exhausted and downhearted. Marco called to Adrian from the entrance to lower the drawbridge; there was no response. Natalia and Ricardo called him as well, but as hard as they tried, Adrian still gave no signs of life, and the bridge remained raised. Marco looked at the building sullenly and turned toward Bruno. He didn't have to say a word. The Italian sauntered through the air, over the moat, and then floated like a ghost over the greenish walls of the tower. Not five minutes had passed before the bridge descended with its habitual racket, the entryway gates all raising in unison. They crossed quickly. Bruno waited in the doorway.

All he said was "Adrian's friend has returned."

The teenagers exchanged uneasy glances, unsure of what to do next. Hector was the first to decide to go outside, and the others weren't far behind him. Adrian was in the middle of the courtyard, dressed in a gray shirt and dark pants. He fought with his usual focus, although his face had a new glow: it was joy, unbridled joy, almost mania. He didn't seem to have noticed them leave.

Hector looked at the rooftop. There was the enemy, sword in hand, dressed in his usual gray clothing. Although his movements seemed as agile as ever, at times he glimpsed a slight hesitation in them.

Dario had perceived the group's presence in the courtyard, but in his mind it was nothing more than background noise, as irrelevant as the tower's shadows or the cobblestones on the ground. For him, only Adrian and his sword existed; there was nothing else in the world. And he knew that he needed full concentration to win that battle. He'd thought that he was completely healed, but he soon realized his mistake. As the fight began, his right thigh started to bother him.

"How can they do that?" Lizbeth asked in a low voice. "It's impossible. How do they know they're parrying each other's attacks? I don't get it. I swear, I don't get it."

"They're mad," Ricardo said. He didn't bother lowering his voice. "That's what's happening. They're both mad, it's as simple as that."

Just then, Marina took a few steps toward them, as if looking for a better angle to view the demented duel. Hector thought he saw the boy from the rooftops direct his gaze at her. It only lasted a second, a gesture that didn't go further. Adrian made a quick jump forward, aware of his adversary's distraction, and thrust a diagonal blow up and to the left, gripping his sword with both hands. Then he sheathed his sword in a rage. His opponent remained completely still; he seemed ready to drop his blade. He brought his left hand to his chest, as if he wanted to check the seriousness of the injury that Adrian had inflicted.

Despite the distance, the two boys looked directly at each other, motionless, one in the courtyard and the other on the rooftop. Hector was conscious of the force from that exchange of glances and of the intensity of Adrian's hatred. The harsh wind blew his hair from side to side, as if it were a golden flame. It was impossible to discern his opponent's expression; he was too far away. Suddenly, he sheathed his sword, turned his back on the courtyard, and took off running. Before long he disappeared from sight, hidden by the uneven line of the rooftops. Adrian remained still for several moments, then he headed toward the tower with long strides.

They moved to one side to let him pass.

"And now what?" Rachel asked, once Adrian had vanished inside.

"I don't know," Hector replied.

They didn't see Adrian when they entered the tower, but they could hear him in the basement. Ricardo approached the spiral stairs at the same instant that the boy rushed up them at top speed, adjusting his belt. He was wearing two sheathed swords: the one he'd just been using in the courtyard, the other a beauty in black metal with a silver grip. He grabbed a shirt hanging from a chair and put it on over the gray one he wore. Then he opened a wardrobe and removed a thick red woolen overshirt. He wrapped it around himself.

"Where do you think you're going?" Marco asked.

"I have things to do outside," Adrian answered. He was trying to arrange the scabbards of his swords in such a way that they didn't obstruct each other, and he didn't even look up from them as he spoke.

"Of all of the bad ideas you've had . . ."

"Coming here takes the cake, yes. But Denestor Tul drugged me with his damn pipe, so it really wasn't my fault, right?" He grunted, satisfied, when the swords were arranged to his liking. "And now I'm going. No matter what you say."

"It will be dark soon. You don't know how dangerous it is to leave at nighttime."

"Neither do you," he said, passing by without making eye contact.

After a moment's hesitation, Marco went for him. He grabbed him roughly by the shoulder and forced him to a halt.

"Adrian! Listen to me! I'm not going to let you kill your—"

He didn't finish the phrase.

Adrian turned and cast an immobility spell, so fast that they could hardly make out his words. A layer of bluish energy surrounded Marco's body, which froze, suspended. His mouth remained half-open in midsentence, one hand raised in the air, the other emphasizing his half-finished phrase.

Everyone was astonished. Even Bruno seemed impressed.

"Since when are you able to do magic?"

"Since forever. I'm not at your level, but I know enough to defend myself." Adrian pulled down his shirt so they could see the various pendants and talismans around his neck. "I'll be fine outside." His past insecurity suddenly flashed across his face. "Listen . . . don't paralyze me or anything like that, okay? I'll be fine. Really."

"I don't intend to." Natalia shrugged her shoulders. "Go do what you have to do."

"And I am not going to interfere in matters that do not concern me in the least," Bruno pointed out.

"What are you going to do?" Marina asked. "Do you want to kill him? Is that your goal?"

Adrian took a step back, surprised by the question. He nodded emphatically.

"Of course I'm going to kill him," he said. "What do you think I've been preparing for?" He looked at Marina, puzzled, as if he couldn't understand why she'd ask him such a question. "He killed me, remember? That bastard killed me. He didn't know me, had no idea who I was, but that didn't matter to him . . . He thrust his sword in my stomach. And I hadn't done anything to him and he . . ." There was so much rage in his words that his voice choked in his throat. ". . . He killed me."

"I'm going with you," Ricardo said, and walked resolutely to the chair where he'd placed his weapons.

Adrian shook his head.

"I have to do this alone. If not . . . what sense will any of this make?"

"The same amount of sense it makes now: none," Lizbeth groaned. "Think carefully about what you're going to do, little boy."

"I've done nothing else for weeks now."

He finally headed for the door. For a moment, Hector thought of stopping him, of trying to persuade him to forget such madness. It seemed inconceivable that he was actually thinking of killing the other boy. He recalled how euphoric Adrian had been at the top of the serpent fountain, or how playful he'd seemed making that rude noise with his hand in his armpit the first night they spent at the tower. It seemed impossible that the Adrian of back then and the one now in front of him were the same person. But then he remembered Marina, besotted with the dark-haired boy as she sat by the well, and something unsettling and viscous stirred inside of him, a nauseating feeling that almost made him wish Adrian good luck on his quest. He looked away as he passed by, embarrassed by his own thoughts.

"Adrian." Madeleine called to him just as he was about to open the tower gate. The boy turned to look at her. "Kill him," she said.

Adrian nodded, opened the gate, and left the Margalar Tower for the first time in four months. Outside, dusk awaited him, bathing the ruins of Rocavarancolia in its bloody glow.


At that very moment, twenty-eight servants wandered to and fro through the rooms and hallways of the castle, pale, drawn, all dressed in the same worn black uniform. Most of them were long past the appropriate age to be carrying out their duties; they were slow and clumsy, and could barely keep up with the filth and chaos that was gradually taking over. Thus was the kingdom's decline also reflected in the servants of its fortress.

But those twenty-eight servants fit Hurza's purposes perfectly. The first Lord of Assassins remained enveloped in the cocoon of brilliant light, fortifying the body which had been given to him. Meanwhile, he watched, observed, and learned, peering out through those empty, tired gazes.

He watched as Lady Serena passed through one of the walls and glided through the air, cold and distant. She paid no attention to the servant, who was trying to clean mold off a picture and was damaging the paint in the process. In one of the hallways, through the eyes of another servant he saw Ujthan, the tattooed warrior, standing still in front of one of the great sets of armor that lined the wall. It was of studded steel, and by its height and build it must have belonged to a troll. Ujthan trembled as he studied it, moved almost to tears. He didn't notice the servant passing by him, either. Hurza couldn't imagine what daydreams filled the warrior's mind, but he assumed they were plagued with scenes of battle, combat, and death.

Then he looked at Enoch, the hungry vampire. He was sitting at one of the tables in the castle library, surrounded by books as dusty as he was. His enormous eyes avidly read the thick volume in front of him. From time to time he looked at the servant who stood next to the library's double doors. The vampire caused an intense revulsion within the servants that Hurza could feel like a constant throbbing in his temples. Twenty years before, out of desperation, Enoch had bit a servant and almost killed him. A member of the guard saved the poor wretch at the last moment, when scarcely any blood was left in his veins. All of the servants remembered with immeasurable disgust how Enoch's sharp fangs had sunk into his jugular and slurped his blood.

"Oh. Yes, yes, yes . . ." The vampire turned toward the servant again, his bony shadow multiplied and projected by the candles and torches above the tall shelves crammed full of books. "And how could we forget Lady Fang? Do you know what she did? Do you?" He smiled, revealing a set of dirty teeth. "She resisted the attack from Thickbeard's fleet on Mistletoe Island for six long years." He felt so much admiration reminiscing about the heroic acts of his race that his voice faltered. "She and her hordes of vampires fought back the unthinkable after Rocavarancolia reopened the vortex that joined the kingdom with that cursed world . . .

Oh . . . What abuse my race has suffered. History is so unjust!" He turned his attention to another book. His skeletal hands practically pounced on it. "And what they tell me about Lady Irhina and Balderlalosa, the first vampire queen and her . . ."

Hurza stopped listening. An invisible presence had just entered the library. The servant sensed the current of air and the muffled sound of bare feet on the ground. It was Rorcual, the kingdom's useless alchemist, he realized. He was following Enoch as usual. The vampire sought to forget his misfortunes by reliving the glories of his race, unaware that only a few feet away someone had set aside their own wretchedness to spy on him.

This council had little to do with those who'd betrayed Hurza and his brother. Most of them were pathetic beings, poorly drawn caricatures of the wonders they'd been destined to be.

*Is this why they killed us?* Hurza wondered. *Is this where they wanted to end up?*

Of all of them, only Esmael was worthy of the magnificent Rocavarancolia that Hurza had known, the Rocavarancolia that he and his brother had lost control of. Hurza still asked himself how it happened. How had they not realized that they were living alongside others who were not only as powerful as them but—even worse— didn't fear them? He'd tried to convince Harex that there was still time to suppress the treason that was brewing in the heart of the kingdom, that it was still possible to get back on course. They only had to do away with several conspirators, the most powerful, and annihilate them to subjugate the others. He still remembered his brother's words:

"If we do that, they'll know that we feel threatened. They'll know that, in a way, we fear them. And that will foster more traitors. No. Killing those vipers will only serve to show others that they are able to bite us, and so sooner or later one of them will do it. It's time to leave. It's time to let ourselves be taken out of the picture."

"I'm not afraid of anything," Hurza had replied.

"That's why I'm the king and you're my servant," Harex answered.

Hurza looked through the eyes of the two servants who in that moment were in the bedroom of the regent of Rocavarancolia. The ancient Huryel lay half-buried in the aqueous blankets of his

enormous bed, submerged in an uneasy slumber. A spectacular necklace hung around his neck and a delicate bronze tiara crowned his
head: these pieces were part of the Jewels of the Iguana, the most
powerful magic objects in the kingdom. As he looked at them,
Hurza felt a pang of rage and hatred. Denestor Tul was with the
regent, although Huryel didn't seem to be aware of his presence.
Hurza forced his gaze away from the jewels to observe the demiurge.
The sorcerer was worn out, and his decline was all too evident. He'd
long surpassed the peak of his powers, but even so, one only had to
glance at him to understand that, when the time came, he'd be a
tough nut to crack.

Denestor sighed.

"In the end you'll bury us all, old friend," he said. He reached his
shriveled gray hand toward the regent's bluish forehead and stroked it
tenderly. Huryel's skin was viscous to the touch, covered with a fine
film of water.

The regent's eyes suddenly opened. Two thick tears slid down his
cheeks. One of them seeped through the pulsating gills on his neck.

"That's not my intention, Denestor," Huryel said. His voice bubbled,
but sounded much clearer than it had in the last few weeks. "It's those
damn hags and their damned potions. They won't let me go." The
regent coughed forcefully. "Even in my dreams they give me their disgusting concoctions. Ah, may demons take them . . . take them away
. . . In the end I'll have to order Esmael to kill them so they'll let me
die in peace."

Denestor smiled. Lady Scar knew that now that she had his support
she would become regent without a problem, but she still took great
care to keep Huryel alive. The guardian of the Royal Pantheon wasn't
interested in the power that came with the role of regent. The only
thing she wanted was to keep Esmael away from it.

"Your time hasn't come yet, Huryel. Don't deprive us of your company, for now."

"Sweet-talking demiurge. There's no clarity left in my mind, only
slime and rot."

He coughed again. He passed a trembling hand over his wet lips and
asked, "How is the harvest?"

"Eleven remain alive."

"Are you sure those witches aren't giving them potions too?" he groaned. "So much stamina is starting to seem suspicious, don't you think?"

"They're just lucky," he answered. "They managed to get into the Serpent Tower fast enough. Without magic, most of them would be dead already."

Denestor wondered what would happen if Huryel found out that three members of the council were betraying the kingdom and helping the children. The demiurge sighed. As much esteem as they felt for one another, Huryel was still regent of Rocavarancolia. He knew very well what his duty was, and, like it or not, he'd fulfill it without hesitation: the conspirators would be exiled to the desert and the harvest would be exterminated. And that would mean the end of the kingdom. He felt a twinge of guilt to think that it would be best for all of them if Huryel died. With Lady Scar as regent, there would be nothing to fear.

Huryel tilted his head to be able to look out the windows. Darkness fluttered through them, agitated by the howls of the pack and the wind. A flaming bat sparkled in the distance.

"How long until that damned moon comes out?" he asked.

"Ninety-nine days."

"Ninety-nine eternities . . . A few months ago I dreamed of Lady Dream. Or that old nutter dreamed of me, I don't know. She assured me that I would survive long enough to see the Red Moon again. I didn't want to believe her, but, as you see, she's on her way to being right."

"Did she show you anything else in the dream?"

"That's not enough for you?" Huryel grumbled. He grimaced as if someone had just struck him a blow. He huffed, groaned, raised one hand, and let it fall on his chest. On each one of his fingers he wore at least three rings, all different and magnificent. More pieces of the Jewels of the Iguana. "It doesn't end, Denestor. This agony of mine doesn't end." The sigh that he let out sounded as if his throat were full of water that was suddenly about to boil. "I'm going to take cruel advantage of you, Demiurge. I have something to ask you. And since I'm the damn regent, you can't refuse me, or I'll make Esmael cut off that ugly head of yours."

"Ask whatever you like."

Huryel gave him an unfocused look. All of his fatigue and suffering were present in those squinting eyes with their dirty whitish color.

"Kill me. Make it stop. Life is pain. Finish me off and let me rest. Free my soul from this crushed body . . ."

Denestor stammered.

"I . . . I can't do that, Regent . . . You can't ask me that . . . No. I . . ."

"I knew it. You always were sentimental. If only I had the strength to do it . . . But I'm so weak that I can't even die." His eyelids closed slowly and more tears flowed from his sad eyes.

Denestor waited until he was completely asleep before he left the room. He felt his muffled heartbeats pounding against his chest and at the same time, they seemed very far, as if at the bottom of a deep abyss.

He nodded at the guard who watched over the regent's chambers and began walking up the hallway. The joints in his scrawny knees creaked with every step he took. Thinking about Huryel's death made him think about his own. He sighed again. He'd been alive for too long to fear death, but even so, the uncertainty over what might await him on the other side made him dread the arrival of that moment.

As he turned the corner he encountered a servant leaning against the wall, noticeably unwell. He was doubled over, with his hands on his temples. The vase that he'd been cleaning was scattered in shards around him. For a moment, Denestor considered continuing on his path, but the still-fresh memory of the dying Huryel and the idea of his own death made him stop in front of the pale little man.

"Are you unwell?" he asked.

The servant gave a start on hearing his voice. He looked at him with empty eyes and blinked slightly.

"It's just weakness, Master Denestor, nothing more." His lower lip trembled without control. He swallowed, recovered himself, and kept talking as he passed a hand over his forehead, which was beaded with sweat. "This has been happening to us often as of late, but we recover quickly. I'll clean up this mess right away, not to worry, master."

Denestor nodded. It wasn't the first time he'd seen signs of weakness in the castle servants, but for some time now they'd all seemed more affected than usual.

"And since when did you say this extreme weakness has been troubling you?" he asked. He squinted his eyes and moved closer to the servant.

"It started with the death of our colleague, but it's gotten worse over the last few weeks."

Denestor took from his tunic a small beetle made from a cameo and the points of a comb. He squeezed it and a soft silver light emerged from its shell. The artificial insect jumped onto his shoulder. A faint light surrounded the gray man and the pale servant.

"It's not the first time that one of you has died violently. During the final battle many of you died on the north tower when the enemy dragons attacked us."

The servant nodded. The terror of that memory showed in his eyes.

"It was horrible, Master Denestor. Horrible."

"I imagine so. Did it take you a long time to recover from it?"

"No. In a couple of days we found ourselves able to carry out our tasks without any decrease in our faculties."

"But this time it's different," Denestor murmured. He fingered the collar of his tunic and felt along it from right to left and left to right. He had to stand on tiptoe to examine the servant's face. His pallor shifted to fright. "What do you feel exactly?" he asked. "What do you all feel . . ." he corrected himself.

"It's difficult to explain, master. It's an intense cold, a terrible emptiness, and"—he brought a hand up to his temples before continuing—"an excessive weight here. And sometimes"—he sighed heavily—"sometimes we have the feeling that we're drowning. We feel like our lungs are filling up with water, with salt water."

Denestor frowned. The map of wrinkles that was his face furrowed even more. He looked directly into the servant's eyes, searching them for some symptom of illness, madness, or witchcraft. He found nothing, but a sinister shiver ran down his spine, an ominous foreboding that gripped his insides and dried up his throat.

On the other side of that gaze, Hurza shifted restlessly in his cocoon.


Adrian returned at dawn. He went down the stairs, one sheathed sword still in hand, and collapsed on the bed in the same clothing he was wearing when he left. Very few of them were able to sleep while he was gone, and Hector wasn't one of them. He'd spent hours tossing and turning in bed, unable to stop picturing Adrian floating over the moat and crossing through the walls of the Margalar Tower, as ghostly as Lady Serena.

*He killed me*, he'd said before he left the tower, and Hector grew more certain that that was what had happened, or maybe some other occurrence almost equally tragic. The boy from the rooftops had killed Adrian, and Bruno's magic had made something new occupy his empty body, something completely foreign to what had been Adrian. Or maybe that tremendous darkness was already inside of him, waiting for the moment to take control.

"I couldn't find him," Adrian mumbled, although no one had asked him anything. "But tomorrow I'll try again. It's only a matter of time before I track him down."

Mistral sat up in bed to watch him. The shapeshifter had spent almost an hour paralyzed, a victim of Adrian's immobilization spell. It was hard for him to believe how easily the boy had gotten away from him. It was humiliating. How could he protect them from Rocavarancolia if the city was already inside of each and every one of them? It appeared in Natalia's gaze when she stared into space, in Lizbeth's nightmares, in the change in Madeleine, and in the tension with which Hector sometimes looked at Marina . . .

"Marco."

Adrian had turned toward him.

"I'm very sorry about earlier," he said. "But I couldn't let you stop me, understand?"

"It's nothing," he assured him.

Adrian was the one whom the city affected most, without a doubt. He now belonged to Rocavarancolia in body and soul.

Hurza stretched out a hand in the vibrant luminosity of his chrysalis. He sank his nails, still tinted brownish gray, into the cocoon's surface and began to tear at it. He did it in one single motion, from top to bottom. Then he stood up slowly as the chrysalis's walls of energy ripped and fell around him like the petals of a flower just opening. Belisarius's body was still recognizable, but it radiated an energy and vigor that it lacked before.

The first Lord of Assassins held the palm of his hand before his eyes and closed it tightly. Magic energy crackled around his fist as he watched in satisfaction—a dirty gleam of silver with black lightning. It wasn't even close to what he'd been able to conjure in the past, but it was a good start. He walked over the damp planks of the sunken ship. Parts of his body were still covered in Belisarius's bandages, dirty scraps of rotten fabric that gave him the appearance of something recently dug up.

The plan that he'd outlined was very simple: first the book, then the boy.

# DO NO HARM

Hector rose to the surface coughing and spitting out water. He didn't know what hurt worse: his pride or the blow he'd just gotten. It was the third time that morning that he'd ended up in the stream. In that stretch, the water reached up to his chest and flowed calmly and peacefully. He looked around for his staff. He saw it several yards ahead, carried off by the current. He swam toward it, grabbed it, and headed to shore, trying to ignore Ricardo's laughter.

"You fell like a sack!" he shouted from the wall at the top of the bridge. "I give you a score of nine out of ten. You get better with every dive!"

"Revenge," Hector growled.

He left wet footprints on the pavement as he climbed up to the bridge with his staff in his right hand. He and Ricardo had figured that they might end up in the water, which was why they were only wearing shorts. As soon as he saw him arrive, Ricardo was prepared; he raised his staff and crossed it before his face, which was insultingly dry.

"You've come back for more, I see," he commented with a smile. "Haven't you had enough?"

"Revenge," Hector repeated. He scaled the wall in one jump, twirled his staff, and approached Ricardo in a threatening manner.

Above them shone the Rocavarancolian sun. There was no one in sight and all was completely still. The others were in the tower, except Adrian, who had left once again to hunt down the boy from the rooftops; for now his efforts had been in vain, but he didn't give up. A black bird perched on the rooftop of the tower let out a litany of cackles and then took off in flight. The tiny salamanders that lived in the river swam next to the shore, searching for the repulsive water bugs they consumed.

The two friends greeted each other theatrically atop the wall of the bridge, arranged themselves in fencing poses, each more forced and ridiculous than the last, and, shouting in unison, resumed combat. The wall was so narrow that it was difficult to move and keep their balance at the same time. For a few minutes they crossed their weapons slowly, thrusting simple blows that they parried effortlessly. Little by little they increased the speed of their attacks. They looked each other in the eye, focused and smiling, until the intensity of the fight made their smiles disappear.

Ricardo struck from the left, quickly, thrusting one blow after another. Hector dispelled them as fast as they came, without missing, but with less and less precision. Besides parrying the attacks he had to constantly adjust his position on the wall to keep from falling again. Ricardo feinted to the right, Hector played into his hand and got a blow to the side that made him completely lose his balance. But before he fell he had just enough time to grab Ricardo by the arm.

"Revenge!" he shouted happily as he dragged his friend into the river.

"You cheater!" Ricardo howled when he emerged from the water. He shook his head, spraying water droplets in all directions.

"I'm sorry, I'm sorry . . ." Hector said, without feeling sorry in the least. "Listen: it was the only way to get you to take a bath. It's no excuse, but I'm ashamed of my behavior."

Hector reached the shore before his friend completely recovered. He hoisted himself up and sat, his legs dangling in the water. Ricardo joined him a couple of minutes later.

"You're a dirty rat," he growled, rubbing his eye. "No wonder you're getting so thin: it's because you're evil, it's eating you up."

"Being evil makes one thinner and sleeker," he said, a half smile on his lips. "And it's much more fun."

Hector had to admit that the "Rocavarancolia diet," as Rachel sometimes called it, had had a miraculous effect on him; he had no idea how many pounds he'd lost in the last few months, but he estimated he was close to his ideal weight. He looked out of the corner of his eye at his reflection in the water. His face had lost some of its roundness, and his hair, that unkempt black mane that reached his shoulders and that Lizbeth always insisted on cutting, made it look even thinner. His reflection looked like some melancholy vagabond, to the point that sometimes he hardly recognized himself. Natalia had said that every day he looked more and more like a street musician.

The changes weren't limited just to his physical appearance. He'd also changed mentally. He was more determined and sure of himself. And although it was silly, all of those changes scared him. It was as if somehow the old Hector were being exiled from his body, as if his own being were forgetting him, just like the people he'd known on Earth had forgotten him. That loss of identity, that emphatic abandonment of everything he'd been up until now, made him dizzy. He tried to think about it as little as possible, but sometimes he couldn't help it.

Ricardo looked back, toward the top of the Margalar Tower. The star on the sphere had already reached a quarter to nine. He sighed and dropped backward, onto the riverbank.

"You know something?" he said. "I think yesterday was my birthday . . . Or maybe it's today, it's difficult to say in this place. I was born the fourth of March, seventeen years ago . . ."

"Oh." Hector didn't know what to say.

He fell back too, with his arms crossed behind his head, and let his gaze wander across the sky. He couldn't remember the last time he'd used certain Earth terms. In Rocavarancolia, day always followed day in a constant cycle. Names had no meaning there. Why call it Tuesday if it was exactly the same as the day before and the day after? What did it matter if it were December or March or always autumn? There weren't seasons, there weren't any natural signs that indicated the passing of time, there weren't even stars to guide them. It was like living suspended in time.

"Happy birthday, I guess," he finally said.

"Thanks, I guess." He began to whistle very softly. "And do you know whose birthday is next week?" He imbued his question with a mysterious singsong tone.

"Not me. I was born July tenth."

"No, idiot. I know it's not you. Marina. Marina turns fifteen."

"Oh," Hector said, and closed his eyes. Every time he heard her name he felt a pleasant warmth spread throughout his insides.

"I don't know . . ." Ricardo said. He whistled for a few more seconds before speaking again. "I thought it would be a good idea to spend that day in the cemetery. She likes that place, you know. And maybe you, in an act of chivalry, could make her a pretty bouquet with the flowers around there. A nice gift, you know."

"Pick flowers? She'd look me up and down, and she'd get all sulky. No, she likes living flowers, not cut . . ." Hector stood up abruptly. The conversation had taken a complicated turn. "What are you talking about?" he asked, with exaggerated curtness. "Why do I have to give her flowers?"

"Hector, Hector, Hector," Ricardo crooned. "It's time you realize: everyone knows you're crazy about her."

"What are you talking about?!" He covered his mouth, aware of having raised his voice. He shook his head with the same resolve with which, if his life were hanging in the balance, he would have denied at that moment that it was daytime. "That's ridiculous, it's silly. I don't know where you got that idea, but forget it. I don't like that girl a bit. Not at all. Less than zero. You must be . . ." He was breathless from talking so fast. Ricardo's grinning face made it clear that he was giving himself away. "Oh . . ." he managed to say. "Everyone?" he asked, in a thin voice. "Everyone knows?"

"Of course. Sometimes you stare at her so hard that it makes me want to smack you."

"Does she . . . ?" His heart pounded in his chest. He took his legs out of the water, as if it was burning him. "Does she know?"

"Thank heavens, Marina is smarter than you. So yes, I assume that she knows." He shrugged his shoulders. "It's not like we've talked about it, of course, but . . ."

"Is this because I pulled you into the water?" he asked. "Is this how you get revenge?"

Ricardo started laughing.

"Maybe. But that doesn't mean it's not true." He punched him in the shoulder. Hector frowned. "When are you going to say something to her already?"

"Say what?"

"I don't know, something."

"Something!" He laughed. "Wait, wait. I know! I'll invite her to go for a walk among the skeletons! And then maybe we can go feed Caleb's hyenas, or listen to the howls of the mountain monsters. It will be delicious. A perfect romantic evening."

Ricardo looked at him with eyes the size of dinner plates.

"You're an idiot," he said.

"No, I'm a realist."

"Sometimes that's the same thing," he said, amused. Hector smiled in spite of himself. Ricardo's spirits had greatly improved after their underground adventure. Being on the verge of death had been good for him.

"What I mean to say is . . ." He shook his head. It seemed absurd to be talking about this subject. However, it felt important that Ricardo understood. "Okay, I like her, it's true," he admitted. "But look, look at where we are: Rocavarancolia, the capital of horror, the land of nightmares . . ." He jumped up and walked along the bank, pointing left and right like a circus ringleader showing off the attractions. "Take a look around! Ruins, black magic, monsters everywhere! And there'll be many more when the Red Moon comes out! Did I mention the disintegrating spells? Or the stab wounds to the stomach?" He lowered his arms and shook his head. "We're in Rocavarancolia. This is no place for love or any such nonsense . . . Love can't save us."

"I insist: I can't believe what an idiot you are."

"And I can't believe that you don't understand what I'm saying."

"All I can hear is nonsense. Excuses. But hey, it's your life, do what you want."

Hector dropped down next to him once again. He still felt hot. He plunged his hand in the river and splashed his face.

"So, you like her?" Ricardo asked.

"Ugh." Hector smiled. "A lot. I . . ." He swallowed. "How can I not like her? Have you seen her?" He smiled even more thinking about her. "She has the most beautiful eyes in the world." He didn't want to go any further but he couldn't stop himself. He no longer saw ruins or desolation; he could only see her. "When I look at her, everything makes sense," he said. "When I look at her, I know who I am and why the world's turning. It's for her, for Marina."

"You're in love."

"I know. It's a pain in the ass."

Suddenly something made him turn around. It was such a strong premonition that before he finished turning he knew who he would find behind him. Natalia stood there motionless, her eyes very wide, an indecipherable expression on her face. She carried two sandwiches in her hands.

"Idiot," she said bleakly.

She dropped the sandwiches and took off running back to the tower. Bewildered, Hector saw her cross the drawbridge, and he immediately understood something so obvious that he was astonished that he hadn't realized it sooner. Something moved behind him, a fragment of darkness that he glimpsed out of the corner of his eye, a black streak that jumped from the bridge into the river. He turned quickly, and although he didn't see anything, he knew that Natalia's shadow, the one that always followed him, was no longer with him.

"I messed up," he heard Ricardo mumble. "I guess not everyone knew."

Natalia had locked herself in a room on the second floor and refused to talk to anyone. Lizbeth tried to find out what happened, but neither Ricardo nor Hector said anything. The girl didn't insist, although they clearly saw that she was dying to do so. Hector solemnly went up to the common room. Marina was on the second floor, talking quietly with Maddie, but he didn't even look at them as he passed by. He felt so guilty that it was hard for him to focus.

He threw himself on his bed, one arm folded over his face.

But why exactly should he feel guilty? For feeling something for Marina or for not feeling the same for Natalia? He gazed up at the roof beams of the tower. The senselessness of the situation confused and enraged him equally. He believed without a doubt what he'd told Ricardo: there was no room in Rocavarancolia for silly love affairs. They weren't in high school; they were in a city that could kill them given the slightest opportunity. He tried to clear his mind of all thought. He needed to calm down, to stop this insufferable pounding that had started in his temples.

After a while, Lizbeth's head appeared at the top of the stairwell. "Natalia wants to talk to everyone," she said. For once, she spoke slowly. Rather than merely looking at Hector, she seemed to study him as if he were a highly interesting specimen.

"What about?" he asked, alarmed.

She walked the rest of the way up the stairs. Rachel was behind her. Seeing them appear, one after the other, emphasized what a strange pair they were: one of them tall and thin, all knees and elbows, the other short and round, full of an energetic sweetness.

Rachel sat on the edge of Hector's bed while Lizbeth remained standing, her arms crossed, not taking her eyes off him. It took her a few moments to answer.

"I don't know," she said. "She didn't say, but it's important."

Hector nodded slowly. Rachel looked at him with a smile on her lips. The boy frowned.

"It's okay. Let's go see what she wants."

Lizbeth grabbed his hand before he could get out of bed. She grasped it firmly and tenderly.

"You always have to try to do the least amount of harm possible," she said, "but sometimes doing harm is inevitable. It's not your fault. It's nobody's fault."

He looked at her without understanding. Rachel nodded complacently, as if her friend had uttered a fundamental truth.

"That's life," Lizbeth went on. "That's just how it is. Don't worry about it. In a lot of situations there's no good guys or bad guys, winners or losers. The world, most of the time, is gray."


The world was dark, terribly dark.

Under the water, the shadows were like gigantic celestial bodies crammed into a tiny sky. Not even the weakest ray of sunlight penetrated the surface: down below everything was darkness: areas of moving silhouettes that crowded one on top of the other. Hurza walked along the bottom of the ocean, submerged up to his ankles in the slimy sediment that stretched across the Rocavarancolian seabed. He was dragging a dead mermaid by the arm. The creature's tail flapped behind it like a limp banner. It was the ninth one he'd killed. The eyes of those beings tasted of salt and scales, and their memories were full of underwater currents, games among the seaweed, and turbulent love stories. The amount of vital energy that they provided was minimal, but it was better than nothing.

The mermaids of Rocavarancolia hardly resembled the ones from the linked world of Trumaria, the only mermaids that Hurza had known until then. Those were creatures of unheard-of beauty, with long, silky hair and silvery tails. He and Harex had made a quick raid to that world during their first years in Rocavarancolia. There they'd murdered seventeen sorcerers, and robbed the Sacred Harpoon from the royal palace, a magnificent jade weapon enchanted in such a way that there was no surface it could not cut, no target it could not hit. He remembered the intense pleasure that ran through him as he threw that harpoon into the lava pit of Rocavaragalago. He believed he heard the scream of its magic as it was eradicated.

From the underwater darkness surged another shadow. It was an immense alabaster head, more than forty-five feet long, that lay at an angle in the seabed. The water had eroded its features, almost erasing them completely. The mouth of the head was open, and he dragged the mermaid's dead body toward it, to the statue's hollow interior. The cadaver rose slowly and joined with those of its eight sisters floating at the top.

Hurza looked up; although the light didn't reach the bottom of the sea, he was aware that it was still daytime up above. He had only to peer through the eyes of the castle servants to know that the brightness of the dull Rocavarancolia sun still reigned in the sky. He sat down in the muck and closed his eyes in the darkness, waiting silently for night to enshroud the world so he could finally get started.

"I see things . . ." Natalia began. They all sat at the main table on the ground floor. Adrian was there, too, he'd returned while Hector had been upstairs. "This isn't something that's only happened to me here. I saw them on Earth. I've seen them forever, since I was small. I call them elves, although they're not like fairy-tale elves. They're shadows."

She told the story exactly as she'd told it to Hector, without revealing that he already knew about it. Hector didn't mention it either. He remained silent, sitting on a bench with his hands resting on the edge. He tried not to look at anyone; at first he felt everyone's glances orbiting around him, but he managed to avoid each and every one of them. Then the group's attention focused on Natalia and they forgot about his presence.

As he listened to her talk, Hector felt a strange, bitter sadness. With each of her words he realized that he'd lost something that until then had only belonged to the two of them. He remembered the warmth of her hand in his during their first nights in Rocavarancolia. He thought of that clumsy hug in the library, and he felt emptier still. Then the fleeting movement that he'd sensed near the river came to his mind, and he wondered if Natalia's shadow had abandoned him for good.

The girl stopped talking. She'd finished her story. For a while, the table remained silent. Ricardo was the first to break the silence. Before he spoke he shook his head, as if he couldn't believe what he'd just heard.

"And you waited until now to tell us this?" he asked bluntly. "We've been here more than four months, and you're telling us now?"

"I had my reasons, okay?" Natalia replied, morosely. She tried to hold Ricardo's gaze, but she wasn't able to. "I'm telling you now, right? They're not like my elves from Earth, they're dangerous. If you don't get that, then it's your problem, not mine."

"Are they here now?" Rachel asked, leaning forward at the table. They all looked around.

"There's one on the ceiling, above the door to the courtyard," Natalia answered unwillingly. Many of them glanced up in that direction, and she shook her head. "You can't see them. Only I can. As soon as you looked, it jumped onto a table and then climbed down a wardrobe."

Mistral stared at Natalia with a furrowed brow. In Rocavarancolia there were so many entities that didn't have an actual physical body or that could only be seen in certain circumstances or by certain people that it was hard to know which ones she was referring to. Even he wasn't sure he knew all of them. Apart from the ghosts of Rocavarancolia, most of them safe within the infinite room in the castle, there were spectral creatures that lived between dimensions, there were shapeless terrors born from defective spells, there were phantoms of dead phantoms . . . And so many others. He'd speak to Denestor. The demiurge would find a way to determine which creatures the girl was talking about.

"Does anyone else want to tell us anything?" Ricardo asked. It seemed like he'd taken Natalia's secret as a personal affront. "Anything important that's been hushed up for reasons that only you know?"

Everyone was silent for several minutes. Some exchanged uncomfortable looks. Hector lowered his head and sighed. He couldn't tell them about the warning mist; the voice in his mind had made it very clear what would happen if it came out that they were receiving help. And what if he wasn't the only one keeping a secret? What if they all had something to hide?

Suddenly Madeleine cleared her throat and leaned back in her seat.

"I don't know if it's important or not, but for some time I've had really strange dreams," she said. "Do you remember what I told you about the pictures that I painted on Earth? The ones where I drew broken lines so that they looked like they were covered in spiderwebs? Well, my dreams are like that. Exactly like that. They're more or less all the same: I'm wandering through Rocavarancolia and I see everything through those cracks, those marks that entangle everything . . ."

Lizbeth gasped. Then she brought a hand to her chest and went still.

"I forgot about your pictures! My goodness!" She stretched across the table and reached her arm toward Madeleine as if she meant to take her by the hand despite the distance between them. "I'm having the same dreams! Exactly the same!" She lowered her voice. "I dream that I have a veil over my vision." She waved her hand in front of her eyes, and continued talking. "It's like I'm looking through a cracked window. And everything's a different color, not the color it should be, more warm and intense. They're your dreams! Your pictures!"

Madeleine nodded.

"That's my dream, you're right."

"This is very odd," Rachel said. "I don't dream. I haven't dreamt since we arrived. At least not that I remember. And on Earth I always remembered my dreams."

"Has anyone else dreamed the same thing as Lizbeth and Maddie?" Marco asked. No one answered. Some shook their heads, and others just remained silent. "Any other dreams that seem strange?"

"Sometimes I dream that I'm writing," Marina said. Hector glanced sideways. She looked more insecure than usual, even uncomfortable. "The weird thing is that when I'm awake, as hard as I try, I can't write anything . . . It's like I'm only inspired when I sleep."

"Do you remember what you write?" Marco asked.

"No, I always forget. When I dream I know it's important and sometimes I even realize that I'm asleep, and I tell myself that I have to remember it when I wake up, but I never do. As hard as I try, I forget everything as soon as I open my eyes."

"What about you, Bruno?" asked the shapeshifter, looking at the Italian seated at the opposite end of the table. "Have you had any strange dreams recently?"

Bruno shook his head.

"My dreams now are identical to the ones I had on Earth." Just when it seemed like that was going to be his whole response, he went on: "I dream that I'm on an empty stage without any scenery or decoration, facing a theater full of seats that stretches as far as the eye can see. Only the first row is filled. That is where the dead people sit. All the people who died because of me, I mean. My parents are there, my aunts and uncles, my grandmother . . . The children from the nursery school, my servants and tutors . . ." He seemed as if he was about to add another name, but after looking at Madeleine he let it go. "They're all watching me without blinking. They seem anxious. In the dream it looks like they're waiting for something to happen. An act, a magic trick. I don't know. I don't know what the dead people want. From time to time they look at the curtains that cover the theater entrance, as if they're waiting for more spectators to appear."

"How awful," Rachel murmured. "And then what happens? Do more people come? Do you do what they're waiting for?"

"What happens?" Bruno shook his head again, slowly, mechanically, like the gadgetry inside a precise watch. "Absolutely nothing happens. I stay still in front of the dead people until I wake up. And when I go back to sleep I return there, to that same empty stage, and throughout the entire night the dead and I look at each other."

"You're crazy, you know that?" Adrian said. He was leaning back in his chair, his feet propped up on the table. He'd conjured a small fireball that he rolled between the fingers of his left hand, first in one direction, then in the other. His eyes followed the sphere's movements without blinking. "Really, really crazy."


Natalia and Lizbeth stayed in the tower while the others went out to explore the city. The first said she was kind of tired, and the second said she "was going to use the afternoon to tidy up the tower a bit," although it was clear that what she really meant to do was keep Natalia company. Hector was grateful for the Russian girl's absence. What had happened had affected him deeply and having her nearby didn't help the situation. With Marina it was different. They hadn't exchanged a word or a glance all day, but there was something friendly in that mutual avoidance, something comforting. Sometimes he had the impression that she was watching him and that she only looked away when his own gaze was searching for her.

Adrian accompanied them until they crossed the Scar of Arax, then he said his farewells and took off through the air toward the flat roof of a five-story building. They saw him pat the head of a red gargoyle before he finally disappeared from sight, his hand on the hilt of one of his swords. The others carried on in silence. They'd spent several days exploring the northeastern part of the city, particularly the area between the cemetery and the outskirts. The only noteworthy thing they'd discovered in that time was the ruins of another tower of sorcery. Mistral knew that it was near impossible that they'd find anything useful in that part of the city, since it was the most damaged during the conflict; most of the vortices used by the enemy army to invade Rocavarancolia had been there: those streets and plazas had been witness to the ferocity with which attackers and defenders alike had fought during the first stages of battle.

After a few hours of walking aimlessly, they ended up wandering along a wide esplanade littered with debris. The façades of the scorched buildings that lined the disaster area watched them like gloomy giants about to collapse. The wind had free rein throughout the area, drawing meaningless symbols among the dust and rubble, and ruffling their hair and clothes.

Hector crouched down to pick up a pretty piece of clear blue tile with an iridescent eye in the center, which looked like it had been part of a mosaic. When he got up, Marina was in front of him. He hadn't heard her come near; it looked like the wind had deposited her there as if by magic. The girl smiled, although she seemed somewhat tense. She brushed her hair, waving in the wind, away from her forehead.

"How are you?" she asked him.

She knew, of course she knew. She'd known from the beginning. Hector returned the smile and looked into her eyes, trapped by the whirlwind of feelings that her mere presence awoke in him.

"Fine," he said. "I'm fine."

She nodded, satisfied, as if that frugal response were more than enough, as if, in fact, she hadn't expected anything more. She was about to leave, but she suddenly stopped, turned toward him, and touched his cheek so softly and swiftly that Hector thought he might have imagined it. Then she walked back to Rachel, who was hanging around, poking her staff at some broken ceramic as she pretended not to look at them.

When they finally set off back to the tower, he and Marina walked next to each other, not exchanging a word or glance, but close enough that they could stretch out their fingers and touch.


"She hasn't said a word to me all day, can you believe it?" Lizbeth told Hector, shortly after they arrived back at the tower. "Not a word. She spent the whole time lying on the bed staring at the ceiling. When you arrived she went out to the courtyard." She fixed her hair quickly, in an automatic gesture. "Why don't you talk to her?"

"And what do I tell her?" he asked.

"I don't know. But tell her something. It can't go on like this."

"Just ignore her," Maddie advised. She was peeling a pear with a small knife. She was the only one close enough to hear them. "It's best just to leave her alone for a few days. It will pass. And don't feel bad, that's silly. You didn't kill anyone."

"But . . ." He bit his lower lip.

He didn't know what to do. Following Madeleine's advice would be his preferred option, but only because that seemed easier, not because he was convinced that he was making the right decision. That was precisely the path that the old Hector would follow: he'd let it go, not do anything, and hope that things would resolve on their own.

He shook his head.

"I have to talk to her," he mumbled, and walked toward the courtyard. Lizbeth smiled. Madeleine shrugged her shoulders and took a bite out of the pear.

Natalia was sitting on the wall that surrounded the courtyard, looking absently at the ruined city. Hector watched her for a few minutes from the door. He took a deep breath and crossed the plaza. He went up the steps that led to the top of the wall and once he was there, he called to her.

"Natalia."

She didn't even turn around. The wind rustled her messy hair.

"Go away."

"This doesn't make any sense, okay? I don't know why you're being so . . ."

"I told you to leave."

"You're my friend. I don't want you to have a hard time because of something I did or said. You can't—"

"Just leave!" Natalia finally looked at him. There was so much rage in her face that Hector felt like he got slugged right in the chest. He took a step back.

"I . . ." he began.

And then he could feel them. Natalia's shadows had jumped from the wall and were pounding on his back; he felt them with the same certainty as he felt the ground beneath his feet or the fury that made his friend shake. They writhed and twisted, dozens of them, perhaps hundreds. The shadows hissed behind him, a pandemonium of evil whispers spoken in languages born of darkness and fog. The only thing he managed to understand, between words so foreign to anything alive and human, was his own name. Hector imagined a mountain made of darkness and shadows, a black tsunami ready to sweep him away. If he looked back, he would see them. If he looked back, the shadows would tear him apart.

"Natalia! No!" Lizbeth ran across the courtyard toward them. "Please stop! Stop it!"

Natalia looked at the girl approaching them. Then she looked at Hector's back, trembling, her mouth agape.

"Oh my goodness . . ." she whispered.

Behind Hector they heard a long hiss. He turned around, his heart in his throat, just in time to see the last of the shadows scatter and flee his field of vision. Natalia's creatures were like dismal clumps, remnants of darkness of the most diverse shapes and sizes. For a tenth of a second he saw a dark being in the form of a monstrous comet, covered in pseudopods of black mist.

"I saw them." He looked at Natalia. The girl stepped back toward the stairs, pale, shaking. "Your shadows . . . I saw them."

"Leave me alone!" the girl howled, and took off running. In the blink of an eye, she sped past Lizbeth, who tried to stop her with no success.

Hector heard something beyond the wall call his name again, something that wasn't endowed with a mouth or vocal cords. This time he didn't turn around.

Night slowly crept in and swallowed the Rocavarancolian sky. Shadows spilled out among the ruins and erased the outlines of buildings, turning them into ghostly silhouettes nestled in the black of night. Darkness flowed like sticky tar down the sides of the mountains, slithered up the walls of the castle, and seeped through embrasures and windows.

The two guards at the main gate remained firmly at their positions, their features hidden by masks shaped like the heads of dragons. Behind the gate, the pack paced listlessly from side to side. In the fortress, all was calm and silent. Enoch turned the page of his book with shaking hands. He was reading the story of the Battle of Despair, one of the bloodiest to take place during the war that Rocavarancolia fought against the linked world of Esolvilda. That campaign marked the first great defeat of the kingdom and put a dead stop to the aspirations of conquest of King Graya, the successor to the throne of the late Harex. But that meant nothing to Enoch; what truly mattered to him was that during that battle the first documented heroic act of his race had occurred. One hundred and twenty vampires achieved what all of the armies of Rocavarancolia had failed to do in five years: defeat the armies of General Mercy, a legion of warriors whose reputation for invincibility had been proven throughout the crusade. The vampires fell upon them with the ferocity that came from knowing they were defeated. Combat lasted an entire day, and in that time the two factions exterminated one another. There were no prisoners or survivors. According to legend, the last vampire, pierced by half a dozen lances and at the brink of death, leapt upon Mercy and killed him in the midst of a sea of corpses.

"Esolvilda . . ." Enoch whispered, full of pride. His voice barely awoke any echoes in the enormous room.

The library occupied the north wing of the main building. It housed thousands of volumes, and held most of the literary works of Rocavarancolia as well as a wide selection of books from linked worlds. There was a second library in the fortress, smaller and more select, where the magical compendia were kept, books of spells and grimoires, but Enoch tried to stay away from it; the magic there gave him a headache. The room's silence was so sepulchral that the air seemed like it was embalmed.

Suddenly a strong odor of fresh blood hit him, fast and unexpected like a slap in the face. Enoch got up at once, his eyes wide, staggering. He looked around. The aroma was so piercing that his entire being twisted under its spell. It came from outside.

He threw aside the chair as he stumbled toward the door. He hurried down the hallways, using the walls and furniture in his path as support and to gain momentum. Enoch was incapable of containing his excitement. As he turned a corner he collided with something he couldn't make out and fell to the ground. For a few seconds he advanced on his knees. He finally got up, clinging to a torn tapestry, and continued his journey.

He climbed the stairs of the main tower. The aroma that tugged at him was the only thing in the world; the rest of reality had been plunged into darkness and shadow. The only thing that was real was that mark in the air and the emptiness in his belly.

The smell was coming from the main hall. He took off running for the door, his arms raised and his mouth open wide. He pushed it and it swung inward, so quickly that he stumbled again. The smell was so dense that he could almost taste the flavor of blood in his throat. On the ground, over an immense pool of dazzling red, lay three decapitated cadavers. In some far-off place in his mind, Enoch identified them as the mermaids of the reefs, but he didn't even wonder how they'd ended up there—he just got down on his knees and crept toward the bodies, thirsty.

Until he saw the stranger sitting at the council table. Enoch froze as a sudden current of panic shot through him. There was something diabolically wrong about the individual. He was sitting at the head of the table with his legs crossed, dressed only in strips of dirty cloth. He was a brownish color, emaciated, his ribs pressing against his chest as if they might break through the surface; his arms were long and without a trace of musculature; his head bald and thin, with sunken cheekbones and eye sockets. But the most striking thing about him was his eyes: their gaze held such an unlikely strength that it seemed out of place in that body. In his right hand he held a crystal sword.

Someone spoke behind Enoch in a bewildered, uneasy whisper. "Belisarius . . ."

Enoch turned around but saw no one behind him. He was so shocked that it took a moment to realize that the voice he'd just heard belonged to Rorcual. He looked back at the stranger. Yes, the alchemist was right. It was Belisarius, although at the same time it wasn't. The old mage had never given off such resounding energy.

"No," said the thing sitting at the table. "Belisarius is dead. I am Hurza."

The doors of the throne room shut loudly at the exact same moment that an invisible force constrained Enoch's body and held it still. The vampire tried to scream but it was nothing more than a pathetic whistle. Magic roiled in the throne room, in a surge of silver, of ash. The tentacles of the Sacred Throne waved from side to side, sensing imminent death.

The man got up from the table and walked slowly toward the kneeling vampire and the invisible alchemist. There was something insect-like in his walk, like a scavenger, a nightmare in motion. The first Lord of Assassins bared his teeth, showing the world the fangs that had been growing while he recovered underwater. They were black and sharp, and behind them lurked a darkness even more bottomless than the night sky or the depths of the sea.


"If the blond one uses magic, the other won't stand a chance," the Lexel twin in the black mask and white clothing commented.

"But he won't use it, you ignorant rat," his brother replied with scorn. "That would undermine his victory, and he knows it. He wants to confront him on equal footing. And that's where the magic sword comes in. As long as the other boy has it, he's guaranteed to win."

Esmael yawned. He was sitting between two crenels on the castle's north tower. Beneath him was a small terrace that bordered the edge of the structure. That's where the two twins sat, next to Ujthan the Warrior and one of the fortress servants. None of them was conscious of the presence of the Lord of Assassins above their heads. The three council members were too busy watching Adrian and Dario through the winged spyglasses. As was to be expected, the twins had placed bets over which of the teenagers would emerge victorious.

Ujthan laughed between his teeth.

"What does it matter. Those two will never find each other. If one of them's in the north, the other's looking for him in the south. Fate doesn't want their paths to cross."

Esmael knew that it wasn't fate that kept both of them from encountering each other, but rather Dario's efforts to avoid his adversary. To tell the truth, the boy's behavior disappointed him. At the start, Dario had been the member of the harvest that had awakened the most interest in him.

Esmael looked to the east. Over the prison floated the light-haired kid, way up in the sky, scrutinizing the ruined city. Dario was to the southeast, close to the neighborhood in flames, well hidden in an old building. Adrian quickly descended to the rooftops and continued his hunt on foot, tireless, unrelenting. For some time now, the Lord of Assassins had been inclined in favor of the blond. He liked the insane intensity that burned in his eyes; it made him feel nostalgic for better times.

The pack began to howl and run in the courtyard. Esmael cast a thoughtful glance in their direction and frowned. It wasn't strange for those creatures to go crazy all of a sudden, but there was something in the way they now lifted their heads that Esmael did not entirely like. They almost seemed to be calling attention to a particular spot high above them.

He froze on the battlement. The wind had carried with it a foreign sound in the night, a scream that wasn't a scream, but a choked whistle.

The Lord of Assassins straightened and listened carefully to the sounds coming at him, his eyes half-closed, his brow furrowed. He ignored the howling of the wind and the restlessness of the pack. He removed his focus from the insipid talk below him and paid attention to the night. For a short while he remained still and attentive, like yet another gargoyle sitting on the cornices and overhangs of the castle, until a new sound reached him with terrible clarity. A sound that hadn't been heard for over thirty years: the sound of a body being torn to pieces by the throne of Rocavarancolia.

Esmael leapt into the void. With a furious beating of wings, he managed to halt in front of the terrace, even though every last fiber of his being screamed that there was not a second to spare.

"To the throne room, Ujthan! Now!" he ordered. Then he turned to the servant, who had stepped back, scared by his sudden appearance. "Tell the guard and the servants to spread out throughout the tower and the main building! Lexel, watch the windows! Let no one leave!"

He took flight once again, forcing his wings to carry him at maximum speed. He turned in the air and burst in through a window in the façade at the exact moment that someone seemed to be leaving the room in a hurry, closing the door behind them. It took Esmael barely five seconds to cross the room from one end to the other. He saw the cadavers of the mermaids, and the mountain of dust that had once been Enoch. He understood that the blood of those unfortunate creatures had been used to lure the vampire.

He didn't stop to open the door but threw himself right through it. As soon as he landed in the hallway, in the midst of a storm of splinters, several dark metallic shapes fell toward him. Someone had just hurled the heavy suits of armor that lined the front of the main hall at him. Esmael hardened his wings and in two flaps he sliced one of the suits of armor to pieces while he evaded the other two.

The hallway crackled with pure magic rushing to meet him: it was a silvery blaze that made the walls reverberate and tremble as it passed through. The black angel spun a dispersing spell with his fingers as he catapulted to the front. The temperature in the hallway quadrupled. The paintings, tapestries, and furniture shook and turned to ash.

He fought through the current of blazing air, grasping the walls of the stone hallway with the claws of his right hand and propelling himself forward while he held his left hand out, stopping the heat spell and thrusting it back to its source.

He turned the corner and watched as the five doors at the end of the corridor all closed at once. He stepped forward, on the alert. To his left were the stairs that led to the lower level and two of the doors that had just closed; on the opposite side were the other three doors, one of them enormous, situated next to another flight of stairs. He heard the muffled sound of footsteps behind the first door to the left. He jerked it open using magic and entered at top speed, already preparing a spell of devastation and ruin. He was met by a servant, who shouted and backed up so quickly that he fell onto the rug. Esmael growled and ran back out. A potent burst of sorcery suddenly manifested in the adjacent room; it was a roar of magic that made the door to the room vibrate. They hadn't even bothered to try to hide it.

Esmael flew across and opened the door. It led to a small room, half-empty, in the middle of which floated an infinity of entwined magical threads—vividly colored, pulsating rings that curled up and died like fish out of water. He took one of the strands in his fingers. The trace of magic wrapped around his index finger and vanished. The rest of the magic residue followed the same course. The black angel brought his fingertips to his nose and sniffed.

Ujthan found him in the same posture several minutes later. The gigantic warrior had come running from the balcony, and despite his extreme girth he wasn't even panting. The only thing that had sped up his heart rate was the massacre in the main room. He stopped in front of the door with a scimitar in one hand, a lance in the other, and his face astir with excitement.

"What? What?" he asked. He looked from one side to the other, eager to find something to kill.

"He transported himself outside," announced the black angel without looking at him. He rubbed the tips of his fingers with a thoughtful expression. There were a number of dampening spells in the castle that made it difficult to execute transport magic within its walls—as difficult as performing destructive magic, but the intruder had managed both. "Summon the council immediately, Ujthan." A smile crossed his lips. "These are turning out to be very interesting times."

★★★

Hurza stumbled through the dark passageways of the castle, on the verge of fainting. His desperate ploy had worked: Esmael believed that the transport spell had carried him far from the fortress, when he still remained within it. The brief skirmish with the black angel had depleted his power to such an extent that a spell that transported him any further would have exhausted it completely, and given the circumstances, that would have meant his death. The little strength that remained was barely enough to keep him alive.

If he'd learned anything throughout his life, it was to expect the unexpected. That was why he could accept the paradox of having assassinated the last vampire of Rocavarancolia, only to discover that his grimoire was cursed in such a way that only a vampire could touch it without being destroyed. That was nothing more than a blow dealt by fate, something that he could concede and tolerate.

What he never could have imagined was that all of his plans could come so close to failing because of a stupid alchemist. It was so ridiculous, so bizarre, that despite the pain that twisted his insides and seared his throat, he couldn't stop laughing. It was quiet laughter, a grotesque mumbling that burst from his brownish-gray lips.

Rorcual had taken so many potions and concoctions in his attempts to make himself visible that he'd ended up poisoning every last cell of his body. The alchemist's eyes had not only provided his memories and his vital essence; they'd also spilled all of the poison absorbed throughout his long years into Hurza's body. Rorcual had managed to survive by taking close to a dozen antidotes a day, whereas Hurza had no choice but to use magic to keep that torrent of venom at bay.

He stopped under the arcade at the end of the passageway. Further along it branched into two: one branch descended to the catacombs, while the other led to the floors above. He leaned back against the stone and closed his eyes. A locating spell was approaching him, coming through the air in waves like a multicolored serpent. Hurza conjured a spell of interference and cast it over the magic as it passed by him, ignoring him completely. Then he bared his teeth and swallowed a scream. It wasn't only the venom that affected him: he'd forgotten how disturbing it was to assimilate the essence and memories of a vampire. He'd absorbed practically all of Enoch's memories, but his essence had torn him up in the process. He still felt the bitter taste of dust in his throat. No, he didn't like killing vampires. The withered souls of those creatures always rebelled at the hour of death.

He closed his eyes and tried to calm down, distance himself from the pain, and analyze the situation with a clear head. His predatory gaze peered out through the eyes of the servants scattered throughout the castle. He saw hallways opening, rooms and terraces; different perspectives that gave a general picture of what occurred in the fortress and its surroundings. The hallways were still filled with members of the Royal Guard and Denestor's creatures. The entire castle garrison was on alert, somber men stuffed into old chain mail who walked quickly, their weapons at the ready, accompanied by dozens of the demiurge's creations. They were outside as well, flying over the fortress and the surrounding cliffs, alert to every movement and trace of magic. The Lexel brothers completed the exterior surveillance, each of them levitating at opposite ends of the fortress, wrapped in the chaos of their garments as they whipped in the breeze.

Dozens of seeking and following spells flooded the passageways, some too powerful for Hurza to evade in his current state. He smelled them coming in his direction, dragging the stench of silver with them. It would still take a few minutes for them to reach him, but once they did, he was lost.

The first Lord of Assassins of Rocavarancolia squinted his eyes and forced himself to breathe slowly. There was only one place for him to go.


The throne room reeked of massacre and butchery. The servants had already removed the mermaid corpses and the invisible remains of the alchemist, but they hadn't yet cleaned up the blood or the pile of dust that had once been Enoch. Denestor Tul, standing in front of the throne, asked himself if he'd be the next to die. Sorrow and melancholy overtook him.

The diminished Royal Council had taken their places at the meeting table. The seat of honor remained vacant, as did the seats for

Mistral and Lady Dream, and of course, Enoch and Rorcual. The last to arrive had been Solberinus, the castaway. Denestor noticed the faint smile that crept across the man's face as he watched the servants remove the corpse of the last mermaid.

"He used the blood to attract Enoch." The little gray man walked toward the meeting table, lifting the hem of his robe to avoid dragging it over the bloody stone. "The vampire was without a doubt his main target. The alchemist's presence must have been somewhat unexpected."

"Or maybe not. Rorcual had that idiotic habit of stalking Enoch. Maybe the murderer knew." Lady Serena floated near the Sacred Throne with a thoughtful expression; the tentacles that had cut Rorcual to pieces lay across it harmlessly. The ghost let out a listless sigh. The deaths of the vampire and the alchemist had affected her deeply—not because of the loss of their lives, but out of pure and simple envy: she could not die.

"In the name of all the heavens," groaned Ujthan. "Who in their right mind would want to kill these two good-for-nothings?"

"They're killing us off," Esmael said. He stood behind a chair, his hands gripping the back of it. "That's what they're doing. First Belisarius, and now Rorcual and Enoch. If this keeps going, soon even Caleb, the crazy hyena guy, will have a chance to be on the council."

Lady Scar looked up and studied the black angel carefully. Not for a moment had she suspected that Esmael had been involved with the murders. She was convinced that there was something more sinister than his participation in this. And that was a disquieting thought. It was disturbing to think that they were up against something darker than Esmael.

"He transported three mermaids from the bay into the castle and used battle magic within our walls. And what I find most surprising: he managed to avoid you." Seeing the grimace on the black angel's face, she hurried to add, "No, it's not an insult or a recrimination, I just want to have an idea of what we're up against."

"We're up against a great sorcerer," Denestor pointed out, now seated. A servant with shaking hands served him a glass of wine at his request. "That much is obvious."

"It is, it is," continued Lady Scar. "But . . . where did he come from? He couldn't have just appeared in Rocavarancolia out of thin air, no matter how great a sorcerer he may be."

"They left someone behind." Ujthan the Warrior straightened up in his chair and looked at all of those present. "The enemy left one of their own in the city with orders to exterminate us if he saw the slightest possibility of our recovery."

"Foolishness," said the demiurge. "If someone wanted to destroy our hopes, it would be easier to kill the children than come to the castle to kill us."

"What do they want?" Lady Scar asked. "What are they looking for? Just death? Or is there something else?"

"Right now we're not in a position to know." Denestor pointed to one of the magic meters that wandered through the throne room. They were small creatures with wire feet, made from ashtrays, cups, and porcelain doll heads. "And we won't find out with my knick-knacks or with any magic, I assure you. And neither will we be able to contact the spirits of Rorcual and Enoch, just like we couldn't with the servant and Belisarius."

"So what do you propose, Demiurge?" grunted the Lexel twin dressed in black. He received a look of hatred from his brother. "That we stay here, sitting on our hands, waiting for another one of us to die? Is that what you want?"

"Not at all. I'm only pointing out that we'll find the same dead ends that we found in the case of Belisarius, but that doesn't mean that we can't look for new courses of action." He looked out of the corner of his eye at one of the servants, pale and stooped, awaiting orders at the room's entrance. He had a very clear idea of what would happen next, although he didn't care to share it with the rest of the council. Not at the moment, anyway.

Esmael glanced at the empty seats that had belonged to Enoch and Rorcual.

"So we agree we're up against a high-caliber sorcerer and the only thing we know for certain is that he's going to a lot of trouble to exterminate us." He brought a hand to his face and stroked his cheek slowly, thoughtfully, without taking his eyes off Denestor Tul. "And three members of the council have already died. I wonder . . . It's trivial, something insignificant that has nothing to do with what's going on, but I might lose sleep over it if I don't find out once and for all." He squinted his eyes. He leaned forward, his gaze fixed on Denestor Tul.

"Where is Mistral, Demiurge? Where is the shapeshifter hiding while we're being slaughtered?"

Mistral was about to lose his patience and return to the tower when the demiurge's blue butterfly appeared. It slipped in through an opening in the roof of the bathroom in the courtyard and fluttered in the small cubicle until it landed on the wall, right in front of the shapeshifter.

"I was just about to leave, Denestor," he told the butterfly. "You've taken your time showing up."

"Listen to me, Mistral. You have to leave the Margalar Tower as soon as possible."

"By all the heavens and hells, again, no." It was ridiculous that all their conversations began the exact same way. "Listen, today I—"

"No, Mistral, no. You listen to me. Listen to me just this once in your life: Enoch and Rorcual are dead. They were murdered in the castle last night."

That news left the shapeshifter frozen. He supported himself against the wall with his right hand and leaned forward, almost grazing the body of the artificial insect with his nose.

"Who?" he managed to ask.

"A sorcerer. That's all we know." The butterfly's voice had no inflection whatsoever. "He evaded the castle's protections to enter and he did it again to leave. We don't know who it is or what they want. We don't know anything, except that every last one of us could be in danger."

"And the children?"

"If he's after the children as well, there's little you can do to protect them. You must leave the tower, do you hear me? For some time now your presence here hasn't been necessary, and all you're doing is putting them in danger. Even more so, if that sorcerer means to finish off the council and find out where you are."

"I . . ." Mistral brought a hand to his forehead, dazed. The butterfly fluttered around him.

"You have two days," the demiurge warned him. "If you haven't left the tower by then, you'll leave us no choice but to take action. We'll find a way to remove you from here by force, do you hear me?"

★★★

Ujthan climbed the twisting stairs that led to his rooms. Several hours had passed since the sorcerer had assaulted the fortress, but his nerves were still on edge. His heart beat frantically, a persistent thumping that made his blood boil. Death had visited Rocavarancolia, and its aroma had permeated every last stone of the castle. And that brought back so many memories that he could barely hold back his tears.

As soon as he opened the door, he had the feeling that something wasn't right. He folded his arms in front of his chest without crossing the threshold. His left hand stroked the tattoo of the whip that adorned his right shoulder, while the other hand brushed against the handle of a scimitar tattooed on his left shoulder. Ujthan's fingers sank into his skin, grasping the painted weapons and extracting them from his flesh with a hiss. Then he took a step into the room. The beating of his heart suddenly stopped. What now seized him was the tense calm that marked the start of battle.

He crossed the short hallway. The door to his bedroom was open. Before him was his bed, unmade, the blankets on the floor. Two heavy suits of armor flanked the bed, and an endless number of weapons decorated the walls. There were also banners and tapestries that depicted the most glorious battles of the kingdom. A taxidermied horse to the right, next to the window, was equipped with a golden shield and a dark saddle.

The intruder stood with his back to the door, looking at a tapestry.

"I've been waiting for you," he announced in a guttural, worn voice before turning slowly toward Ujthan.

It took the warrior a few seconds to recognize him, and it was more by the scraps of bandages covering him than by his features.

"Belisarius . . ." He stepped backward. "What enchantment has brought you back to the land of the living?"

"I'm not Belisarius, although I wear his body. The old man gave his life so that I could live again. I'm Hurza, founder of the kingdom you now defend."

"Hurza?" Ujthan grunted. This couldn't be happening. "The Eye-Eater died centuries ago. You can't be him. No magic can return life to something that's been dead for hundreds of years."

He took a step forward and raised his scimitar. The creature that claimed to be the first Lord of Assassins didn't even flinch as he watched him approach. He exuded such an aura of power that the warrior felt all the hair on his body stand on end. He'd never encountered anything like this. He cracked his whip and stopped barely two yards from the intruder, his sword ready to unleash a blow. The way he saw it, he couldn't lose.

"You won't be able to defeat me with those weapons." The creature pointed a listless finger at the scimitar. "You can try it if you like, and share the fate of Rorcual and Enoch, or—better yet—you can sheathe them and listen to what I've come to propose."

The intensity of the creature's gaze made Ujthan shake from head to toe. He felt a deadly cold running through the inside of his skeleton, a gust of ice that bit into the very heart of his bones. Those eyes had seen everything.

"Speak. Speak quickly, before I cut that ridiculous neck of yours."

"You won't do it. Because I know you, Ujthan. I know who you are. I know what you want. And I can get it for you." Hurza smiled. "I bring you war, a war like you've never dared to dream of. And you need only swear your loyalty to me to get it."

# THE PALACE

Hector removed his black cape, wadded it into a ball, and tried to force it into his leather pouch. He'd found it the day before while searching through a trunk in the tower, and he was immediately taken with it. Lizbeth smiled to see him struggling with the cape, unable to make it fit inside his bag. She had warned him that it was too big for him and that he'd get tired of it before long, but Hector hadn't paid any attention to her. He'd resisted until they arrived at the square with the tower of sorcery, but ultimately he had to surrender and accept that Lizbeth was right.

"Tonight I'll trim it for you," she said. "It's going to look great, you'll see." She took the cape from his sack, unfurled it with two shakes, and looked it up and down, left to right. Her eyes squinted, looking back and forth from the cape to Hector. "Yes, with a little here and there, it will be more than perfect." Then she nodded, folded the cape with astonishing ease, and slid it into the bag in such a way that not even a corner stuck out.

Hector smiled and thanked her.

They were heading west, beyond the prison where they'd awakened months ago. The only one missing was Adrian, who was once again on the hunt for the boy from the rooftops. Rachel walked in front and Marco was right behind her, immersed in thought. Madeleine, Marina, and Ricardo were behind them, and Bruno and Natalia brought up the rear, one with his staff and the other with her halberd.

Hector looked at the Russian girl with a furrowed brow. He hadn't spoken a word to her in the two days since the incident in the courtyard, and as far as he was concerned he had no intention of doing so for some time. The memory of those whispering shadows still frightened him. He couldn't help but wonder what might have happened if Lizbeth hadn't appeared. Just as he was thinking about it, he felt Lizbeth's hand slip into the crook of his arm, squeezing it tightly.

"She wants to say she's sorry, but she doesn't know how."

"She doesn't have to, nothing happened," he said coolly.

"I want to apologize too. I messed up. You didn't have to go talk to her. I'm sorry, I'm really sorry. I was wrong to tell you what to do . . ." She shrugged her shoulders. "I know very little about matters of the heart, love and all that." She let out an uncomfortable, somewhat sad giggle. Then she sighed. "You should have listened to Maddie. Redheads know more about those things."

Hector felt a deep current of affection toward his friend. He was tempted to hug her, but a trace of his old shyness stopped him. Instead he said:

"It wasn't your fault. I didn't go because you told me to; I went because I thought it was the right thing to do. We were both wrong."

They hurried to join the others, arm in arm. A flock of black birds broke out in laughter above, and Hector couldn't help but think that for some unknown reason they were laughing at him.


They entered an area made of wide, ruinous avenues. Rubble was heaped up everywhere, and the few buildings that were still standing were in such bad shape that any access seemed impossibly risky. In fact, one structure came collapsing down right next to them as they watched. It wasn't the first collapse they'd seen, but something about the cloud of dust that arose disturbed Hector. For a moment it looked like an immense skull floated in the air, with a demented, wolf-like smile embedded in the bony whiteness.

As soon as they came to the first crossroads, Mistral took command of the group and indicated to Rachel which direction she should take. He attempted to do it in the most natural way possible, but his tone of voice sounded more authoritative than usual. The girl gave him a strange look.

"What's up with you?" she asked him. "You're bossier than ever today?"

He laughed and gently encouraged her forward, trying to hide how perturbed he was.

To begin with, mere chance had kept them from visiting this part of the city, but later the shapeshifter himself intentionally kept them away. Among the ruins and dilapidated buildings that were scattered through the area was a splendid palace, in such good shape that he knew the group would want to explore it as soon as they laid eyes on it. Mistral had decided that would be the last place he'd show them before abandoning them to their fate; the visit to what was without a doubt the most beautiful building in Rocavarancolia would be his way of saying goodbye.

The palace was in the middle of an avenue, opposite a long line of large, sturdy houses with gabled roofs covered in gargoyles. Rachel was the first to see it. She stopped in her tracks, amazed, her eyes wide open. It was the only building on that side of the street, but it filled the space with more forcefulness than the other thirty that spread out opposite her.

It was gray stone, in a rounded U shape, and something about its angles and arrangement on the grounds was calming. It seemed to make her think that not everything in the city was awful. What caught her attention most was the gigantic dome that crowned its center: a marvelous construction of black and emerald crystal. Underneath the dome, in the middle of the façade, a large oval window opened, surrounded by dozens of smaller windows so narrow that they looked like scratch marks in the wall.

"It's beautiful." Lizbeth brought her hands to her chest, in awe. "Just beautiful . . ."

"We have to see the inside," Madeleine said. Her eyes sparkled. She turned toward the others; her glare shot through them like a dagger. "With all the ruins and shitholes you dragged me through, if you even think of saying we can't go into that wonderful place, I'll never speak to you again," she warned.

No one contradicted her. Mistral smiled contentedly. He couldn't remember ever seeing Madeleine so excited, and that in itself made guiding them there worth it.

They advanced slowly, with Hector bringing up the rear. The palace was free of the warning mist. The only area nearby where the black mist gathered was around one of the houses across the way, far enough to not be of concern.

The courtyard was a labyrinth of winding paths that unfurled among what must have once been landscaped plots, but were now nothing more than segments of parched earth. They headed for the black-and-green tile staircase that led to the main gate, keeping a close watch on the windows scattered across the palace walls. All they could see through the center of the main window was darkness.

They waited at the foot of the stairs as Rachel climbed them, leaning forward, as if listening for magic. The girl placed her hands on the iron door and nodded as she confirmed what the shapeshifter already knew: the place was free from enchantments. She took the bar that served as a handle and tried to open it, first pushing, then pulling. The door rattled, but didn't budge.

"It's stuck," Rachel muttered, her hands on her hips. "We'll need some muscle up here if we want to get in."

Before Ricardo and Marco climbed the stairs, Bruno waved his staff, drew a strange symbol in the air with his left hand—and the double door opened inward without a sound. The first thing they saw was an area of dense shadows, a curtain of darkness that led to a large entrance hall, illuminated by a delicate green light.

They gathered around Rachel on the last flight of stairs. The air in front of the door was incredibly pure, nothing like the stale odor of the enclosed spaces they were used to encountering on their explorations throughout the city. Hector breathed in deeply, filling his lungs with the unexpected freshness.

Rachel, after exchanging a glance with Marco, entered the palace. At once, the shadows from the entryway clung to her body like a wavering cape.

"Nothing," she announced from the darkness, and her voice broke into a chorus of musical echoes. "There's no trace of magic. Come in, but don't get too far away from me until we check the whole place."

They came to a stop in a round entrance hall with gray stone walls and flooring. The ceiling, in contrast, was a heavy assortment of huge iron plates that didn't seem to fit with the rest of the palace; this structure felt ominous, as if at any moment it might fall and crush them.

Two large staircases were located on either side of the entrance hall, of the same black-and-green tile as the stairway outside. From where they stood, the twin staircases seemed to sink like fangs into the grid of the ceiling at a strange, forced angle.

They hadn't gone two steps outside the shadows when they all stopped at once, looking up, mouths open in shock.

What they'd thought was a ceiling wasn't as such. As they left the darkness their perspective changed, and they could now see the palace as it really was. For a brief moment, Hector thought that the framework hanging above their heads had just exploded, and the explosion remained frozen in time, just like the flames in the burning neighborhood, leaving the forged plates hovering motionless. He had to blink several times to understand what he was seeing. The plates that he had first thought were all level were actually suspended at different heights throughout the palace.

He stepped back into the shadows, and the scattered plates became one again, forming a ceiling without visible cracks. It was no more than an optical illusion: if he squinted his eyes, he could see that the plates hovered in different planes.

"The rooms are in the air . . ." he heard Marina say. "Good grief! They're floating in the air!"

It was true. The palace had only one floor, an astonishingly vast floor in which dozens of rooms of various shapes and sizes floated. The only thing they all had in common was their bases, made of the same forged iron. Most of them were three stories tall and measured more than two hundred yards long, while the smallest ones were mere foundations for decorations and statues. Most of them didn't even have walls.

The stairways didn't sink into the false ceiling like they'd thought, but rather curved off into the void until they were lost in the shifting emerald fog that swept across the top of the structure. From each main staircase sprouted dozens of flights, which themselves branched into more offshoots of green-and-black tile, twisting in the air until adjoining the edges of the floating rooms. That display of rooms and staircases produced a prodigious sense of harmony: it was as if the whole world had suddenly become light, as if reality, existence itself, was less heavy and oppressive within those walls.

"It's magnificent," Ricardo exclaimed, as captivated as the others.

The teenagers spread out throughout the entryway. Mistral watched them go in, incredulous, bathed in the crystalline emerald light that filtered in through the dome. The shapeshifter smiled.

"I'm going to kill you guys," Maddie said. "You make me live in a filthy tower when there's a palace here . . . I'm going to kill you."

"The Margalar Tower may be ugly, but it's safe," Marco reminded her. "And if you have the ridiculous notion that we're going to move here, you might as well forget it."

"Besides, Hector would be dead in this place within a week," Rachel added. "Don't you remember how much he likes falling down stairs?"

"You were nicer when I couldn't understand what you were saying," Hector replied.

Rachel stuck out her tongue and said something in French that made Ricardo burst out laughing. The echo of his laughter traveled up the stairs, rebounded off the platforms, and was lost in the high ceiling, enveloped in fog.


They took the staircase to the left. The first flight soon broke off into three large branches. Rachel chose the one on the right, which went downward in a sharp curve before dividing into another two flights of twisted stairs. As they progressed along that colossal roller coaster they saw an endless number of rooms and halls. They saw bedrooms; living rooms with velvet couches, crystal footrests, and hanging swings; passageways with fountains and iron benches . . .

What struck Hector most was that, just like with the false ceiling, the perspective from above was also deceptive; it changed with practically every step they took, turning the palace into a place of constant mutation. A room looked at from above was completely different when seen from below or from the side. Everything fluctuated, flowed. It was a crazy game of perspectives and architecture. A room glimpsed from a stairway looked like a jungle overflowing with vegetation, half-hidden by the ferns that hung from the neighboring platforms,

THE CHILDREN OF DARKNESS

but later, from above, it became an elegant bedroom. From another curve in the staircase, the same room appeared empty.

Rachel guided them to the palace's main hall, the only room completely enclosed by walls. The girl approached the oval door in one of the walls, touched the handle, waited a few seconds, and then opened the door. The darkness on the other side was so thick that it looked like there was another door behind the first. Rachel crossed the threshold with Bruno right behind her.

"Can you light it up a bit?" Ricardo asked.

"Wait a moment. It might not be necessary."

A tiny spark had appeared on the ground in front of them, a brilliant flickering that projected very slowly upward, transforming into a growing column of light that didn't stop until it reached the ceiling high above. Just ahead, another column took form, in the same way as the first. Little by little, scattered throughout the floor, more columns formed. The light that they emitted lit up the great room, and the darkness became bright.

"It's a ballroom," Madeleine whispered with admiration.

Mistral nodded, although he knew that it was much more than that. All types of events had been celebrated in that room, from pyromancer tournaments to concerts by the fabulous singing birds of Alarán, not to mention sorcerer duels and royal weddings. It was said that on one occasion, they'd sacrificed an albino dragon there for the greater glory of the kingdom.

The kids went down the stairs that led to the gleaming floor of the room. On the wall to their right they saw the gigantic window they'd seen from outside. The lower third of it was covered by black curtains, most of them drawn, while up above two large green curtains opened to the left and right.

Opposite to the entrance rose a small stage containing various metal statues. Hector and Marco approached as the others spread out through the room. It was an orchestra composed of seven musicians as bizarre as the instruments they were poised to play. A humanoid creature with rat-like features held two sticks in its paws, about to strike against the drum in front of it that was riddled with holes. Among the musicians was another human-like being, with inky black skin and a magnificent pair of red wings folded at its back. It held a dented violin in one hand and a bow with strange protuberances in the other. From the side of each statue jutted a metallic butterfly: a key to wind them up.

"Automatons," Hector said.

He turned to look for Rachel, who was looking through the curtains and out the large window with Lizbeth and Marina. He was about to call her when he saw that Marco, beating him to it, had started to wind one of the musicians, a slender blue being with bulging eyes and gills on its neck. He didn't seem to worry whether the thing might be enchanted. As he wound it, the creature straightened and brought a twisted flute to its lips. When the mechanism was fully wound, the automaton blew on the flute as its metallic fingers moved rapidly over the holes. The first sound that emerged from the instrument was an impressive bellow, then a soft and sweet melody unraveled in the air, with the cadence of a nursery rhyme turned waltz.

"Music," Marina whispered. She brought a hand to her mouth, moved. "I'd forgotten about music."


After leaving the ballroom, they went from platform to platform, always with Rachel in the lead. The condition of the palace was almost as surprising as the structure itself. There was scarcely any dust or dirt, and although some of the rooms appeared to be purposefully empty, the majority were in perfect condition, as if the residents had left only a moment before they arrived.

In the afternoon they took a break to have a snack. They sat on wooden benches surrounding a small pond. They barely talked. The place seemed to encourage silence and daydreaming.

Shortly after they resumed their exploration they discovered a large room full of empty bookshelves. The shapeshifter wandered among them just like the others, aware that they wouldn't find anything there. The room had been an important library of magic, but some time ago the books that weren't taken by magicians from linked worlds were moved to the castle.

Another branch directed them to a platform with a series of walls that led to more than twenty great wardrobes, with silver-framed mirrors on every door. Rachel hurried to open the closest one, and its contents made her gasp excitedly. The wardrobe was filled with dresses, each one more splendid than the last. The girls pounced on them immediately. Natalia was the only one who stayed where she was, huffing indignantly at her friends' behavior.

"There's men's clothing too!" Marina exclaimed. She darted toward Hector, grabbed him by the arm, and dragged him toward the wardrobe. Before he could even react, she was taking garments from inside and holding them out in front of him, evaluating which ones would fit him better.

Ricardo broke out in laughter when Madeleine approached him and dragged him to a wardrobe. Mistral smiled. There was a new glimmer in his friends' eyes, a return to former times, when looking through wardrobes and chests was a marvelous pleasure. Bruno and Natalia were the only ones not to partake in the commotion, and even though the girl was frowning, her eyes went to one of the open wardrobes, as if there was something there that she couldn't help but look at.

Rachel hugged one of the garments to her tightly. It was a beautiful black blouse, with fitted cuffs edged in silver. She held the shirt in front of her, took the end of one sleeve in hand, and commenced dancing among the mirrors and wardrobes, humming the song that the flutist had been playing on the dance floor.

Lizbeth grabbed a white dress with a long pleated skirt and imitated her friend, twirling with it around the room.

The shapeshifter observed the scene with his arms crossed. As he watched Rachel and Lizbeth, he realized that he'd just found the perfect way of saying goodbye.

"Listen," he said. He was nervous, in spite of himself. "I just thought of something. It's silly, I admit, but even so . . . I don't know, I think we deserve it. What do you think if, for a change, we just relax for once?" He smiled from ear to ear. "Forget Rocavarancolia, forget everything for a while. Let's have a party!"


Hector stuck two fingers between the shirt's stiff collar and his throat and tried to create some space in between. The suit made him itch all over; his skin was so used to rough fabric that the unexpected softness made him uncomfortable. He examined his friends out of the corner of his eye, wondering if they felt as strange as he did stuffed into the clothes that the girls picked out for them.

Marco and Ricardo wore suits similar to his: silk shirts and pants, lightweight shoes, and tailored jackets. Ricardo's, like Hector's, was a somber black, with white trim on the sleeves and neck, and fit him so tightly that in some places the fabric puckered as if the seams might split at any moment. Despite his size, however, Marco's suit fit him like a glove. The girls had chosen a white outfit with gray trim for him.

Bruno wore a long dark green overcoat, a black vest and pants, and a green shirt with cuffs that leapt out from the sleeves of his coat like tiny whirlwinds. But the most impressive part of the ensemble was his emerald top hat with black edging on the brim. Hector had to admit that the getup suited him, although given his lack of expression, he looked more like a porcelain doll than a live person.

"Do you really think that this is a good idea?" he asked. "I am clearly referring to throwing a party in this location. I do not know if it is appropriate, given the circumstances."

"It's not going to be a real party, just a little music and dancing," Marco replied. "A bit of fun will do us good for a change. Don't worry, we'll leave before it gets dark."

"I do not like to dance," the Italian said, after one of his customary long silences.

"Have you ever done it?" Ricardo asked.

"No. But I know that an experience of that nature will not be in the least gratifying to me."

Hector looked him up and down, sighed, and shook his head.

They'd been waiting for a while on the flight of stairs that led to the room where the girls were getting ready. Sometimes they heard whispering and laughing inside. Hector ran a hand over his head. Before the group had split into separate rooms to change, Lizbeth had quickly arranged the boys' hair, gathering their messy locks into ponytails that, while improvised, seemed capable of withstanding gale-force winds without coming undone. Only Bruno wore his hair down; it fell in long curls beneath his top hat.

Hector leaned against the handrail and toward the expanse of emerald fog that swirled below the domes. The light was different up there; it was warmer, friendlier.

"Are you there?" he heard Lizbeth ask through the door.

"We've been waiting forever," Ricardo answered.

"We're finished, here we come."

"Don't look at us directly or you'll go blind!" Rachel warned, before slowly opening the door.

Hector blinked incredulously as he saw them come out, as surprised as he'd been at any of the many wonders that he'd witnessed in Rocavarancolia. It had been worth the wait. To say they looked magnificent was an understatement. The hairdos that Lizbeth had improvised for them paired perfectly with the dresses they wore—wonders in light cotton and silk in black, green, and white—and with the elegant sparkle of the jewelry that adorned them. There must have been makeup in the room as well, as some of them wore eyeshadow and lipstick. The boys were all speechless. They were so used to their everyday disheveled state that the transformation was almost magical.

"What happened to you guys?" Natalia asked them, frowning. "Are you all dumb?" Her hair, swept up in a tall bun, revealed her tiny ears, which had gone completely red.

"Dumb and blind," Ricardo answered, enacting a bow as he removed an imaginary hat. "I'm convinced that there's never been such beauty in these rooms."

"What an idiot!" Natalia exclaimed, while making a scornful face that couldn't hide the shadow of a smile.

Rachel returned Ricardo's bow with as much grace as she could manage. She wore a white dress with a skirt in the same soft green tone as her matching shrug. Given how thin she was, the dress was big on her, but the girls had managed to fasten it with pins in the proper places. The only jewelry she wore was a wide silver choker with a red stone in the center.

"It's not the clothes, it's us," she said, raising her hand in an affected gesture. "When you're as pretty as we are, a little wash and some silly clothes are all you need to be even more stupendous." Then she smiled, took two quick steps forward, and puckered her red lips. "Can you believe it? I've never worn makeup before! How do I look?"

"Beautiful," Mistral replied. They all were.

Despite their differences, most of their dresses had a similar cut: they were ballroom gowns with full flared skirts, and they wore shoes with low heels.

Without a doubt, Natalia was the biggest transformation of them all. Her dress was of white silk, with embroidery along the neckline and a black bow around the waist. A pearl necklace accentuated her neck, which seemed more delicate than ever. She couldn't stay still; she kept reaching up to touch her hair and make sure it was still in place, or she'd tug at the folds of her dress to adjust it.

The most beautiful, as always, was Madeleine. She wore a green dress that matched the color of her eyes. She also wore an emerald necklace that graced her deep neckline. The dress was so tight that when he saw it, Hector couldn't help recalling the time he'd glimpsed her naked in the tower.

Although the redhead was the most gorgeous, in Hector's eyes Marina outshone her and all the others so overwhelmingly that to him, she was the only one on the stairway. She was the last to come out, fighting with her left strap, which insisted on sliding down her shoulder. She wore a sleeveless black dress with an open back and no embroidery. Lizbeth had brushed her hair back, securing it with hairpins and a pretty silver tiara.

Lizbeth's dress was the simplest, full and white, with a large bow at the waist. She was radiant, but more due to the expression on her face than her attire. Lizbeth looked at each and every one of them as if they were her creations, as if she'd been the one who made them and gave them form. Pride and joy shone in her chestnut eyes.

"You're all so beautiful," she said. "Just beautiful."

To the side of the stage they found a winding mechanism that activated all of the automatons at once. There was a knob next to it, and although the instructions nearby were quite enigmatic, they guessed that they could use it to select the number of musical pieces they wanted to hear.

The seven automatons began to straighten as Marco turned the butterfly key on the stage, with the others scattered close by. The musicians' heads adopted poses of strict concentration while their multicolored hands and paws hovered over harps, violins, and other instruments. From inside came a restless clattering, as if they were impatient to begin their task. The black creature unfurled its red wings at the same time as it raised the curious violin to its chin and positioned the bow over the strings. An ape-like automaton removed the grates that covered the piano in front of him and placed his furry fingers over the keys.

When Marco fully wound the mechanism, all of the musicians began to play. A frightening squeal echoed through the room, so unpleasant that they all covered their ears. Even the windows vibrated. There was no time for concern: within that out-of-tune racket they soon heard the unmistakable sound of music. Little by little the rhythms fell into place, harmony overtook chaos, and that frightening noise transformed into something different: a sweet, slow melody that compelled them to move.

Rachel practically threw herself into Marco's arms. They were the first to start to dance, with more enthusiasm than rhythm. Then Lizbeth took Maddie by the waist and began dancing too, laughing and getting provocatively close to Bruno. The Italian stepped backward, clutching his staff, as robotic in his movements as the orchestra behind him.

Hector had the strange sensation of having fallen into a dream, a dream made of music and the flickering of light from the columns. Someone took him by the arm, not too forcefully, but firmly. He turned to find Marina looking right at him. He felt as if the ground was pulled from beneath his feet.

Marina pointed with her chin toward Natalia, who was chatting nervously with Ricardo a few yards away, not yet having decided to dance.

"Tell her she looks very pretty, go on." Marina pushed him in the direction of the pair.

"What?" he whispered, incredulous. She was the one he wanted to tell that to. She was so radiant that his heart stopped every time he looked at her.

"Go tell her. Go. Go. And stop looking at me like you've never seen me before."

"It's just that . . ." He swallowed. They spoke in whispers. The music surrounded them, rocked them. They might be standing still but they'd already started to dance. "It's just that that's always how I feel whenever I see you. Every time I look at you . . . it's like I'm seeing you for the first time . . ."

Marina blushed. She smiled. She brought a hand toward her tiara, stopped it halfway, and put it back behind her.

"Stop talking nonsense. Tell her how pretty she looks, go, or I won't let you dance with me."

Hector nodded enthusiastically, aware of the seriousness of the threat as he approached Ricardo and Natalia. As he saw him come near, Ricardo stepped away from the Russian girl so quickly that she frowned.

"You look very nice in that dress," Hector told her. Natalia turned toward him, surprised by his appearance. "You look very pretty. Seriously."

She looked hard at him and there was so much relief in her face that for a second Hector was afraid she was going to cry. But suddenly the girl smiled; it was an honest smile, marvelous and new, a lightning bolt that lit up her face.

"Thank you," she said in a thin voice. Her smile widened. "You look very handsome too. But I'm not going to dance with you, so don't even think about asking me." She stuck out her tongue. "I've already got a partner, you know?" And in no time she was at Ricardo's side, who, laughing, took her in his arms and lifted her up in a masterful demonstration of agility.

"They make me want to dance on air," Madeleine said. She looked up toward the ceiling with a dreamy look and turned around in circles.

"Do you really want to?" Bruno asked. Something in his posture had changed. His natural rigidity had softened, not entirely, but enough to notice. "I can cast a spell that will allow you to do so."

Madeleine looked at him for a few seconds, a half smile on her lips. She seemed moved by the Italian's invitation.

"No, no," she said finally. "I'd end up breaking a bone, I'm sure of it. I prefer the ground." She stretched her arms toward him in an elegant movement. "Will you do me the honor of being my partner?"

Bruno blinked slowly. For a moment, there was doubt in his eyes. Then he nodded even more slowly still. He leaned his staff against the wall, and then abruptly encircled Madeleine by the waist with one hand while he took one of her hands in the other. Mistral stopped dancing with Rachel just to observe the miracle. Lizbeth, dancing next to them, stopped also, as shocked as the others.

"Let me lead, okay?" Madeleine asked. Bruno nodded so energetically that his top hat jumped on his head. When the shapeshifter saw the pair

THE CHILDREN OF DARKNESS

begin to dance he smiled with satisfaction. Yes, that was the farewell that they deserved. He left Rachel, and after bowing to Lizbeth, began dancing with her.

Marina and Hector were face to face at one end of the room while the others danced a little further away. She looked him in the eyes, a mischievous smile appearing on her lips. He could barely return her gaze.

Marina put an arm around his shoulders. Hector looked at her, hesitant, so dazed by the contact that, although he knew what was expected of him, he was afraid to do it. She shook her head, took his hand, and guided it around her waist. The heat that radiated from her body beneath the silk extended in slow waves through his hand.

"I don't know how to dance."

"It's easy. Follow the music and try not to step on me." He laced the fingers of his right hand through hers.

He smiled, nodded resolutely, and let himself be carried away by the automatons' music. He didn't even blink, his eyes fixed on hers, the most gorgeous eyes in the world.

"Are you real?" he asked. "Are you really real?"

"No," Marina answered without a moment's hesitation, looking back at him with the same intensity. "None of us are, didn't you know? We're only illusions in an enchanted city. If you close your eyes very tightly, we'll all disappear."

"Then I'm never going to close my eyes again."


Dario watched them dance through the enormous window. He couldn't make out the music, but occasionally the wind carried with it a faded note that, paradoxically, made him feel even more distant from the scene taking place through the glass. The Brazilian was crouched between two hunchbacked gargoyles at the edge of the rooftop, as motionless as they were. Anyone seeing him would have taken him for another stone statue. His head was covered by the hood of his cape, and his sack lay at his feet, full of food.

He'd been spying on them for so long that his legs were cramped. Every time he saw Marina in Hector's arms he felt a void exploding in his stomach, a voracious emptiness that sucked up his insides, his mind, and his soul. But he couldn't look away. He'd never seen anything so lovely: she was radiant in that black evening gown. He cursed himself for being so stupid.

"I could kill you right now," he heard from behind him.

The emptiness inside him turned to pure ice. He got up slowly, rubbing his legs to get the blood circulating again. Then he turned around. Adrian was behind him, wrapped in a tangle of red clothing whipping in the wind, his sword in hand. He pointed it at Dario's neck.

"It would be so easy, so simple . . ." He made a quick movement from left to right, as if practicing the cut to his throat. "Just like that . . ." he whispered. Then he took a step back and sheathed his weapon. He wore a second sword, sheathed next to the first one.

"It doesn't have to be like this," Dario said. He took off his hood so that the other boy could see his eyes. "Listen . . . I didn't mean to hurt you on the stairway. The only thing I wanted was to get away and be left alone. It was the sword that—"

"Take it out."

"No."

"Then this will be much easier than I hoped." Adrian drew his sword once more. The whistle that it made coming out of the hilt sounded like the hiss of a serpent.

Dario squinted his eyes. If he'd learned anything in the countless fights that he'd been in throughout his life, it was to judge his adversary by his gaze. That way he could tell if he was confronting a braggart who would flee at the first chance or someone who wouldn't give up, no matter what it took. He drew his sword, too. On rare occasion had he seen determination like Adrian's.

"You can't win," he warned. "It's a magic sword. It does what it wants." As if echoing his words, Dario felt the weapon pull forward from him, ready to take command of his hand at the first opportunity. "It doesn't matter how skilled you are, it will find a way to kill you."

"Thanks for the warning."

Adrian rushed at him. Dario stopped the attack, his weapon held waist high. At that moment the sword took over and thrust forward and up, changing the angle at the last second to attack the right side, which was completely exposed. Adrian deflected the blow, but stumbled as he did so. He bumped into one of the gargoyles with his hip and recovered himself just as Dario's sword leapt to his throat, eager for blood. Adrian retreated and looked at Dario's weapon, impressed. "You can't win."

They jumped on one another in the blustery twilight. The wind swirled around them while the blows and counterblows fell swiftly. From time to time a stray note came from the palace, an echo of muffled music that interspersed with the sound of steel on steel. Through the cracked window they danced and laughed, unaware of the other dance taking place just yards away.

Adrian ducked, avoiding his enemy's blade slicing his throat by mere inches. He had to launch to the left to dodge another attack. The Brazilian waited for Adrian to collect himself before charging again.

It was an uneven battle and Dario knew it. Adrian wasn't only confronting him—he was fighting against the will of Dario's weapon. It was surprising that the fight was lasting so long; it was even more surprising that his opponent got an occasional chance to go on the attack.

The duel brought them to the middle of the rooftop. They fought in absolute silence, each darting his eyes back and forth between his enemy's gaze and his hands and feet. Dario stepped back. They watched each other, panting, sweaty. For a moment the Brazilian was tempted to ask Adrian to take out the second sword that he wore on his belt to even out the fight. But he quickly tossed the idea aside. One of the things he'd learned on the streets of São Paulo was to never squander the advantages that one might have.

He sprung again. Adrian met him with a smile. Once more the blows fell with ruthless speed. They twirled and danced, their teeth bared, their hearts frenzied. After one of Adrian's devastating attacks, Dario felt his weapon turning in his hand as it found a flaw in the enemy's defense. This time Adrian couldn't stop the blow or avoid it. The blade passed through him from one side to the other, entering through his stomach and exiting his back, with such force that his feet left the ground. For several seconds they remained motionless in the midst of night, looking at each other in that insane stance. Then Dario stepped back, dragging the sword with him. Adrian fell on the rooftop and slowly rolled toward the row of gargoyles. There he stopped, looking at the sky, his breath faltering.

"I told you," Dario mumbled. He approached the sack that he'd left by the eaves, slung it over his shoulder, and looked at Adrian. "I told you," he repeated. His lower lip trembled. He sheathed his sword and took one last look at the party through the glass. No, that world wasn't for him; he could never belong to a world where there was music and light. He belonged to the darkness, to violence, to cold. The only warmth meant for him was that of freshly spilled blood. "I told you. I told you. I told you."

He staggered away with his hand on his side, covering a deep gash that Adrian's sword had left in the last assault.

If he had looked back, he would have seen the collapsed boy rising up from the rooftop, beginning to wave his hands and chant between his teeth. The pendant in the shape of a three-eyed baby's head that he wore around his neck began to shine, but promptly dimmed as a cry of pain interrupted the song and the spell.


In the palace, time was diverted from its usual course. Hector noticed that it had a new and magical cadence; he felt it pass not just in the quickened beating of his heart, but in the music, the dancing, and above all, the rhythm of Marina's body. The softness of the curve of her waist and the heat of her hand in his gave him a warm sense of belonging, and made him dizzy. They danced in sync to the automatons' melody, twirling on the dance floor. Their reflections moved beneath their feet like misty phantoms, radiantly and swiftly.

Wrapped up in the feeling that time had slowed down, he saw Lizbeth and Rachel: they'd stopped dancing and were whispering cheerfully in the middle of the ballroom, so close to one another that their foreheads were almost touching. Both beautiful and bright in their evening gowns, perfect ladies in a marvelous world made of music. The smaller girl gathered her skirt and spun around twice. Rachel brought her hand to her mouth and broke out in laughter before repeating the pirouette herself.

Hector changed direction with Marina and lost sight of his friends. His dance partner smiled and her eyes, the most gorgeous eyes in the world, focused on his. Hector felt the need to hold her even more tightly, to draw her close and finally let flow that torrent of feelings that had flooded him since the first time he saw her. His body couldn't contain so many feelings; it was impossible, completely impossible. Once again the music made them turn, and she separated from him, only a little, to return immediately, even closer than she was before. Marina's hand tightened its grip on his shoulder, and his hand slid from her waist to her hip.

Once again the dance brought him in view of Lizbeth and Rachel. Lizbeth pointed to the choker that her friend wore around her neck, with the red teardrop in the center. Rachel said something, made a gesture of agreement, and brought her hands to the clasp that fastened the jewelry as the other girl held her hair away from her neck.

Hector sped up his moves, pulling Marina with him. The girl let out a peal of laughter and fell into his arms. The music took a turn and the dance slowed. There was no longer any space between them. He was aware of every curve of her body, every pleat in her clothing, and her quickened breathing entwined with his.

They spun once more, and Lizbeth and Rachel appeared before him again. The first held the choker around her throat, her small fingers about to close the clasp at the back of her neck. Rachel watched her, smiling, and distractedly scratched at her throat right where the necklace had been in contact with her skin. Hector and Marina turned in unison, and the girls were lost from sight. It took a moment for him to realize what he'd just seen. In his mind the image of Rachel scratching her neck exploded like a bomb. His next thought was that the red of the choker's teardrop was the same red of Rocavaragalago, the color of the cathedral made from the Red Moon. He stopped thinking there and then.

He dropped Marina so quickly that the girl almost fell down. Hector turned toward Lizbeth and Rachel at light speed.

"Don't put it on!" he howled, but it was too late. Lizbeth's fingers had fastened the clasp.

The stone in the choker flashed just once. As if echoing that brilliance, two red stars shone in Lizbeth's eyes. Her gaze, always happy and lively, clouded over with a scarlet gleam that seemed to surge from hell itself. Her expression became distorted, her features twisted, and her face turned into a bestial mask. The girl hunched over as if all the weight of the world fell suddenly upon her shoulders. Hector ran shouting while Marina struggled to regain her balance.

Lizbeth growled. It was not a human sound. It was the beginning of a howl. The same howls that came from the mountains every night. The Red Moon reflected in the girl's eyes, scarlet and bloody.

All of a sudden she leapt at Rachel, who watched, stunned, unable to react. Hector saw Lizbeth's arm launch toward her, the hand transformed into a frightening claw. The impact against Rachel's throat was savage: the blow knocked her off her feet and sent her flying several yards before she landed and lay completely motionless. Hector reached Lizbeth, trying not to think of the horrible crack he'd just heard.

"Lizbeth!"

He tried to grab her, but she escaped in one jump, growled, and pounced on him, baring her teeth. That was not Lizbeth; that thing had nothing to do with his friend. The red blaze of her eyes blinded him momentarily. He violently attacked the shadow descending on him. His knuckles collided with Lizbeth's jaw as the girl's claws tore at his clothing and scratched the skin underneath.

Lizbeth fell to the ground and rolled over onto four legs, growling and drooling. Hector heard cries behind him; someone called to him, asking him to back away. Another voice yelled at Bruno. And the automatons' music kept flowing across the dance floor, oblivious to the chaos. It was the same rhythm that he and Marina had danced to only seconds before. Lizbeth leapt at him, her face twisted in a ferocious grimace. Hector made no effort to avoid her and met her head on. The girl's mouth closed only inches from his face. He shoved her to the side with his left hand and kept pounding her with his right. Finally, a devastating blow left Lizbeth unconscious and sent him staggering.

He was still for a few moments, in the same position he'd been left in after knocking Lizbeth out. Time had stopped completely in the ballroom; Hector closed his eyes slowly, wishing that it would never resume. With his eyes shut, everything was warm and comforting, and with time at a standstill, nothing could ever hurt him again. Everything would be okay. Through the tender darkness of closed eyelids, nothing could reach him.

But time did continue when someone behind him announced in a weak voice:

"She's dead."

"No . . ." he whispered, and pointed to Lizbeth. "She's breathing, she's still breathing . . . No . . ." He turned and saw Madeleine kneeling beside Rachel.

"She's dead," the redhead repeated, louder this time. She turned to the Italian, who stood stock still, his eyes bulging, mouth agape. "Bruno! Do something! She's dead, damn it!"

At that moment, Natalia screamed.

# THE REVELATION

The castle courtyard was in an uproar as creatures pounced, writhed, and howled. The pack had gone completely mad. The guards at the gate exchanged a worried look. They hadn't been this agitated in a long time. One of them rammed its forehead against the bars of the gate, and the entire door shook.

The biggest, a majestic gray specimen, leapt up on the stump of a dead tree. It raised its head and howled in such a way that the castle itself seemed to shudder. The others crowded around, growling and snorting. The lattice of black veins that covered their eyes gave them an even more savage look, as if they were peering out through broken windows or delicate spiderwebs.

Lady Serena watched them, disgusted, from a terrace on the south tower. The threadbare curtains that hung from the doorway rustled next to her like ghostly creatures. She deeply despised those beasts. Everything about them repulsed her, from their dirty, smelly fur to their twisted claws.

"There is death in the city," Ujthan's booming voice announced suddenly from behind her. "They can smell it."

Lady Serena spun around when she heard his voice. She hadn't noticed him come in. It was disturbing that such a large man could be so stealthy.

"It's not just death they can smell," she assured him. She looked him up and down, never hiding the scorn she felt toward him. "What are you doing here, Ujthan?" she asked. The area of the castle where he'd found her was uninhabited, and it was unusual to see someone wandering around.

"I was looking for you." The shadows in the room fell upon his tattooed face, giving him an even more sinister look than usual.

"Have you become Esmael's emissary?" asked the phantom queen. "Are you taking Dusty's place as the black angel's messenger?"

"I don't mean to bother you, Lady Serena," he mumbled. "And no, I'm not here on Esmael's behalf. I'm here because of another matter."

An enchanted current shook Lady Serena. She felt the subtle vibration of a silent field extending around her. The ghost looked at the warrior, intrigued. Ujthan was unable to perform magic. He was a warrior and a merciless assassin, but there wasn't a shred of magic in his body, save for the tattooed weapons that covered him. But without a doubt, she saw him manipulate something in the shadows with unsteady hands, a bewitched object.

"I come on behalf of someone who can fulfill your most longed-for desire," he said. "Someone who can grant you oblivion and extinguish the parody of a life that you lead."

The ghost laughed. Enclosed in the magical field, her laughter caused not the slightest echo.

"Ah, such nonsense!" She floated toward the middle of the room. "This again?" She laughed once more. "Tell Esmael to quit this foolishness. He doesn't have my—"

"It's not Esmael who sends me," Ujthan insisted. The warrior's voice was so curt that Lady Serena narrowed her eyes. She suddenly realized that there was something strange about him, an aura of dark energy that didn't at all match Ujthan's essence.

"Who are we talking about then?" she asked sternly. "And no more games."

Ujthan's only answer was to sink his fingertips into his left cheek, right next to the tattoo of a dagger. Lady Serena watched as he gently pulled at a shadow located next to the weapon's blade. The ghost went on the defense and began to draw a protection spell with one hand. Before she could complete three movements she stopped, astonished.

It wasn't a weapon that Ujthan extracted from his flesh. It was a living creature, a brownish being that began unfurling before her eyes in a nightmarish vision. She couldn't tell what was arm, torso, leg, or head; it was all the same amalgam of dun flesh and black bandages that surged from the warrior's face and spilled out onto the floor like a waterfall of lumpy gelatin.

Once it was completely separated from Ujthan, the creature shook like a dog right out of the water, straightened up, and took a step toward Lady Serena.

She recognized him instantly. It was Belisarius. The spirit narrowed her eyes. *No*, she corrected herself, *it's Belisarius's body, but something else is inhabiting it. Something much more powerful and terrible. Something very old.* The ghost, in spite of herself, shuddered.

"Allow me to introduce myself," the creature said. His voice was that of devastation; his voice was the herald of death and pain.


They went down the stairs that led to the palace courtyard immersed in a tense, almost palpable silence.

Ricardo walked in front with Lizbeth in his arms. The paralyzing spell that enveloped her emitted a bluish glow that bathed them both and spilled onto their feet, illuminating the steps as they walked. The girl's tense fists looked more like animal claws than human hands; it even seemed like the nails and fingers had grown. Her face remained contorted in a demonic grimace. They hadn't been able to remove the choker from her neck: it appeared to be welded to her flesh.

Hector stopped halfway down the stairs as the others reached the courtyard. They were still wearing their party clothes, and the contrast between their attire and what had just happened made everything feel even more absurd and unreal. He watched them from the stairs and wondered how they could have been so reckless. They'd forgotten where they were, and that had cost them dearly.

"Lock her in the dungeons. Bruno will stay with her," he ordered. His voice was firm, although he felt very little conviction. His legs trembled. "Maybe she'll recover when she wakes up and she'll go back to being herself. But we can't risk it." He turned to the Italian. "If the spell wears off before you get to the tower, paralyze her again."

"I will," he said. There was something strange about Bruno. His face showed his usual indifference, but his eyes suddenly darted from Lizbeth's body to Hector on the stairway to the window at the entrance.

"You always have to try to do as little harm as possible, but sometimes doing harm is inevitable," Lizbeth had told him at the tower, and Rachel had nodded by her side. The memory of the girl's eyes clouding over with the red from the choker shocked him like whiplash. He shuddered.

"What about you?" Maddie asked. She hugged herself at the foot of the stairs, frozen stiff from a cold that had nothing to do with dusk. "What are you going to do?"

"I'll take charge of Rachel."

"Hector . . ." Marina took a step in his direction. She was the only one crying.

With difficulty he resisted the impulse to step back. He felt the need to move away from her, to put as much distance as possible between them. The memory of the warmth of her body seemed like blasphemy after what had happened, an insult to Rachel, to Lizbeth, to the whole world. No, there was no place for happiness or love in Rocavarancolia, or for anything remotely similar. Rocavarancolia was darkness and death. There was nothing else. And he'd been an idiot for letting himself think otherwise.

*How long does it take for a corpse to grow cold?* he suddenly wondered.

"Go back to the tower. Lock Lizbeth up there. I . . ." His voice faltered. He avoided Marina's gaze; he avoided all of theirs. He wanted them to leave. He wanted to be alone as soon as possible so he could find a dark place to collapse, a place where no light would shine.

"Go. I'll take care of Rachel," he repeated.

"My story . . ." Marina whispered.

Hector nodded after several seconds. He shrugged his shoulders.

"That's what happens now, right?"

He turned the corner to enter the building again when Marco stopped him. He strode toward him, his eyes glassy. For a moment, Hector thought he was about to attack him, but what he did was even more surprising: he hugged him tightly. Hector was still, dazed by the German boy's sudden gesture.

"Whatever you do, don't bury her underground," he whispered in his ear. "If you do, the echo of her conscience will filter into the soil, and she'll never stop talking. Let her rest. Let her truly rest."

Then he hugged him even tighter, almost leaving him breathless, and finally let him go. Hector looked at him, bewildered, unable to understand all that Marco's words implied. In that instant, what had happened in the ballroom was the only thing that mattered.

As soon as they left, Hector returned to the palace. The false ceiling hung once again above his head. The light that entered through the domes grew fainter by the second. The beauty of the place was obscured by the growing darkness. He hadn't gone two steps when his knees finally gave way; he had no choice but to sit down in the middle of the entryway to avoid collapsing. The knuckles on his right hand throbbed with pain, as if a tiny heart beat in each one. The memory of his fist as it impacted with Lizbeth came to mind so clearly that it made him retch.

"Do no harm . . ." he managed to whisper.

He got up shortly after, but only to sit back down on the closest stairway. He still wasn't ready to go back up and face Rachel's body.

He heard the wind outside, that Rocavarancolian wind that was now as familiar to him as his own body and thoughts were distant.

The monstrous spider in the frock coat was leaning over Rachel's body, wrapping her up in its silk. She had already covered her up to the waist and continued her task with such concentration that she didn't see Hector approaching, sword in hand. When he'd already crossed most of the distance between them, the creature turned toward him. Four of its eight eyes were bathed in tears.

"I'm so sorry, child. So sorry . . ." Her head swayed with sadness. Her voice was an unpleasant viscous burping sound, almost like she was drowning in her own saliva.

"Get away from her."

"I must bring her to the Scar of Arax, where the dead lay. That is her place now. The dead should be with the dead."

"I won't let you throw her to the worms." He pointed his sword at her. His voice burned in his throat. "Rachel deserves much more than that. So much more."

The spider twisted her head to look at him, then lowered it at an impossible angle and fixed her eyes on the dead girl. Her chelicerae waved without creating the slightest sound. She stepped back slowly, her attention focused on the sword. Hector lowered it but did not sheathe it. The knuckles on his right hand kept throbbing.

He approached one of the curtains and pulled at it with force. The curtain detached with a loud crack, so quickly that he had to jump aside to avoid being covered by it. The fabric was too large and heavy for what he had in mind. It didn't take much to cut it with his sword; he tore it sloppily on the diagonal. Then he took a long, deep breath, gathering his strength for what came next.

He wiped away tears with the palm of his hand and moved toward the motionless body, his sword now sheathed, the curtain in his arms. He looked at Rachel, astounded, unable to believe that just a little while ago she'd been dancing and laughing, and now she lay still, in the middle of the dance floor, as limp as a broken toy. He crouched down next to her and removed the spiderweb. Then he wrapped her in the cut piece of curtain. He did it delicately, as if afraid of waking her. Next he lifted the body in his arms. It hardly weighed anything. And that lightness overwhelmed him even more.

"It's almost like she's empty," he said.

"She is empty," Lady Spider answered. "What matters is no longer there. It's gone."

Hector nodded, and he left the ballroom with the body in his arms. Lady Spider followed behind him, keeping a safe distance. She continued after him as he left the palace behind and went into the ruined city. The darkness was a thick cape that shrouded the world itself, just like the curtain shrouded his friend's body.

That minuscule funeral party passed through the blustery Rocavarancolia night: the young boy with his dead friend in his arms and the spider behind. They crossed the Scar of Arax using one of the planks that led to the other side. Once there, Hector stopped to find his bearings. The city was different at night, as if the chaos of ruins that formed it were even more disorganized. Something shifted in the darkness: fierce, yellow eyes that watched them from an alleyway; whatever it was, it didn't make a move in their direction.

Hector looked around, completely lost. He wasn't even sure which direction they'd come from to get there. To his left was a tall marble pedestal upon which perched a dozen black stone eagles, their wings raised. He'd never seen it before.

Something flapped in the night. He turned again to the pedestal, but the eagles were motionless, nothing but still rock. Looking forward again, Hector glimpsed a rapid succession of metallic flashes quickly approaching. He was about to place Rachel on the ground to unsheathe his sword when he realized that it was the metal bird that habitually stalked them, with that human eye held fast in its beak. He'd never seen it so close before. He remembered the rag birds that Denestor had conjured in his bedroom a thousand years ago; although the materials for each of them were different, something in their design linked them, as if they were the work of the same artist.

The bird landed barely two yards from him, deposited the eye on the ground, and let out a croak that sounded like *Come*. It picked up the eye again and took off in flight. It didn't go far. It landed on the porch of a black house with a spiked roof and sinister weathervanes and shook its wings impatiently, waiting for Hector to follow it.

As soon as the boy began walking, the bird took off again. Hector followed it through the labyrinthine streets of Rocavarancolia. From time to time the metallic bird glanced back to make sure he was still there. Lady Spider stayed behind them, with her slow and clumsy gait, rubbing her four hands as if she were stiff from cold.

It took them over an hour to arrive, and throughout the whole journey, Hector didn't recognize a single street, not even when he saw the deep hollow of the cemetery appear after they crossed the red brick wall. Hector was surprised by how many lights were shining below. It was like peering into a magic scene, a set made of shadows, sparkles, and flashes that hardly resembled the city around them, as if trying to compensate for the sky devoid of stars that hung above Rocavarancolia. The bird entered the cemetery and perched atop a marble obelisk.

The voices of the dead rose up to greet them as soon as they stepped on the south ramp that led to the hollow.

"She doesn't belong here! Take her away! Take her away! We don't want her here with us! Leave!"

"Poor broken girl, poor dead girl . . . What emptiness she leaves behind. What silence. What sadness. Bring her, bring her. We'll cover her here with us in the warm darkness."

"No! Let her rot far from here! Very far! Get her cold bones out of here! Take away that flesh that doesn't feel and that blood that doesn't run!"

"Don't listen to them. Leave her with us. We'll sing her lullabies. We'll honor her memory, and she'll never be alone."

"Shut up!" howled Lady Scar, moving rapidly toward Hector from a small square. The dead went silent.

The guardian of the Royal Pantheon carried a torch that lit up a vast circle around her. Her skin, pocked with scars and sores, radiated in a ghostly way under the direct light, making her seem paler and more gaunt than usual. She looked as if she might come apart at any second; Hector wasn't surprised to see that she was missing an eye. Lady Scar waited until he'd crossed the last few yards downhill and then, without saying a word, she turned her back on him and headed for a slope that led down between two identical mausoleums of blue stone and thin green columns. The metallic bird left the obelisk and glided to the woman's shoulder.

The grotesque woman guided him through the cemetery. The lights hurled their shadows against vaults and tombs, sometimes making them appear immense and other times small and insignificant. They walked for several minutes, until they came to a stop at a half-erected mauso-leum. Only two of the four walls of the structure had been raised. They were tall and made out of reddish stone covered in hieroglyphs. The two walls formed a corner without a roof above a marble platform with a simple white tomb in its center.

Lady Scar left the torch in a metal bracket that stuck out from one wall. Then she grabbed the slab that covered the tomb and slid it effort-lessly to the side, propping it up vertically against the tomb. She turned to Hector.

"The dukes of Barinion ordered this mausoleum to be built for their dying daughter just days before the enemy passed through the vorti-ces," she explained. "I suppose the dukes, as well as the little girl, ended up in the Scar of Arax, I don't know . . . Whatever happened, nobody will complain if you leave her here."

That tomb wasn't what Hector had hoped for after listening to Marina's tale. There was nothing grandiose or memorable about it, nothing that made it special. The half-constructed mausoleum went unnoticed among the rest of the tombs and vaults, but other than that it was a good place. And it was much better than the Scar of Arax.

Lady Scar approached Hector. A waft of sweet rot instantly surrounded him: a smell of life beyond life, an organic aroma that grew in secret in the furthest reaches of dying forests. The woman extended her scarred arms toward him.

"I'll take her," she said in a broken voice. "This is my job. Guardian of the Royal Pantheon, commander of the armies of the kingdom, and gravedigger . . ."

Hector hesitated for a moment but then handed over Rachel's body. Only when that frightening creature freed him of the weight of the cadaver was he aware of the exhaustion that had settled in his arms. He let his arms drop to his sides, and tried to ignore the shooting pain coming from the knuckles of his right hand.

Lady Scar carried the body wrapped in a curtain toward the tomb and placed it inside, with the abrupt clumsiness of one not used to providing a delicate touch. Then she took the slab and placed it once again over the tomb. The sound of stone hitting stone resounded strangely in the unfinished mausoleum. It was a macabre, resistant crack, a sound that made Hector clench his teeth and caused his hair to stand on end. It could well have been the sound of the clasp of Lizbeth's choker as it closed around her neck. Hector went back to reliving in his mind the instant those two bloody, glowing coals overtook his friend's chestnut eyes.

"That's what's going to happen," he said. "What happened to Lizbeth . . . That's going to happen to all of us."

He wasn't talking to Lady Scar, or to the spider who stood several steps behind. He was talking to make that nightmare real, to extract the truth. But more than anything, he talked to free himself from the terrifying red stars that had exploded in Lizbeth's eyes.

"The Red Moon will change us," he went on. "It will change us, like it changed Lizbeth."

Lady Scar remained silent, not knowing what to say or do. She had seen everything. The bird that carried her eye had been perched on one of the rooftops in front of the palace, and from there she'd witnessed the duel between Adrian and Dario, and Rachel's death.

"It will change you, but it doesn't have to be as traumatic as the change in your friend," she finally said. She spoke very quietly, in a vain attempt to make her voice not sound as horrible as it naturally was. Her mangled throat was not made for consolation. "There are kinder transformations, more—"

Hector interrupted her:

"Is that why you brought us here?" He clenched his fists. He'd never felt so much rage and so much helplessness. "To turn us into monsters?"

"Monsters?" asked Lady Spider.

"Rocavaragalago and the Red Moon will increase your magic essence," said Lady Scar. "In most of the cases this increase will be accompanied by physical and mental changes. The transformation is necessary, child, to prevent all of that new energy from killing you. It would scorch you."

"Damn you." Hector took a step back. "Damn you all."

He shook his head. There would be no horrors fleeing the red walls of Rocavaragalago. They would be the monsters: the children that Denestor Tul brought from Earth, the harvest of Samhein.

He looked at Lady Scar with rage.

"How could you do this to us?" he asked. "What kind of creatures are you?" His fists were clenched and he trembled with fury. "You took everything from us! You tore us away from our world! You made everyone forget us, and now this! Now this! No . . . No one could be more despicable than you."

Lady Scar squinted her one eye and stepped forward. She hadn't expected any gratitude from Hector, but she was hardly prepared for such scorn, as justified as it might be.

"Curse all you like, little boy." Her voice had turned icy. Hector's fury had incited her own. "Scream all you want. You can curse me and the entire universe . . . It won't change a thing. The Red Moon will come out and Rocavaragalago will be set in motion. There's nothing you can do to stop it."

"Monster," Hector said. He put so much hatred and rage into that word that it was like he was uttering it for the first time. Lady Scar showed him the broken and blackened ruins that were her teeth. Hector's hand went to the hilt of his sword. The woman's rotten aroma was now imbued with a new odor, a smell of poison and threat.

"Yes," growled Lady Scar, drawing out the word in an evil hiss as she leaned toward him. "That's what you'll all become: monsters . . . Look at me, child, and consider your future. There is no hope for you. Your bodies will change with the Red Moon, some to such a degree that they'll be unrecognizable. And not just your bodies. Your soul itself will turn dark. And that darkness will carry you very far. By the time the Red Moon sets, there will be nothing human left in you. Do you hear me? Nothing."

Hector removed his hand from his sword handle and looked at the grotesque woman, astonished. He'd just understood something so obvious that the revelation left him breathless for several moments.

"You too . . . Good lord . . . They deceived you too? You were like us . . . and the Red Moon turned you into . . . that."

Lady Scar let out a growl.

"Get out of my sight!" she howled. She tried to avoid the memory of past times—when her skin was smooth and her heart pumped blood through her veins, not slime—to no avail. "Go with the others! Get out of here, run, run, run!" She made an abrupt gesture with her hand, sweeping him toward the path. "Run back to your friends. And you better carve that girl's face into your memory—that girl you love—because soon you won't be able to look at her without wanting to throw up."

The mention of Marina made him stumble. He couldn't take his eyes off Lady Scar. Those swollen, scarred extremities, the frightening scars that covered her pale body, had now taken on a new and terrible meaning. He suddenly imagined Marina transformed into something similar, and he felt dizzy.

He took two quick steps backward. The spider's shadow fell over him for a second as she stepped out of his way.

He turned toward her. For a moment the arachnid's monstrous face was in front of his; the eyes hidden behind monocles appeared black and exaggerated, with an expression of bewildered stupidity in them. The daggers of her chelicerae were covered with grayish, viscous spittle. Would one of his friends end up becoming a creature as terrifying as that?

"Monsters," Hector whispered, but it was no longer an insult; it was a cold premonition. "Monsters, monsters, monsters . . ."

He turned his back on the mausoleum and took off running.

★★★

He didn't need the metal bird's guidance to get back to the tower. He moved like a specter through the dark streets, a shadow among shadows. He cried throughout most of the journey; they were tears of rage, pain, and helplessness. He couldn't stop thinking about Rachel, Lizbeth, and Marco and his words on the palace staircase, of the Red Moon and what would happen to them when it came out . . . In his mind, in his turbulent thoughts, there was no room for peace or hope.

When he caught sight of the tower in the distance, he stopped and forced himself to calm down. He cleaned his face with his sleeve. He wanted no evidence on his face that he'd been crying; he drew his sword and checked his blurry and distorted reflection on the blade. Then he continued his march. The star on the façade had reached the height of ten to nine.

Madeleine, Marina, Natalia, and Bruno waited on the first floor of the tower. The redhead and the Italian were sitting alone, one at either end of the large room. Marina and Natalia, on the other hand, were together on a divan covered in hides close to the stairway. The Russian had her legs folded up on the seat and hugged her knees, inconsolable. By Marina's posture, Hector understood that she'd been trying to comfort her. When he saw his friends, another wave of anguish passed through him. He couldn't stop picturing them as horrible creatures, as monsters covered in scars and sores. He remembered Lizbeth's transformation once again, and the savage way she leapt upon Rachel to deliver that fatal blow.

Madeleine was the only one who got up when she saw him come in. She approached him and kissed him on the cheek without a word.

"Is it done?" she asked.

He stared at her for a while before nodding. Madeleine was the only one who'd taken off her party dress. She'd put on an ugly dark robe, old and wrinkled. And even so she looked almost as radiant and beautiful as she did in that marvelous green dress. It was impossible to believe that all that beauty could be lost with the coming of the Red Moon.

"It's done," he said. To his surprise, his voice didn't waver, despite the grief and weakness that he felt. "Where are the others?"

"Ricardo is downstairs with her," Madeleine said. The redhead looked at him strangely, as if she didn't recognize him or there were something about his face she hadn't noticed before. "Adrian still hasn't returned. And we don't know where Marco is. He left as soon as we got back."

"He said he had something important to do, something that he couldn't put off any longer," Marina added from the divan. Hector didn't even look at her. If he looked at her now he would collapse, he was sure of it.

"Something to do? What?"

Madeleine shrugged her shoulders and Hector frowned. Marco knew more about the nature of the cemetery than he should have, and that gave new meaning to all that the boy had done for them. Without him, things would have been much harder; without him, Hector doubted that they would have survived this long.

Suddenly a vivid memory from the day of their arrival came to his mind: Alexander had wanted to go after weapons in the Scar of Arax, and the German, as he looked for a way down, had thrown several stones over the edge. That had been on purpose, Hector realized. Marco knew that something dangerous awaited them down there, and that had been the signal to put them on guard.

But how did he know so much about Rocavarancolia? Was someone helping him, like Lady Serena had helped himself, or was there something else? And where did he go? What did he have to do that was so important?

Mistral walked through the streets of Rocavarancolia, covering his ears with his hands so as not to hear the howls coming from the mountains. He'd been tempted to block his ears, to turn them into two blobs of useless flesh so that terrible sound wouldn't find a way inside of him. But it was too late. The howls of the pack were etched on his mind, just like Alexander's scream as he was trapped by the curse of the Serpent Tower.

Everything had been useless. His presence had made no difference; he had brought nothing but death and suffering. A tiny voice in his mind assured him that he was wrong, that he'd prevented many others from dying, but he didn't take notice. It was a voice that came from such a far distance, and so weak that he didn't seem to believe it existed.

First he'd killed the German boy, strangled him with the same hands that he now pressed against his ears. Then he'd sacrificed Alexander to save Adrian and Natalia. And now Rachel was dead, a victim of the senseless idea of having a party in Rocavarancolia.

But could it have been any other way? How could he expect to save them when his first act had been assassinating one of them? He shook his head. His goal wasn't to save the children. His goal was to save the kingdom. Or at least it had been, at first. But then what? What happened next? Why had he stayed in the Margalar Tower for four long months?

"Because I promised Alexander," he whispered. "I promised to watch over his sister."

Was that his true motive? No, that was the excuse that he'd clung to all this time. His true motive was something else, not the promise, but who he'd made it to: Alexander. That was the key. He remembered the redhead facing the end with a strength that disarmed him. But what was the difference between being brave and just pretending to be? Was it the same as the difference between being a monster and pretending to be normal?

He remembered Alexander again, after he found him crying while Adrian lay on his deathbed. The shapeshifter had asked him a similar question then: if the result was the same, what difference was there between being a hero and pretending to be one? The redhead had showed him, unequivocally.

Mistral repeated Alexander's reply in a strangled whisper:

"I know I'm lying."

He left a dark alleyway and encountered the broken edges of the Scar of Arax. He approached, stumbling, his hands still on his ears. He stopped at the very same edge of the crack that King Sardaurlar had created with his magic sword. The whiteness of the skeletons that lined the enormous gulf radiated a dismal glow in the darkness. Dozens of empty eye sockets watched him; fleshless hands pointed to him with the insolence with which death points to life. In the Scar of Arax the bones of men and monsters were mixed; skeletons of friends and enemies lay together, unified in the emptiness and silence.

For the first time in more than a century, Mistral thought of other times, of another world, a land with a hot, blazing sun, starry nights, embraces, and sweetness. He tried to remember what he was called in that place, but it was impossible. Rocavarancolia had snatched his name in the same way that it had snatched his humanity. It didn't matter. He was Mistral, the metamorph, the shapeshifter, another monster. A pathetic monster who had fooled himself for months, pretending to be normal. That's what it all came down to.

He took a step forward, before the anxious gaze of endless skulls, and jumped into the Scar of Arax. The rattling of the skeletons as they shook echoed in the night, louder and louder as the blind worms hurried in his direction. But Mistral couldn't hear them. In his mind he kept hearing, over and over again, the howls of the pack in the mountain and the screams of Alexander, trapped in the doorway.

Bruno had deactivated the cold spell in the dungeons and, although the temperature was back to normal, he noticed a strange dryness to the air, as if the molecules of the basement still hadn't recovered from the sudden change of atmosphere. There were no longer any provisions in the cells, and Hector figured they'd been moved to the rooms upstairs.

Ricardo was crouched in front of one of the cells, still in his party clothes. He didn't even look at him when he entered the room. His face, his posture, even his shadow reflected a deep despondency. Hector approached him. The ground was full of puddles.

His stomach clenched as he saw Lizbeth. He grasped the bars, choking back sobs. The sight of the reddened knuckles on his right hand made him immediately pull his hands back and hide them, as if they were somehow obscene. The girl lay on the floor, curled up in a ball, her dress soaked and muddy.

"Bruno put her to sleep right after he left her in the cell," Ricardo explained. "She became . . . She became very violent. She threw herself against the bars, and we were afraid she'd hurt herself."

Hector nodded.

The process that had begun when the choker clasped shut around Lizbeth's neck had not yet finished. The girl was changing physically. Her hands were more stretched out, the fingers longer, and the nails had taken on a copper tone bordering on black. Her feet had burst through the buckled shoes that she'd worn for the party, and when he saw them Hector couldn't help thinking of paws. Her face was changing as well: her lower jaw had projected forward, while her forehead seemed to have been pushed back. With every passing moment there was more animal in Lizbeth and less human. Hector closed his eyes and breathed deeply. They kept hearing the howls coming from the mountains.

"Werewolves," he whispered. "That's what they are. Werewolves. Monsters . . . That's why they kidnapped children from the linked worlds. They want monsters . . . Rocavaragalago won't open a door to hell. We're the ones who will be transformed into monsters. That's why we're here."

Ricardo stood up beside him, startled, and looked at the stairway, as if he was afraid someone might be listening.

"Are you going to tell the others?" he asked in a weak voice. "Will you tell them what will happen when the Red Moon comes out?"

"You knew," Hector realized. Ricardo sighed.

"I wasn't sure," he said. "The text was confusing and I . . . I simply couldn't believe it. I resisted, I . . . I didn't want to believe it. I chose the simplest explanation, and besides, it fit so well with the original text that I almost began to believe it was the truth . . . But it's not . . . At least not entirely."

"Monsters . . ."

Ricardo tilted his head and rested it against the bars.

"Don't tell the others, please. Don't do that to them. It won't do them any good to know."

Hector didn't answer. He was unable to take his eyes off Lizbeth, curled up on the floor. Her chest rose and fell, slowly; her breathing was an intermittent grunting, threatening even in sleep. That thing lying there on the floor of the cell looked nothing like his friend. Was there some way of reversing the process? Was there a way to avoid what was going to happen when the Red Moon came out? Flee to the desert, maybe?

No. There was no hope. Lady Scar had made that very clear. There was no way out. No possible exit. What he looked at in the cell was his destiny.

"Monsters," he repeated again.

★★★

The hand in the alleyway was still, with the palm held upward, like that of a beggar seeking alms. The arm that stuck out from between the bars looked more like an extension of the stone wall than something that was once alive. The scales that covered its seven fingers were stained with the mud of the alley, the claws covered in dirt. Dario had left a piece of meat on the enormous open palm with the absurd hope that the monster might revive once it felt the food in its hand. Now he sat in front of the arm, rocking slowly. The blood that ran down his side mixed with the mud that dirtied his pants and boots. Dario fell on his side, as if sleeping, his eyes still fixed on the motionless palm.

Esmael saw him collapse in the muddy alleyway and remain as still as the dead hand. The black angel was crouched on the rooftop of the house facing the alley, with his arms lightly resting on his thighs.

Around him, the city huddled in the shadows, large and dark. It almost seemed like he could hear it breathing. Rocavarancolia smelled of devastation. Finally, that night, it had shown itself in full splendor; it had finally shown what it was capable of. Esmael thought of it as a gigantic beast who, after a massacre, lay satiated in its den.

The lone boy was dying in front of him. In the Scar of Arax, the worms had already become aware of the German boy who, in a fit of madness, had decided to end it all among the skeletons of a thousand horrors. That pointless and cowardly act had surprised Esmael; it was hard for him to imagine the boy would go to such extremes, but Rocavarancolia was an expert in bringing out the worst in people.

One of the girls had discovered that in the cruelest way. The choker with the fragment of the Red Moon had sped up her change. Esmael had heard tales of those enchanted jewels, but this was the first time he'd seen their effects. Only in times of crisis, when Rocavarancolia needed a large number of troops and couldn't wait for the coming of the Red Moon, were the artifacts used. The jewels could accelerate the metamorphosis of the harvest, but the resulting creatures would never develop to their full potential. Lizbeth would never undergo the full change; she was condemned to remain in a hybrid state between her old self and the one that she would have been transformed into by

Rocavaragalago and the Red Moon, by primordial magic instead of that clumsy substitute.

Esmael looked to the east. In the sky, after months of pitch black, a single star shone. He wondered if the children would find any comfort in its light, if it would give them a little hope to discover that faint brilliance where before there had been nothing but darkness. He hoped not. He hoped they wouldn't be fooled by appearances and they'd understand that star foretold nothing good. That star was known as the Emissary, and it was the first of many that would populate the night sky of Rocavarancolia before the coming of the Red Moon.

Hector and Ricardo returned to the others as soon as they heard Adrian's agitated voice upstairs. The boy turned to watch them coming up the stairs. His clothing was in a lamentable state, wrinkled and covered in blood.

"What happened to you?" Hector rushed over to him. "Are you hurt?"

"I'm fine. I'm fine," Adrian answered. His voice sounded raspy and his face was so pale that he almost looked like a ghost or someone revived from the dead. His lips were crusted with dried blood. "What about Rachel? What's this about Lizbeth killing her? What . . . ? What the hell happened here? What's this idiot trying to explain to me?" He gestured to Bruno, standing behind him with his top hat in his hands. "Where's Lizbeth?" He looked around, his head wobbling on his neck, as if it wasn't securely attached. "And Marco? Where's Marco?"

Hector didn't answer any of his questions. He just watched Adrian's demented expression in silence: his madness seemed to have reached a new level. The boy had crossed another threshold that night. Behind him, Bruno twirled his top hat nonstop, from one side to the other. Would Rachel appear in his dreams now? Would she take a spot among the audience that observed him night after night? And where were Natalia's shadows at this moment? From what corners were they stalking them? Would Marina keep writing stories that became reality?

*What are we?* Hector wondered. The only answer that came was the constant throbbing of the knuckles on his right hand. He'd leapt upon Lizbeth without a moment's hesitation; he'd acted instinctively, as if violence was something innate in him, as much a part of his essence as his own flesh. *What are we, and what are we going to become?*

He shook his head, looked at Ricardo out of the corner of his eye, and sighed heavily.

"There's something you should know," he announced.


Lady Spider stopped a moment as she discovered the distant sparkle of the Emissary. She uttered a long musical clucking, and after rubbing her four hands with delight she resumed her task with greater dedication than before. The appearance of the first star always put her in a good mood.

She completed another turn around the mausoleum, still secreting her silk. She then climbed up the wall of fabric that she constructed and let herself drop down the other side, reinforcing the interior wall.

In a little more than three hours she'd raised a striking cocoon twenty-five feet tall that soon roused the interest of the dead.

"Spin a pillow for me, Lady Spider!" one requested. "I'm sick of the wood of this coffin, it scratches my skull!"

"A cover for my tomb!" another called. "Please! Please! To hide me from view of the sky and the Red Moon!"

Lady Spider, not paying any attention to them, persisted in her task, humming an old lullaby. Her first intention had been, simply, to improvise a few walls and a ceiling for the unfinished mausoleum, but as she began the work, a sudden fit of inspiration made her change her mind and embark on a more ambitious project.

First she'd constructed a tunnel of webbing from the path to the pantheon entrance and then, using the passageway and the walls of the building as supports, she'd begun to raise a bell-shaped structure. Once that was finished, she thought she'd add projections and wall hangings, and maybe, to top it all off, a crown of spikes. She'd set out to make that mausoleum the most striking in the entire cemetery.

The appearance of the Emissary wasn't the only thing that had helped to improve her mood. Doing something for the dead girl filled her with pride and joy. She would have liked the bad-mannered boy to be there; she wished he could see what she'd created to honor his friend.

"A monster?" She let out a little chuckle as she dropped halfway down the mausoleum, grabbed on with her claws, and proceeded to secrete circles of silk. "Would a monster do this, ungrateful child? No, no, no . . . A monster wouldn't do this, I assure you." She danced around the white walls, imagining how embarrassed the boy would feel if he were here. It wasn't hard to imagine him asking forgiveness. "Of course, of course I accept your apology; not another word about it, my good boy. I understand the moment was painful and anyone's nerves would be on edge in a situation like that . . ."

"What do you think you're doing?" she heard from the bottom of the mausoleum.

Lady Spider froze, clinging to the silk wall with all eight extremities. She turned her head and saw Lady Scar on the other side of the path. She had her arms crossed in front of her chest and regarded the white webbed construction with a half-curious, half-irritated expression. Lady Spider's jaws opened in a slobbery smile.

"I couldn't leave the mausoleum like this," she explained. "The Red Moon is coming, and bad weather will come with it. I thought it would be best if the girl had an actual roof over her head . . ."

"A roof over her head?" Lady Scar let out a strange noise, strangled, almost a laugh. "Go ahead. Waste your time however you like."

"It's not a waste of time. Oh no, no, no . . . I'm doing it for the girl, yes, but not just for her." She looked away from Lady Scar to glance at the lone star shining up above. "The boy will learn. When he sees the beautiful mausoleum that I've built for his friend, he'll have no choice but to realize that we're not monsters. He'll learn. Yes. He will, he will." She looked back at the scarred woman, searching for approval in her face so that she didn't feel ridiculous. To her relief she found it; at least, she thought so. "He shouldn't have called us those terrible things. No, he shouldn't have done it. That was bad."

"That's what he sees."

"No. No. That was bad. Very bad." Lady Spider grabbed a thread from her web with three hands and pulled on it to test its strength. Two eyes now watched Lady Scar, four were focused on the task at hand, and the last two were still fixed on the Emissary. "He's not looking. He doesn't know how to look. So he can't see the truth. No, he can't."

"And what truth is that?" asked Lady Scar.

"We're not monsters," the spider answered without a moment's hesitation. All eight eyes looked at her once again. The glow from a nearby torch made her monocles sparkle. "We're beautiful," she said. "We're marvels. Just like this world that surrounds us, like the coming moon. Monsters? No. We're not monsters. We're miracles."

# THE AFTERMATH

The days after Rachel's death were slow and bitter. A heavy grief spread through all corners of the Margalar Tower, snatching their breath and leaving them exhausted. Time was filled with empty hours, blank spaces that contained nothing. They wandered aimlessly throughout the tower or sat by themselves, without looking at each other and barely speaking. The magnitude of what had happened and what was yet to happen overwhelmed them. Rachel was dead, Marco had disappeared, and the creature that had once been Lizbeth remained locked up in the dungeons. The passing of time became a sinister curse. Every minute that transpired brought them closer to the fateful moment when the Red Moon would transform them as well.

"Let's flee to the desert!" Marina begged them, with tears in her eyes. "It can't be worse than what waits for us here!" She pointed to Bruno, visibly upset, trembling from head to toe. "We have a magician. No, we have three! Adrian and Natalia can help there . . ." Hector saw the Russian girl frown at hearing her name. She had stopped trying to learn magic some time ago. "We'll bring all the talismans and charges that we can and . . . and . . ."

"We can't flee from the moon, Marina," Ricardo said, the very image of desolation. "We'll have it over our heads even if we go to the desert, even if we run to the end of the world . . ."

"But Rocavaragalago will be far away!"

"The horrible woman from the cemetery said that there's nothing we can do to avoid the transformation," Madeleine reminded them. The tone of her voice made everyone look at her; there was resignation in her words and an iciness more typical of Bruno. "It doesn't matter where we run. To the desert or to the sea . . . It doesn't matter. The Red Moon will change us. And I know what I'm going to become," she added. "Lizbeth and I had the same dreams. They were identical. You don't have to be very smart to know what that means: I'll transform into the same thing that she did."

"You can't know that," Ricardo contradicted her, after a long, uncomfortable silence. Her words were a crushing blow to everyone. "You can't be sure of that."

"Can't I?" She turned to him with extraordinary calm. "I've never been more sure of anything in my life, Ricardo. Absolutely nothing," she declared. Hector looked at her, surprised. She wasn't the same person who'd started talking minutes before. She had changed, and in a certain way it was as shocking a change as Lizbeth's: Madeleine was growing up before their eyes. "I'll become a wolf," she announced.

And any doubt they may have had in that respect vanished the next morning when they discovered that she was the only one that could get close to Lizbeth without her going wild. She was still hurling herself frantically against the bars as soon as anyone took a step toward her, but with Maddie it was different. Once she saw her come in she grew calm, let out a growl that almost sounded like a question, and began pacing the cell, back and forth, without looking at her, waiting, perhaps, for her friend to set her free.

Madeleine moved closer to the dungeon gate. Ricardo begged her to be careful, and she indicated that he shouldn't worry.

Lizbeth had only needed one night to complete her transformation. That had been enough time for her to double in size, for her back to curve and for her legs and arms to turn into four sturdy limbs with massive paws. A tangled coat of long brown fur covered her entire body. Her face had grown outward in the form of a misshapen snout and a powerful jaw. Her mouth contained two sets of concentric fangs; the second, halfway down her palate, was larger than the exterior one, and each of them curved inward like hooks. There was no indication whatsoever this being had once been human. The new Lizbeth exuded energy and strength. She radiated brutality. There was no trace of the choker with the embedded red stone; it was as if the wolf flesh had absorbed it.

"In my dreams I look through those eyes as well," Maddie said, both hands clutching the bars that separated her from Lizbeth. "And I looked through them before, on Earth, every time I stood in front of a canvas and wanted to paint a picture . . ."

Of all the changes that had taken place in Lizbeth, that was the most disturbing. Her eyes were lined with thick, shadowy black veins that turned her gaze into a pair of shattered windows. There was no trace of her sweetness or her humanity, and even so—most shocking of all—those eyes were the only thing that resembled the old Lizbeth.

The wolf stood up on her hind legs, supported her front legs on the bars, and stuck her snout through them to sniff Madeleine. The monster's fangs were only inches away from the girl's face. Maddie, far from being intimidated, stroked the wolf's shaggy, rough fur through the bars.

Lizbeth rubbed against her hand like an animal eager for affection. Hector watched the scene with a knot in his stomach. That frightening creature had killed Rachel while he was dancing, lost in a moment of absolute, and, as he now understood, undeserved happiness. That creature had been his friend, he'd laughed and cried with it, they'd shared misery, fear, and joy, and now she was nothing more than a brutal animal. And Madeleine was destined to become a similar being. The city had snatched her brother from her, and now it meant to snatch her beauty and her humanity.

"Madeleine, move away from her," Ricardo pleaded as he took a step toward the dungeon. Hector was convinced that his friend's thoughts ran parallel to his own. He wasn't afraid for Madeleine's safety. He knew, as they all did, that Lizbeth wouldn't hurt her. He only wanted her to keep away because the proximity between them reminded him that this was Maddie's fate, a fate that awaited them all: to transform into something alien, to be lost in strange bodies in an incomprehensible world.

The wolf dropped to all four legs when she saw Ricardo approach. She bared her teeth and growled once again. Between the cracks in the first set of fangs they could glimpse the second.

"No, Lizbeth, no," Maddie urged. "Ricardo, don't get any closer, please, you're making her nervous. Easy, Lizbeth, easy."

"Don't call that thing Lizbeth," Natalia said in a thin voice. She was leaning against the wall, next to the door, with her arms crossed in front of her chest, pale as a cadaver. "That monster is not Lizbeth. And she shouldn't be here. No, no . . . We should do something about this. We should . . ." She stopped speaking. She brought a hand to her throat, as if trying to keep a word from escaping her lips.

"Kill her?" Marina finished for her, appalled. "Is that what you want to do? You want to kill her?"

"No one's killing anybody," Hector asserted. He didn't look at Marina. He'd been avoiding her since the night before. Whenever he saw her he recalled the warmth from her body, and that memory made him tremble. If she hadn't been so close . . . If he hadn't been so unforgivably lost in her arms, maybe he would have realized sooner that Rachel's choker had a piece of the Red Moon embedded in it. He clenched his fists. If he hadn't been in love with Marina, Rachel would probably still be alive.

"I do not think it's advisable to kill Lizbeth," Bruno intervened. "And not just because it would be a disproportionate and amoral measure. We should keep her alive so that we can study her and learn from her. Among the books I've found are several that deal with lycanthropy and various transformations. I should like to investigate whether Lizbeth's current state is irreversible or not." He looked at Madeleine. It was shocking to see that there was more emotion in Lizbeth's eyes as she looked at the redhead than in the Italian's.

Bruno was the only one who hadn't changed out of his clothing from the night before. He was still wearing the topcoat, black jacket, green shirt, and annoying top hat on his head. Hector wondered what made him remain in the clothes that the rest of them had so hastily taken off.

"Keeping her locked up is cruel," Madeleine said. The wolf had lain down in the middle of the cell and was watching her closely, attentive to each and every one of her words.

"But we don't have a choice, Madeleine," Hector said. "We can't let her go. It would be dangerous. You understand that, right?" He'd just imagined her sneaking down to the dungeons in the middle of the night and opening the door of the cell to let Lizbeth escape. And then, the next image that came to his mind was of all of them murdered in their beds, where the wolf had surprised them as they slept. "Promise me you won't free her, please."

Maddie clutched the bars and took a long look at the monster behind them. Then she nodded.

"I . . . I promise."

"Smart girl," Adrian said as he entered the dungeon. "If you let her go, the first thing she'll do is tear open your throat. No doubt about it."

They hadn't seen him all morning. He'd showed up with messy hair and baggy eyes, looking like he hadn't slept a wink. He carried a bulky package on his back from which jutted the hilt of a double-handed sword, another weapon added to the two he wore on his belt. He looked like someone about to embark on a long journey. He adjusted his sack on his shoulder and looked at the beast in the cell while he scratched his ear with gusto. Lizbeth stood up once again and growled, her wolf's mane bristling.

"Poor Lizbeth. What a terrible fate," he said. He sighed before adding: "She really didn't deserve to end up like that. She was always so kind and caring with everyone . . ."

"Where do you think you're going?" Ricardo asked, pointing to the bundle on his back.

"Away from here. I'm leaving the tower. For good."

"What do you mean?" Marina asked.

"I mean I'm leaving," he repeated. "And let's not make a scene, okay? We all knew it had to happen sooner or later. This isn't the place for me. You know it as well as I do."

"And where are you going?" Hector asked. It didn't surprise him to realize that he didn't really care whether Adrian stayed or not.

The boy shrugged his shoulders.

"I don't know. Here and there, I guess. There's so much to see in Rocavarancolia, and I don't want to miss anything."

"He beat you, right?" Ricardo said. He'd been studying him with the same intensity that he devoted to texts when he was translating. "You've been training for so long, and when you finally find him, he wipes the floor with you."

"I almost won," Adrian replied.

"But you didn't. He still has the upper hand, right? And you think it's because he's been on his own in the city since the beginning? That's why you're leaving? You want to toughen up like him?"

"You're wrong on all counts. My leaving has nothing to do with that kid. Last night I made a mistake. It wasn't the right moment to confront him. I was wrong and I admit it, but I'm not bothered. My time will come."

"You're going to wait for the Red Moon to rise," Marina said. "Then you'll look for him."

Adrian smiled. It was clear that the idea of transformation excited him. He wasn't afraid of the Red Moon. One only had to see how his eyes shone at the very mention of it to know that he was longing for its arrival.

"It's the city that sets the pace," he said. "You still can't hear it, but you will, you'll see. Rocavarancolia sings, and we dance to its rhythm."

"Maybe I should leave too," Bruno added. He'd taken off his top hat and spun it in his hands. "That way you'll be free from my influence. Given what has happened, my presence here is doing nothing but putting you all in grave danger. Maybe the best thing would be to move to the tower in the square. There I could continue my investigations but not be too far—"

"What are you talking about?!" Madeleine whirled toward him, provoking an uneasy growl from Lizbeth. "Have you forgotten what happened underground? We'd all be dead without you!"

"No. You're not going," Hector said, definitively. "We need you. You and your spells."

"But you don't need me for anything," cut in Adrian. He took a bow, bending low and waving his left arm. The bracelets and pendants that he wore jingled with the movement. "I'm going. Rocavarancolia calls, and it's not polite to make her wait any longer. She's been waiting for me for a long time. Obviously I'll stop by to visit you from time to time . . . As long as nothing kills me out there, of course."

Natalia groaned and pressed herself even harder into the wall.

"Are you sure of what you're doing?" Ricardo asked.

Adrian looked at him with uncertainty, then shook his head, let out a loud laugh devoid of humor, and hurried out of the dungeon. When he passed by Natalia he flipped his hair dramatically. The Russian stared daggers at him, but said nothing. She was pale and her hands trembled.

"He's crazy," Marina said after they'd heard him go up the stairs. "That's what's happening: he's crazy."

"Well, let him take his craziness far away," Natalia snarled. "We don't need it here."

When they left the dungeons, Lizbeth began to howl. It was a plaintive and terrible sound, similar to the one from the mountains, but not muffled by distance. It was deafening to hear it so close. Bruno turned, brandished his staff, and, after waving it toward the door, began chanting a spell that they'd never heard him perform before. As he went on, Lizbeth's howl grew quieter. When she was silent, Bruno lowered his staff, reached an arm before him, and traced a strange arabesque with his fingers.

"What did you do to her? How did you make her quiet?" Marina asked.

Bruno shook his head in his robotic, precise way.

"I created a wall of silence on the door of the dungeon, and then I anchored the spell to her so that it doesn't dissipate. Lizbeth will keep howling inside, but we will not be able to hear her."

"Thank heavens . . ." Natalia said.

Hector looked back as he climbed the stairs. He wasn't the only one. The door that led to the dungeons was closed and thanks to Bruno's spell, not the slightest sound crossed through it. But Lizbeth was there, howling, chained to the wall.

*Everything is fragile and fleeting*, Hector thought. He felt kind of dizzy. *Everything's always just one step away from collapsing . . .* He focused on Madeleine, in front of him on the stairs. Every one of her steps, as always, was elegant and sublime, a dance step in time to music that only she seemed to hear. Hector's eyes followed the smoothness of her arm as she braced it against the wall. Madeleine was beauty incarnate. *It doesn't matter how many doors we close or how many spells protect us: the Red Moon will tear us all to pieces.*


After three days of waiting in vain for Marco's return, Hector decided that it was time to go looking for him. Since Rachel's death, the only one who had left the Margalar Tower and not returned had been

Adrian. The others didn't seem to want to go back into the city, and it was easy for Hector to understand why. That tower was their only oasis in the midst of the constant threat that was Rocavarancolia. The temptation to stay indoors and leave only when absolutely necessary was too strong.

"We can't wait any longer," he said. "We have to try to find Marco. Or at least try to find out what happened to him."

They were eating at the table in the courtyard, all except for Madeleine, who'd gone down to see Lizbeth and still hadn't returned. The redhead spent hours in the dungeons. At first, Hector had had qualms about her spending so much time alone with the wolf. Even though deep down he knew that Lizbeth wouldn't hurt her, he couldn't help thinking that if something did happen, they wouldn't be able to hear her from the other side of Bruno's wall of silence. But Madeleine was immovable, and he had no choice but to give in.

"He's dead," Marina said, pushing away the plate of food that she'd barely touched. "If Marco's not here, it's because he's dead. He's not coming back and we're not going to find him, no matter how hard we look."

For some time now, the dark mood that had taken over his friend had ceased to surprise him. In fact, at that moment, he shared her pessimism. There were so many questions surrounding Marco's behavior, but he was starting to suspect that they'd never be answered. Even so, alive or dead, they had to try to find him. They owed it to him. And not just that. Hour by hour he watched the others' spirits decline. It was hard not to give in to the temptation to just let go, to surrender to grief and pass the time feeling sorry for themselves. But he couldn't let that happen.

They needed to leave the tower, face Rocavarancolia once again, not allow the darkness to be the end of them. Looking for Marco would give them a reason to live.

Curiously, it was Bruno who fueled their hopes of finding him alive.

"You are wrong, Marina," he said. He'd opened his grandfather's watch at one end of the table and was fiddling with its insides while he ate. "If he were dead, I would know it," he pointed out. "I would see him in my dreams, and that has not happened. He is still alive, I'm sure of it. What we need to find out is what's keeping him away from the tower."

"I don't want to go out there," Natalia said, her voice so soft that the only one who heard her was Hector, seated at her side. She looked at him out of the corner of her eye and shook her head. "No, I don't want to leave."

"You can stay in the tower if you want," he told her. "No one will say anything."

Natalia hung her head and snorted.

"I don't want to stay here either," she said.

They left the following day, just after dawn. An oppressive silence loomed over them as soon as they crossed the tower gate. The only hint of color in the group was the green of Bruno's top hat and over-coat; the others dressed in plain, dark clothing, muted blacks and grays. It was clear that the Italian had permanently adopted that attire. The day before, Maddie had asked him why he insisted on wearing that same clothing. He took off his top hat and looked inside, as if it might contain the answer.

"I like it. It's just a matter of aesthetics." Hector thought he noticed a slight hesitation in his voice, as if he were keeping something to him-self, something he didn't dare to confess.

"Whatever. But wash it once in a while or you'll stink."

Bruno then said three words, shook his left hand twice, and his clothing regained the crisp, bright quality that it had lost over the last few days. The stains disappeared without a trace, and even the tiniest wrinkle was instantly straightened out.

"That won't be a problem in the least," he stated.

When he saw him cast that simple spell Hector understood the real reason behind the clothes. They made him look like a magician. Not a wizard from a book or movie, but rather an illusionist from a fair or a vaudeville performer: the type of magician who went onstage, just like he went onstage every night in his dreams.

As soon as they left the drawbridge, the gap that Rachel had left in the group became apparent. Her absence had somehow been diluted within the walls of the tower, but outside it was painfully obvious. Rachel had always headed their marches, and now that emptiness in front was drummed into them with every step that they took. After a few moments of hesitation where no one seemed to want to take the lead, Hector stepped up. Luckily for him, Ricardo and Bruno recalled the places where Rachel had detected magic quite faithfully. And when his own memory or his friends' recollections weren't enough, he had the warning mist to alert him.

They started out at the palace and its surroundings; they thought maybe something had compelled Marco to return to the scene of the tragedy. Only Bruno and Ricardo dared to go in; the others waited outside, sitting on the steps, their backs to the building, avoiding the sight of it. Their friends returned over an hour later, and had found no trace of Marco inside. They devoted the rest of the day to exploring the northeastern part of Rocavarancolia.

They wandered for hours through ruined streets and plazas, in the shadows of shacks, twisted towers, and derelict mansions covered in crystallized ivy; they walked through gardens with blackened soil marked by the footprints of dragons and giants, and they peered into seemingly bottomless pits of fleeting swirls of light.

It didn't take Hector long to realize the futility of their search. Rocavarancolia was enormous and was so full of nooks and hideouts that only a miracle would lead them to find Marco. He could be any-where; they could have passed him within inches without noticing. But Hector refused to give up. He had to keep the group moving. A futile search was a thousand times better than staying at the Margalar Tower, doing nothing.

From time to time, Bruno levitated above the ruined buildings and scrutinized the city below, his green coattails flapping behind him, his hands on his top hat to keep it from blowing away.

"Are there any spells you could use to find people, or anything like that?" Hector asked, when he landed after one of his ascensions.

"There are. I have five searching and tracking spells cataloged, but all of them are beyond my abilities."

The second search day was as fruitless as the first. They scoured the eastern part of the city, without reaching the cliffs or crossing the crack that split Rocavarancolia in two. They returned to the gigantic statues' enclosure, and the beauty that so dazzled them upon discovery now only made them nervous. They looked sidelong at the statues, as if waiting for some new trap to jump out and ensnare them.

By late afternoon they'd reached the amphitheater where Caleb and his hyenas lived. The beasts began to growl from their corrals as soon as the kids passed through the gates. Three of them were already approaching menacingly when Caleb appeared, eyes bulging out of his sockets, terrified they'd come to finish what they'd started weeks before. It was Marina who asked him about Marco.

"The big kid with dark skin who was with us. Have you seen him?"

"I don't see anything. I don't know anything. Nothing." He'd wrapped his arms around a hyena's neck and looked at them in horror. "I don't know. I don't know. The children come and go. And I never know a thing. It's not Caleb's fault that he doesn't know. Please, don't hurt Caleb's children just because Caleb is stupid, please, my children don't . . ."

Their hopes of finding Marco alive were dealt a swift blow on the third day, when they decided to search the area by the cliffs and the lighthouse. They were walking around the edge of the cliff, inspecting from above the shifting chaos of the half-sunken ships, when a voice behind them made them turn around. It was the man with the straight blond hair who they'd run into once before. He carried a large sack on his shoulder and advanced with a strange swaying motion, as if walking on solid ground were difficult for him. Hector couldn't help but focus on the two harpoons he wore crossed at his back.

"You're not looking in the right place," he told them as he headed toward the cliff. His voice was harsh and bitter, the voice of someone who'd lived for many years in absolute silence. "The boy jumped into the Scar of Arax to feed the worms. If you want to find him, maybe look for him there, though I can't say it'll be easy."

Ricardo and Natalia stopped him in his tracks. The girl wielded the halberd with both hands, and the boy had his sword halfway out of its sheath.

"You're lying," Ricardo said. "Marco would never do that."

The blond man revealed his blackened teeth in a mocking grin.

"With everything that's happened to you so far, you still come at me with what someone would or wouldn't do?" He shook his head. "Haven't you learned anything from this city?"

"Marco would never do that," Ricardo insisted.

"Your Marco jumped into the crack the same night that your friend started howling. He probably understood what was coming and decided to end his life. Good for him. And now, get out of my way, or I'll feed you to the mermaids."

For a moment, Ricardo and Natalia remained defiant in front of the man with the harpoons. Hector hurried between them.

"Enough," he said. "Let him go."

"Smart boy," gurgled the man as he went on his way.

Hector wrinkled his nose as he noticed the stench of rotten fish that he gave off. He watched him as he walked away. There was nothing monstrous about him; he was gaunt and dirty, but undoubtedly human. The Red Moon hadn't seemed to have affected him, or if it had caused any changes, they weren't visible on the surface.

He reached the end of the cliff, fastened the sack between the harpoons on his back as if they were a harness, and began to climb down using his bare hands. Hector approached the very edge to observe the peculiar man's progress. He descended the steep cliff face with the agility of a monkey, and actually seemed more comfortable climbing down the cliff than walking on level ground.

The man jumped onto the broken deck of a ship covered with algae and mollusks. Hector shifted his gaze to the lighthouse and wondered if he could be the main character from Marina's story.

"Either he was wrong, or he's lying," Bruno said. He took off his hat and looked inside, a gesture that was becoming familiar to all of them. "He's not dead. If he were, I'd see him in my dreams."

"We'll keep looking for him," Hector assured him. "If he's alive, we'll find him."

Only as he moved away from the edge did he realize that he hadn't felt any vertigo—not for a second—as he looked over the steep decline.

A piercing hum woke Esmael.

He opened his eyes immediately: there was no transition between sleep and waking, not a single moment of confusion. He went from a deep sleep to being completely alert. The black angel hung inverted from one of the exterior platforms of the crystal dome that had been his home as of late. He opened his wings and dropped down. It was late at night in Rocavarancolia, so dark that for a second he thought he was falling into a bottomless abyss. The sky was covered in a thick blanket of clouds that blocked the light from the few stars that shone above the city; not even the light of the Emissary, the brightest of all of them, could penetrate the dense barrier. Esmael caught a rising current and let himself be lifted upward. The hum had ceased once it achieved its goal of getting his attention.

Weeks before, he'd scattered finding spells throughout Rocavarancolia, all with the same target: Mistral. But the damned shapeshifter must have been well protected, and those spells had been nothing more than a useless waste of energy. Many had dissipated with the passing of time, and others had fallen victim to the creatures thirsty for magic that prowled the city; although one, it seemed, had managed to remain active and continue the search.

And now it alerted its creator that its mission was a success. Esmael felt the pulsation of the spell pulling him toward the south. Before his eyes he saw a fine thread of light unfurl. He would find his target at the other end.

He glided over the city, following the winding trail of magic. As he advanced, it became more defined. Either Mistral's protection spells had worn off or the shapeshifter no longer cared if they found him. Esmael flew over the Scar of Arax toward the west, toward its birthplace, to the exact point where His Majesty Sardaurlar had thrust his sword thirty years ago. Something wailed in the distance; it was a weak sound that perfectly matched the gloomy night that loomed over the city. The trail to the shapeshifter ended in the middle of the scar, in a mountain of bones heaped against the north wall of the crevice.

The black angel landed near the scar's edge. He folded his wings and walked right to the brink. The gigantic skull of a warrior mammoth crowned the top of a massive pile of bones; its eye sockets were like blind suns that watched him with apathy. He looked down. Yes, without a doubt: Mistral's trail led inside.

Esmael made himself intangible and jumped into the crevice. The worms of Arax posed no danger to him, but he wanted no interruptions during his search. Crossing the skeletons of the scar gave him an unpleasant, suffocating sensation. It was hard to concentrate on the trail with so much death spread out around him. But there he was, sparkling among jawbones and skulls, staggering between tibias and rib cages.

*This is where death lies at a standstill, this is where we'll all end up sooner or later,* thought Esmael as the bones of the dead passed through his own. He shook his head to free it from such dismal thoughts and concentrated on the pull of the spell.

He followed it to an opening in the bottom of the scar; it was wide enough that he could pass through it in a solid state, but he didn't resolidify until he crossed to the other side. The opening led to a curve of one of the many passages that ran underground in Rocavarancolia. The shapeshifter's trail continued along the stone path, heading west.

He moved through the passageway after the faint thread of light. He walked clinging to the ceiling like an enormous insect. He disliked entering the city's web of underground tunnels. His wings weren't made for those narrow pathways and he felt constricted, out of his element. He remembered the skirmish that had taken place in tunnels similar to those during the battle of Rocavarancolia, when he confronted the traitor Alastor, who was guiding enemy forces toward one of the war towers. Esmael had been close to death dozens of times over the long defense of the city, but he was never so close as on that occasion.

The darkness around him was gray and unpleasant, the air so dry that it was devoid of any aroma. Maybe he was walking into a trap, similar to the one that the unknown sorcerer had laid for Enoch, only this time maybe he'd used Mistral's trail as bait instead of mermaid blood. But Esmael wasn't a stupid vampire blinded by hunger: he was a black angel, one of the deadliest creatures the world had ever known; no, if this were a trap, he wouldn't be caught off guard.

To Esmael's relief, the stone passageway led to a wide hallway, lit up by a foggy emerald light. He dropped from the ceiling and crouched in the entryway, alert. Mistral's trail ended inside.

Esmael recognized the space as one of the many storehouses of food that were scattered throughout the city. The rows of stacked-up barrels had long since come tumbling down and most of the casks had shattered on the ground. Red spiderwebs covered the walls and the top part of the arcade that led to the hall, adding to the chaos. The only source of light came from the phosphorescent abdomens of the spiders as they napped in their webs. The ceiling wasn't very tall and lay just below the Scar of Arax; the bones that had fallen through its cracks were piled in heaps on the floor of the grotto.

Mistral sat on the largest of these mounds. He rocked slowly, forward and back, his legs bent in such a way that he rested his chin on his knees. Esmael couldn't remember the last time that he'd seen a shapeshifter in its original form. It was a rare occurrence: shapeshifters abhorred their true bodies and did their best to hide them. Esmael understood. There was something extremely pathetic in their appearance. Maybe it was their likeness to a dull plaything, a hastily assembled doll . . . All shapeshifters without exception looked like crude marionettes made out of long white cords, laced together to form something almost humanoid. They never stood more than five feet tall, although they looked very compact, as if it took hundreds of feet of rope to give them form. Mistral was smaller than average, just over four feet tall, and looked even smaller still atop the mountain of bones.

Esmael approached slowly, looking disapprovingly at the dusty and abandoned room. Several dozen albino scorpions scurried out of one cask, swarmed around frantically, and then equally frantically returned to their barrel once it was clear that Esmael was not suitable prey.

"What do you think you're doing here, Mistral?" asked the black angel.

The shapeshifter looked at him, surprised. His face was composed of woven white strings that tried to imitate human features. The nose was several poorly tied knots; the mouth was no more than an empty space between two taut cords connected at the ends; the eyes, two sunken holes that seemed deliberately dug out to reflect a desperate melancholy. Mistral, without taking his eyes off Esmael, plunged his long braided fingers into his chest and rummaged around for a minute.

"Woe is me. I forgot to recharge my shield spells," he mumbled apathetically. He'd extracted a metallic amulet in the shape of a hexagon from his thoracic cavity. He sighed, threw it away, and resumed his rocking.

Esmael waited several seconds before insisting again.

"What are you doing here?"

"Waiting for everything to collapse," the shapeshifter answered, still rocking. "This is as good a place as any to wait for the end of the world.

Do you want to join me? There's plenty of room and abundant provisions—if you don't have anything against bats and rats, that is."

"Humor is not one of your few virtues. Don't go down that road. I asked you a simple question, and I want a clear answer."

"I already told you: I'm waiting for the end. There's no hope, Esmael. Our world is collapsing. And although it's the least that we deserve, I don't want to watch it happen. Call me a wimp if you like. Or a coward. I don't care. I'm staying here. Where I can't hurt anyone and where no one can hurt me. Unless that's exactly why you've come . . . Have you come to kill me, Lord of Assassins?"

"Kill you? What utter foolishness. You're a member of the council, and you've been missing for months. That's why I'm here. I was looking for you."

"Are you worried about me?" Mistral asked sarcastically.

"If you're trying to irritate me, you're doing a good job," he growled. "No, I wasn't worried about you. I wanted to know if you were alive or dead, yes, but not because I'm the least bit interested in your health. Let me say this again: you're a member of the Royal Council of Rocavarancolia. That means you have certain responsibilities to fulfill. And if you can't honor them, another must take your place." *Someone I can persuade that I'm a better choice for the regency than that appalling Lady Scar,* he might have added.

"Responsibilities!" exclaimed the shapeshifter. "Our world is crumbling, and you come to me about responsibilities? There's no hope, Esmael. You should know better than anyone. Rocavarancolia is finished."

"Just a couple of weeks ago you would have been right, yes. But every day the Red Moon is closer to emerging, and there are still children left alive."

"They will die. They will all die. One after the other, until not a single one is left. And that will be the best thing that could happen to us. Listen to me, we deserve extinction. We've earned it, pure and simple. We're evil and perverse, murderous and depraved . . . We're monsters. Monsters!" Mistral hit the ground in rage. "And nothing we can do will ever change that," he added bitterly.

It was then that Esmael saw the clothes. They were wrapped up on the ground, very close to where Mistral sat. It only took him a second to recognize them. It was the suit that Marco had worn to the party that had ended so badly for Denestor's kids, the same white suit in which he'd jumped into the Scar of Arax. And as soon as he saw it, Esmael knew where Mistral had been over the last few months and what he'd been doing. The realization sent a shiver down his spine. He blinked, shook his head, and looked at the shapeshifter, his bewilderment plain on his face. Mistral kept his head down, never looking at him, still unaware that he'd been found out. The next realization left Esmael as stunned as the first: Denestor knew about this and was protecting the shapeshifter. How many others were in on the conspiracy, Esmael wondered. Lady Scar? Lady Serena?

He took a deep breath. The consequences of all this began to play out with crystal clarity in his mind. For the first time in thirty years, Esmael's pulse quickened. He'd never been so close to fulfilling his dreams, he realized. He had only to drag that pathetic creature before the regent and make him confess, and thereby change the direction of the kingdom's future government. Huryel would have no mercy. He couldn't—the laws of Rocavarancolia were very clear regarding interference with the harvest. All of those implicated would be exiled to the desert. Lady Scar might not be a part of it—though he doubted that—but her aspirations toward the regency would fall apart with the expulsion of Mistral and Denestor from the council.

He shifted his glance from the heap of clothing to watch the shapeshifter, who kept rocking, indifferent to the black angel's long silence. The regency awaited him, and then . . . Esmael couldn't believe his luck. It made him dizzy just thinking about it. Without a doubt, the situation would be dangerous and complicated. Huryel wouldn't be content with exiling those guilty of interfering with the harvest. He'd also have no choice but to terminate all of the harvest contaminated by their influence. Every last child from the Margalar Tower would be executed. Only Dario would remain alive, the eternal loner. But the Brazilian's essence was strong, and would be more than enough to open the vortices again. A new beginning for the kingdom, with him in charge: just what he'd always wanted.

It would be risky, he knew that. All of Rocavarancolia's hopes would rest on one single boy. There were less than two months before the Red Moon came out, and if Dario survived until then, everything would be fine . . . And besides, he'd be the one protecting him from the shadows, as he'd done so many times, as he'd done the night that Dario almost died from blood loss after his duel with Adrian. For decades he'd been using his stealth and skill for killing, but he had no difficulty whatsoever using them now to protect the boy's life.

Suddenly Mistral raised his old doll's head and stared at him. Esmael smiled scornfully. The time had come; the hour had come to take the fate of the kingdom in his hands. However, just as he was going to announce to Mistral that his foolish conspiracy had been revealed, the shapeshifter spoke:

"Do you remember your name, black angel?" he asked. Esmael blinked, confused. He hadn't expected a question like that. "The name you had before they brought you here. Do you remember it?" Mistral moved his braided head from one side to the other while he continued his manic rocking. "Because I've been trying to remember mine for days . . . my real name, and I can't . . ."

"My name's always been Esmael," he answered. He looked at the balled-up clothing out of the corner of his eye, as if he were afraid it might have vanished while Mistral distracted him with his bizarre question. "I didn't see a reason to change it," he added.

Traditionally, the majority of those transformed by the Red Moon changed their name shortly after; it was a way of breaking with their old life. If he remembered correctly, he was the only one of his harvest that decided to keep his name. He was too proud to discard his past. It might have been insignificant compared to all that awaited him in Rocavarancolia, but it was his.

"I remember the day that we, the shapeshifters, chose our names." Mistral had stopped rocking. Now he remained still, his dark, hollow eyes staring vacantly. "We met in front of Rocavaragalago and threw all of our belongings, to the very last, into the lava. We stood naked in front of the cathedral and we renounced our names. There were four of us: Mistral, Alisios, Lady Breeze, and Hurricane . . . I don't know whose idea it was . . . *Winds of change*, someone said, *the winds of change are blowing . . . We'll adapt to them.*" He sighed. "And those damned winds took them all. They killed Alisios when she tried to infiltrate the court of a linked world, posing as a chamberlain. Lady Breeze and Hurricane died in the battle for the city. Their remains are in the Scar of Arax; I carried Lady Breeze there myself. She unraveled in my arms."

Esmael remembered the nauseating feeling that had seized him as he crossed through the skeletons in the scar. A shiver ran down his spine and split when it reached the stem of his wings; it was a bolt of ice that left him frozen. There was the possibility, although negligible and remote, that he had just crossed over the bones of one of his friends.

He thought of Dionysius, the gigantic drunk with the eternally tearful eyes, with whom he'd shared a tent during the conquest of the world Alfilgris. He always carried a studded mace with him. He didn't let it out of his sight even when he slept. He loved it so much that he'd even given it a name; Esmael tried to remember what it was, but he couldn't. Dionysius had died in the first charge from the enemy armies. An ogre on horseback snatched the mace from his hands and crushed his face with it.

He remembered Lady Fiera, radiant and wild Fiera, a black angel like himself; he remembered how she laughed, as if each bout of laughter could create a new, perfect world. She had taken him under her wing after his transformation and had helped him familiarize himself with his new body. With time he'd surpassed her, both in power and in the hierarchy of the kingdom, but that didn't matter: the link forged between them was too strong to allow ambition or envy to test them. Lady Fiera had died defending the south of the city from Balgor's hordes of dragons. When she fell she was so drenched in blood that she yelled, between peals of laughter, that she'd transformed into a red angel.

The list of names was unending: Malazul, Coldmouth, Dorna, Sandor, Lady Hyena, Valaka, Drog . . . All had died in the last defense of the kingdom. Glorin, Tajnada, Lady Lenta, Lady Essence . . . Esmael shifted his gaze back to the heap of clothing, and suddenly it seemed extremely risky to entrust the fate of the kingdom to one boy alone. Two months was a long time, even longer in Rocavarancolia.

"We lost many in that battle," he affirmed in a hoarse voice. Something in his tone aroused the shapeshifter's interest.

"I'd already lost what was most important a long time before, Esmael," he said. "I lost my name, my true name, and with it all the good that there once was in me. And now I renounce the one I have.

No, I don't want to be Mistral. I give you my name, murderer. Do with it what you will. Throw it into the moat at Rocavaragalago, if that's your wish. Let it burn. Let us all burn."

Esmael stared at the shapeshifter for a while without saying a word. Once more, he tried to recall what Dionysius's mace was called, but he couldn't. He groaned, frustrated, and looked around him. A river of death flowed above his head. And every last one of the skeletons that lay between the broken walls of the Scar of Arax had once had a name, every one of them: from the most vile and despicable creature to the most noble and valiant, from those who gave their lives for the kingdom to those who did the same trying to destroy it. But, in the end, names were nothing more than words, lifeless characters. What was truly important was that all of those cold bones had at one time been surrounded by flesh, beating hearts that pumped blood through veins, eyes which looked at all of creation, hands to touch with . . . All of that death had once been alive.

The regency could wait, he decided. There was no need to report the shapeshifter immediately. He would wait until the Red Moon was imminent to visit Huryel and reveal Mistral and Denestor's conspiracy. The temptation was strong, but he would wait. He owed it to Lady Fiera, to Dionysius, to Coldmouth, to Glorin . . . and not just them. He owed it to all of the kingdom's dead, all those who perished for its glory. He couldn't fail them. He couldn't let his own ambition cause Rocavarancolia's ruin.

He slowly left the passageway, without saying goodbye to the shape-shifter, who still rocked in the greenish darkness, oblivious to his exit. When Esmael made himself intangible to ascend to the surface, he was very careful not to cross the Scar of Arax again. He didn't want to feel any bones inside his body other than his own.

It was over a week before Adrian showed his face again at the tower. They'd crossed paths with him several times while they searched for Marco, so they hadn't had reason to worry. From what he told them, he simply wandered from one place to another. He wanted to see it all, he assured them; he didn't want to miss a thing. Hector wondered how long it would be before he showed up in Bruno's dreams.

He was waiting for them at the tower when they returned after yet another day of fruitless searching. He sat at a table on the ground floor, a book open in front of him and three others piled up by his side.

"I want to keep learning magic," he told them. The greetings they'd exchanged had not been very effusive, but Adrian didn't seem to mind. "And as hard as I try I can't find a single book of magic in the whole city, at least not one written in a language I can understand. I've taken the liberty of choosing a few from the library. I hope you won't mind lending them to me for a while," he said, looking at Bruno. "I give my word that I'll return them in the same condition."

"You could have taken them just like that, right?" Natalia said.

"Who do you think I am? That wouldn't have been polite at all."

"It's not polite to go to someone's place when they're not home and start searching through their things, either."

"You should do something about that temper of yours, Natalia. One day you'll blow a vein."

"If you've decided to leave the tower, that's it: you've left. Come visit if you like, but do it when we're here."

Bruno thoroughly inspected Adrian's books. He didn't normally limit access to the small library that he'd compiled over the last few months, but he did like to maintain strict control over the whereabouts of each book. For a whole week he'd turned the tower upside down just to find a study on magical cats that Natalia had misplaced. They finally found it at the bottom of a laundry basket.

Hector watched the Italian with concern as he examined the books. Bruno was pale, and with each passing day he seemed increasingly tired, but not without reason. He didn't just participate in the search for Marco with the others; he also reviewed his books over and over again in search of spells that he might have overlooked that would help them find their friend. But it wasn't just Marco that occupied his time; he was dedicated to learning about lycanthropy and other transformations to try to find a way to reverse Lizbeth from her beastly state, and he also needed to prepare for what might happen when the Red Moon came out. Not a day passed that he didn't try a new spell on the wolf, but so far all of his experiments had failed. Hector urged him to slow down a little when he found him passed out in the dungeon one morning.

"You're going to wear yourself out," he scolded him sternly. "And we can't risk anything happening to you. You're too important to us."

"That's exactly why I'm doing what I'm doing, Hector. Given the circumstances, I'm the most qualified to find a solution. Don't you agree?"

"And what if there isn't a solution?" he asked him, as he looked at the caged beast.

Bruno was silent for some time before answering:

"There is. There has to be. And I swear that I will find it."

The Italian placed the books that Adrian had requested one on top of the other and nodded his head mechanically.

"You can take them," he announced, after a few moments. "Although I should warn you that only one will be truly useful to you. The spells and incantations compiled in the others are completely out of our reach." He put one hand on the thickest book on the table, a book covered in creased red leather. "And this isn't a book of magic," he said. "It is a treatise on dragons, with no useful sorcery within its pages."

"Well, not everything has to be about studying, right?" Adrian said, smiling from ear to ear. "Let me amuse myself with something."

He left shortly after. It seemed he wanted to spend the night in a turret full of mysterious noises that he'd found near the square with the serpent fountain.

Soon after Adrian left the tower, Hector approached Natalia. Adrian's visit and Bruno's clear state of exhaustion had been food for thought, and he needed to discuss something with her.

The Russian was sitting on a chair at the opposite end of the tower, with her feet propped up and her chin resting on her knees. Her eyes were half-closed and she held a piece of meat in her hand that she nibbled at listlessly from time to time.

"Do you have a minute?" he asked her.

"Yes, but just one," she responded sharply. "As soon as I finish eating, I'm heading to bed. I'm worn out from all of this moving back and forth. When are we going to stop looking for Marco?"

"When we find him."

"What a waste of time," she griped.

"It's what we have to do. He would do the same for us, don't you think?"

"No, he wouldn't. Think back: he left, Hector. Marco left. He abandoned us. And do you know something? I think the guy with the harpoons is right. I think Marco understood what was going to happen to us as soon as he saw what happened to Lizbeth and he decided that the best thing was to kill himself. And he went to that horrible place and jumped."

"Do you really think that?" he asked in a worried voice. She shrugged her shoulders.

"Who knows? I'm so tired I can't even think. I went to the pantry to get some fruit, and look what I brought back." She shook the meat in her hand, and a light rain of grease fell on the table. "A piece of who knows what . . ."

Hector smiled and sat next to her. Marina watched them from the other end of the tower, but he looked away immediately, without allowing his gaze to cross hers. Soon after he heard the girl walking upstairs.

"What do you want?" Natalia asked, suspicious.

"To talk to you." He rubbed his chin before continuing. "I know that you don't like magic, but the way things are, it would be good if we had another mage. Adrian's gone and we can't depend on Bruno for everything."

The others were still useless when it came to magic, and it wasn't for lack of trying.

On every attempt, Hector felt a boiling of strange energies inside him that never seemed to reach fruition. He recited the words and performed the appropriate gestures, just as they were explained in the books, but right as he neared the end, when he could feel the spell activating just beneath the surface, it fizzled out to nothing.

"You know it's really hard for me to learn a single spell," Natalia said, frowning.

"I know, but I also know that you do end up learning them. Look at where we are now and everything that's going on. We're going to need all the help we can get, and we can't afford to let anything slide. I'm not asking you to reach Bruno's level, just that you learn some basic spells that could help us in a pinch."

Natalia hung her head.

"I don't know, Hector . . ." she said quietly. She ran a hand through her hair and huffed. "I don't know what to tell you. Especially not now, when I'm so tired . . . I promise I'll think about it, okay?" And without saying another word or giving him a chance to speak, she got up from her chair and left.

Hector watched her disappear up the stairs, looked up at the ceiling, and sighed, dejected.

"It's not easy being the boss, is it?" Ricardo asked him. He was sitting with Bruno at a table nearby, charging talismans while the Italian remained silently buried in a book, so deeply focused that he seemed worlds away.

"What are you talking about?" he asked, turning toward him. "I'm not the boss of anything."

"Whatever you say," Ricardo said with a smile on his lips.

# FREAKS AND WONDERS

Days passed by, and still they found no trace of Marco. They explored every inch of the prison where they'd woken up so long ago: they went from dungeon to dungeon, sticking together as a group, peering through the cracks in the walls, wandering through the outskirts of the burning neighborhood, trying to ignore the screams of the unfortunate wretches trapped there. They walked around the chasms that opened up northeast of the city, and although it took all their courage, they also approached the immense red cathedral of Rocavaragalago. The mere vision of that gigantic building made from lunar rock made their hearts shrink: the tall striated walls rose up toward the cloudy sky with abominable coldness. They didn't find anything there either.

"And what if something dragged him underground?" Marina asked, the morning that they passed near the point where the monstrous bat had caught her.

"No!" Natalia turned toward Hector, frightened. "You're not thinking of making us go back down to that awful place again, right?"

"What chance would Marco have of surviving on his own down there?" Ricardo asked.

"None," Hector answered. He looked at Marina out of the corner of his eye and remembered how he'd climbed down behind her without once stopping to consider the possible risks. Everything was different now. The caverns underneath the city were something they could rule out completely. Going down there was tempting fate, and he wasn't up for letting that happen. But a little voice inside his head dared to ask, *And what if Marina disappeared down there again? Wouldn't you drag everyone to go after her?*

*No, I wouldn't,* he answered, and knowing that was true was disheartening.

On the afternoon of the eighth day of their search, the group headed toward the cemetery in Rocavarancolia. Until then they'd done everything possible to avoid that place, but their options were running out. Hector had no choice but to be consistent and proceed to that area. When it became clear where they were going, he noticed that everyone grew uneasy.

Hector could still recall the look on their faces when he'd described the mausoleum where Lady Scar had carried Rachel.

"It can't be." Marina shook her head when she heard it. "An unfinished mausoleum? No. It's impossible. That's not the tomb from my story."

That error in the script—that mistake in Marina's prophetic tale—cast an even darker shadow over the group's mood. Since then the topic of the cemetery had become taboo. No one talked about visiting their friend's tomb or mentioned the possibility of looking for Marco there. At first, Hector thought that his friends' behavior was because they didn't want to confront that half-constructed tomb, that mockery of fate: knowing about it wasn't the same as having to see it with their own eyes. Then he realized that the explanation was even simpler. Visiting Rachel's tomb for the first time would mean accepting that she was dead.

A flock of black birds followed them on their slow journey toward the cemetery, harassing them with their cackling. When they were less than a hundred yards away from the hollow, Marina stopped, raised her bow, and, without bothering to aim, shot an arrow into the cloud of birds. One of them fell, pierced right through. The rest immediately fell silent and changed direction. Marina put her bow away, brushed her hair from her eyes, and continued on. Hector had never seen her so serious and somber.

The appearance of the silk cocoon took them all by surprise. It was like a huge white finger pointing to the sky.

"What the heck is that?" Ricardo asked.

Marina's eyes opened wide when she saw the strange white structure. She shook her head, incredulous, and announced in a voice charged with intense emotion:

"That's the tomb from my story."

Hector watched the incredible construction rise up before their eyes as they went down the slope that led to the hollow. It was an actual tower made from spiderwebs. It was over sixty feet tall, and, although its appearance was somewhat inconsistent, it was clearly solid. Six horns curved upward from the top, also made from spiderwebs, although much more compact than the rest of the structure.

They walked toward it, escorted by the voices of the dead buried in the cemetery.

"Visits from the kingdom of the living! Brush your skulls and shine your rib cages! Make your skeletons sparkle!"

"Colors. I can't remember them. I've forgotten them. What color was the sky? Green? Was it green? Someone, please do me the favor of telling me what color the sky was?"

"In the cavern there was an iridescent dragon. I'd never seen anything so beautiful. It was the last thing I saw, that's for sure. But it was worth it. Yes, living was worth it, if only to see the magnificent creature that killed me."

They stopped in front of the silk arcade that led inside the mausoleum. Blankets of web hung down from up above, delicate curtains that together formed the exterior walls of the unprecedented construction. Two of the curtains fell over the arcade entryway, acting as a double door. Hector unsheathed his sword and pushed one of them aside. After ensuring that the weapon's blade didn't stick to the web, he tested the consistency of the second curtain with his hand. The idea that they could get stuck to that thing so that the spider could later make a feast of them was too disconcerting to ignore. The webbing was soft and not at all sticky. It even felt pleasant to the touch. He remembered that long nighttime journey with the spider at his back, walking in silence, always a few yards away. He shook his head. What would make a being like that create a monument such as this? He didn't understand.

They entered one at a time, in silence. Natalia stayed behind the others. She stopped shortly after going through the silk doors, looking at everything with wide eyes. The light of day was scarcely visible through the silk walls, and a melancholy darkness spilled out into the corners. When Hector's eyes adjusted to the shadows, he could see that stalactites of spun silk hung from the ceiling. He couldn't say if he liked that construction or not. The presence of the tomb and what it contained kept him from making a judgment one way or another. But one thing was indisputable: that was the most striking monument in all of the cemetery.

The teenagers gathered in a circle around the tomb. Only Natalia remained at the entrance, her arms wrapped around herself. They looked at one another, uncertain, not sure of what to do next. Should they improvise some kind of ceremony? Say a few words in honor of Rachel? With Alexander they hadn't done anything of the sort, but he hadn't left a body for them to honor.

Suddenly Bruno placed the palm of his hand on the silk covering the tomb. Madeleine, after a moment's hesitation, placed hers on top of the Italian's. Hector was the next to follow suit. Then it was Ricardo and Marina's turn. Hector looked at Natalia, still in the doorway. The girl let out an anxious sigh and began walking slowly toward them. It was clear that every step required a great deal of effort. She finally reached the tomb and placed her hand on top of the others'.

They remained silent for some time, barely moving, their eyes fixed on the web that covered Rachel's tomb. She was there, only a few inches away, cold and still, dead in the darkness. Hector closed his eyes. *Can she feel our warmth?* he wondered. *Does she know that we're here with her?*

"If something happens to me, I want to be cremated," Ricardo said suddenly. "And then throw my ashes in the sea." He turned his head toward Bruno. "I'm sure that wouldn't be very difficult for you to do, right? Walking through the air, I mean, and scattering my ashes out away from the shipwrecked boats . . ." The Italian shook his head. Ricardo smiled and kept talking. "My mother loved the sea . . . When she died we spread her ashes in a small cove near where we spent the summers. Who knows, maybe the magical currents of this world will take me back to her someday."

"I do not have the least interest in what happens with my body once I am dead," Bruno said. "It is only a body. Why should I worry about it once I'm done using it?"

"We'll stuff you and stick you on top of the tower," Marina said.

"Nobody will know the difference," Ricardo claimed.

Maddie let out a giggle. Hector smiled. It was the first time he'd heard her laugh since the night at the palace.

"What are you doing? Have you gone crazy?" Natalia took her hand away and looked at them all intently. "Shut up already! Nobody's going to die!"

"We will all die." In the shadows, Hector couldn't see Bruno's eyes as he spoke, but he imagined that his gaze was as icy as ever. "Sooner or later we shall all die. It is an inherent part of life and is common sense. Everything with a beginning has to have an end."

"Bury me here, in the cemetery," Marina said. She had already asked Hector several weeks ago, but now her voice was less solemn than before: more like someone talking about what they wanted to eat the next day or what kind of clothing they were thinking of buying. "Do you think there are other mausoleums without owners? I wouldn't want to be outside here, with all of that chatter day and night. It would give me a headache."

"No! Shut up!" Natalia took a step back, her fists clenched.

"The wind carried my brother away," Madeleine murmured. "It can carry me away, too. Yes, that would be a nice way to go. Cremate me like Ricardo and scatter my ashes throughout the city. From up high. From way up high . . ."

"That's enough! Stop talking about death!"

"Calm down, Natalia," Ricardo said. "No one's planning on dying tomorrow. Don't be afraid. We're just—"

"Just shut up!" she shouted, in hysterics, before running out of the mausoleum. The spiderweb door waved as she passed through, as if saying goodbye.

Hector was the first to react and go after her. Natalia sped down a dirt path, and it took all he had to catch up to her. The dead would not shut up.

"Run, little girl, run! Don't let them trap you! They'll tear out your soul and suck the marrow from your bones! They always do!"

"What a lack of respect! Running through the cemetery! Damn you! Stop reminding us of movement!"

Hector reached her as she was heading for one of the ramps that led out of the hollow. He took her by the arm and made her stop and turn toward him. Tears streamed down the girl's face.

"What's going on?" he asked her. Natalia looked behind Hector, horrified. He spun around but didn't see anything. "It's your shadows. It's not because of Rachel, or the Red Moon. It's the shadows."

"Here everything is darkness and shadow," a corpse murmured sadly.

Natalia gave a tug to free herself from Hector, but instead of running again, she closed her eyes and hung her head.

"They won't leave me alone, you know?" She wept bitterly. "They're everywhere and they're trying to drive me insane."

The others caught up to them. Madeleine and Marina stood behind the girl, while Ricardo and Bruno hung back, close to Hector. The Italian seemed to stare at everything with interest, his head tilted at an angle.

"They growl at me . . . They threaten me," mumbled Natalia. "They appear out of nowhere and whisper horrible things. They leap when I least expect it . . . and just when they're about to reach me they break away and point with their twisted claws. I . . ." She swallowed. Hector pulled her toward him and hugged her tight. "They're everywhere. And they want to hurt me . . . They want to drive me insane. They hate me. I've done them no harm, but they hate me . . ."

Hector was moved when he noticed how fragile the girl was in his arms. At first he'd attributed her behavior to Rachel's death and the revelation of what would happen to them when the Red Moon came out. After what happened in the palace, Natalia had been gloomy and silent, but they'd all been acting that way to some extent since then.

"We'll help you however we can, okay?" Madeleine said. "There must be something we can do to keep those things from stalking you."

"Help me?" Natalia pulled away from Hector and looked at all of them, her face twisted. "What are you going to do to help me if you can't even see them? You can't do anything! Nobody can!"

"We'll try to find out what those creatures are," Bruno assured her. "I have some theories. As soon as we get back to the tower I'll start—"

"But I already know what they are! And that makes it even worse! I know what they are! I know! They're not elves! They're not shadows! They're ghosts! Do you hear me? They're ghosts!"

"Ghosts?" Marina asked. "What do you mean?"

Natalia grabbed her wrists and began twisting them, visibly nervous. She looked around, away from the group. Her lower lip trembled. Hector wondered what monsters she might be seeing just then and shuddered. The girl closed her eyes.

"I found out the night at the palace," she began. "When . . . When it happened . . . When Lizbeth killed . . . There was something else, something you didn't see . . . At the same time that Rachel fell to the ground, on the ceiling, right on top of her . . ." She spoke so haltingly that it was hard to follow the thread of what she was saying. ". . . A hole opened up in the air, as if the world was torn open. And the shadow emerged through that hole . . . First the arms came out, so long that it seemed like they'd never end. One after the other, so many that I lost count . . . Then the rest of the body came through, black and swollen . . . It was something repulsive, slimy and dense; it was like smoke, like liquid smoke, if that's even possible . . . When it came all the way through, it clung to the ceiling, looked at me with rage, and jumped out of sight." She opened her eyes and faced the group, swiping at the tears that ran down her face. "It appeared right when Rachel died! What can it be but a ghost? Rachel's ghost! And it hated me!"

"Your assumption is understandable, Natalia, but those entities are not ghosts," Bruno said. She looked at him with a furrowed brow. "If you will allow me to explain, I think I am in a position to shed some light on the nature of those creatures." He brought his hands to the brim of his top hat and turned it around one hundred and eighty degrees before continuing. "You already know that Rocavarancolia is a place that is conducive to crossroads between dimensions. The fabric of reality here is fragile and malleable, and it's relatively easy to break. Hurza and Harex, the city's founders, took advantage of that to open vortices that connected this world with others, and Denestor Tul used that same feature to go to Earth to bring us here. Those shadows of yours, Natalia, are inhabitants of another plane, beings that dwell in the folds between the different dimensions."

"But it showed up when Rachel died . . ."

"Sometimes those types of creatures behave like insects. Just like a moth is attracted to a flame, they're attracted to different phenomena.

It could be that the species stalking you is particularly attracted to death. Maybe every time someone dies in Rocavarancolia a small vortex opens between this world and theirs, and they are forced to cross into this plane. It is just a thought, of course. I would have to investigate the subject further in order to—"

"And why am I the only one who sees them?"

"You are mistaken. You are not the only one who can see them; you are the only one they reveal themselves to openly, which is notably different. Remember that Lizbeth and Hector were both able to see them once. And when that beast attacked you shortly after we came to Rocavarancolia, one of those beings defended you. Marina could see it, although at that time she could not tell exactly what it was."

"Well, what does this all mean? I don't get it! Why do they help me if they hate me?"

"Maybe exactly for that reason," Ricardo ventured. "Maybe they hate you because something stronger than them compels them to help you. And maybe they don't find that all too amusing . . ."

"Oh. What a smart boy, what a feast for the worms your brain will be," a dead voice gurgled from a nearby grave. "Crying girl, scared girl, they hate you because when the Red Moon comes out they'll have no choice but to obey you. That's why they hate you, and that's why they're trying to drive you crazy."

They all turned toward the tomb. It was a large grave made of white stone, cracked on the sides, the slab half-covered with moss. From below, one of the dead spoke:

"They loathe you, they detest you . . ." It was impossible to tell if the voice belonged to a man or a woman. "They'll dance themselves to exhaustion on the day you die . . . Because when the Red Moon comes out they'll be forced to submit to your will. You'll be their mistress, their owner, their lady. The queen of the dark shadows. Some call them onyxes, others call them sibyls . . . What does it matter what their name is? They're the teeming darkness, the death that embraces you, the kiss that suffocates you . . ." Its voice hummed like the buzzing of a thousand insects. "With every violent death, a door opens, and they're forced to go through it. Poor creatures, they're drawn to the violence, but they're unable to find their way back home. That drives them insane. They must stay in a world that isn't theirs until their very essence is stamped out." It let out a demented laugh. "Oh, child, what a powerful witch you'll be when you're bathed in the light of the Red Moon. If only I had eyes to see it!"

"Witch? Me, a witch?"

Bruno hurried over to the tomb.

"Do you know what we are going to become?" he asked the grave's occupant. "Do you know what the Red Moon will transform us into?"

The dead creature didn't answer his question.

"The darkness that trembles, leaps, and kills." In its indescribable voice there was now a trace of nostalgia. "I saw it, did you know, dear children? I was with her when she launched her army of shadows at the bastion of the mad sorcerer who dared to raise arms against the king-dom. How beautiful Lady Umbra was, how lovely . . . Her hair was made of snakes; her eyes, beetles . . . her hands, twisted spiders; and her wrists, scorpions . . . With each of her movements she conjured legions of murderous shadows. I have no hard feelings toward her, don't get me wrong. Her army defeated the sorcerer and led us to vic-tory; it wasn't her fault that they slaughtered us, too. Once they started killing, it was impossible to stop them. They didn't discriminate between friends and enemies."

No one moved a muscle as the dead voice spoke. They remained frozen in place, their eyes glued to the white stone tomb. They breathed slowly, dazed before the rambling discourse from the tomb's occupant. The rest of the cemetery kept quiet.

"What will we be? What will we transform into?" Bruno insisted.

"A witch, I'll be a witch . . ."

"You'll be silence," announced another of the dead. The voice came from a black marble tomb and was atop a burial mound adorned with the statue of a crying woman on her knees.

"You'll be rain and snow, warmth and life. Flower and scythe," added another.

"Freaks and wonders. Atrocities . . . Miracles . . ." offered a third.

Little by little, a veritable chorus of dead voices surged from the earth. The amalgam of voices made their hair stand on end.

"Wing, snout, claw, and thirst," the dead crooned. They could almost hear them rock inside their tombs to the rhythm of their monotonous quivering. "Fang and fire, perdition and screams. That's what you'll be. Yes, that's what you'll become. Nothing more and nothing less. Walking death and night that takes human form . . . You'll be putrefaction and carrion, oblivion and twilight . . ."

"Let's get out of here, please," Natalia begged in a thin voice. The earth thundered beneath their feet. "Let's get out of here."

Hector looked around. He was surrounded by singing dead people and shadows he couldn't see. He nodded. They'd had enough.

"Let's go," he said.

They set off quickly toward the hill, followed by the voices of the dead that still clamored underground. Their chatter continued even as the teenagers left the cemetery. They sang the same refrain incessantly, all lost in delirium, until their consciousnesses dozed off and their voices were finally hushed.

"You'll be new life and frenzy, madness and destruction," said the final dead voice, the first who'd spoken to them. As its strength dwindled, the volume of its dusty speech diminished. Its last phrases were nothing more than whispers, so weak they couldn't penetrate the stone slab. "And sometime later, you'll be us: bones, dust, and rot. You'll be silence, then nothing. Then, perhaps, legend."

# THE DAYS BEFORE

Sarah was in the front yard, giving her final touch to the snowman that she'd made next to the porch stairs. Bundled up in a red winter coat that was too big for her, the girl took a step back and looked thoughtfully at her creation. After a few moments, she took a twisted carrot out of her pocket and stuck it in the very center of the large ball of snow at the top of her creation. She placed two large black buttons up above, and then, to finish the job, she traced a wide smile under the carrot. She took another step back and nodded, content. Then she turned toward Hector:

"Come on! Come over here! Doesn't it look great? Am I brilliant or what?!"

He was on the other side of the street, his hands in his shirt pockets. That day he wore a long dark green cape with frayed edges, and the strong north wind had wrapped it around the handle of his sword. He untangled it without taking his eyes off Sarah. The girl called him again, but like so many times before, he ignored her. It didn't occur to him for a moment to approach the house. If the dark tentacles that surrounded it weren't enough, during his last visits he'd begun to glimpse what was actually hidden behind the illusion: the head of a gigantic black rock creature that rose up from the ground, all mouth, fangs of stone, and hungry madness. He ignored the true nature of the building and concentrated on memorizing every detail of the scene prepared to lure him: Sarah's chestnut hair, the stairs he'd gone up and down so many times, the sun shining through the windows of his room . . . The vision that the carnivorous house showed him was more complete than his own memories, and that, precisely that, was what made him go back time and time again, even though he knew it wasn't real. It was the most effective way he'd found of retaining his past.

Through the living room curtains he could see his mother's silhouette, walking toward the kitchen. Sometimes she peered out the window or went out onto the porch to ask him inside, but that wasn't usually the case. His father, on the other hand, he hadn't seen even once.

Sarah approached the gate and called him again, now more urgently. When she started to cry and asked if he was mad at her, Hector couldn't take it anymore. He turned his back on the vision and hurried down the street, fighting the temptation to look back. Maddie waited for him around the corner, sitting on the ground, leaning against the wall of a dark shack.

"You're sick in the head, Hector," she said, stretching out her hand so he could help her up. "What you're doing is sick, dangerous, and strange."

"I guess I'm sick, dangerous, and strange."

"You don't say," she said, pretending to yawn.

They headed back to the tower. Madeleine interlaced Hector's arm with her own. He glanced at her discreetly. She looked so pretty. Her hair had started to grow back, although it was a long way from its former luxuriance. Seeing her, he couldn't help but think of Lizbeth and what she'd become. He felt a pang in his stomach.

"Stop looking at me that way," Madeleine told him. "You're making me nervous, you know?"

"And how am I looking at you?"

"You know how. Like I'm going to start howling at any moment. It's annoying."

"I'm sorry," he said. "It wasn't my intention, I promise . . . But sometimes I can't help but think about what's going to happen. And if it's already horrible for everyone, in your case, well, in your case . . ." He wasn't able to finish the phrase.

"In my case, exactly the same," she said. "What makes me more special than Lizbeth? Or Marina?" she asked, narrowing her eyes.

"That you've already lost more than anyone," he answered. "And we promised your brother we'd take care of you."

"And you're doing just that. But controlling moons is out of your league. At least for the time being. We'll see what Bruno ends up being capable of."

The Italian had already achieved the impossible: he'd given them hope. They saw him immersed in books day and night, his eternal top hat on his head, his overcoat on. And although trying to read emotions in his face was still a losing battle, seeing him so active encouraged them, it made them believe that there was a chance of cheating fate. Hector knew they were deceiving themselves. There was no way of escaping the Red Moon, and not just because Lady Scar had told them so; he felt it in his very bones. But he wasn't going to be opening their eyes any time soon. In fact, he envied them. Waiting without hope was even worse.

Night fell. The wind had changed direction. It now swept the ground from the west and eddied in slow spirals through the streets. Although it was cold, the temperature didn't drop as low as other evenings; those repetitive days in the ruined city were now being left behind. A new season had come to Rocavarancolia, and the monotony that they'd grown used to was a thing of the past. Between the violet patches of twilight, twelve stars shone brightly in the sky, all of them in the east. Most were grouped into two different constellations; Marina had named them the Trident and the Teardrop, inspired by the shapes they formed. But one star, the first to have appeared and the brightest of them all, floated apart from the rest, distant and cold, as if it refused to be a part of a group. It seemed less like a star and more like ice encrusted in the night sky.

A pair of flaming bats flew overhead. When they saw them, the two teenagers instinctively shifted their gaze to the southeast. In the distance they heard the cries of the people who burned in the neighborhood of flames, far enough to ignore, but not so far that they couldn't see the gleaming tongues of frozen fire pulsing in the twilight. That sight was still as horrific as the first day they saw it. Madeleine's arm tightened around his own. They quickened their pace.

It didn't take them long to reach the slope that led to the bridge over the stream. To the east they saw the shimmer of a tiny aurora. It barely measured a foot long and floated five feet off the ground, illuminating the walls of a porticoed square with its changing brilliance. Hector watched its melancholy radiance for several moments. It wasn't the only aurora that had appeared in the city over the past week. There were dozens scattered throughout Rocavarancolia, some almost touching the ground, others way up high. In Bruno and Ricardo's opinion, they were the remains of the vortices that had once united the kingdom with other linked worlds.

They resumed their march. As always when they approached the tower, Hector made a supreme effort not to look at the clock on the façade that maintained its fateful countdown. And without exception, he failed. They hadn't gone halfway across the drawbridge when, unable to resist, he looked up.

The star had already passed ten. According to Bruno's calculations, there were less than two months before it coincided with the moon.

Maddie tugged at his arm to draw his gaze away from the sphere. He lowered his eyes and smiled like a child caught red handed. They went into the passageway that led to the tower gate. It was closed, but they didn't need to call. Bruno had enchanted it so that it opened if any one of them were near.

The tower was silent, and they didn't see anyone around. Marina, Natalia, and Bruno had gone to spend the afternoon in the small haunted woods that they'd recently discovered, and apparently they weren't back yet. The forest was a beautiful place full of translucent ferns and trees where they could hear the songs of endless invisible birds. The girls had insisted on going there for a walk, and after a great deal of effort, they ended up convincing the Italian to take a break and go with them.

"Is anybody home?!" Hector shouted.

"In the courtyard!" he heard Ricardo yell.

Hector headed out there while Madeleine went off to the dungeons. The girl did everything for Lizbeth: fed her, brushed her, and even tried to give her a bath once. Hector, on the other hand, did everything possible to avoid going down there.

He opened the courtyard door and went out. Night was beginning to close in completely in the Rocavarancolia sky. He looked at the gate he'd just passed through. He felt a twinge of unease for Marina and the others. It was strange they were taking so long.

Ricardo was a few yards from the entrance. His torso was bare and the palms of his hands were wrapped in bandages. Weapons were piled up at his feet, most of them lances with different blades and lengths. More than two dozen improvised targets were placed throughout the courtyard, the largest ones leaning against the wall and the rest propped against chairs and planks. Ricardo was already a strapping young man when he came to Rocavarancolia, but recently his muscle mass had increased considerably. His muscles looked as if living beings had sought refuge beneath his skin.

"If you're trying to show off, I'm sorry, there's no one watching," Hector said when he reached his side.

"I didn't want my clothes to get sweaty, that's why I took them off," he explained in a somber voice. "Although the truth is I haven't been sweating much . . ."

"What is it you're trying to do?"

"See how far I can throw," he said, as he chose a lance from the pile.

The weapon he held measured more than six feet long and was made of dark wood with a grooved steel point. Ricardo didn't even need to gather momentum before he threw it. It left his hand at a frightening speed, whistling across more than a hundred yards to the target and landing in the exact center with a crack.

"And I'm seeing it and I still don't believe it." Ricardo shook his head. The lance's handle still quivered from the impact. "No, I don't believe it."

Hector looked back and forth between his friend and the targets. What he'd just witnessed was impossible. And it wasn't a strike of luck. There were six other lances in the bull's-eyes of many of the other targets. One of them had been hurled with such force that a third of the shaft had penetrated the wood.

"Marina will be mad when she finds out your aim is better than hers," he said, trying not to seem too impressed.

Ricardo smiled weakly.

"It's a time of change, Hector. I'm stronger, faster, and more precise. And I swear this morning I woke up with more muscles than I had last night." He grabbed another lance and threw it as he stood up. It landed cleanly in the center of another target. The plank shuddered and fell with a crash. "Something's happening. And I'm not just talking about me. Look at Bruno: he's capable of performing spells that just recently would have left him unconscious for hours . . ."

Hector nodded. The Italian's capabilities were growing before their eyes. It had been that way since day one, but recently his progress was speeding up. A week before, he'd descended, floating, down the tower stairs, pale as a ghost, his eyes bloodshot with black light. He'd managed to cast one of the seeking spells that had been out of his reach until then, and he said he'd found Marco's trail. It led them to the edge of the Scar of Arax, right where the man with the harpoons told them their friend had jumped. They stood for a long time in front of the river of bones, dazed, silent, reluctant to believe that Marco would have chosen to go out in such a way.

Ricardo selected another spear and began playing with it, tossing it in the air and catching it as it fell.

"It's the Red Moon," he said. "It's affecting us just like it's affecting the whole city. It's still weeks before it comes out, but it's already starting to change us."

Hector approached the pile of weapons and chose a light-looking spear with a wide point with serrated edges. He raised it above his shoulder, and after practicing the motion a couple of times, he threw it with all his might as he jumped forward. The weapon sliced through the air and fell only twenty yards from where they stood, at the foot of the target he was aiming for.

"It's not just starting now," he said. It hadn't been a great throw, but it was much better than he'd hoped for. "It started as soon as we arrived. Rocavaragalago has been changing us from the beginning. That's why Bruno's power grows day by day . . . Or why your skills and strength have improved. And look at the rest of us. You've seen how we handle our weapons; okay, we're not experts or anything, but it's impossible to learn so much in so little time, even with a teacher as good as Marco was. And remember Rachel: she learned the language of Rocavarancolia at an astonishing speed."

"That's not so odd. There are people who have an extraordinary gift for languages."

"But to that extent? We're not talking about an Earth language . . . This is a language of another world, a language that she couldn't possibly have any frame of reference for. And look at me." He raised his arms and turned around so that his friend could get a good look. "Remember what I looked like when I came here."

"I remember, Fatty." He smiled and threw the spear, which flew straight and true into the bull's-eye of another target.

"And now I'm skin and bones. And it's not just because of the food around here and the exercise, I'm sure. Rocavaragalago has been molding all of us since we arrived."

"Well, now it's speeding up."

"At least with you and Bruno," he said. "I don't notice anything strange."

"You will. It's coming, Hector." He put a hand on his shoulder. "Sometimes I close my eyes and think I can almost see what I'll be like when that moon comes out." He sighed, his eyes fixed on one of the pierced targets. "What's going to happen to us?" he asked.

Hector shrugged his shoulders.

"Madeleine will become a wolf, and Natalia a witch. Right now, that's all we know."

Madeleine a wolf and Natalia a witch . . . Saying it out loud didn't help make it any more real. At least the Russian girl's transformation would probably be a lot less traumatic than what was in store for the redhead. Maybe that was one of the reasons why Natalia's mood had brightened so much over the past few days.

"When the Red Moon comes out, I'll control those shadows," she'd said, from time to time, clenching her fists in rage. "And the first thing I'll do is order them to disappear and leave me alone . . . Or maybe I can make them kill each other. One way or another, I'll be free of them forever."

Since what happened in the cemetery, they never left her alone. She always had someone nearby to keep the shadows from harassing her. And it was clear that Natalia liked having them look out for her, although she didn't express it openly and even complained bitterly about the lack of privacy.

"Next you're going to go to the bathroom with me!"

"The bathrooms are too small for those shadows of yours to make trouble for you there, so we'll wait for you right outside, that's enough,"

Madeleine replied. "If you want us to leave you alone, get into a wardrobe and stay there as long as you like."

Bruno had several books in his library on witches and witchcraft, and after finding out about their friend's destiny, they all wanted to read them, especially the concerned party. At first, the drawings weren't very reassuring: they showed disfigured men and women, their faces covered with pustules and boils and insects that looked like they formed part of their very flesh. Above all else, Hector was repulsed by a picture of a woman with no eyes, with wasps in the empty sockets and long hairy worms instead of hair. There were others with crustacean pincers instead of hands, scorpions in their mouths, and other, worse, details that were truly nausea inducing. Natalia went pale when she saw them, but Bruno quickly calmed her down, in his cold and robotic manner:

"It is not real. Witches and warlocks change their appearance with the intention of causing fear in their enemies. Everything that you see in those pictures is false, either enchantments or makeup. In your case, the Red Moon should not alter your physical appearance."

"So, I'll be just as ugly with or without the Red Moon?" She'd regained her color after the Italian's explanation.

"There is nothing ugly about you," he answered, incapable of understanding that Natalia's question was just a joke. The girl blushed, and the hint of color softened her features in such a way that it was hard for Hector to imagine her looking like the witches in the pictures, even if it was on purpose.

According to what they read, witches and warlocks were considered minor practitioners of magic, and only on rare occasion did they reach the height of power that great sorcerers achieved, but there was something that made them tremendously special, a feature that only they possessed: it was called Dominion.

"Lady Sargasso had the power of controlling any plant that grew underwater," Bruno explained. "It says that during the war with Arfes, she created an army of giants made from algae and coral that destroyed the enemy fleet. And there was Lady Nighthawk, who controlled the storm clouds when it was nighttime, or Celsidro, who had power over the eagles. All witches and warlocks can dominate one aspect of reality, and, depending on which it is, some are more powerful than others. Controlling the leaves of a larch tree is hardly the same as, for example, having hurricanes obey your command. Or controlling those shadow creatures, like you do."

"Dominion," Natalia whispered, looking straight at a spot on the tower that the others couldn't see. "Did you hear that, little monster? When the Red Moon comes out, you'll be under my power," she said. "You'll be mine . . . And then we'll see who's afraid of who."

And maybe it was a figment of his imagination, but Hector thought he heard an evil hissing sound come from behind him. When he turned around, of course, he saw nothing.

Hector helped Ricardo carry the lances to the armory. Night was upon them and the others still hadn't returned.

"They're fine," he assured Ricardo when he saw the way he looked at the main gate as they headed toward the stairs. "Bruno's with them. Nothing bad can happen to them with him around."

After they dropped off the lances, they went into the dungeons.

The creature that once was Lizbeth leapt from Madeleine's lap as soon as they opened the door and left the spell of silence behind them. The enormous brown wolf charged the bars, baring her double row of fangs and growling menacingly. It was a terrifying sight. Even more so with Maddie inside the cell.

"Lizbeth! No!" The girl pulled hard on the chain, but the wolf didn't flinch. She howled, growled, jumped down, and ran from one side of the cell to the other, her cracked eyes staring at them.

It didn't matter how much time went by; that monstrous beast seemed incapable of getting used to their presence. She went mad as soon as she saw them. And Bruno was her least favorite. As soon as the Italian appeared in the doorway, the fury that came over her was so great that not even Madeleine dared go near. Bruno had cast spells on her repeatedly, trying to find a way to reverse her transformation and bring back their friend, but the only thing he'd achieved was that the wolf now hated him with murderous intensity.

Maddie looked at them from the cell, surprised by their presence. It was rare for someone besides Bruno or herself to come down to the dungeons.

Hector sighed and took a step forward. The subject he wanted to talk to her about made him uncomfortable—even more so after the conversation they'd had on the way back to the tower—and the presence of the growling, snapping wolf didn't help.

"All right," she said, looking at them suspiciously. "What's on your mind?"

"It's a delicate matter. I'm not sure how to ask you this . . ." Hector began. He looked at Ricardo, pleading for help, but his friend shrugged his shoulders. It was his idea to talk with the others about the possible changes they'd been noticing, therefore it was his responsibility to see it through. "So I'll be direct and unpleasant." He took a breath before continuing. "Have you noticed anything strange recently? We think the Red Moon has already started to affect us, to really affect us, and it could be that you—"

"I can't believe it. Who was I talking to just now?" She looked at Hector, frowning. "Are you asking me if I'm growing hair in places where there wasn't any before? Or if I'm starting to grow a tail?"

"Uh . . ." was all he could manage. In spite of himself, his cheeks burned. He took another deep breath. "I don't know, anything that doesn't seem normal to you . . . At a glance you look just the same as always, but . . ."

"No. Nothing's happened to me." She approached the bars and looked at them with her sparkling green eyes. "Everything is in its place, and is exactly as it should be. I'd show you, but none of you are prepared for something like that."

The girl smiled malevolently, and although it was perhaps a trick of the light, Hector thought her teeth were bigger than they should have been. Maddie lowered her hand to the snout of the wolf, who rubbed her head against her palm, watching them all the while.

"You'll tell us if anything happens to you? Whatever it is?"

"Are you afraid that I'll eat someone before the moon comes out or what?" She crossed her arms across her chest and glared at them. "Are you thinking about locking me up with Lizbeth?"

Hector didn't know what to say. His only intention had been to see if the girl had started to feel the change coming on. Until then he hadn't even thought about what to do with her once the Red Moon came out, nor had it even crossed his mind that Maddie could become dangerous before that happened.

"If you think you might become a risk to us, will you tell us?" he asked.

"If I realize that I could cause you any harm, I'll lock myself in a cell," she answered.

The door to the dungeons opened at that moment and Natalia peered her disheveled head through the opening.

"Just in case you're interested, we've got some serious problems, very serious," she said, her face somber. "And it's Marina's fault."

Ricardo and Hector exchanged a worried look and left the dungeon. Outside they met Bruno and Marina, waiting in the stairway, him standing and her sitting down; the girl was even paler than normal. Hector breathed a sigh of relief to see that she was okay.

"What happened?" he asked Bruno, glancing sideways at Marina. The girl brushed her hair out of her face and groaned softly.

"We had a small accident on our way back," the Italian answered. "Nothing serious; as you can see, we're all in perfect condition."

"Marina activated a weird spell in the street!" Natalia exclaimed. "She wasn't looking where she was going, and she stepped on a star drawn on the ground and set a demon free. Even a blind person would have realized it was a curse!"

"I didn't see it, smarty-pants!" the other girl grumbled, staring daggers at her. "It could have happened to anyone!"

"But it happened to you! Everything happens to you!"

"That's not true!"

Hector took a deep breath and asked Bruno to tell him what happened. Madeleine arrived from the dungeon just in time to hear the Italian's explanation.

"Natalia summarized it perfectly. A spell was activated by Marina's step. It was a security spell. That stone slab must have been in the entryway to an important building, although all that was left of it was a pile of rubble. We can assume that the enchantment formed part of their security system. They had chained a protector demon to the stone, and when Marina stepped on it, the demon was freed. It was a grotesque being, a headless, hunchbacked gray giant with four arms and a multitude of tentacles covered with eyes that sprouted from its back and chest."

"It had a huge mouth at the height of its stomach, full of long black fangs," Natalia added, and mimed an exaggerated shiver. "And it smelled like rotten food! It was so awful!"

"Everything happened so quickly that it had snatched Marina before I could react."

"It was revolting," the girl cut in. Her voice was barely a whisper. She'd rested her head on the palms of her hands and kept her eyes on the ground. Madeleine approached her and stroked her hair. "It shook me from side to side . . . I screamed and screamed. I couldn't do anything else. It raised me to its mouth and then . . . then . . . ."

"I tried to petrify them both," Bruno continued. "I didn't want to cast anything more expedient for fear of hurting Marina, but the demon was protected from direct magic, and the spell only turned her to stone. It threw her to the side and then came for me."

"Marina broke into pieces when the monster threw her!"

Hector looked at the girl, horrified. Marina looked defeated. She bit her lower lip and sighed.

"All I know is that I fainted," she said. "The last I can remember is that thing's fangs in front of me and then everything went black. I lost consciousness."

"Marina shattered into pieces when she hit the ground," Bruno continued. "But I knew I could save her as long as she remained turned into stone, so I focused on the demon. Like I said, it was protected against direct magic. First I raised a force field around Natalia to protect her, and then I took off, the monster behind me, keeping just enough distance between us so it would think it could catch me. It took the bait and followed me. Once I thought it was far enough from Natalia and the pieces of Marina, I faced it and threw a building on it."

"You did what?" Hector leaned forward. He couldn't have heard correctly.

"A displacement spell. I hurled a three-story building on top of it. I pulled it up from its foundation and threw it on him. It seemed like the most effective and fast solution, given the circumstances. I could have done something else, of course . . . but I didn't have time for subtleties, not with Marina in pieces . . ." He took off his top hat, looked inside it, and planted it firmly back atop his head. "We had to find every last fragment and put them back in place before I could reverse the spell and turn Marina back to flesh and bone. That was what really delayed us. We couldn't allow even the slightest error. It was a laborious process."

"A puzzle . . . That's what I became. A puzzle scattered in the middle of the street. So horrible. My head hurts and my mouth tastes like sand . . ." She opened her mouth from time to time and stuck out her tongue while she made a disgusted face. Then she got up from the stairs, leaning unsteadily against Madeleine. "Can we go now, please? I'm dying for a drink of water."

Once they were upstairs, they spoke some more about what had happened. Natalia told them how shocking it was to see Bruno being chased by that tentacled horror. The Italian assured them that it wasn't risky; the only thing he was worried about was using up his magic reserves. He knew how truly complicated it would be once he'd dealt with the monster and had to reassemble Marina. Hector couldn't stop picturing her on the ground, in pieces, an image that enraged and terrified him in equal amounts. When Natalia started talking about how complicated it had been putting the pieces together and holding them in place while the Italian joined them, he couldn't take it anymore. He turned toward her and looked at her sternly. He had to struggle not to raise his voice.

"If Bruno hadn't been with you, you'd both be dead," he said. "Both of you. And if that happened, it wouldn't have been Marina's fault. No. It would have been your fault." Natalia huffed in the chair that she'd plopped down in. It was clear that she knew what was coming next. "We can't keep taking risks with only one magic practitioner when we should have two. Not given what we know about this city."

"I can't believe it. She gets us into this, and you take it out on me."

"Marina made a mistake this afternoon, that's true," Ricardo intervened. Natalia looked at him with a scowl. By the tone of his voice it was obvious he wasn't going to take her side. "But you've been making a bigger one for a long time now. Hector's right: you need to go back to learning magic, and you need to do it as soon as possible."

"But I don't want to!" she exploded. "Besides, even if I learn, I'll never be able to do what Bruno does! How was I going to throw a house on that thing?"

"No one's asking you to learn how to throw houses," Hector said. "Only that you learn what's necessary to save yourself and the others if it comes down to it."

"You're going to force me to learn magic?" Natalia looked at them intently. "Is that what you're saying? No matter what I think?"

"If you don't give us a choice, yes, we will," Ricardo said.

"Oh, and how are you going to do that? Tie me to a table and put books in front of me?"

"Isn't there a spell that can get rid of that damn stubbornness of hers?" Ricardo asked Bruno.

The Italian shook his head.

"Despite the apparent increase in my capabilities, the magic that alters behavior is still out of my reach."

"You're overcomplicating this," Madeleine pointed out, shaking her head. "There are easier ways of doing things. Leave it to me."

She approached the Russian, who kept her eyes on her, hunched in her chair. The redhead got down on her knees in front of Natalia, took her by the hand, and looked her in the eyes. When she spoke, she did it in such a soft yet deliberately threatening tone that Hector felt a stitch of unease in the pit of his stomach.

"There's the possibility that one day our lives will depend on a spell that you didn't want to learn, dear," Madeleine said. "And if that happens and we die, it will be your fault and your fault alone, do you understand me? Can you live with that weight on your conscience? I couldn't, I promise you."

Natalia looked at her in silence, her eyes very wide. Madeleine smiled. It was an open and friendly smile, but something akin to a veiled threat peered through. Hector again thought that her canines were bigger than he remembered.

The Russian let out a loud sigh, groaned, and reluctantly got up.

"All right, all right," she conceded. "Idiots. I'll try to learn what I can. But not because I want to. I'll do it so that I don't have to listen to you ever again."


No one had much of an appetite that night, and the chatter at the table was uncomfortable and forced. Marina still seemed affected by what had happened and ate even less than usual. She was the first to get up, excused herself from the group, and went out into the courtyard to get some air while the others finished their dinner. Hector wasn't far behind her. He was worried about his friend.

The night was cooler than usual, and an unfamiliar quivering mist surrounded everything in the courtyard; it was a film of sparkling dampness that gave reality an otherworldly consistency. The statue of the spider king had never looked so real; it gave the impression that at any moment it would descend from its pedestal.

Marina sat with her legs crossed on a cushioned chair, and she'd halfheartedly covered herself with a blanket. With each of her exhalations, a trembling flower of mist burst forth from her mouth and quickly vanished. Hector shook his head.

As much as it weighed on him, he was in love with her. And it was exhausting having to fight that feeling day after day. He loved the blue of her eyes, the way that she walked, the way she tied her hair back. He loved her silences, her words, the sound of her footsteps . . . But he wasn't about to surrender. No, he wouldn't succumb. He'd drawn a line between them that neither of them should ever cross again. There was no place for love in Rocavarancolia, of course not. Love couldn't save them in that horrible city. It didn't matter how loud and strong his heart screamed; he wasn't about to listen.

He walked toward her, but avoided looking at her directly. He plopped into the chair next to hers and looked at the sky, up at the sparse stars of Rocavarancolia, before speaking.

"You're not okay," he said.

She shook her head. She did it abruptly, a quick side-to-side shake.

"No, of course not," she replied with ill humor. "How could I be? A creature without a head tried to devour me for stepping on the wrong slab, turned me into stone, and then I broke into pieces. That would be too much for anyone, you know?"

"But not for you. And there aren't many people who can say they've been broken into pieces and lived to tell the story."

The chill of her glare completely disarmed Hector.

"You're really bad at consoling people," she shot back in a gruff voice. "And since when do you even worry about me?" she asked. "Are you tired of not paying me any attention or what?"

"No . . . I . . ." Hector leaned back, already regretting the impulse to go after her. "I pay attention to you, of course I pay attention to you . . . Where did you get that idea?"

"You've been avoiding me since the night at the palace and you know it."
"That's just your imagination," he lied. "I'm not avoiding anyone, why would I?"

"That's what I'm wondering."

"Well, you're wrong, seriously." He shifted uneasily in his seat. "Maybe . . . maybe I seem more distant than before . . . but it's not because of you, I promise, it's because I have a lot going on in my head. Everything that's been happening to us . . . What's waiting down the line . . ."

"Yeah, sure." She brought the blanket up to her chin without looking at him. "So much going on in your head, sure . . . But that doesn't stop you from talking to the others, does it? Or going for a walk with Maddie, right?"

"I . . ." Hector brushed his hair from his forehead and sighed. He felt gripped by a terrible inability to think clearly. "It's that . . ." He swallowed. "I'm just thinking about the night of the dance, okay?" he began hurriedly, without knowing very well where that was going to take him. "About Rachel and the choker and that I should have realized sooner that something was strange about it. But I was distracted by dancing with you and—"

"You're avoiding me because you feel guilty about dancing with me?" she asked. The tone of her voice made it clear how much that idea offended her.

*I'm avoiding you because I love you*, Hector thought, and it was such an intense thought that for a second he was afraid she'd been able to hear it.

"I'm avoiding you because I can't avoid myself," he said instead. His strong desire to cry at that very moment made it clear that this wasn't as far from the truth as he might have thought. "Because I couldn't save Rachel. I wasn't fast enough . . ." His voice cracked in his throat. "I was a second too slow, only a second. If I'd reacted a second earlier, I would have been able to save her. I'm sure of it."

Marina stared at him, her hands clutching the blanket tightly. She looked at him with an impenetrable expression, as if she didn't know how to react. She shook her head and sank down in the chair.

"I . . ." she began. She sighed again. "One second, one single second, and the whole world changes forever. Something you did, something you didn't say . . . and now there's no going back. It's surprising how much can happen in such a minuscule amount of time." She contemplated the pitch-black night beyond the wall. "I was about to put on that choker myself," she said. "Madeleine tossed the jewelry that she found on the bed and we started choosing what we liked best. And I saw the choker with that red stone, and I loved it . . . I thought, *Look how nicely that will go with the black dress.* And just as I stretched out my hand to grab it, Rachel beat me to it and took it. If I'd seen that choker a second earlier, it might have been me in that dungeon right now."

They both sank into a strange silence, a heavy silence that Hector was eager to break, but as hard as he thought he couldn't come up with anything, and he had no idea of how to console Marina. The silence between them extended in the cold night, and neither knew how to end it. Until Marina spoke:

"Natalia is right," she said. "I wasn't looking where I was going. I was caught up in my own thoughts, thinking how pretty the haunted woods were, about how much Lizbeth and Rachel would have liked it, and . . . I was distracted, and like a fool I stepped on that thing. And it's true: if Bruno hadn't been there with us, that monster would have killed us both . . . and it wouldn't have been Natalia's fault, whatever you say, it would have been mine. Only mine." She sighed. "It doesn't matter what we do. This city will end up killing all of us."

"Don't say that, don't even think it."

"How can I not? Like today . . . What would have happened if Bruno and Natalia hadn't found all the pieces? Or if they'd placed one, only one, a millimeter off?"

He'd asked himself those same questions over and over again throughout the night.

"But they found them all. And they put them where they needed to go. That's what matters. We'll find a way to defeat this city. I'm convinced that somehow it will all end well."

At that precise instant, despite the circumstances and all that had occurred, Hector realized that he didn't say it just to cheer her up: he firmly believed his words. "It can't be any other way. It wouldn't be fair."

"Fair?" Marina broke out in laughter. "You're talking about fairness in this place? Are you feeling okay?" She took a hand from under the blanket and rested it on the arm of Hector's chair, then she leaned in toward him. "Look me in the eyes and tell me that you truly believe this will all end well," she said.

Hector blinked, confused. He couldn't hold her gaze, but it wasn't because he didn't believe what he was saying; if he looked in her eyes, all of his efforts to forget what he felt for her would be reduced to nothing. If he looked in her eyes, the only thing he could tell her was that he loved her. And he couldn't allow that to happen.

"You see?" Marina said, misinterpreting his hesitation. "You can't." She gave him an affectionate pat on the arm and got up from her chair. "At least I know it's hard for you to lie to me. That's something."

"It's not that, it's not that . . ." he said hurriedly as she was already making her way back to the tower.

"Then what is it?"

Hector shrugged his shoulders. The cold of night froze him stiff inside. He couldn't tell her what he was thinking; he couldn't tell her he'd like nothing more than to spend his whole life looking at her. The battle inside him raged. He gazed up at the stars, searching for inspiration, searching for words that could save him. But the only thing that happened as he stared at the cold Rocavarancolian stars was that his recent flash of optimism fell to pieces. How could he have thought even for a second that all of this would end well? How dared he? There was no happy ending for Alexander, Rachel, and Marco. They were dead. Rocavarancolia had killed them.

No, now he understood. Clearly, this story didn't have the slightest chance of a happy ending.

Marina, tired of waiting for his response, shook her head and started walking toward the door, but before she got there she stopped again, one hand resting on the doorknob.

"Not everything that happened in that ballroom was horrible, right?" she asked in a weak voice.

"No," he answered. "For a moment . . ." He stopped suddenly, conscious of what he was about to say.

"Don't even think about going silent on me now. Finish the sentence. For a moment what?"

"For a moment, I was completely happy." And although he couldn't see it, Hector knew that Marina smiled.

# THE FIRE

The days passed, laden with shadows and omens. One afternoon at dusk, several dozen nebulous silhouettes congregated in the heavens and flew above the city. For hours the teenagers watched from the tower battlements. Bruno couldn't explain the phenomenon. They didn't look like ghosts, or living beings, but like something in between. Creatures from another dimension, perhaps, like Natalia's shadows. The beings, mere stains of light, ended up vanishing with the arrival of nightfall.

Another day, they ran into a pack of globular creatures, transparent, as big as elephants, that floated around a ramshackle house completely enveloped by Lady Serena's mist; they clung to the façade and sank the protuberances jutting from their heads into the building's walls. Within each entity they saw small storm clouds full of lightning bolts. Hector thought that they were feeding on the house, but what they were ingesting he couldn't say. Maybe magic?

That same afternoon, shortly after returning to the tower, a shout from Ricardo made them run out to the courtyard. Beyond the moat, in a garden among the ruins, several creatures were enmeshed in fierce combat. There were almost fifty of them, all of the same species, with red, wiry fur; they looked like squirrels without tails.

It was an actual battle royal without apparent sides, a free-for-all where mercy was neither requested nor granted. The creatures' fierceness astonished them. The fight lasted more than two hours and only ended when one single animal was left alive. It let out a pitiful howl after finishing off its last companion, as if it realized in that instant what had just happened. It took off running from the yard, whimpering and casting horrified glances as it looked back.

The entire city was changing.

There was movement in the streets, more life, and—something they liked enormously—more color. The withered vines that covered some of the façades were replenished, and among their now-green leaves small flowers with blue petals began to emerge; miraculous blades of grass burst forth in the ruined gardens of parks and courtyards—not many, but enough to make a huge impact on their former desolate grounds. And with each new dusk more and more stars took their positions in the dark sky of Rocavarancolia, shining embers that tried to break up the darkness. One night in particular, one whole area of the sky that had up until then been a spotless black was covered by dozens of tiny, pulsing stars. It was as if an invisible hand sprinkled them across the celestial vault. The small fragments of aurora scattered throughout the city also grew in number, though to a lesser degree. The largest of them all was located over the pits where one of the bathtubs deposited its cargo. The aurora, a silky curtain of violet and scarlet, as tall as a man and as wide as three, turned slowly in place, casting radiance and sparkles in all directions. The idea that all of those whirlwinds of light had once been doorways to other worlds was dizzying.

On the façade of the Margalar Tower, the star reached the height of ten fifteen, and six days later it reached ten thirty. There were forty days before the Red Moon arrived. When Bruno commented that they'd been in Rocavarancolia almost half a year, it was hard to believe. Natalia insisted he'd made a mistake in his calculations; it was impossible they'd been there so long. Marina also said there had to be some error, but for the opposite reason: she had the feeling that much more time had passed since Denestor Tul had taken them from their world.

"I did not make the slightest miscalculation. I am one hundred percent certain that on Earth it is April twenty-second," he said. "Four years ago today my grandfather gave me his watch." He took it out from the pocket of his overcoat and looked at it studiously. It had stopped the exact moment that they'd arrived in Rocavarancolia, and so far all of his attempts to get it working again had failed.

"It's your birthday!" Marina exclaimed. "Why didn't you tell us?"

"Because it is not relevant" was all he said.

He delicately grasped the little wheel located on one side of the watch and began turning it. When it was completely wound, there was no movement in the hands. Bruno shook his head and placed the watch back in his pocket, with the chain still hanging out, swinging from side to side. Something in that pendulum-like swaying caught Hector's attention, but he couldn't say what it was. He shrugged his shoulders and didn't give it another thought; it was just a watch chain. He soon forgot it.

Hector collapsed onto his bed and tried to remove himself from everything around him. He wanted to find out if the Red Moon had started to affect him in the same way that it had already affected Ricardo and Bruno, but he didn't notice anything out of the ordinary, and he didn't know if he should feel happy or disappointed.

Marina and Natalia had both assured him they hadn't noticed anything either, although he had serious doubts with regard to the former. Marina had never eaten much, but lately she'd barely eaten at all. When he asked her about it, she reassured him that everything was fine, that she'd just gotten into the habit of snacking between meals, and that's why she was never hungry when they sat down to eat together. That same day, Marina ate with an unusual appetite; when she finished she showed him her empty plate and asked in a sarcastic tone if she could be excused from the table now that she'd eaten everything. Hector didn't comment then, or the day after, when she set her plate aside, barely having touched it.

The one area in which there'd clearly been no improvement was the group's aptitude for magic, Natalia's included. The Russian girl had taken her decision to learn magic seriously, but for all the hours she put into it she didn't achieve much; it was extremely difficult for her to master even the simplest spells. According to Bruno, her concentration was lacking. She spent three days trying to learn the spell of intangibility, but she still hadn't succeeded.

"This is nothing but a waste of time," she admitted to Hector one afternoon. She'd just taken a bath in the stream and her hair was still damp. "I'm exhausted and I'm not getting anywhere. And that puts me in a bad mood." She snorted. "And being in a bad mood puts me in a bad mood. I get the impression that I'm always angry."

"Well, you are always angry. You're an insufferable grouch."

"I hate you."

Hector thought it would go much more smoothly if Bruno helped her, but the Italian didn't seem to have any interest in doing so. All he'd done was select the books that he thought were most appropriate for her, and that was it. He had more important things to focus on, he insisted. Bruno was not only growing more powerful as time went on; he was also becoming bolder, as was evident the afternoon he informed Hector that he'd decided to explore the city on his own.

"There are places I intend to go that I consider to be high risk," he said. "It is even likely that I'll go back to the underground passageways of the city. I am not capable of guaranteeing the safety of anyone coming with me, and that is why I prefer to go alone."

Hector wasn't too worried about Bruno going off by himself in Rocavarancolia; it was clear that he was the most prepared out of all of them to do so. What worried him was their fate if something happened to them and the Italian wasn't close at hand.

"Nothing I can say will change your mind, right?" he asked.

"I understand your concern. I know it is risky, but unfortunately we have run out of options. Time is short, and there are no answers in the books we have gathered so far."

"Do you really think you're going to find something that will help us? Do you think there's anything out there that can stop the Red Moon from transforming us?"

The Italian took his time before answering:

"I promised to find a way to avoid it, and that is reason enough not to relent," he said.

Hector remembered that Alex had promised Adrian he'd take him home. Rocavarancolia wasn't a place to make promises.


Denestor Tul stroked his cheek while he watched how Belisarius leaned over the table where he'd soon be assassinated. The demiurge was witnessing the scene from the perspective of the servant who, unaware of the tragic end that fate had in store for him, awaited the old man's orders in the doorway. Denestor wasn't just seeing through his eyes; he also had access to all of his thoughts, all of his feelings. He noticed the soft rug beneath his worn sandals, breathed the air of dust and old age that emanated from the study and its occupant, and was even able to feel the accumulated exhaustion that the servant felt after a long day of working in the castle.

Belisarius turned his bandaged face toward him and muttered something that Denestor couldn't comprehend. He had to resort to the thoughts of the servant, who was more accustomed than he to the old man's murmurings, to understand his words:

"Turn on all the lights. I want the study to be well lit tonight," he'd said.

The servant, and Denestor Tul with him, hurried to fulfill the command. First he lit the candles and torches next to the door. Then he walked toward the candelabras at the opposite end of the room. When the servant was halfway across, almost at Belisarius's table, Denestor Tul paused the image that he was extracting from the common memories of the servants. The demiurge stopped stroking his cheek to tap his chin. He thoroughly examined the scene in front of him. The horn that would be used to murder Belisarius was at the head of the table, next to the pile of scrolls atop which the old man rested his bandaged hands.

Denestor focused his attention on the table. Besides the chaos of parchments and the horn, there was a mounted owl, a little engraved box which, if Denestor remembered correctly, shrieked when opened, and two books of ancient history, one dedicated to the origin of Rocavarancolia and the other to the dark times of the spider kings. On top of that book was an inkwell with a quill and two large black wax candles.

The servant had been the first to die. He'd been attacked as he lit the candelabra at the back of the room, next to the door that led to Belisarius's sleeping quarters. According to Ujthan, the assassin must have been hiding in that room. He decapitated the servant with a single slash. Then he went after Belisarius. The sequence of events, as well as the way the crimes were committed, got Denestor's attention. The assassin carried a weapon capable of severing a head in one blow, but curiously he hadn't used that weapon on the second victim. He'd preferred an old horn to finish off Belisarius, and then he'd taken the servant's head with him. No, the two murders didn't make sense.

"Who would have thought that at my age I'd be playing detective," he mumbled to himself.

Denestor was in two places at the same time. While his mind wandered through the memories of the castle's servants, his body was in the lower levels of Highlowtower, sitting in a gigantic chair with articulated legs. At the other end of the room, one of the servants lay resting on a straw mattress. Between them was the demiurge's latest creation: a large galvanized fish barrel from which extended two jointed black tubes which were connected to the helmets that Denestor and the servant wore on their heads. The barrel was full of feathers, hourglasses, and pulverized walnut shells. It had taken Denestor some time to prepare that invention. It was a living creature, with limited intelligence, but perfectly suited for its task: it allowed the demiurge's mind to project itself into the minds of others and access the memories they held.

He suspected the illness that afflicted the castle servants, that exaggerated weakness that made them wander around like lost souls, was something more than just an effect of the murder of one of their own. And besides, he couldn't forget the chilling premonition that had assaulted him as he peered through the eyes of that one servant. He could be wrong, of course—maybe all of this was nothing more than an absurd waste of time—but the assassin left so few clues behind that he had no choice but to examine all of them.

He watched the motionless scene for several minutes. This was the memory of the dead servant, assimilated by the hive mind that formed the castle's staff. If he played it again, he'd see how the unfortunate wretch reached the candelabra, raised the hand in which he carried the long lighter used to light the candles, and died before he got to the first one. Denestor didn't want to be with him in that terrible moment; he'd already done it once, and he flatly refused to feel yet again the intense pain and cold with which the servant's life had come to an end. So instead he accessed the mind of the servant he had here, on the mattress. Here he could search among the servants' collective memories, so he could find the recollections of the first one to arrive at the scene of the crime.

The view that now surrounded him showed two cadavers: that of the decapitated servant in the corner and that of Old Belisarius, slumped at the table. He stopped the image at the exact moment where he had a complete view of the table. He studied the scene with care. Then he substituted it with the image extracted from the memory of the dead servant. Besides the two cadavers, there were subtle differences between them. The positioning of Belisarius's chair was different, for example, and the parchments before him had been moved.

But there was something else. He set aside the memory of the dead servant to enter once more into that of the living one. At the edge of the table, barely an inch from the cadaver's outstretched hand, he discovered three small blue stains, very close to the spot where the horn had been. Denestor examined them closely. He couldn't touch them, but he didn't need to to know they were fresh. Those stains weren't there when the first servant, the one lying dead in the corner, entered the room. He confirmed that the ink was the same as the liquid in the inkwell which sat atop the book. There was a quill sticking upright from a small base next to it. He studied it in detail. It was a long tube of white bone with a black feather; the point was stained with ink, as fresh as that which had marred the table.

He started the memory of the assassinated servant from the exact instant that he entered the room, and stopped it when he had the best view of the pile of documents over which Belisarius leaned. The first thing he found was that there were also stains of fresh ink on the bandages wrapped around the old man's left hand. Next, Denestor fixed his attention on the scrolls. There were almost twenty, heaped up messily. The end of one of them, a dirty grayish scroll located second in the stack, stuck out among the others. The writing was fresh and he managed to read the first three lines of the text. Denestor Tul frowned. They were written in a language unfamiliar to him.

He exchanged the dead servant's memory for those of the living servants who were in charge of searching and arranging Belisarius's office. He watched them, jumping from one to the next, as they restored order to all the chaos. He saw one of them gather the parchments that Belisarius had on the table. The gray one wasn't among them.

The demiurge squinted his eyes. He was on to something.

Whoever had murdered Belisarius didn't just take the servant's head: he'd stolen the parchment. Denestor was convinced that the old man had been writing on it shortly before the servant arrived; the stains on the bandages and table were proof of that. Belisarius's vision was almost nonexistent; therefore it must have required great effort for him to write with so little light. Why hadn't he called on one of the servants to help him? The answer was obvious: so that no one knew what he was writing; so no one could do exactly what Denestor was doing now, spying on what he wrote. The demiurge examined the text that he glimpsed among the pile of papers again, traced in that strange language.

Denestor went back to tapping his fingers on the center of his chin. He was sure that if he found out what language it was and managed to translate it, he'd be closer to solving the mystery of the castle murders.

"You can take off the helmet," he ordered the servant as he did the same. "We're finished for today. Go back to your duties."

The servant sat up slowly on the mattress and took off the contraption that engulfed his head. His movements were crude, hesitant. The flickering pallor of his face came into view. He blinked, dazed, and looked at the demiurge.

"I hope I have been helpful to you, my lord," he whispered in a weak voice.

"You have been, my good friend. You have been," he assured him, smiling.

But his fit of good humor disappeared when he looked at the servant's empty gaze. His emotionless eyes seemed to watch him from an infinite distance, from a place where neither cold nor heat existed. Looking into that gaze was like looking into a void.

And on the other side of those empty eyes, the first Lord of Assassins lay in wait.


The ten-pointed star reached the position on the sphere that would read as ten forty if it were a sundial. The day was cold, the coldest they'd had since they'd arrived in Rocavarancolia. The buildings and ruins awoke smudged with frost, and a fine layer of ice had formed over the stream. Weather in the city had become completely erratic: an unusually hot day might follow a day of the harshest winter.

Marina and Hector walked through a twisted alleyway to the square with the towers, each wrapped in a thick cape. They walked slowly, in no hurry whatsoever. From the west came the flying bathtub with its singing pilot at the helm. His voice was barely audible in the distance. It was the first time in several days that they'd gone out in search of provisions. In the last few weeks they'd subsisted on the provisions they'd stored, but they were running alarmingly low on fruit and they'd decided to dedicate a day to stocking up.

Bruno and Ricardo had gone out to intercept the two ships beyond the scar, while Marina and Hector were in charge of the third. Natalia had preferred to stay in the tower and keep battling with the magic books, while Maddie kept Lizbeth company in the dungeons.

"Come on!" Marina urged him. Her cheeks were red from the cold. "Tell me! I told you. Two boys. One was named Marcos, he was in my English class . . . The other was a cousin of a friend of mine, it was at her birthday party, in one of those ridiculous kissing games, truth or dare." She tugged at his arm. "How many girls have you kissed?"

Despite the bitter cold, it was a clear day, the sky a magnificent blue. The few clouds they saw were so faint that they looked like unfinished drawings.

"This conversation is making me uncomfortable," he answered. He remembered Natalia's fleeting kiss in the darkness, but before he could even feel guilty, he quickly pushed it out of his mind. "I don't know how it started, but I want it to be over." He gently shoved her forward. Marina gave him a sulky look.

They'd ended up on one of the main streets in the area. Marina walked a few yards ahead of him, until she suddenly turned around and pointed an accusing finger at him.

"None! You haven't kissed a single girl! That's why you don't want to say! You're embarrassed!"

"Why are you torturing me? What did I do?"

"I'm sorry, I can't help it." She looked at him over her shoulder and winked. "You're charming when you blush."

"You wicked, sadistic girl." Hector smiled maliciously. "I could make you blush if I wanted to, you know? But I'm a gentleman and I won't."

"Empty threats," she laughed. "You can't embarrass me with anything."

"I saw you naked," he let out suddenly.

She stopped short and turned to look at him head on.

"You're lying!" But she brought her hands to her face when his expression made it all too clear that he wasn't. Hector's smile grew when he saw her turn red. "No! You didn't! Oh! When? When?"

"Shortly after we got here. I saw you and Madeleine. You didn't close the door all the way when you were taking a bath."

"You spied on us? Some gentleman you are!"

"I got my just deserts. I fell down the stairs . . ."

"Oh, *that* day!" All of a sudden she smiled, arched an eyebrow slyly, and rushed over to him.

"Did you like what you saw?" she asked him, looking him in the eye.

Hector was painfully aware of how close she was, her smell, the heat of her body less than an inch away from his. Marina's hair was tangled and there was a minuscule wood shaving caught in a lock of hair that fell across her face. He had the urge to remove it, but his hands remained still. If he tried to touch her, he would die, he was sure of it—if he reached out a hand to caress her, he'd be struck down before he could touch her.

Rocavarancolia would kill him, or worse: it would kill her.

And suddenly, as if to confirm that prediction, the wind carried a new sound: a horrible chant unrelated to the sailboat scarecrow, a crude and unpleasant litany.

Marina stepped back after seeing his expression change. The sparkle in her eyes went from mischievous to alert. She took the bow from her left shoulder into her hands. Hector unsheathed his sword and looked around.

"What is that?" the girl asked, an arrow at the ready.

"It's coming from the square," he whispered.

They walked the rest of the way in silence. It was only one voice singing, in a language that didn't seem possible for a human throat. They reached the large sinkhole at the end of the street, right at the entry to the square, and sheltered in place as they looked on.

The petrified monsters and warriors stood motionless in the square, their shadows spilling out at their feet, immersed in that perpetual battle that neither side would ever win. A flock of black birds guffawed at the top of one of the tall stone trees, huddled against one another to protect against the cold. The sun shone directly on the glass tower, and its light, reflected off the web of cracks on the façade, was blinding.

Marina was the first to see him.

"It's Adrian." She pointed to the middle of the square.

The boy was sitting on the back of the petrified dragon, leaning lazily against its left wing. He held an open book in front of his face, a thin volume covered in red fabric so worn that it looked like it was wrapped in scarlet spiderwebs. He was the one singing that horrible tune. More than singing, it seemed like he was trying to imitate the crackling of flames. From his neck hung a variety of amulets, pendants, and necklaces, all emitting a faint bloody glow.

Marina and Hector approached him after exchanging a puzzled glance. Adrian seemed even smaller on the dragon's back. As soon as he laid eyes on them, he stopped singing, closed the book, and gave them a warm smile. Hector frowned. The horrible litany had stopped, but he felt as uneasy as before, and not knowing why made him all the more nervous. There was something strange in the square. Something that hadn't been there before.

"Now you're singing to the rocks?" Marina asked, at the feet of the rampant dragon. The monster's claw was just above her head. She pressed her outstretched hand against the beast's chest and looked up. "You spend too much time alone. If you come back to the tower with us, we'll let you sing to the spider in the courtyard."

Adrian let out a chuckle and patted the stone dragon, like a rider satisfied with his mount's performance. His hair was scorched and he had soot marks on his face and clothing; one in particular completely covered his right eye, as if someone had punched him in the face.

"The offer is tempting, but no, sorry. Giant spiders aren't my type."

"Whatever. He's charming when you get to know him." She shielded her forehead to get a better view. Now and then, reflections from the glass tower surrounded the boy like a garment made of light. "Okay, can you tell us what you're doing?"

Adrian scratched his head; the question seemed to make him uncomfortable. It took him a long time to respond.

"The last time I came by the tower, Bruno gave me more books about dragons, and, well . . . I've learned some pretty interesting things about them," he explained. "Apparently they're very resilient. They're probably the toughest creatures out there. It's because of their metabolism . . . They can adapt to their surroundings and survive for years in the most extreme conditions."

"Are you saying that this dragon is alive? Get out! You can't be serious!" Marina exclaimed. "For all we know it could have spent centuries turned into stone!"

"Thirty years. It's only been thirty years," Adrian said. "What you see here is part of the battle that was the end of Rocavarancolia and closed the doors to other worlds."

Adrian set the book down on the dragon's back and jumped down in two leaps; the first took him to the end of the monster's tattered wing, and the second directly to the ground. He landed barely two yards from Hector. A strong odor of ash emanated from him. Hector frowned even more.

"Even so," Marina said, "thirty years is a long time."

"It is, yes. And despite that, I assure you there's a chance that it's alive," Adrian said. "Okay, it's a slight chance, but it's there."

"You're pulling my leg. The spider from the courtyard won't like you if you make fun of me, I'm warning you."

"No, no. Listen: A sorcerer from Yemei turned Belaicadelaran, the greatest of all the dragons from his world, into crystal," he explained. "The animal was like that for more than five hundred years, until another sorcerer decided to revive it so that it could fight in a war. It was a complicated spell, and it required a great deal of effort, but he finally did it: he brought the dragon back. Five hundred years, Marina . . . Five centuries as crystal didn't kill it. So why would a handful of years as stone?"

The girl looked at the monster's half-open jaws. The dragon's eyes were bulging and enormous, focused on a group of riders that were harassing it with their lances. Marina seemed impressed.

"And why are you singing to it? You want to entertain it until it becomes flesh and blood again?"

"I'm not singing. It's a restoration spell." He ran hesitant fingers through his singed hair, as if he wasn't very sure if he should continue. He grimaced and watched Marina, focused on her reaction. "I want to wake it up," he announced. "That's what I want."

"You want to wake a dragon," she repeated after a moment, her jaw dropping. "Does that really seem like a good idea to you?" She gestured to the immense beast with both arms. "It's a dragon!"

"A dragon from Transalarada, to be exact . . . Isn't he beautiful?"

Marina shook her head.

"Very beautiful, yes. You can't be serious."

"I'm very serious. But don't worry. The restoration spell is out of my reach. Not even Bruno could perform it . . . It takes more magic than we have, much more. Who knows? Maybe when the Red Moon comes out, we'll be able to revive it." He smiled. "Can you imagine what we could do with a dragon?"

"And can you imagine what a dragon would do with us?" She turned toward Hector. "Are you hearing this? He wants to wake that thing up! Say something! Don't just stand there in silence!"

But he was barely paying attention to the conversation. He couldn't stop looking at Adrian while he tried to figure out what was wrong with the square. He squinted his eyes and looked around slowly. He looked at the faces of the men and monsters in battle around him. It was a compendium of ferocious grimaces, of gestures of pain or simple exhaustion. He rested his gaze on a grotesque being with a scorpion's tail that screamed mutely, split in two by a lance so big that it had to be wielded by two armored creatures at the same time.

"Hector? Are you listening to me?"

He suddenly realized what was wrong. It was quiet. The silence in the square was greater than usual. It was almost absolute. He only heard the sound of the wind and the occasional squawk of a bird. From the square, they'd always been able to hear the screams of those who burned in the district in flames. It was a disturbing, distant murmur, as much a part of the place as the petrified creatures. But it was gone. The screams had stopped. And the silence—and what that silence implied—was so terrible that it hurt.

Hector looked at the marks of ash and soot that covered Adrian's face. Then he looked down at Adrian's hands. The back of his right hand was blackened, and his shirtsleeve was burned. A shiver ran through his spine, a slow shiver that cut into his spine vertebra by vertebra as it climbed.

"What did you do?" he asked him in a whisper, barely parting his lips. He clenched his fists tightly.

The look Adrian gave him was one of complete indifference, and that enraged him all the more.

"Hector?" Marina asked, confused.

"What did you do?!" he repeated. He took a step toward him, but Adrian didn't budge.

"I don't know what you're . . ." he began. Suddenly his face lit up. "Ah . . . You're talking about—"

"The people . . . The fire . . ." He bit his lower lip.

"I killed them," Adrian answered, his voice swollen with pride, his eyes shining. "I killed them all. I went into the flames and finished them off, one by one. It took me hours."

"My God . . ." Marina brought her hand to her mouth and took a step back, horrified.

"You've gone crazy," Hector whispered. He couldn't believe what he'd just heard. "You've gone completely mad."

"Why are you looking at me like that? I did something that someone should have done a long time ago. I put an end to their pain."

Hector imagined him going in through the chaos of the silent flames: a small blond figure immersed in a labyrinth of frozen radiance, sword in hand, his shadow multiplied at his feet, searching for the places where those poor wretches screamed. He saw him floating in the air before cascades of flames, passing immaterially through walls of fire to reach every last one of them who'd been trapped in that inferno.

"How many people did you kill?!" he yelled, enraged. He pushed Adrian up against the dragon, grabbing the collar of his cape with both hands.

"They weren't people," he answered, in a condescending tone. "They were monsters. Horrible things . . . You should have seen them. Frightening creatures with bulging eyes and deformed limbs, grotesque beings with two heads . . ." He freed himself from Hector's grasp with a shove and got even closer to shout in his face. "And they'd been burning alive for thirty years! Do you hear me?! Burning for thirty years! Do you think they were upset by what I did?!" He pointed furiously to the neighborhood in flames. "They'll be thanking me! I put an end to their suffering! That's called mercy!"

Hector grimaced. Adrian couldn't fool him.

"Mercy? You're saying you did it out of mercy? You want to wake up a dragon who's spent years turned into stone . . . and you don't stop to think that there might have been a way to save all those people?" He hit the dragon with all his might. Several chips of rock scattered. Then he made himself breathe slowly, still staring at Adrian. It was beyond belief that the kid in front of him could be the same boy he'd met just months before, climbing a fountain and dressed in ridiculous pajamas; the same boy who took off running every time he saw a flaming bat. "Why did you do it?" he asked. The calm in his voice was completely at odds with the rage that consumed him.

"They weren't people," he insisted again. "They were monsters."

"Why did you do it?!" Hector howled. His hand flew to the hilt of his sword. He grabbed it, but he didn't draw it.

Marina cried out and tried to step between them, but Hector only had to move to the side to get out of her way.

For a second, it seemed like Adrian was also going for his sword, but instead, he shifted back and looked him in the eye.

"Because their damn screams distracted me from the spell," he whispered. "Are you satisfied? That's why I did it. So they would shut up, once and for all."

No one said anything for several moments. Atop the stone tree, the ugly black birds cackled.

"You're a monster," Hector murmured. Something dark and sinister twisted inside of him. "You didn't need the Red Moon to transform you."

He took a step back. And then another. If he didn't back off, he'd leap at him. If he didn't move away, he'd let his rage take him, and he'd beat him until one of them ended up lying on the ground.

"You feel it, right?" Adrian moved in his direction. The tone of his voice had changed. Now it was almost friendly. "The fire. You feel it. I see it in your eyes."

"Shut up," Hector hissed. He wanted to hit him. He wanted to pound his head to pieces. He wanted to kill him.

"Yes. I can see it. You feel the fire. It's begging you to hurt me."

"You're insane!" he shouted. He took another step back, shocked in spite of himself that Adrian could have described so accurately what he was experiencing. It felt like liquid fire was running through his veins. He still hadn't let go of the hilt of his sword, and his whole being demanded he unsheathe it and launch himself at Adrian.

"I've felt that fire since Bruno brought me back to life," Adrian said. "It won't let me sleep, and sometimes I can't even think. That fire is what made me go and look for that kid . . . That fire is everything. It burns me, it scorches me, it consumes me. And it will consume all of you."

"Don't listen to him." Marina grabbed Hector by the arm and pulled him away. He dropped his sword immediately. "Don't pay any attention to him. You're right: he's insane. This city has driven him insane."

"This has nothing to do with insanity." Adrian faced her. "It has to do with being awake! Denestor was right when he told us that he brought us to the place where we belong. On Earth I was blind, and I can see now! Here we'll be what we're meant to be!"

"Murderers?" Hector asked scornfully.

"No," Adrian answered, and pointed vigorously to the dragon. "We'll be power, do you hear me? Without weakness, without fear. We'll be everything we want to be. Fighting it doesn't make sense! Can't you see that?"

"I'd rather not tell you what I see," Hector said. Marina's hand still on his arm comforted him. He felt his rage ebbing away, but the memory of that fire still burned in his mind. He didn't want to think about it. He wasn't ready.

Adrian turned his back to them and, after casting a levitation spell, began to ascend the dragon's spine. When he reached the top, he faced them and looked down from up high, his cape whipping in the breeze, his eyes sparkling.

"As much as you fight, as much as you struggle, you can't stop it. You'll succumb to the fire too. And the only thing that makes you different from me is that I already started down that path."

"We'll never be like you," Hector said.

"That, I suppose, is something that only time will tell."


"The demiurge is getting too close," Hurza said, his voice like a hungry tomb. "I must kill him. I can't delay it much longer."

THE CHILDREN OF DARKNESS

"Yes, yes . . . Denestor must die. Yes, yes . . ." whispered the witch seated at the other end of the table. She was a grotesque woman, decked out in a tattered wedding dress. Underneath the dirty, dusty silk of her gown waved the blue vipers that covered her. There were dozens of them twisted around her body, endlessly shifting their positions.

Lady Serena watched her with poorly concealed disgust. Lady Venom was the latest addition to Hurza's small group. The witch, an unpleasant creature who lived in a cave in the mountains, was also part of the Royal Council of Rocavarancolia. She'd taken the place of Rorcual, who'd been assassinated by the same being who had just announced that the time had come to kill Denestor Tul.

The phantom didn't understand why Hurza would include the witch in his scheme. Lady Venom was extremely stupid, a crazy woman who had nothing to offer. No, she didn't know why Hurza wanted her, but there were so many things she didn't know about him that she was beginning to accept she'd never understand his actions and motivations. The first Lord of Assassins was a mystery to Lady Serena, something incomprehensible. And he was the only one capable of freeing her from her existence as a wandering soul, which was all that really mattered.

"All I need is my grimoire to do it," he assured her the first night they spoke, surrounded by the sphere of silence. "Once I regain the power that I deposited in its pages, I can give you the rest that you deserve."

"You can't," Lady Serena said. "Because it's no longer the book that you knew. A blood spell protects it, and only a vampire can use it now without being destroyed."

"I know. Fate had me assassinate the last of that species before I knew of that detail, but fate shall also bring a new vampire to Rocavarancolia."

"One of Denestor's kids?"

Hurza nodded.

"The Margalar Tower already stinks of bloodsucker," he said. "When the Red Moon comes out, the change will be complete, and I'll be closer than ever to accessing the book's power. And I promise that the first thing I'll do when that happens is kill you."

"And what will you ask of me in return?"

"Your absolute loyalty until then, of course. There are those in Rocavarancolia who won't view my return or my plans in a positive

290 JOSÉ ANTONIO COTRINA

light. Maybe I have no other choice but to confront them before I'm truly prepared. If that happens, I'll need your skills to defeat them."

"And if I refuse? What's to stop me from telling Denestor and Esmael what I know? As you've said yourself, at this time you don't have the power to destroy me."

"I wouldn't be able to stop you from betraying me. That's true. And the demiurge and the assassin would finish me off. Yes. They would destroy me, without a doubt. And with my death, you'd likely lose the last chance of reaching oblivion. Is it worth it to take such a risk?"

Lady Serena didn't answer. The answer was clear.

The ghost scanned the small table where they sat. Besides the unpleasant Lady Venom and Hurza himself, there was Ujthan, the immense warrior who'd become the most loyal champion of the reborn Lord of Assassins, and Solberinus, the castaway. It was surprising to see how that man had prospered in Rocavarancolia. He'd gone from being a mere victim of the lighthouse to holding a seat on the Royal Council, and now, at Hurza's whim, he formed part of the conspiracy. As with the witch, she wondered how useful Solberinus could be in his plans. The castaway might have been a born survivor, but aside from that he was just a normal, ordinary human. Lady Serena also wondered how Hurza had bought his loyalty. He'd promised Ujthan a war, he'd promised her destruction—what could Solberinus desire?

The five of them were gathered in a windowless diamond-shaped room with black walls and no decor. The only things of note were a small dark chest, located in the middle of a ledge halfway up one of the walls, and a wardrobe that looked like a casket standing upright. The room was located inside the castle, but it was protected by a magic so ancient and powerful that not one of the castle's inhabitants knew of its existence.

It was Ujthan who led her to it two weeks before, each of them wrapped in a spell of silence and another of darkness. The warrior stopped in front of a shabby curtain in the middle of a hallway in the south wing of the fortress. Lady Serena once again had the dubious pleasure of seeing Hurza emerge from the warrior's flesh, as if he were nothing more than another weapon engraved on his body. Once he set foot on the ground, the first Lord of Assassins advanced within the sphere of silence until he touched a specific spot on the curtain. Suddenly, the threadbare curtain turned into an embossed bronze door.

"The paradox room," Hurza explained as he grasped the door handle. "Only those guided here by someone who's already been inside are able to see it."

As soon as they went in, Lady Serena focused on the black chest. She immediately felt a pulsation of an ancient power coming from inside of it, a flow of energy so deep that it was hard for her to resist the impulse to approach it and open it.

Since then, they'd had two meetings there already. This was the third.

"The demiurge must die, yes, yes, yes," the witch repeated, rocking forward and back. A light sprinkling of dust and grime fell from her dress to the floor.

The death of Denestor Tul. That was the reason why Hurza had gathered them there. It was clear that the time had come that Lady Serena so feared: confronting the rest of Rocavarancolia. She'd harbored hope that her treason would not be necessary. Once Hurza collected the energy deposited in his grimoire, he could confront Denestor as well as Esmael. But the old demiurge's investigations were beginning to prove dangerous. If he stayed on course, it wouldn't be long before he discovered that the threat that hovered over Rocavarancolia came from its past. The language that Belisarius had used to write on the parchment was an ancient dialect of Nazara, the first linked world, the language that the followers of Hurza and Harex used. There were very few references to this dialect and to the cult of the two brothers, but they did exist. If anyone could find them, it was Denestor.

"Killing him won't be easy," the ghost assured them. "He's the most powerful demiurge that Rocavarancolia has had in centuries. In the war I saw him confront the conclave of Faraian's wizards, and his spells were the only ones that were able to defeat him and his creatures."

"I know more than enough about Denestor Tul's abilities," Hurza commented. His features were still those of Belisarius, but at the same time they weren't. It was as if two different faces struggled to dominate that brownish flesh. The eyes were bigger, the nose, which before had been bulbous and swollen, was smaller, and in the center of his forehead a small bony protuberance had begun to emerge. "I don't like the idea of confronting him directly. That's why I need an alternate plan." Hurza leaned back in his seat. The palms of his hands rested on the edge of the table like thirsty spiders. "And that's why I gathered you here. We must find a simple way of terminating the demiurge."

"What if one of my children pays him a visit?" Lady Venom said as she dramatically stretched out one of her arms. A viper peered its head through her sleeve, hissed, and went back into hiding. "Or poison in his drink, perhaps? I know a concoction that will turn his blood to water and shatter every last one of his bones."

Hurza didn't even bother to respond. By the look he gave the witch, Lady Serena understood that he despised her as much as she did. Which made her wonder again why he'd included the hag in his plans.

"I should be the one to kill him. That goes without saying. I should kill him with my own hands. The demiurge of Rocavarancolia deserves that honor."

Lady Serena shuddered. She closed her eyes for a second, unable to believe that she was there, thinking of the best way to kill Denestor. She didn't feel particularly connected to him, of course, just as she never felt connected to anything that was alive, but the demiurge awoke certain sympathies in her. She pushed the thought firmly away. She couldn't allow herself the luxury of feeling compassion. She must shield herself from that nauseating sentiment. Let the demiurge die, yes, let all of creation fall if that was the price to pay to end her misery.

"Ideally his death would appear to be by pure coincidence," Solberinus commented. Lady Serena didn't recall having heard him speak in any of the Royal Council meetings, but he always spoke in the meetings in the black room. "Yes. That would be best. Another murder on the council would be counterproductive given the situation; on the other hand, if it appeared to be an accidental death—"

"Sorcerers don't have accidents," Ujthan broke in. "Much less demiurges. They always have their creatures nearby to save them from any trouble."

"So we have no choice but to be subtle," Solberinus pointed out.

"An ambush! We'll take him by surprise!" The witch pounded the palm of her left hand with her right. "We'll jump him when he least expects it and tear him to pieces!"

"Still, even if we catch him off guard, he won't give up without a fight," Lady Serena pointed out. Once again she remembered Denestor in the battle for Rocavarancolia, mounted on a bronze dragon, surrounded by a myriad of his creations, facing the seventeen magicians of Faraian. He managed to kill four before they stopped him. "And we can't allow the luxury of a drawn-out confrontation. The disturbances caused by magical combat would attract the whole city, no matter how powerful our spells of interference and camouflage might be . . . We must finish him quickly."

"With one single blow," Lady Venom hissed. "An unerring, precise blow."

"Maybe I can facilitate things," whispered Ujthan, rising from his chair. He reached round his back and sank his fingers into his right shoulder blade. By the expression on his face it was clear that he wasn't completely sure of what he was doing.

Lady Serena watched as the warrior's fingers grabbed one of the tattoos from his back and slowly extracted it from his flesh. First a long curved handle emerged, made of bone and carved with countless runes, then came the blade of a green steel broadsword, covered with the same runes as the hilt.

"I got this sword in Nago," Ujthan explained as he held the weapon before them. It was over six feet long and he held it with one hand, with the same ease with which he would have handled a piece of cutlery. "It's one of the mythical weapons from that world," he continued. "Its name is Glosada, Killer of Sorcerers."

Hurza studied it with interest. It was unusually wide, and around the runes the green of the blade took on a more brilliant tone. Lady Venom bared her blackened teeth and leaned forward.

"It reeks of power . . ." she whispered. She clutched the edge of the table, and instantly the wood around her fingers turned a nauseating yellow color. "What is it? What is it?"

"In Nago they began a crusade to kill all the magic practitioners in their world, and this was the most powerful weapon they forged to fight them," Ujthan said.

Lady Serena observed the sword brandished by the warrior with admiration. There were hardly any magical weapons left in Rocavarancolia. The armies of the linked worlds had taken all they could find. If they'd known of the magic arsenal engraved on Ujthan's body, they would have ended his life immediately. She shifted her gaze toward Hurza and saw a strange light in his eyes, a mix of greed and eagerness. Ujthan continued:

"It absorbs the magic of whomever it touches," he explained to them. "A mere scratch is enough to leave the most powerful sorcerer dry, without a trace of energy left in his body."

"I want that sword," Hurza ordered in an authoritarian tone. Ujthan swallowed and tried to hide his consternation from those around him. He felt as if every last one of his tattoos had suddenly turned to ice.

"I would gladly give it to you, my lord," he said. His voice trembled, and this made him feel all the more insecure. "But . . . but only I can wield the weapons linked to my body. If anyone else tries to brandish them, they turn to dust . . ."

The first Lord of Assassins looked at Ujthan carefully. Throughout his entire life, the warrior had confronted the most frightening creatures in more than a dozen worlds, had fought an endless number of battles, had stared death in the face a hundred times, but nothing compared to being the target of the Eye-Eater's gaze. Every time Hurza looked at him it was as if one of his long, sharp fingers plunged into his soul. Without thinking he grasped Glosada more tightly. It was then that he realized the tremendous mistake he'd made. He'd just revealed the existence of that weapon on impulse, in an attempt to be useful, but what he'd actually done was reveal to Hurza that he had in his power a weapon capable of defeating him. And in doing so he'd completely lost that advantage.

"I want to try it for myself." Hurza smiled coldly. His smiles were almost worse than his gazes. "Let me hold one of your weapons, Ujthan. Any one of them. Let's find out for sure that what you say is true."

The warrior hesitated once again. He looked at the other occupants of the table, searching for support and coming up empty. Then he sat back down in his chair. He had exactly one hundred and twenty-eight weapons tattooed on his body, and he loved them equally. They all represented something special, from the first one he'd obtained to the last. Those tattoos formed part of his being. What Hurza was asking of him was the equivalent of asking him to cut off a hand or a foot.

"I give my most solemn word of honor that what I say is the truth," he insisted. He managed to make his voice sound firm this time. "No one other than me can use my weapons—"

"I've been betrayed so many times that I promised myself never to trust anyone." Hurza stretched out a hand to the warrior and looked directly at him. Ujthan felt those cold fingers plunge inside him once again.

He took a deep breath and nodded. He had no choice but to give in. It was very hard for him to choose which weapon to hand over. He finally opted for a longbow that he'd obtained in his first battle. They had sent him specifically to kill an enemy lookout, and after he'd done it he kept the bow as a trophy. He set Glosada down on the table, extracted the bow from his wrist with trembling fingers, and handed it to Hurza.

As soon as the Eye-Eater's hand closed around the bow, it turned to dust. Hurza nodded, satisfied.

"When this is all over, when there is no one left to confront me, we will find a way of disconnecting this sword from your flesh without destroying it," he said as he rubbed his hands to discard the remains of the bow. His eyes settled again on the warrior, somber and terrible. Ujthan hesitated again, but then nodded. Next, Hurza looked at all of the others gathered in the room. "We have now decided what shall deliver the blow, but we still must decide how and when we're going to do it."

"If I may be so bold," the castaway interjected, shifting in his chair. "I think I have an idea that might suit us to perfection."

The ghost, the witch, the warrior, and the monster reborn listened carefully to his words. It was an actual outline of a plan, and as she listened, Lady Serena wondered if Solberinus was improvising or if this was something that he'd prepared beforehand. The plan wasn't very complicated, and therein lay its main virtue. Only Lady Venom had objections, but no one cared about her opinion. Despite that, the meeting stretched for several hours. The assassination of a demiurge was not something that could be left to chance.

Finally, when it was barely two hours before dawn, Hurza called an end to the assembly. Lady Venom was the first to leave; she'd been asleep during the final part of the meeting, but no one had taken the trouble to wake her. Ujthan, still affected by the loss of his bow, was next. He walked hunched over and gloomy, stroking the place where the weapon had been engraved on his body. He looked at Hurza out of the corner of his eye as he passed but said nothing; he'd sworn obedience to that monster, and the promise of a warrior was sacred: now his destiny and Hurza's were linked. Solberinus left after him, visibly pleased. The weak glimmer in his eyes was that of a dark, tortured soul who suddenly found some joy in his existence. Lady Serena and Hurza were the last to withdraw.

The ghost hesitated before crossing the threshold. She stopped and looked at the black chest on the wall; for a second she had felt a strong outburst of magic inside. Lady Serena felt strangely empty. Planning Denestor Tul's death had affected her more than she expected. That wasn't going to stop her, of course, but it did bring up issues that she hadn't really cared to consider before. Until then, for example, she'd had zero interest in what Hurza's plans were. She knew he wanted to control Rocavarancolia, but she didn't know why—if all he longed for was power or if there was something else.

She decided that the time had come to find out more.

"What's inside the chest?" she asked. "I feel magic boiling inside of it. And it's eager magic, magic that wants to be free."

Hurza turned toward her and watched her with an impenetrable expression.

"Nothing for you to worry about," he answered, after a few moments of silence. "When that chest opens, you will no longer be with us."

"And I'll pay a high price for it," she answered. "I'm betraying the kingdom I once ruled over. I'm betraying everything I was in life, everything I believed in . . . That's why I need—"

"Betrayal?" Hurza interrupted her abruptly. His eyes were wide open. "You dare speak to me of betrayal? You and your people have corrupted the essence of Rocavarancolia, you've diverted it from its mission, from its true path." He lowered his voice so that it became a venomous whisper. "You've turned it into a mockery."

Ujthan peered around the door to see what was delaying them, but Hurza closed it in his face with a hand gesture. Then he turned to face the ghost once more.

"Do you want to know what the chest contains?" he asked. "I'll tell you: inside are the remains of my brother Harex, founder of this kingdom you claim you are betraying." He took a step toward her and spoke again, his voice choked with rage. "We raised this city out of nothing," he said. "We brought the Red Moon down from the sky, sculpted Rocavaragalago, and opened doors to other worlds. We're the ones who've been betrayed. They murdered us. We gave them life, power, and they killed us. And you speak to me of betrayal?! No, this is not betrayal: this is justice."

Lady Serena looked back at the chest. The magic that lurked inside was far from being dead. It was living, pulsing like the heart of a sleeping sun. It was then that she understood what it contained.

"The horn of Harex . . ." she whispered.

"Yes. That's right." Hurza nodded, calmer. "And his soul inside. Waiting for centuries for the moment to come back to life. And when he does, when he's in a mortal body once again, we will take our seats at the head of the kingdom, and everything will be as it should have been from the beginning. Oh, yes. This time we'll make sure it happens."

"But I still don't understand . . ." Lady Serena said. "What is it you're looking for? What is the true purpose of Rocavarancolia that you speak of?"

Hurza seemed ready to answer, but suddenly the expression on his face changed. He stroked the horn that was growing from his forehead and smiled.

"Enough questions, Lady Serena. You know everything you need to know," he said. "And allow me to remind you of something I told you in our first conversation. Do you want to stop me? Do you want to betray me? Go ahead. I won't even try to prevent you. Go talk to the black angel if you wish and tell him what you know. If you do, I'll be damned—but so will you." And without another word, he left.

The ghost took one more look at the chest and followed him, even more confused than before. The bronze door closed behind them, and all was silent.

For a long period nothing moved in the room with the black walls, until suddenly the dust under the seat that Lady Venom had occupied began to move. At first it formed small whirlwinds, restless waves that collapsed as soon as they were born; then, little by little, the dust gained control of itself, and its movements became more fluid and precise. Slowly but surely, drawing a stubborn trail on the dirty tile floor, the remains of what was once Enoch the Dusty moved toward the crack between the bronze door and the floor.

Hector woke up at dawn, out of breath and drenched in sweat. He'd had a horrible nightmare, but he'd forgotten it as soon as he opened his eyes; only the anguish that it caused remained. He sat up in bed and looked around, dazed and frightened by the bad dream in spite of himself. It seemed brighter than normal; a sullen light filtered in through the open hatch in the ceiling. Hector thought it was strange to see it like that: they always closed it at nighttime. When his eyes adjusted to the shadows, he saw that there were two empty beds: one was Bruno's, the other Marina's. The Italian had assured him that he'd never go out at night and Hector figured he must be downstairs, with his nose in his books or trying a new spell on Lizbeth. He got out of bed, threw his cape around his shoulders, and headed for the roof. Natalia shifted in her bed, and as he looked over, he saw the girl was awake and watching him.

"Marina's up there, she went out a while ago," she whispered, and before he could say anything, she wrapped herself up in the blanket and turned her back to him.

Maddie and Ricardo were also awake; neither of the two moved or looked at him, but he could tell by their breathing and their forms under the sheets. Hector himself had spent hours trying to fall asleep, only to fall into a nightmare. They were uneasy, and not without reason. What Adrian had done had upset all of them, even Bruno. The Italian had had to sit down when he heard the news, and that made it all the more disturbing.

"And what if I did something wrong when I healed him?" he wondered. "It was practically my first spell, and maybe I made a mistake . . ." He stopped there. He removed his top hat and began twirling it obsessively as his gaze went from one of them to the other, hoping for a response.

"You have to stop blaming yourself every time something bad happens," Madeleine said. And to add to his agitation, she took the top hat from his hands, planted it firmly back on his head, and sat down in his lap. She looked him in the eyes for a long time before she spoke: "Despite what you might think, you're not the center of the universe, and you're not responsible for everything that happens around you, okay?"

The Italian stammered, but ended up nodding. Since then he'd been silent, even more absent than usual. Hector wondered if he was mulling over Maddie's words.

He went up the improvised stairs made from boxes and a barrel, and then climbed through the opening. Outside, the cold night air and an unpleasant wind that couldn't decide which direction to blow in awaited him.

Marina was leaning against the battlement, looking to the east. The girl wore a scarlet cape over the sleeveless shirt and shorts that she usually slept in. The indecisive wind whipped her hair around. She tried to control it with her hand but it was a losing battle. Hector called to her softly before he hoisted himself up and outside: he didn't want to startle her by appearing out of the blue. She turned, brushed her unruly hair out of her face, and smiled. It wasn't a huge smile; it was somewhat forced and tainted with sadness.

"You can't sleep either?" he asked when he reached her.

Marina shook her head. She seemed completely dejected.

"It's Adrian. I'm horrified by what he did." She shuddered as she remembered it. "Is that what we're going to become? Heartless creatures?"

"I . . ." What could he tell her? That everything would be fine? That they'd never turn into anything like that? And how could he say that when he had no idea what was going to happen? The confidence with which he'd faced Adrian was long behind him. Now he only had doubts. "I wish I knew, I wish I had an answer . . . But I don't. I don't know what's going to happen to us. And it's terrifying not knowing. Even more so after what happened this afternoon, after I was about to . . ." He didn't finish the sentence. He noticed that he was out of breath. He had avoided thinking about it, but now the memory of the fire and rage was too strong to ignore.

Marina looked at him without saying anything. Hector was quiet and looked at the shadowy city. Three more stars had appeared, and he could clearly see the glow from the closed vortices that burned sporadically. Something howled in the distance. He wondered if Lizbeth was doing the same in the dungeon.

"If you hadn't been with me in the square," he began, still refraining from looking at her, "if you hadn't touched me like you did and when you did . . . I would have attacked him. I would have . . . Because Adrian was right." He brushed his hair away from his forehead, but the wind immediately blew it back in his eyes. "I felt the fire: it was burning me. My veins were inflamed, and every last fiber of my being was begging me to kill him."

Marina's hand searched for his atop the battlement. He pulled his back before she could touch him, but he did it in such a way that it seemed like a fortuitous movement, rather than an abrupt one.

"Well, then I'm glad I was with you," she said, ignoring the rebuff. "Mostly because you didn't stand a chance. Adrian's better with a sword than you, and he knows magic. You wouldn't have lasted two seconds."

"I know. He would have given me a beating . . . or something worse. But that's not what worries me." He supported himself on his crossed arms against the crenel. "It's the fire. That fire that consumed me, that desire to do harm." He looked at her. "Was it me? Or was it the Red Moon? And if that's the effect that it causes in me, what am I going to turn into when it comes out? What if Adrian's right about that too? What if in the end I turn out like him?"

"You're not like that. You're not like Adrian."

"I don't know. I don't know anymore." He shrugged his shoulders. "I think I can officially confess that I'm scared to death."

"That makes two of us," she said. She took a deep breath, as if finding the strength to continue. "Because I feel the effect of the Red Moon too," she confessed. "Something's happening to my eyesight." She smiled sadly at his worried glance. "No, it's not what you think. I'm not losing my vision; it's the opposite, actually. It's improving. I can see better and better all the time. I can see farther and more clearly. Even at night." She pointed to one of the new specks of light that had emerged in the west. "Look over there, toward that vortex or whatever it is, can you see it?"

"I can see it." It was far away, but not too far away. He saw the violet and scarlet glimmers of the small aurora twisting in the night like a ghostly rose with all the wrong colors.

"It's surrounded by butterflies," she said. Her voice shook. "They're transparent, but I can see them perfectly. They're carrying little pieces of magic in their legs, who knows where. Maybe they eat it, or they're making nests. I don't know." Two tears slid down her cheeks. "They only come out at night. I think they're so fragile that sunlight would kill them."

Hector shifted his gaze from that vibrant source of light to look at her. Marina also seemed fragile right then. She had always been pale, but now she was even more so. The color of her skin was closer to white than to pink.

"That's not all, is it?" he asked. "It's not just your vision. There's something else." He suspected why she hadn't told him that her vision was improving until now: something else was changing, and she knew it would show on her face as soon as she started talking, whatever it was.

"Yes . . . I . . . It's not . . ." She ran her hand through her hair and huffed. Hector realized she was making a huge effort to tell him this. "What you said to me the other day, that I hardly eat, remember?" He nodded. "It's not what it looks like. Cooked food doesn't appeal to me, the mere sight of it makes me sick. It started a few weeks ago and it's getting worse. But I wasn't lying when I told you that I eat well. I swear, I'm not trying to deceive you . . . I eat when no one's watching because it's disgusting and it scares me, but I can't help it, it's the only thing I fancy." Her voice cracked in her throat. She took a breath and went on. "The same food Madeleine sets aside for Lizbeth. That's what I eat: raw meat." She covered her mouth with the palm of her hand, surprised at having revealed her secret.

Hector gripped the crenel tightly, as if he were in a ship at the mercy of a storm, and at any moment he might be tossed overboard. He closed his eyes for several seconds, searching for something to say. This time he found it.

"I don't know what awaits us," he repeated. "The Red Moon might come and turn us all into horrible creatures . . . Or maybe Bruno might find something that can free us from this curse . . . Or maybe Rocavarancolia itself will kill us tomorrow and end this nightmare . . ." He shook his head. For a moment he thought maybe that was best, that maybe the path Marco had chosen was the most sensible. He rejected the idea, horrified. "But if it happens, if we make it to the end alive, if we have no choice but to witness the coming of that moon . . ." He looked her in the eyes before continuing. "Whatever happens, whatever comes to pass, I'll be with you. I promise. I won't leave your side. I know it's not much comfort, but . . ."

Marina smiled.

"It helps," she said. "Of course it helps."

She started to move closer to him, but hesitated and stayed where she was. She brought a hand to her neck and bit her lower lip.

"But . . ." she began. She'd suddenly turned red.

"What?" he asked.

"Tonight I need something more," she said without looking at him. "Starting tomorrow, that promise of being by my side will be enough . . . But tonight there's something that . . . I . . ."

"What is it?" he asked, his heart pounding.

"Nothing, nothing . . . It's nothing . . ." She hesitated. "It's that . . . Tonight, just for tonight: will you hold me? Even if it's just for a moment. Just a hug. Just that."

Hector was frozen on the battlement, as paralyzed as the creatures in the square. He nodded slowly. He could do it; of course he could. In fact, he wanted nothing else but to hold her in his arms: feel her body against his and never let her go. He clumsily put an arm around her shoulders; she turned to him and buried her face in his chest. They both trembled. For a moment Hector's right hand lay still at Marina's side. It was hard for him to move it and cross that damned line that separated them.

*Just this once. It will just be this once*, he thought.

They embraced in the fading darkness of the Rocavarancolian night, desperately, as if they were the only two people left in the world. As if the emptiness were closing in on them and they only had each other.

Above the Margalar Tower, above the clouds, halfway between the auroras and the stars, enveloped in shards of murky shadows, Hurza watched them.

And a new star, cold and distant, emerged in the night. A new aurora lit up in the ruined city. And the Red Moon continued its path through the darkness of space, as colossal as a gigantic drop of blood spilling from the wound of some primordial entity.

# THE TROLL

Twenty-seven days remained before the arrival of the Red Moon.

On the clock, the star was at eleven, so close to the scarlet sphere of the moon that they almost touched. Hector, in spite of himself, looked at it again that morning as soon as he stepped outside of the tower, unaware that the clock with its ominous countdown would soon lose all meaning for him.

"Staring at it isn't going to make it stop," Ricardo told him.

"I'm sure that would be easier than shutting those two up," he mumbled grouchily as he nodded his head toward the tower. They could still hear the shrieks of Marina and Natalia, who were wrapped up in their thousandth argument that week.

"You're right about that," Ricardo said. "What the hell's going on with them?"

Hector shrugged his shoulders. He didn't understand his friends. Recently they'd spent most of their time arguing, almost always for the most insignificant and absurd reasons. Today the tension between them had reached a new level and they'd ended up screaming at each other with such violence that even Bruno peered his head around the stairwell to see what the fuss was about. Ricardo and Hector couldn't take such a hostile environment and decided it was best to disappear for a while. Besides, it was impossible to mediate between them, as any attempt to do so only succeeded in making them forget their argument long enough to turn on whoever interrupted them. Madeleine was the smartest of them all: as soon as she caught a whiff of a confrontation she disappeared speedily into the dungeon, taking refuge behind the spell of silence linked to its door.

"They're going through another phase, that's all," the redhead told them. "When it's over they'll be better friends than ever, believe me."

"But what if they kill each other before that happens?" Hector asked, not entirely joking.

"Well . . ." Maddie's lips formed a malicious smile. "Then, problem solved, right?"

Ricardo hurried him along with a look when the noise in the tower intensified. Marina shouted at them to come and give their opinion about whatever it was they were discussing, while Natalia screamed that they shouldn't even think about getting involved. The boys picked up their pace, almost running across the drawbridge.

"Did you find out what they're arguing about?" Hector asked.

"I think one of them picked out a shirt that the other wanted to wear today . . ." He sighed and pushed him to walk faster as he cast a fearful glance behind. "Or something like that. It wasn't very clear to me, and I didn't really want to find out."

They went into the streets of Rocavarancolia with no other goal than to pass enough time for things to calm down back at the tower. By chance they ended up in the southeast part of the city, near a destroyed lot that they'd never paid much attention to. It looked like it had once been home to a large building, but nothing of the structure remained except a fragmented wall around the perimeter and heaps of rubble here and there. In the middle of the yard a new vortex had appeared. It hadn't been there the last time they'd passed by, less than a week ago; it was a brilliant spark of light, about a foot and a half tall and eight inches wide. They walked toward it, advancing with care over the irregular terrain full of cracks and sinkholes. The greenish-amber light of the vortex soon illuminated both of them, and the ancient portal hovered five feet off the ground, beautiful and blinding, like a jewel made out of energy. Hector reached a hand upward, without touching it. The play of the light tinted his skin with bright colors. This had once been the door to another world.

"In half a year a vortex to Earth will open up," he said. He hadn't thought about it for some time. The Red Moon occupied so much of his thoughts that it was hard for him to think about what might happen after.

Ricardo stared at the flower of light that turned in front of them.

"That's what Denestor said," he pointed out. "I suppose that's when they'll give us the opportunity to go home. We signed in blood. It's in the contract." The bitterness in his voice was clear.

"Each year I will be given the opportunity to return home or remain in Rocavarancolia if that is my desire," Hector whispered. He didn't know if those were the exact words, but he doubted they were far off. "And they'll do it. Denestor couldn't lie to us. They'll let us leave if we want."

"Oh, sure." Ricardo shook his head. "Sure they will."

"Go back . . ." Hector smiled scornfully. "And where do you suppose we'll go back to? No one remembers us on Earth. No one. And when that happens, the Red Moon will already have transformed all of us. How could we go back like that? We'll be monsters."

"Maybe that's how legends are born on Earth," the other whispered. "All of those stories about werewolves, vampires, and the rest . . . Maybe they were just like us: people who wanted to go home."

They both watched the vortex in silence for a long while, lost in thought.


The sea was so turbulent it looked as if it might escape the seabed. The waves that pounded the cliff rose up like enraged columns of furious water and dirty foam. Ships crashed against one another under the constant onslaught of the ocean, and a few went under for good. Beneath the turbid water, beasts from all parts of the ocean congregated: silver whales floating motionlessly while sea serpents swam around them; jellyfish the size of warships propelled themselves, as luminous as suns plucked from the sky; titans with a thousand tentacles battled endlessly against the armies of sharks that plagued them. Mermaids took refuge in the deepest trenches and watched, torn between terror and awe, as immense shadows came and went in what used to be their territory, not that long ago.

From the top of the lighthouse, Solberinus watched the water. Even he wouldn't dare to climb down below, with the ocean in such a state.

He'd had more than enough of that in his early days in Rocavarancolia, when he'd had no choice but to coexist with the storms and the marine monsters, when each day was a struggle to survive, with no encouragement but the messages from the lighthouse. Those letters had helped to keep him alive for years; without them he wouldn't have had the strength to survive. But in the end it had turned out to be nothing but a horrifying joke, another mockery from the cursed city.

"Put yourself in my service, castaway, kneel before me and I, in exchange, will make your greatest desire a reality," Hurza the Eye-Eater had assured him.

"You will?" he asked, skeptical that he could fulfill such a promise. "You'll destroy Rocavarancolia for me? Lay this city to waste until not a stone remains? Because that is the only thing I long for."

"I will. I give you my word that sooner or later I will destroy this place. Yes, Solberinus, believe me when I tell you that few promises I've made throughout my life will be as easy to fulfill as that one. And I won't stop at destroying Rocavarancolia, I swear to you. I'll turn this world to pieces and wrench the Red Moon from the sky. There will be nothing left. Not even ashes."

Solberinus only had to look into the eyes of that frightening creature to know that he was telling the truth.

He gazed at the raging water. He knew the rhythm of the tides and knew there would soon come a brief period of calm; the sea would become still for a while before kicking back up again. Then they would kill Denestor Tul. Solberinus smiled fiercely. He was thinking of paying Rocavarancolia back in spades for all the pain it had given him.


The influence of the coming star was noticeable throughout the whole city. Creatures that had been hibernating for months woke from their long slumber and returned to life. From one of the many wells in Rocavarancolia a half-bird, half-lizard creature covered in greenish mud emerged. It squawked twice and started to fly with great difficulty, until it perched at the top of the triumphal arch which commemorated the end of a forgotten war. It stayed there for some time, cleaning off— feather by feather and scale by scale—the mud that covered it. The crocodiles that slept submerged in a flooded passageway opened their eyes almost in unison and began to crawl through the dark hallways, heading to the surface in search of sustenance. On their way they passed by the grotto where the shapeshifter without a name continued his slow rocking, surrounded by bones, scorpions, and rats.

Not only animals came back to life with the arrival of the Red Moon. In the most remote reaches of a dilapidated mansion, something rustled in an old coffin leaning upright against a wall. The lid fell to the ground with a crash, and a figure wrapped in layers upon layers of cobwebs stumbled out. From the chaos of matted threads emerged a twisted, skeletal hand. Soon, another followed and joined its twin in the task of escaping the tangled cocoon. Spiders ran around furiously while the creature rid itself of the foul blanket that covered it. After a long battle, a human skeleton came to light, without a trace of skin, flesh, or muscles: just bare bones to which strips of web still clung.

The horror opened and closed its fleshless hands, stretched its long arms, and then looked around. Belgadus, one of the most renowned necromancers in the history of Rocavarancolia, had created that creature over two centuries before; it had been formed from the bones of hundreds of dead sorcerers. Belgadus defiled the tombs on the cemetery island of Echicia, a linked world, and in that very place he assembled his aberration, using one bone—only one—from each mage. The necromancer's intention had been to create the most powerful sorcerer to have ever existed, but all he had achieved was a furious creature without a drop of blood in its entire being. Belgadus died, but his creation survived him.

The skeleton discovered a sealed envelope on a tall nightstand next to the coffin. He approached it with a clumsy gait, still pulling off spiderwebs, grabbed the envelope, tore it open, and proceeded to read the letter it contained. It announced that he had just become a member of the Royal Council, and by the date on the letterhead, it was from several weeks ago. Unfazed by the news, the skeleton laid the letter and envelope back on the table and picked up the garment hanging from the back of the chair. It was a human pelt, the skin of Belgadus, torn from his corpse by his own creation. The skeleton put it on with some difficulty. When he was about to pull the mask that had once been the necromancer's face over his head, a sudden movement among the shadows in a corner made him pause.

"What demented freak dares to sneak into my home?" the skeleton asked. He turned as he bent down toward the figure he saw. His voice was a constant clattering: the sound that hundreds of tiny bones would make as they shook inside a bag. "Who despises their own life so much they would spy on me?"

The shadows in the corner quickly cleared, and from them emerged a fibrous brownish man with a small gray horn in his forehead, his nakedness barely covered by scraps of bandages so dirty they looked black.

"Someone who has died frequently enough to value life for what it's truly worth: absolutely nothing."

"That's too long to be a name," the skeleton spat. "Either liven up your tongue or I'll cut it out. I'll ask you again: who are you?"

"My name is Hurza and I'm known as the Eye-Eater."

The skeleton let out a snorting laugh.

"Well, I'm warning you, you won't get much out of me," he mocked, pointing to his empty sockets. Out of one of them, a spider hung from a thread, like a tear.

"On the contrary. A creature like you fits my plans perfectly," said Hurza, and his smile was even more terrifying than the macabre perpetual smile of the being that stood before him. "Listen to me, and listen well, son of Belgadus. I have a proposition for you."


Denestor Tul watched as the book he'd just brought to life flew toward a sky full of clouds beyond the nonexistent ceiling of Highlowtower. It ascended slowly and elegantly, opening and closing its black covers as if they were actual wings. Around the book swarmed more of the demiurge's creations, some flying, others clinging to the walls, most of them in constant movement, giving Highlowtower the look of a frenzied anthill. A small moth, made from pieces of stained glass and candle ends, descended from atop a lamp screwed into a gauntlet and glided to a landing on the demiurge's shoulder.

Denestor sneezed twice, cleaned his nose on his sleeve, and after cracking the joints of his fingers, he resumed concentration on his work. He took another book from the heap piled up on the ground and opened it on the dusty table in front of him. Written over and over in its yellowing pages were the three lines of text that he'd discovered on Belisarius's parchment. Before the day was through, a score of those unusual birds would take to the skies of Rocavarancolia, searching for anything, be it a book, scroll, tapestry, or inscription, that contained a single word written in the same language of the vanished parchment.

At first, he'd tried using magic to translate the gibberish. The demiurge knew that there were two treatises in the castle library that were dedicated exclusively to the art of logomancy—magic specializing in language—but he couldn't seem to find them. They had both disappeared without a trace. It wasn't unusual for books to go astray in that library: some disintegrated without any warning due to the high concentration of mystical energy in the room, others escaped to parallel dimensions, and there had even been cases of books attacking and devouring their fellows. In spite of this knowledge, Denestor thought it suspicious that the only two books on logomancy that remained in the kingdom had disappeared at the same time. He came to wonder if there hadn't been some kind of dark hand involved, but he quickly discarded that absurd hypothesis: at that time he still hadn't spoken to anyone about the stolen parchment, so it was nonsense to think of schemes and conspiracies.

Only when it was clear that traditional magic wasn't going to work did he decide to ask for help. He had no luck there, either. Apparently there was no one in the city who recognized the language or knew of any spell that could determine what it was or translate it. Lady Venom had assured him that she could make a potion that would help, but he refused to drink anything prepared by the idiotic witch. For Denestor Tul, the fact that both that woman and Belgadus's perverse creation were now part of the Royal Council was just further proof of the kingdom's decline.

Neither Esmael nor Lady Scar were able to help, although both promised to investigate on his behalf and keep him informed if they learned anything. The black angel had been strangely solicitous: to the demiurge's surprise, he had treated him with a deference that was unlike him. That change in character concerned him; it made him fear that Esmael was plotting something.

"I'll pull some strings. I'll consult books that you don't have access to, and I'll see what I can find . . ." he said, while he studied with half-closed eyes the phrases Denestor had written down for him.

They were under the bulbous dome where Esmael had lived for years. Until then, on the few occasions that Denestor had visited, the black angel had received him in the exterior walkways, but now, for the first time, he invited him inside.

"I'd be profoundly grateful if you did," he said. "We have very little, I admit. But maybe it's enough to put us on the trail of the assassin."

Esmael raised his gaze from the parchment to look Denestor in the eye.

"Have you asked Mistral?" he said, and Denestor thought he detected a mocking tone in his voice. "For years he undertook espionage jobs in a large number of linked worlds. Maybe he knows the language in this document."

"The shapeshifter is still indisposed," he responded. "I asked him, but he didn't give me an answer . . . Not an answer that made sense, in any case."

"Is it my name, Denestor?" Mistral had asked him excitedly as he clutched with trembling hands the parchment where Denestor had written Belisarius's unintelligible words.

"Did you bring my name? Read it to me, please . . ." he said, handing it back to him. "I don't understand it."

Esmael shook his head, apologetic, or at least pretending to be. The demiurge perceived a hint of amusement in his eyes. He knew the black angel had visited Mistral more than once, and that worried him. In the state the shapeshifter was in, there was always a chance he would say too much, and if Esmael found out he had interfered with the harvest, everything would fall apart. It would be the end.

"Those poor metamorphs all end up crazy sooner or later." Esmael tapped his temple with a finger. "So much change confuses them, until they end up forgetting who they are," he said. "Maybe later I'll pay him a visit . . . Maybe I can convince him to abandon that depressing grotto and take shelter in a place more appropriate for a member of the council."

Denestor himself had tried to persuade Mistral to return to the castle, but all of his efforts had been in vain. The shapeshifter barely listened to anyone; he just sank deeper and deeper into madness, into that ridiculous obsession with the name he'd had before the Red Moon transformed him.

"We must have hope. Maybe he'll regain his sanity on his own," he said.

"That is a vain hope, Demiurge, a vain hope. And we must take into account that Mistral has never been known for being sensible."

No, Denestor hadn't had much luck interrogating the inhabitants of Rocavarancolia. No one knew anything. Not even Lady Serena had been able to help, even though Denestor seemed to remember that she had some notions of logomancy. The ghost had looked at the text with an absent expression, and then shook her head listlessly.

"I'm sorry, Demiurge, I can't help you," she'd said.

And that was why, finally, Denestor had no choice but to resort to his own arts. It would be a much slower path, but sooner or later he would have results. He focused his attention on the book in front of him.

He turned the pages one by one, caressing each one with exquisite care, feeling an infinitesimal part of his own essence transferring inside the book. Thanks to his power, life took hold in the object, previously inert; he noticed a shudder inside him, a painful sting that he was already more than accustomed to. The pages that he touched trembled; beneath the rough cover he could hear a distant pulse, growing stronger by the minute. The book gave an abrupt shiver on the table, and Denestor hurried to calm it. Soon he would free it to fulfill its mission.

And if they failed, if the books didn't find anything that could help him, he'd look for other alternatives. He was a demiurge, a warlock capable of creating anything he could imagine—and if there was one thing he had a surplus of, it was imagination. Sooner or later he would find out what Belisarius had written on that parchment. It was only a matter of time.

The book shook again, raising another cloud of dust that made him sneeze once more. The demiurge shifted in his chair and gestured toward a nearby rack. The five creatures hanging from it immediately jumped to the ground and from there to the table. They were small articulated brooms, with four dustpans on their handles. Denestor moved the chair back and watched as his creatures set to work on the table and its surroundings. It was odd, but there seemed to be more dust in the tower lately than usual. As much as his creatures cleaned, there was always more.

"I'm probably disintegrating," he said in a loud voice. "You know, old man: thou art dust, and to dust thou shalt return."

As soon as he uttered those words, he remembered that Lady Dream had prophesied he would die soon, and unease loomed over him. He straightened in his chair and looked behind him, as if he feared that something was stalking him at that precise moment. But only his creations filled Highlowtower: dozens of miraculous beings that twirled, ran, jumped, or stayed motionless, awaiting orders from their master.

Denestor shook his head, shooed his unease away with a gesture, and waited for the cleaners to finish their work before he could continue with his, oblivious to the frustrated dust which shouted his name in vain.

The demiurge's books flew over Rocavarancolia. Most of the time they just glided, opened wide, riding the quick air currents, only flapping their covers occasionally to vary the course. The pages, rustling against one another, produced a low, almost inaudible whispering. The books read themselves as they flew through the skies of the ruined city.

Hector looked up at them as he and Ricardo returned to the tower. As far as they could see they were nothing more than points of darkness silhouetted against the sky's clarity, but there was something in their flight and their shape that made it clear they were not normal birds. He didn't have time to speculate: Ricardo went tense next to him, and alarm flickered in his eyes.

Something was coming. Hector felt it in his bones. There was a hissing, a current of air that leapt at them from behind. Both teenagers turned around together, drawing their swords in unison to come face to face with shadows. Darkness hung before them, a torn and broken darkness flapping in fury, clouding the day. They took a step back.

"One of Natalia's shadows," Hector whispered.

The creature, a dark curtain ten feet tall and two wide, floated above them and contorted in a ferocious manner. The dozens of thin extremities that covered its torso shook in the air like angry whips.

The shadow's head, an oval topped with tangled horns of gloom, stretched to the right. A spiral tentacle shot out from what must have been the mouth and pointed to the west.

"Heeeeeeeeeeeeeector," the thing said.

He shuddered to hear his name. He almost dropped his sword.

"Natalia's in trouble." Ricardo grabbed him by the arm and pulled him forward.

Hector stumbled a few steps, still staring at the entity that called his name. The shadow retreated, moving to one side as it pointed to the west.

"Heeeeeeeeeeeeeector," it repeated.

He nodded and gripped his sword tightly.

"Take us to her," he pleaded.

The darkness retracted its extremities and let the wind carry it away. It was like watching a jellyfish pulsating underwater. The creature's elegance was extraordinary. They ran after it. Hector bit his lower lip, tense. Since he'd come to Rocavarancolia they'd chased after flying bathtubs, screams, metal birds, and now sinister shadows. He couldn't help but think about the lighthouse on the cliff, deceiving ships with its unholy light so that they'd shipwreck on the reefs. That was how he felt in pursuit of the dark creature: running toward his doom for the thousandth time.

The shadow entered the square with the three towers. It twisted up high like a comet that had escaped its orbit and was euphorically enjoying its freedom. Hector and Ricardo took refuge in a hollow close to the wooden tower and inspected the square from there. The shadows had taken over. They were everywhere: gliding over the petrified battlefield like crows anxious to feast on the remains, clinging with misty pseudopods to the tower façades, hanging from the trees, twisting around the frozen warriors and monsters . . . They came in all shapes and sizes, all the same color, so dark that it was more like a tear in one's vision than an actual color.

The boys' shock at such a gathering was short lived. It lasted just the time it took them to realize that every last one of the shadows was looking in the same direction: toward the gigantic petrified trees at the opposite end of the plaza, beyond the ruins of the fourth tower. There, in front of the largest tree, a crazed grayish creature roared, hitting the trunk fiercely. Shards of stone went flying with each attack.

The thing crouched at the base of the tree, remained still for several seconds, as if taking a breath, then jumped up to launch another brutal blow at the tree. A piece of stone the size of its head flew off and landed over twenty yards away. The monster howled and took a few steps back. That's when they saw them: Natalia and Marina were inside the tree, taking shelter in a large hole in the trunk. The back of the hollowed-out space was just wide enough to accommodate the two of them, and the entrance was too narrow for the monster howling outside to access. The creature jumped forward, grabbed the stone bark, and stuck one of its long arms through the opening. For several moments it contorted, pressed up against the petrified wood, but it didn't get anywhere. It went back to attacking the stone, and another shower of shards rained down.

The wind suddenly turned the monster's screaming into intelligible words:

"Scorpions and serpents!" it howled. "Months of eating worms and spiders! That's no life for a troll! Fed up! Roallen is fed up! I want meat! I want tender flesh!"

He was eight feet tall, and although he had broad, bony shoulders, his waist was almost nonexistent. His extremities were long and sinewy, and his forearms covered with matted hair. His fingers were long as well, with sharp claws. With each blow more fragments flew off the tree. He was starting to make an opening.

"He's going to kill them . . ." Hector whispered.

Ricardo pointed behind them. Adrian stood at the entrance to the square, close to them, crouched down behind the body of a fallen giant. He watched as the troll continued, unrelenting, his assault on the tree.

"Come on," Ricardo said. He perched at the edge of the hollow and gestured for Hector to follow him.

"Fresh, clean meat!" the troll clamored. "One last banquet after the previous last banquet! By all the fires in every inferno, I swear that Roallen will feast one last time!"

The racket was so loud that the monster didn't hear the two boys running toward Adrian. Ricardo and Hector crouched down at his side, but he didn't even look at them. The fallen giant's legs were bent, and the boy was watching through the space between them and the ground. Hector hadn't seen him since the encounter they'd had in that very place.

"How come you aren't doing anything?" Ricardo asked him, grabbing him by the shoulder. "Why aren't you with them? Why aren't you helping them?"

"Because that monster would destroy me," Adrian answered, tugging his arm away from Ricardo's grip. "It's stronger than me, okay? And it's stronger than you, too. That thing's not your usual Rocavarancolia vermin, it's something else."

"What about your spells? And your magic?" Ricardo asked. Adrian shook his head.

"I'm all out. I don't have a drop of energy left."

"You used it all up trying to wake the dragon," Hector realized.

"If I'd known there'd be a troll attack today, I would have saved some," he replied angrily. "These things always happen at the worst time."

Hector leaned against the giant's forearm and tried to calm himself.

"Don't you have any charged talismans left?" he asked, as he tried to turn a deaf ear to the sounds coming from the tree. "Nothing?"

Adrian looked at them for the first time.

"Nothing," he answered. He pointed to the closest tower. "I was in there, taking a nap to recover, when I heard them scream and came outside."

"What did you see?"

"They both ran toward the tree; the square was full of all those creepy shadows. That thing was behind them, right on their heels. Natalia stood up to it when she saw it was going to catch them, but there wasn't much she could do. The troll took her halberd and tried to slice her in two. That's when a bunch of the shadows descended on it. It tore them to pieces, but it was enough of a distraction that the girls could hide in the tree."

"They couldn't have just stayed in the tower arguing, no . . ." Ricardo grumbled.

Hector risked a glance over the stone giant. The shadows hovered everywhere, giving the scene a surrealistic, nightmarish quality. The tree where the girls hid was swarming with them; they twisted around the trunk and rocked in the branches, clinging to them with tentacles and claws.

"Why are the shadows over there trying to help them, but these ones aren't doing anything?" Ricardo asked. "They're only watching.

If they all attacked together, the troll wouldn't stand a chance. Why don't they?"

"Well, it looks like the majority doesn't have the slightest interest in saving them," Adrian answered. "That's why. They gathered here to watch Natalia die."

"But one came looking for us," Hector said. "It brought us here so we could help her."

"It doesn't make sense," Adrian pointed out. "If what it truly wanted was to save her, it should have gone for Bruno. He's the only one who stands a chance against that thing." He shook his head. "That shadow didn't bring you here to help, it brought you so the troll could kill you, too."

Ricardo cursed and crouched even flatter to the ground as he watched from underneath the giant. The expression on his face was one of total concentration. He was sizing up the troll, Hector realized. His friend remained still in that position for a long while, hardly even blinking.

"You're right. We need Bruno," he said. "We can't get out of this without magic."

"I'll go look for him," Adrian offered. "I'm the fastest of us three and I won't take long. Is he in the tower?"

Ricardo and Hector nodded in unison.

"I smell you! I can smell you!" Roallen yelled just then. Hector felt a sudden knot in his throat at the thought he was referring to them. But the troll kept at the tree. "You smell of life! And here's me, eating scorpions in the desert! More than a year of sand and starvation! It has to end! It has to!"

Ricardo turned toward Adrian.

"Do it," he ordered. "Run. Go get Bruno."

"As fast as I am, that tree can only take so much," he warned.

"Leave that to us. We'll distract him until you get back. Now go. Run as fast as you can."

The boy gave them a firm nod and crouched down. He ran, hunched over, until he reached the hollow. A few instants later they saw him emerge from the other side, upright and running at full speed. He didn't look back even once.

"Adrian's right," Hector said. "That tree won't last much longer. It's going to get them."

"We'll wait until the last moment to intervene. That's what we'll do. We have to buy as much time as possible. And maybe we won't even need Bruno. Maybe we can do it ourselves with that . . ." He suddenly went silent. The monster moved away from the tree and was looking around frantically, searching for something. "What's he doing? What on earth is he doing?"

For a few moments the troll was hidden from sight behind a line of lancers. When it reappeared it was holding Natalia's halberd.

"He's out of patience," Hector whispered. He raised his sword. "We have to go," he said urgently. "We have to go now."

He jumped over the giant's body and took off running toward the tree, with Ricardo at his heels. He hadn't taken more than a few steps when he saw a viscous bluish light suddenly surround the troll. They both stopped in their tracks. They were in the middle of the field, in a clearing amid the petrified battle, between a group of goblins and a unicorn reared up on its hind legs, less than a hundred yards from Roallen. The troll stood motionless in midstride, covered with a fine blue film.

"Natalia froze him," Ricardo said. He seemed confused, and Hector understood why: if she could have paralyzed him, why hadn't she done it earlier? Why had they let themselves get stuck in that death trap? It didn't take him long to figure it out.

"Not completely. He's moving. Look. He's doing it slowly, but he's still moving."

The troll, after a few moments of complete immobility, had started walking again, slowly, hunched forward as if battling against a fierce wind. The bluish light of the spell was tearing around him; with each step he took, new cracks and rifts opened in the layer of magic covering him. The spell finally succumbed and Roallen, as if making up for lost time, crossed the distance to the tree in an explosive run, so fast that it took the two boys by surprise. The troll raised the halberd above his head and aimed it at the hole in the trunk.

"No!" Hector howled at the precise moment that Roallen sank the weapon in the hollow where his two friends took refuge.

The troll spun around in the blink of an eye. He pulled the weapon out of the tree as he stepped back. A silhouette emerged along with the halberd, and for an instant seemed skewered by its blade. It was Natalia, kicking at air, clutching the shaft of the weapon with both hands. The point had pierced her cape, but she appeared to be unharmed.

Roallen tossed the halberd and the girl to the right, and faced the two boys. The shadows in the plaza had begun to whisper in grotesque, inhuman voices; it was a growing murmur, the sound of an ocean about to whip into a frenzy.

"Heroes?" bellowed Roallen. "Saviors of damsels in distress? Brave knights? Call the minstrels! Let them write songs in their honor! May they write poems to extol their glory!" The enormous mouth, lipless and out of proportion, opened in a parody of a smile. "Or better yet: bring cooks and stoves. Because that's what we're going to need here."

Natalia stumbled upright. She grabbed the halberd and took a couple of steps in the troll's direction, limping. Roallen didn't even notice her or Marina, who came out of the tree with her bow at the ready, her hair unruly. The troll only had eyes for Ricardo and Hector.

"Hold out until Bruno gets here," Ricardo whispered. "We only have to hang on until then."

Roallen growled. Hector and Ricardo reached him. They stood on guard, their weapons raised. The troll straightened to his full height. He stank of swamp and frenzy, and hunger and madness. The circle of living shadows tightened around them. The whole scene was darkness and whispers.

"You brats don't stand a chance," Roallen warned them. The last remains of Natalia's immobility spell rustled down his back. "Don't kid yourselves. When I want you dead, you'll be dead."

"Leave," Hector said. His voice sounded so strange that he didn't recognize it as his own. "Leave us alone, and it will be like none of this happened. We'll forget you and you'll forget us."

The troll bared his teeth again.

"I'm Roallen Melgar. I've ridden manticores and bashed giants' skulls together in worlds that would scare you stiff." His voice was swollen with pride and rage. "I strangled a celestial dragon with my bare hands and I fought in the battle of Livingsoul. Do you really think you stand a chance against me?"

*Talk, keep talking*, Hector encouraged him in his mind.

Every second they gained was precious.

The shadows hissed. The wind howled. Time stood still in the square. The troll turned around, without taking his eyes off the boys. And then, without warning, Marina shot her bow. Hector and Ricardo watched, horrified. At the same instant, Natalia leapt on the troll, and now they were all forced to attack. A split second later, something blocked the swing of Hector's sword so abruptly that its vibration shot pain up his arm. Roallen had stopped his weapon in midair. The monster's left fist closed around the blade without a care for the sharp edge that cut into his palm. Hector pulled with all his might, but it didn't budge; it was as if it had been thrust into stone. With his other hand, the troll grasped Ricardo's sword, as harmless as Hector's, in the same manner. Roallen smiled. Natalia's halberd hadn't even grazed him. As for Marina's arrow, the troll's thick mane caught it, and it didn't even reach his skull.

Roallen let out an insidious laugh, and just then they heard two cracks. Hector noticed that the weapon he held was now free. The troll raised his arms, opened his hands, and let the broken blades of the swords fall to the ground. Ricardo cursed. Natalia stepped back and stretched out her right hand, ready to cast another spell. The monster's smile widened.

"Now it's time for you all to die," he announced.

The next thing Hector knew he was flying. He crashed violently into a stone horse and fell flat on the cobblestones. Months before, a blow like that would have been enough to leave him out of action, but now it just dazed him. He shook his head and tried to focus. He heard a hair-raising scream in the square, followed by the troll's cackling. Hector looked up. Roallen had just pierced Ricardo with his own shattered sword. The broken point emerged through the boy's back, stained red. Ricardo howled in pain.

He lunged forward in an attempt to reach the monster that was killing him, but Roallen didn't even flinch. Natalia and Marina both lay motionless at his feet. He roared with laughter. Ricardo's hands clutched at the troll's throat and began to squeeze, but Roallen just kept laughing.

"No!" Hector shouted. For one delirious instant he thought that this was no way for Ricardo to meet his end, that there wasn't the slightest glory in being run through by a broken sword wielded by a famished monster. "No!" he repeated, unable to react. It wasn't fair. It couldn't happen like that.

"I am Roallen!" the monster shouted. He gave the weapon a vicious twist inside the boy's body. "Do you hear me, Rocavarancolia? Your son has returned from exile!"

Suddenly Ricardo lay still; his hands let go of the troll's neck and hung lifeless. Then everything went quiet. Even Roallen stopped laughing. The troll, stone faced, pulled the sword free, and Ricardo, dead, fell like a sack between the two girls.

His murderer, sword in hand, crouched swiftly next to Marina, grabbed her by the hair, and raised her head. The girl opened her eyes. That was enough to get Hector to finally move. He took off running, forcing his legs to maximum speed. But it was late, very late. Roallen raised the weapon, covered in blood, ready to thrust it into his next victim. Hector was so far away that he howled in desperation, aware that he wouldn't make it. He shouted, helpless. Ricardo was dead. Like Alexander. Like Rachel. As fast as he ran, he would never be able to save anyone.

At that moment a dark figure charged at the troll. Hector heard the whistle of something sharp slicing through the air, and then the monster's cry of pain and surprise. Roallen brought a hand to his side and growled again. The boy from the rooftops was before him, pointing his sword. He panted, hunched forward, wrapped in two sand-colored capes. His straight hair, long and dirty, covered half his face. His visible eye burned with fierce determination.

"Magic," croaked Roallen, his eyes fixed on the weapon that wounded him. "A baussite sword . . . a weapon for cowards. In the last battle I killed many who carried them. I showed no mercy."

Dario didn't say a single word. All of his attention was centered on the creature in front of him. The sword tugged at his hand, but he did everything he could to hold it back. The troll bared his teeth. Dario wondered if it had been Roallen who'd killed the sword's previous owner. Would such a coincidence be possible? Was that why the sword seemed more eager than ever to leap into action?

Roallen watched him avidly as the wind rustled his tangled mane. Dario still wondered what had made him follow the troll after he'd seen it wandering through the city. It had been a kind of premonition, an impulse that he hadn't been able to resist. As soon as he saw him, he felt a strange certainty: this monster was the key to a mystery yet to be revealed.

Marina started shouting, but Dario didn't even look at her. The girl had discovered her friend's dead body. Hector knelt beside her, averting his gaze from Ricardo and the blood that ran onto the cobblestones. Natalia stood up, coughing. She saw the body next to her and went pale.

"Ricardo," Marina whispered. "No, no, no . . . Ricardo . . ."

"Not now," Hector said, as he placed a hand around her waist to help her up.

The troll and Dario still stared at each other, only a few paces away. Natalia stood as well, her eyes fixed on the body. Her expression hadn't changed since she'd regained consciousness. Two fleeting tears ran down her cheeks.

"Go," Dario ordered as he gestured with his free hand for them not to come any closer. "Leave! Do you hear me? There's nothing you can do!" An almost imperceptible tremor shook his sword before he shouted again: "Get out of here!"

He leapt upon Roallen with that last scream still on his lips. He let his sword guide him. The troll leaned back and dodged the blow.

Hector took Marina by the waist and tried to get her to move. She nodded, shook him off, and started to run on her own. Natalia seemed unsure whether to flee or join the fight, but she finally followed them, after shooting a devastated glance at Ricardo. They stayed on the move; Marina grabbed her bow—lying next to the tree—without stopping.

"Don't go very far," cackled the troll as he bent to avoid another sword blow.

*He's playing with us*, Hector realized. It was clear that Roallen could put an end to the fight whenever he liked.

The troll had no problem dodging the attacks of his opponent with a string of increasingly grotesque pirouettes. It looked like a pantomime more than combat.

"Ricardo is dead," Natalia suddenly whispered.

"Don't think about it!" Hector insisted.

"What about him?!" Marina grabbed him by the arm and tried to stop him. "We can't just leave him here!"

"Yes, we can!" he answered, without a moment's thought. "We don't have a choice. We have to hope he holds out until Bru—"

Everything went dark. All of the shadows in the square had taken off at the same time and flew over them, transformed into a hazy blanket of twisted limbs, bulging eyes, and amorphous wings. Hector gritted his teeth and ran under the heavy black canopy. There was no sky above their heads, only darkness, and it was so thick that it was impossible to see where they were going. Natalia let out a shout and faced the sea of black that hovered over them.

"Get away! Get away from here!" she yelled, trying to scare the shadows by slapping at the air. "Get out of my sight! Go! Get out of here!"

To everyone's surprise, the shadows obeyed—so abruptly that it was as if they disintegrated. Hector glimpsed whirlwinds of darkness out of the corner of his eye, and understood they were echoes left by the shadows as they left their field of vision. The blue sky appeared above them once again, and not a scrap of gloom remained in the square. The sudden brightness blinded them. Hector looked over his shoulder.


Dario took a deep breath and resumed his attack.

The troll jumped from one side to the other, crouching down suddenly as he contorted in the air. His movements were chaotic, senseless, but he managed to avoid Dario's strikes time and time again.

The young boy felt his weapon's growing desperation with each failed attack. He hesitated for a moment, unable to decide between continuing to let it take the initiative or taking control himself, and it was in that slight second of hesitation that Roallen leapt at him and grabbed him by the wrist. He squeezed and twisted it mercilessly, his mouth open in a fit of silent, mocking laughter. Dario felt like his bones were splintering under his skin.

The sword slid between his weakened fingers. He howled in pain. The whole world trembled before his eyes. His legs gave out. Only the troll's hand kept him from falling, as it firmly gripped his shattered wrist. Roallen bent down and picked up the fallen sword, without letting go of his prey. The weapon looked ridiculously small in that paw. His tiny black eyes looked the sword up and down, and then went to Dario.

"You'll need something better than this to defeat me," he said with scorn, and hurled the sword far away.

The troll let him go and Dario finally collapsed. For a second he lay still on the ground, his eyes staring at the blue sky of Rocavarancolia. Tears ran down his cheeks. It was only for a second, but in that interval of time there was no pain, fear, or doubts. One second of peace and calm. Only the sky and him. Then the shadow of Roallen fell upon him and he was thrust back into reality. He managed to raise himself slightly, leaning on his elbows. A few yards away lay the body of the kid from the Margalar Tower.

The troll let out a strange noise, a mix between a chuckle and a growl, and pounced on Dario, who stifled another scream as his destroyed wrist was ground into the cobblestones. Roallen straddled his stomach, and his stench filled the air. Dario took a terrified breath. For the first time in his life, he felt defenseless. The troll's black eyes were fixed on his, and the madness and fury in them was so great that he knew, without a doubt, that he was going to die in the next few moments.

He cursed himself for being stupid enough to get involved in a fight that wasn't his; he cursed himself for not having learned his lesson, for fighting nonstop against Rocavarancolia's designs, for looking for light and warmth in a world that was cold. He cursed himself for being in love.

Roallen went to take a fierce bite. Dario saw the twin rows of fangs closing in on his face. He hadn't yet shut his eyes when the jaws snapped less than an inch from his nose.

"Look at me closely, child," the troll hissed. Saliva spattered his face, hot, viscous. "Look closely," he repeated. "Because this is what you'll see in the mirror when the Red Moon comes out. You have troll blood in your veins. I can smell it. And that just saved your life. Trolls don't kill their own."

And with a single blow, he was left unconscious.


"No!" Marina exclaimed when Dario's first cry reached them. Hector turned without stopping. Roallen was grabbing the sword of his opponent, who was doubled over before him, howling in pain. The troll cruelly twisted his right hand.

Hector swallowed a curse. Marina stumbled in front of him, but he grabbed her by the arms and made her keep running. She looked at him with tears in her eyes.

"It won't be long before he comes for us!" Natalia shouted.

Roallen had leapt upon Dario after flinging his sword far away. The ringing sound that the weapon made as it hit the ground felt like a sneer.

"No!" Marina howled; she squirmed in Hector's arms as she tried to grab her bow. She looked at him, distraught. "Why do you want him to die? What did he do to you? We have to help him!" she pleaded, between tears.

"We can't!" he shouted. "Did you not see what just happened? He demolished us without breaking a sweat!"

"He's coming!" Natalia yelled.

Roallen now ran toward them, leaving the rooftop boy's motionless body and Ricardo's corpse behind. He ran on four legs, at top speed. The sheer power behind his sprint was enough for Hector to know they'd never defeat him in battle.

"We have to hide!" he shouted as he pointed at the ruins of the destroyed tower. "Run toward the ruins! We'll hide there!"

The only thing that remained of the tower was the ceilingless first floor; the rest seemed to have vanished into thin air, as if someone armed with an enormous axe had cut down the building at the height of that floor, and carried the rest of the structure away, without leaving a single scrap behind.

They ran for a crack in the wall. It wasn't the first time they'd visited these ruins. They'd thoroughly explored them shortly after they began their expeditions. Rachel hadn't detected any magic in the chaos of destroyed rooms, nor had they found anything useful.

They stopped at a semicircular room with two large tables in its center and several chairs on the floor. The rug that they walked on was ruined; it was damp, full of holes, and littered with animal excrement.

They made their way carefully through the labyrinth of rooms and hallways, avoiding the wrecked furniture and the walls that had crumbled after years of exposure to the elements. They looked in all directions, immersed in a tense silence, alert to any and every sound. They had no doubt that Roallen was looking for them. Every turn around a corner and every open door meant another chance of running into him. Natalia stopped in her tracks and pointed to the right. The troll was fifty yards away, perched on top of a wall. He was headed south, away from where they were.

Seeing him so far away gave them enough confidence to stop for a moment to catch their breath. It was clear that they weren't going to make it out of the building without being discovered by Roallen. From the top of the wall the monster had an exceptional view of all of the terrain surrounding the tower. Their only option was to wait for Bruno. The troll moved out of sight behind a cracked wall, but reappeared before long. He straightened up and looked around. They flattened themselves anxiously against the closest wall. No one spoke. They even tried to breathe as quietly as possible.

Roallen turned his back once more and continued his search to the south, climbing along the partitions like an immense insect.

"Bruno can't be much longer," Marina assured them in a low voice. "He can't be much longer," she insisted, as if repeating it would speed up the Italian's appearance.

"It killed Ricardo," Natalia whispered. She looked at her friends, and by the expression on her face, Hector realized that she wanted them to prove her wrong. She wanted them to deny it, say it was a mistake— that Ricardo was alive, passed out in the square.

The troll disappeared from sight once again, dropped down on the other side of the wall with a movement as graceful as that of a swimmer jumping into water, carefree. They waited expectantly for several seconds, but Roallen didn't reappear. All they heard among the ruins was the sound of the wind.

"Let's go," Hector ordered.

At that very moment the wall behind him shook and thundered. Two long, sinewy arms went through the partition just as he turned to get away. Marina shouted. The troll's claws closed around Hector's arms and pulled him backward. The impact against the wall was tremendous, so much so that the partition collapsed between them, separating them as it fell. Hector fell on top of a heap of rubble. He rolled onto the ground and tried to get up, but a claw grabbed him by the ankle. Nails as sharp as knives sank into his flesh. The boy howled and kicked the hand that held him with all his might. Roallen let him go at once.

He crawled on all fours for a few seconds. The cloud of dust that arose from the collapse hovered everywhere. He heard Natalia shout, but he couldn't understand her words. His head was spinning, his ears buzzed. He couldn't believe the troll could move so fast. He coughed up a mouthful of dust and tried to get up.

Roallen rose behind him, dirty from plaster and dust, and leapt before he could stand upright. Hector punched him in the stomach, and it was like hitting a rock. It felt like his knuckles cracked, but he also heard the troll wheeze and knew that he'd hurt him. Roallen roared and took a savage bite. Hector barely had time to raise his arms to protect his face. A wave of intense pain made him shriek. He never would have believed that anything could hurt so much.

"You monster!" he heard Natalia scream, horrified.

The two girls charged the troll at the same time. Marina drew the dagger that she wore at her waist and stabbed with all her strength, but the blade couldn't even break his thick skin. Roallen turned on them; Marina managed to avoid his diagonal blow, but Natalia got kicked in the hip and fell to her knees. Hector howled with pain. The dusty ground was spattered with blood. As he watched, new drops fell around him, quick like a storm shower. All of that blood was his, he realized. He brought his hands up to his face and discovered, horrified, that he no longer had a right hand: it had disappeared below the wrist, sliced off by the troll's fangs.

Roallen hovered over him again. Once more he heard a scream, and then a flash of blue surrounded the troll. He became immobilized, paralyzed by the spell that Natalia had just cast. The monster's eyes bulged from their sockets. Another paralysis spell fell upon him. And a third. Hector bent toward the ground, still screaming. The world disappeared before his eyes in a blinding white flash.

When he regained consciousness, Natalia and Marina were trying to carry him in their arms. They ran through a narrow hallway, the partitions destroyed halfway up. Reality was a bloody blur, a coming and going of shadows and gloom.

*They're taking me to be with Rachel*, Hector thought, lost in delirium. *I'm dead, and they're taking me to the cemetery.* He tried to ask them not to bury him underground, but he couldn't manage a single word.

He looked back: he expected to see the spider walking solemnly behind him. But he only saw Roallen, paralyzed. His bulging eyes remained fixed on them, and a demented smile distorted his face even more, a smile that grew as Hector watched. The layers of the spell that covered him were fading. He would be freed from his immobility before long, and then they'd be lost. There was no escape. Alex, Rachel, Marco, Ricardo . . . Rocavarancolia had been finishing them off, one by one. And now it was his turn. The names of his dead companions resounded in his mind as he continued to lose blood.

He lost his footing and fell to the ground. His friends tried in vain to make him stand up. There was no place to run. There never had been.

"Get up, Hector," Marina pleaded, with tears in her eyes. "Please get up."

Suddenly all of the violence he'd thought about in the last few minutes came crashing down. It was a deluge of intertwined images that left him breathless. The screams of the boy from the rooftops, of Ricardo as he died, his own, even those of Roallen himself. Hector felt something moving inside of him: something aflame and furious. It had always been there, within him. It was the fire that Adrian had talked about, but it wasn't just fire: it was darkness, a hungry, thick darkness.

And Hector surrendered to it.

"Heal my hand," he growled, extending his bloody stump toward Natalia.

"There's no time, Hector . . ." she replied. "We have to . . ."

"Do what you can. Just do what you can . . ." he insisted. The determination in his face and his words made her obey.

The pain in his mutilated limb transformed into something distant. He noticed an unpleasant tingling that grew as the spell healed him. It was as if the place where his hand had once been was now covered with hundreds of tiny creatures, all biting him at once.

Roallen roared behind him and started toward them. With each step more magic threads detached from his body, and he gained more speed. They were out of time. Hector pulled his hand abruptly away from Natalia, and at the same time he snatched Marina's dagger.

"What are you doing?" she asked. "What do you think you're doing?"

"I'm going to kill the troll," he answered.

The fire running through his veins was so intense that he couldn't understand how it wasn't consuming him. He stood up slowly. His eyes shone.

"No!" Marina exclaimed.

"Hector!" Natalia glared at him furiously. "Have you gone mad?!"

"Run," he ordered them in a hoarse voice. "Get out of here. Roallen is mine."

He took off, stumbling, never checking to see if the girls obeyed his command. He ran into the wall, and flakes of plaster flew through the air. The hallway fluctuated before his gaze, coming and going in quick waves spattered with shining red points, perfect spheres all with marks down the middle. He blinked several times, the red moons disappeared, and the image came into focus. Roallen ran toward him, his arms raised, his mouth open in a hideous grin.

His stump throbbed weakly, but he ignored it. He still had one hand, and he still had the fire. A sudden green spark in the sky made him look up. He made out an emerald sphere of light approaching from the mountains. And closer still, high in the sky, soared a dark creature, with impressive scarlet wings opened wide. He paid no attention to them. Only one thing mattered:

"Troll!" he shouted. He hurried toward the approaching enemy.

Roallen met him with a powerful right jab to the jaw that he didn't even try to evade. A blinding light exploded before his eyes. He shook his head but remained firm, thrust his arm forward, and stabbed the troll in the stomach. This time the blade cut into the monster's flesh. They both stumbled into another room. The world, once again, was red.

Roallen leapt on him, his mouth open wide. Hector backed up to the left and gave a low kick just as his opponent reached him. His leg swept the ground and tripped the troll, who flew forward into a sturdy wardrobe and crashed to the floor. Hector jumped on his chest and used it as a trampoline to reach the top of the wardrobe. Leaning his back against the wall, he sank his heels into the gap between the wardrobe and the wall and toppled it on his adversary just as he was getting up. The impact on the creature was devastating. Hector landed with a jolt several yards away. Everything was fire. His heart burst into screams in his chest; in his head throbbed suns forged of rage and destruction. He turned in time to see the top part of the wardrobe explode into pieces and Roallen emerge from them, howling his head off, his arms raised above his head as if he cursed all of creation.

On the ground nearby was Marina's knife. He lunged toward it but the monster intercepted him right as his fingers brushed the handle. The collision was brutal, another wave of violence and fury. They rolled around, one over the other. Roallen's claws searched for his face, his body, but Hector was always prepared, dodging to avoid them, casting them aside with a blow. He didn't think. Everything in him was instinct and rage. His body responded to the attacks with a resolution and ferocity that were more animal than human. A door fell apart as they both bashed into it. Once they landed, they flew in different directions, one rolling and the other stumbling. Hector crashed into a heap of rotten lumber and for a second, lost sight of Roallen. They rose again almost at the same time, but Hector was still covered in debris, and that was enough for the troll to attack first. Hector ducked his head to avoid the swipe aimed at his face, but he couldn't avoid the trajectory of the second claw. It sank with such force in his stomach that it lifted him off the ground.

He didn't even scream. He leaned forward and hit Roallen right in the nose; it was a sharp blow delivered out of pure instinct, as if he had always known that flat nose was one of the troll's weak spots. Roallen cried out and leapt away from him. The five talons that had sunk into his stomach vanished. Hector tripped as he tried to move back, and he almost fell to the ground. He had to do a clumsy half turn to keep his balance. He suddenly saw the open jaws of a white stone leopard only inches from his face. Somehow they were now outside, in the square with the petrified warriors. He and Roallen stood between four lancers on horseback and a two-headed leopard over six feet tall.

Hector turned to face the troll. Roallen shook his head from side to side while he held the back of his paw against his wounded snout. The boy jumped toward one of the riders, grabbed the handle of the petrified lance with his one hand, and pulled with all his might, ignoring the savage pain that twisted his insides and the sickening feeling of inhaling blood. The stone gave way with a loud crack and he came away with most of the upper end of the lance. He lowered his arm and charged. Roallen opened his arms wide, as if he wished to embrace him against his chest.

Stone warriors and monsters witnessed this last attack. Some of their faces still revealed the demented savagery of those who seek to kill as they die. When he saw their grimaces of blind fierceness, Hector felt he was losing his footing. What was he doing? What kind of irrational beast had he turned into? His own savagery disarmed him. This creature running toward the troll wasn't him, it couldn't be. He hesitated. And as soon as he did, the fire in his veins went out. He stopped as he reached Roallen; the stone lance slid from his hand and fell to the ground. Hector remained still in front of the monster, looking at him as if it were the first time he saw him. Roallen hissed and knocked him down with a single blow. Hector fell next to one of the petrified dead bodies. For a second he was face to face with it. The warrior had died with his eyes open, and although one of them had been chipped away by the passing of time, in the other he could still see an empty, cold expression.

*Is that what my eyes will look like when I'm dead?* Hector wondered. *What will I see then?*

Roallen crouched before him, his hands resting on the ground. He tried to laugh but he barely had any breath left, and all that escaped his mouth was intermittent gasping. He crawled forward and leaned in to look him in the eyes.

"Did you really think you could defeat me?" he asked in a hoarse voice.

Hector coughed, without the strength to get up. There was no longer any fire in his veins; the lightning had stopped. There was nothing left of the energy that had sustained him over the last few minutes. He was broken. Defeated.

"You damn kid." The troll studied him carefully. "You thought you could defeat me." There was no longer any mockery in his voice or gestures, and what Hector glimpsed in his eyes was admiration. "You thought so. You really did."

Roallen shook his head once more, as if he wanted to scare off an annoying thought. He raised his right claw and prepared to deliver the final blow. Hector closed his eyes.

"No! Get away from him, you filthy thing!" he heard. It was Natalia, and the sound of her voice hurt him almost as much as his stomach wound. Roallen lowered his claw, bared his teeth, and growled. Hector turned in the direction of the voice; he made a huge effort to focus his gaze, but finally he saw what he didn't want to see: there were the two of them, Natalia and Marina.

The troll stood up, not without difficulty, and moved toward them, hunched over and opening and closing his hands. His claws made a clacking sound as they met one another.

"As you wish," he said. "I'll get away from him . . . sure. But only to come closer to you."

"No . . ." Hector whispered, desperate, about to break down in tears. They hadn't obeyed him. They should have escaped while he confronted the troll. At least he would have died knowing that he gave them a chance. Now his death would have no meaning. It would be useless. He hadn't been able to save Ricardo or Rachel, and now he couldn't save them either. He could do nothing but watch. He struggled on the ground, searching unsuccessfully for the energy to get up, but he could hardly straighten his legs.

Roallen moved slowly toward the two girls.

"Stop!" Marina ordered, as she nocked an arrow on her bow.

"Stop?" the troll asked, mockingly. His chest rose and fell in spasms.

The monster was exhausted and bleeding from more than a dozen wounds. He was hanging by a thread, Hector realized. They'd been on the verge of beating him. Marina shot an arrow. Roallen jumped forward and swatted it away, but his movements had lost all of their spirit.

"Who's ordering me to stop?" he asked. "You?" He dodged a second arrow and made a clumsy bow as he approached them, staggering. "Her Majesty I Am Nobody and Princess Cruddy Aim?" In response, a third arrow sank halfway in his chest. The troll pulled it out and threw it aside. "I'm sorry, but the world doesn't work that way. You can't tell me to stop. Little lambs can do nothing but tremble when the wolves come near . . . That's what they do. You can't ask the storm to stop or death to pass you by when the time comes."

"But I can!" exclaimed a stern voice behind them. "Stop, troll! Denestor Tul, demiurge of Rocavarancolia and guardian of Highlowtower, commands you!"

Two projectiles sailed across the square, two steely shadows leapt upon Roallen so swiftly that the troll couldn't dodge them. They were metal shackles, joined by a black steel chain. They closed around his wrists, lifted him from the ground, and dragged him backward, away from the children. Roallen howled. He pulled forward but couldn't free himself from the restraints that towed him away. Another pair of clamps arrived and quickly closed around his ankles. The troll fell forward.

"You're breaking the law, Denestor! You're interfering with the harvest!" he howled, his eyes bulging. "And that's forbidden, do you hear me? Forbidden!"

The mere act of turning his head to look at Denestor Tul left Hector out of breath. There he stood, in the middle of the square, the little gray man who'd taken them from Earth so long ago, dressed in the same robe as on that fateful Halloween night, and although in appearance he was as wrinkled and withered as he was then, both his demeanor and his voice displayed an astonishing energy. Behind Denestor floated a large coat rack with stork wings and a white scimitar whose handle had been replaced by a three-armed candelabra, each arm with a corresponding lit candle. The flame of the middle candle intensified, and the sword flew in a straight line toward Roallen, who was still writhing on the ground.

"You can't interfere!" the troll insisted, out of his mind; from his gaping mouth surged flecks of bloody froth and saliva. "You can't! You can't! It's forbidden!"

"You're right. I can't interfere in what happens between Rocavarancolia and the harvest, it's true," Denestor said, with all the calm in the world. He stepped onto the foot of the coat rack and it flew toward Roallen. The flame on the left candle grew, and the scimitar turned to that side. "But you no longer belong to this city. We exiled you. You shouldn't be here."

"That's ridiculous and you know it! You're interfering! Even a blind man could see that!"

"Denestor!" The bubble of greenish light that Hector saw coming from the mountains had reached the square. It lowered to ground level and after traveling at great speed toward them, stopped suddenly a few yards from Roallen and the demiurge. Lady Serena was inside, surrounded by thousands of minuscule silver lightning bolts. "The troll is right!" she shouted furiously. "You can't interfere! Let him go! Let him go this instant!"

"Let him go?" Denestor looked at her, perplexed. "Have you lost your mind?"

"You're the one who's lost his mind," the phantom hissed. "We are forbidden from interfering. With your behavior, you're breaking the same law that sent Roallen to the desert. Let him go right now, let him go before it's too late." The lightning strikes that surrounded her body intensified; for a moment she was almost hidden behind the web of flashes. "Let the pups deal with him, if they can. It's the city that must judge who lives and who dies, not you."

"I told you, Denestor!" Roallen thundered. "You're interfering! Do you see? Do you see?! Lady Serena says I'm right!" He began struggling again in vain. "Let me go!"

Hector looked at the woman in green, astonished. She was the one who'd bewitched him with the ability to avoid the dangerous areas of Rocavarancolia; she was the one who reassured him that he was the last hope for the kingdom. Why did she want to see him die now? He had to look away. He no longer had the strength to hold his head up. He watched as Lady Scar's metallic bird, with the woman's frightening eye secured in its beak, perched awkwardly atop the helmet of a petrified warrior. The pain kept him from thinking clearly. He brought his hand to the ruins of his stomach and moaned.

"I think Denestor Tul has made it quite clear, my dear friend," said a new voice. The creature with scarlet wings that Hector had seen flying over the plaza had just landed with exquisite elegance in front of the enraged spirit. "The demiurge has no intention of saving anyone. He only meant to apprehend Roallen, without caring in the least what tasks he happened to have at hand. Our unruly friend should not have returned to Rocavarancolia. It was very inconsiderate of him to not have died in the desert."

The new arrival had red wings and intensely black skin, and seemed to glimmer in places; the only clothing he wore was a pair of dark gray pants. There was a wild beauty to him. Each of his steps traced a threat; with every movement came the promise of a swift death. And suddenly Hector recalled having seen a similar creature: in the mansion ballroom, with a violin in its hands.

"Esmael," Roallen stammered. The troll backed away on the ground. His voice was different now; there was not a trace of hostility, defiance, or pride in it, only fear. "Please, please . . . You know how I am, you know who I am . . . It's the hunger, the hunger drives me crazy . . ."

Denestor couldn't get over his shock. This was all inconceivable. Esmael was helping him, while Lady Serena ordered him to free the troll? What was happening? He looked from one to the other, uneasy. Lady Serena was one of the council members who paid the least attention to the laws of the kingdom; she obeyed them, of course, but she wasn't a loyal defender of tradition, not like Esmael or the regent, or himself, until very recently.

"Esmael, please, Esmael . . ." The troll, still on his knees, raised his chained hands to the black angel, begging for mercy. "I beg you, my friend . . . Remember the battle of Livingsoul . . . You and I . . . We were outnumbered and it was just the two of us, back to back . . . fighting like savages, like brothers . . . Remember, Esmael, remember: you and I fought together in the Battle for the End of the World . . ."

"Of course I remember. You saved my life as many times as I saved yours, maybe even more. And I will always be grateful for that, Roallen. But remember that we made it clear what would happen if you returned to Rocavarancolia." Esmael turned toward Denestor Tul. All of his movements looked like rehearsed dance steps. "What is the punishment for returning from exile, Denestor?"

"Death," answered the demiurge. He jumped down from the coat rack and stretched out his hand to Esmael. "But wait, let's not get ahead of—"

"Esmael!" shouted Lady Serena, as aware as the demiurge of what was about to happen. The black angel unfurled his wings, hardened their edges, and decapitated the troll in a single blow, with a movement as prodigious as it was accurate. Roallen's lifeless body collapsed forward, and his head rolled away. Hector gasped, horrified. Esmael's red wings sparkled for a moment in the afternoon sun, gleaming, then he folded them with a loud crack that left tiny pearls of blood suspended in the air.

Hector felt a lump in his throat. No one could have prepared him to witness something as horrible and final as what he'd just seen: an assassination in cold blood, the execution of a helpless being. He'd wanted to kill Roallen only minutes before, but now that he saw his body, it all seemed distant and unreal. The only reality—so categorical and sickening that it made him want to scream—was that this being had been alive only a second earlier and now it was dead, nothing more than empty matter, just a pile of remains at his assassin's feet.

"Case closed," Esmael announced. Then he turned to the specter. "I give my word that now no one will interfere in what the troll does . . . Roallen has paid the price of returning to Rocavarancolia. If he manages to get up, I won't be the one to stop him."

Hector moaned. In his memory he saw Ricardo falling again, Alexander turning to ashes at the gate of the tower of sorcery, Rachel, dead, in the ballroom . . . Life was nothing, life always succumbed, as fragile as glass. He coughed hard and the pain in his abdomen multiplied. A shadow hovered over him. It was Natalia. The girl knelt down at his side and shook her head. There were tears in her eyes. Hector wondered if they were for him, for Ricardo, for those who had died before, or for those who had yet to die.

"You imbecile. You fool. You idiot. No, worse than an idiot. The biggest idiot in . . ." She pointed to his multiple wounds, still crying. She had no choice but to stop insulting him so she could concentrate on the healing spell.

"I kissed you . . ." he said. He reached out his hand to her, trapped in delirium. "I kissed you in the darkness. The light . . . so beautiful, so fragile . . . Don't let it go out . . . Don't ever let it go out . . ."

"You've won yourselves an exile," Lady Serena whispered, looking from Esmael to Denestor. "Both of you."

"No one's getting exiled, ghost," Esmael growled. Killing Roallen had put him in a bad mood. "All we did here was fulfill the law. And no one will banish us for that." He strode over to the spirit. "Why did you want to free the troll? Do you hate your life so much that you want to see all of Rocavarancolia reduced to nothing? Is that what you want?"

Lady Serena shot daggers at the black angel with her gaze. Esmael didn't know what he'd just done. That had been their last chance to delay the inevitable. With the future vampire dead, Hurza would have lost his opportunity to recover the power from his grimoire, and that, probably, would have delayed his plans. But now it was too late. She suddenly felt furious with herself. What was it that she meant to delay? What vain hope had made her try to hinder Hurza's plans, even if it was in such an indirect, clumsy way? To buy time? For what? To see if by chance Lady Scar or Esmael himself found a way to end her life and free her from her promise to Hurza? Why had she done it? To quiet her conscience?

"What I mean to do, Esmael," she said bitterly, in a vain attempt to convince herself, "is to make things right . . ."

Esmael looked at Lady Serena with scorn.

"If you're set on making things right, I advise you to consider changing your name. 'Serena' no longer fits you . . . 'Hysteria,' 'Unwise,' or 'Bonkers' would suit you much better."

The look the phantom gave him was pure ice. No more words were exchanged between them. The spirit took off in flight. They watched her as she disappeared into the blue sky of Rocavarancolia, leaving fragments of lightning and emerald tendrils in her wake.

"Good riddance, you damned lunatic," Esmael murmured.

Hector was barely aware of what was happening in the plaza. All he could feel was the burning and tightness that the healing magic caused inside him. He closed his eyes. He would soon lose consciousness. He noticed how it seemed to slip through his fingers, as if something gently pushed him toward fainting. He opened his eyes again, startled. He needed to see Marina again before he passed out, he needed to leave the world with her image in his memory in case he never woke up again. He saw her a step away from Natalia, her bow still loaded. She aimed alternately at Denestor and at Roallen's killer, and on occasion she shifted her gaze to him. She was also crying, but despite the tears her hand remained steady.

Hector let himself slip away, embracing her image, the memory of her blue eyes, the most beautiful eyes in the world, eyes that he would never see again.


Denestor perceived the magic attack a second before it reached him. It was a potent bewilderment spell, but he had no trouble intercepting it. He wove a mystical barrier with one hand, trapped the spell, and cast it into the sky. Then he faced his attacker as he prepared to repel any other enchantment.

Bruno had just entered the square, flying at great speed, vertically, with the tails of his green overcoat flapping in the wind, his staff in one hand and the other holding on to his top hat. Adrian was at his side. The blond didn't look as comfortable in the air as his companion, and he set foot on the ground as soon as he could. Then he unsheathed the swords he wore at his waist and took off running toward Denestor Tul while Bruno cast another spell. This one was hastier than the first, and, as such, less powerful.

"Enough!" Esmael yelled. He was the one who diverted Bruno's magical attack as he stepped between Adrian and the demiurge. "Steady, both of you! Stop right now!"

Neither obeyed. Adrian leapt upon Esmael with feline agility. The black angel dodged his blows—though he shifted so fast they could hardly see him move—and grabbed the boy by the wrists, raising him in the air.

"I said stop," he said. Adrian made himself intangible at an astonishing speed and Esmael found himself holding up nothing but thin air. The black angel reacted immediately. He traced a spell of confusion and sank his hand into Adrian's ethereal body, causing an electric shock that left him writhing in pain on the ground. "We're done here. Save your rage for when it's needed," he said as he stood up and moved toward Bruno. "One of your own has died today and another is not far behind. Don't you think that's enough for one day?"

Bruno landed in front of them. He didn't change his posture or his expression one bit. He just looked at the black angel and at the demiurge, and then looked at his companions. The birdcage on his staff pointed at the ground, surrounded by a murky stain of scarlet energy. Denestor was ready to disarm the boy if he made a move to raise it. But the Italian seemed to have no intention of attacking. His gaze was fixed on Ricardo's body, dead at the foot of the stone trees.

"Ricardo is dead." Although his voice sounded as distant and cold as usual, it was clear that something in it was about to break. "Who do you say will not be far behind? Hector?"

Denestor nodded.

"No!" Natalia screamed. She jumped up, showing the demiurge the palms of her hands, still tinted with strands of magic. "He's not going to die! I cured him! Did you not see me? I cured him!"

"You healed his wounds, but that's not enough, child." His sorrow was genuine. He'd placed many hopes in that boy. "The bite of a troll is tremendously venomous. Its saliva is deadly. And unfortunately, the sorcery capable of saving his life is far from your grasp."

"What about mine . . . ?" Bruno began. The demiurge shook his head.

"You still have much to learn. And your body still isn't ready for certain kinds of spells."

"You heal him, then!" Natalia demanded. "If you can do it, do it! Don't let him die!"

"That is impossible." The demiurge shook his head. The girl didn't know what she was asking. "I cannot do it. No, I cannot."

"You cannot or you don't want to?" Marina asked, clenching her fists and trembling with pure rage. "It's that stupid law of yours of not interfering, right? That's what keeps you from healing him."

"You've hit it on the head, little girl," Esmael intervened, anticipating the demiurge's response. Denestor looked at the girl, devastated. "The laws of Rocavarancolia are what regulate and give meaning to our existence. And neither Denestor Tul nor myself are inclined to break them, isn't that right, Demiurge?"

Denestor didn't answer. Marina's pain disarmed him.

"If I save him," he explained, "it would only mean that the Royal Council and the regent would order his immediate execution and my exile to the desert. We can't interfere with the harvest . . . It's the law."

"Your laws are stupid!" Natalia exploded. "If you don't save him and he dies, it will be your fault . . . Yours alone!"

"Oh. I suppose I'll have to live with that weight on my conscience," said Esmael with scorn.

At his feet, Adrian moaned. The boy made an attempt to stand up, but as he tried to place his hand on the ground, it passed cleanly through. Bruno walked over to him, with an eye still on the two creatures with them in the square.

"Damn you," Marina whispered, her voice laden with contempt. She fixed her gaze on the demiurge. "This is all your fault," she said. "If it hadn't been for you we would be safe at home! If it hadn't been for you, Ricardo would still be alive! And Alexander and Rachel! And Marco wouldn't have killed himself! You tricked us! You manipulated us so that we thought this was a game!"

"I fulfilled my duty to the kingdom," Denestor said. He wasn't about to be intimidated by that child. Even less so after saving her life.

"As I've done on so many other occasions, and as I hope to keep doing for the rest of my life."

"And you're proud of that? Of serving this kingdom?" Natalia asked. "Your kingdom is worthless. You built it on a mountain of corpses. And what can something like that be worth? What is the value of something built upon piles of dead children? You're sick. I pity you. And you disgust me . . ." She crouched next to Hector and studied his face with a somber expression. She touched his forehead and pulled her hand back immediately, as if she'd been shocked. She bit her lower lip; she looked determined not to cry. "This whole city should burn to the ground. And you, you damned murderers, you should burn with it . . . That's the least you deserve."

Esmael took a step toward her, and Bruno raised his staff in a defensive manner.

"I'm leaving before I decide that one decapitated head isn't enough," growled the black angel. "You see, you silly little girl? Our law of non-interference just saved your life." He spread his wings and took off. He didn't look back as he flew away.

Denestor was left alone with the kids and their reproachful gaze.

"Burn . . ." he heard Adrian whisper. The young boy sat up as best he could, half-sunk into the cobblestones, and tried to grab his head with both hands, but his intangible fingers passed cleanly through his skull. "To the ground . . ." he huffed. He was still dazed.

The demiurge looked at Hector, passed out on the ground. *Essence of kings* was what Belisarius had said when he saw the display of the boy's essence. How little all of that mattered now. He let out a sad sigh. There was nothing left for him to do there, and his presence only made them angrier. He climbed down to the base of the coat rack, gave the order to depart, and immediately the enormous stork wings unfolded, beat at the air, and propelled him upward. The flying scimitar went after them. He felt the children's gazes boring into his back as he ascended. He hadn't gone but a few yards when he halted his creation and turned toward them again. He couldn't leave them like that. The demiurge gestured with his head toward Hector.

"Give him plenty of water and try to keep him cold." He turned to Bruno. "Do you know the impulse spells?" The Italian nodded. "Cast one upon him each day, the smallest you can generate, directly to his heart; that should be enough to keep it beating." It was dangerous magic, devastating at its greater levels; a high-level impulse spell cast over a tectonic plate could split a continent in two. "And spells of snow-white healing every hour, day and night, do you hear me? Day and night . . . It won't purge the venom, but it will keep his organs from collapsing and his blood from coagulating. Listen to me closely: he'll only have a chance if you can keep him alive until the Red Moon comes out, understand? And I won't lie to you: even then it's a remote possibility." He looked at the Italian the whole time, preferring those apathetic, glassy eyes to the accusing looks from the girls. "He will only survive if the Red Moon transforms him into a being capable of resisting troll venom. And there are few, very few, creatures that can do that."

Denestor returned his gaze to the young boy on the ground. *Your kingdom is worthless. You built it on a mountain of corpses. And what can something like that be worth? What is the value of something built upon piles of dead children?* He shook his head, refusing to go down that road. If he did, he ran the risk of ending up like Mistral, rocking himself in the darkness and wondering over and over what his name had been before the Red Moon had transformed him into what he was now.

And Hector, behind his closed eyelids, sank helplessly into a deep unconsciousness, into utter darkness.

# THE TRAP

Dario was in the middle of a wide octagonal room, sword in hand. Six large mirrors hung on each wall, all different: there were oblong mirrors, rectangular ones, mirrors with new and old wooden frames, some carved, some not, some in the form of open jaws, adorned with scales, polished, shining . . . The boy from São Paulo turned slowly in place, horrified. Every single mirror reflected the image of a troll.

And he knew it was his reflection, although each mirror attempted to offer him a different image from the others. Some of the trolls imitated his movements; others remained still, watching him with their monstrous glares; others laughed at him and pointed to him as they beat their chests. One was so enormous that the mirror could barely contain him: he leaned forward like a gigantic gorilla, his knuckles resting on the ground; his fur was a purplish color and his eyes, a sparkling red, were so big in comparison with the rest of his features that it looked like they might fall out. Out of all of the trolls, only one was sitting down. He was small and blue, and his claws were sunk in the thick mat of hair that covered his head, his mouth open wide in a silent scream.

Dario's gaze went from monster to monster. He was unable to take his eyes off them.

*That's what you'll see in the mirror when the Red Moon comes out.* Rage overtook him as he remembered Roallen's words.

He leapt at a mirror and shattered it in a single blow. A shower of glass and splinters fell upon him. The shards fell slowly, and in each of them he could clearly make out the reflection of a tiny troll that laughed at his futile gesture.

He screamed and struck another mirror, a huge oval one with an iron frame adorned with animal claws. It reflected a troll as black as coal; its mane and the coarse fur on its wrists were a bloody red color. He skewered it so violently with his sword that he almost crashed into the mirror. The blade of his weapon went through the glass. The monster brought his hands to his stomach, burst out laughing—and the mirror shattered immediately after.

Dario jumped from one mirror to the next, frantic, enraged, smashing them to pieces as he went, one after another, desperate blow after desperate blow. Soon the ground was a sea of shards from which peered the trolls' mocking faces. He didn't stop until there wasn't a single mirror left intact. Then he collapsed to his knees over the broken glass, exhausted, hanging his head with his eyes closed, his sword fallen to one side. Tears ran down his cheeks. He wiped them away harshly; maybe they, too, held reflections of tiny trolls inside them.

For a few moments, silence reigned in the octagonal room. Then, behind each of the frames of the broken mirrors appeared a troll. They were no longer mere reflections, but real creatures, as solid as he was. Dario tilted his head and shook it in a useless gesture of denial. He couldn't fight against so many monsters, much less against what dwelled inside him, what awaited the Red Moon. It was a lost battle. The trolls closed in on him, slowly, the shards crackling under their feet. Dario closed his eyes and accepted his fate. They watched him with frozen stares. The trolls opened their fangs, in smiles so brutal that the upper segment of their heads seemed about to break off from the lower half. The circle of monsters surrounding him was complete. Dario closed his eyes more tightly. And as he did so, he woke up.

He choked back a whimper, the memory of the nightmare so close that it merged with reality. He raised his hands before his eyes, and the relief at seeing them still human was almost enough to make him cry.

The nightmare had affected him so much that it took him a while to realize there was someone else in the room with him. The bizarre boy with the top hat and the green overcoat was standing at his bed-side, with his magic staff across his back, watching him with an icy expression similar to that of the trolls in his dream. Dario's broken hand flapped, searching for the sword that he left leaning against the bed, but the only thing he managed was to cry out in pain.

"I have no bad intentions," Bruno assured him. But his voice was so unsubstantial, so lacking in feeling or inflection, that it was hard to believe him. No rational person could talk that way.

Dario spun quickly to the other side of the bed, where he'd kept his weapon since Roallen had destroyed his wrist. He grabbed the sword and pointed it at Bruno. He felt the somber tug of the enchanted weapon and for a moment he thought he might lose control, not because he wanted to, but because of the insecurity with which he still used his left hand.

"What do you want?" he asked. His voice broke in his throat. "How did you find me?"

"Magic. Midlevel searching spells, nothing too complex. At least not anymore." He took a step toward the bed. Dario raised his sword and leaned forward, ready to pounce on the Italian at the slightest hint of threat. Bruno raised his hands. "Allow me to emphasize the fact that I am not here with the intention to do you any harm. Quite the oppo-site. They asked me to cure your wounds, and that is why I came."

Dario hesitated.

"You're going to heal me? Who . . . who asked you to?" He couldn't contain himself and before Bruno responded, he added excitedly, "Was it her?"

The young man's face remained as expressionless as always. It was disturbing to have him there.

"Her? No, there was no 'her,'" he responded. "As paradoxical as it may seem, it was Adrian who sent me."

"Adrian," Dario whispered, disappointed. Apparently that lunatic wanted him to be in the best condition for their next encounter. He was tempted to reject the offer, but his wrist hurt too much to refuse. He extended his arm toward the Italian, without lowering his weapon.

Bruno approached him, his eyes focused on the boy's crudely ban-daged hand. The fingers that stuck out were bruised and swollen. Dario felt an agonizing throbbing in each one of them. This time wasn't like the morning after his fight on the rooftops with Adrian, when he woke up in the alleyway and realized that the wound in his side was nothing more than a superficial scratch, not nearly as serious as he first thought. Now the pain was so intense that he'd been tempted to cut off his own hand and throw it far away, as if that might free him from the agony.

The Italian, not bothered in the least by the blade of Dario's sword—inches away from his throat—raised his hands in a magician's gesture and with an elegant movement he placed them around the boy's wrist without touching it. Dario couldn't take his eyes off the boy. His lack of expression was complete; he almost looked like a blank chalkboard waiting for someone to draw a smile, or paint a tear under an eye.

When he began to softly chant, Dario did detect some emotion, but he couldn't tell if it was merely part of the spell. He barely had time to think about it. The reprieve that he felt was immediate. The pain diminished at the pace of Bruno's chant. He lowered his sword, and for the second time since he'd woken up, he almost cried with relief. The pain was gone, it abandoned him, he felt as if his broken bones had joined back together, his destroyed tendons had come back to life, and his bruised flesh was healed. He closed his eyes.

"It is done." Bruno announced.

And indeed, it was. Not the slightest discomfort or pain remained. Dario opened and closed his hand, turned his wrist, first one way and then the other. All of the movements were perfect, everything worked as it should. He looked at the boy in the green top hat, profoundly grateful. He was about to express this gratitude in words when he remembered who had sent him.

"Do you have any other wounds?" Bruno asked. "Anything else that I can heal?"

"No," he blurted rudely. "You're finished here. You can go back where you came from."

Bruno didn't flinch. He just nodded his head as he looked around. He scanned the small room that Dario had made his home; it was on the second floor of a military barracks located in the northern part of Rocavarancolia. If the chaos of the room littered with sacks, blankets, and baskets of food caught his attention, there was no way of knowing it.

"I will not tell Adrian where you are," he said suddenly. He didn't seem to have the slightest intention of leaving. Dario frowned. "I have nothing against you, nor do I wish you any harm."

"Tell your little friend. He has it in for me."

"Adrian is not my friend. He is not anyone's friend." His gaze stopped wandering around the room to focus on the sword. "They told me what Roallen said about your weapon. It is magical." It wasn't a question.

Bruno kept looking at him with that apathetic stare that was so unsettling. Dario shifted uncomfortably on the bed and decided it was time to get up. He felt stupid being wrapped in blankets while the other kid was still there. He managed to stand, still rotating his wrist that had been shattered until then. The Italian took a step back, never taking his eyes off the sword. Dario realized what he wanted and surprised himself by giving in. He took the weapon by its blade and offered the hilt to Bruno. If Bruno wanted to kill him, he could have done it while he slept.

The young mage wielded the sword. He did it clumsily, without grace. The sword stirred in his hand, and Bruno had no choice but to counteract the movement by pulling back.

"It is trying to attack you," he said.

"Yes. That's what it does, it always tries to stab whoever is in front of it. No matter who." It was hard to admit, but it hurt that the weapon turned against him. He felt betrayed. "That's why I hurt Adrian that day. It wasn't me, it was the sword."

Bruno nodded slowly. Dario scrutinized his face, looking for some emotion, any reaction to what he'd said, but there was nothing there. No compassion, no understanding. Just indifference.

"It is the first seemingly magic weapon that I have seen," he began, apparently more interested in the sword than in his words. "I knew of their existence, of course, but in all the time we have been in Rocavarancolia I have not had the chance to see one."

"I found it in the crevice with the skeletons . . . The . . . the troll said that it was a weapon of baussite or something like that. And from what he said, it seems like there were a lot of them." *A weapon for cowards*, he'd pointed out.

Bruno, satisfied with his examination, returned the sword. Dario took it with his recently healed hand, repressed its effort to turn and attack Bruno, sheathed it, and left it next to the bed.

"How's your friend?" he then asked. He'd witnessed the fight between the boy and the troll, from the safety of a rooftop that he'd taken great pains to climb up to after he regained consciousness.

"Hector? He will live or die. We still do not know. We cured his wounds, but we cannot do anything to stop the troll's venom."

"Venom . . ." Dario whispered.

"That is right. The bite of those creatures is highly infectious. And immune to magic healing spells, at least to the ones we know of. If we keep him alive until the Red Moon comes out, there is a chance that he may survive, but it will be a difficult task."

He took a step toward the window. "I should go. Under the circumstances, I do not wish to be away from the tower for too long."

Dario nodded and sat back down on the bed. He resisted thanking him. The Italian lowered his head to go through the window, then something made him stop. He remained still, his gaze lost in the void. He suddenly blinked and turned toward Adrian.

"She did not send me," he said. "Adrian did." His voice continued without the slightest inflection, but now he spoke much more quickly. "But she did ask me to thank you for what you did in the square. You saved her life."

Dario tensed on the edge of the bed. He grabbed his knees tightly and watched the Italian, motionless in the window. They exchanged glances.

"I did what I had to do, that's all," he said.

Bruno moved, finally about to leave, but he hesitated again.

"She also asked me to find out your name," he added, this time without looking at him.

"Dario. My name is Dario," he answered hurriedly. His heart was pounding.

"Dario," Bruno repeated slowly, as if he wanted to try out how that name sounded. "Goodbye, Dario. I hope that everything goes well for you," he said, before disappearing through the window.

After Bruno left, the Brazilian remained sitting there, staring into space as time passed by. He was bewildered by the boy's short visit and, more than anything, by his parting words. He smiled as he remembered how he'd stammered, and he regretted not thanking him then. Not for healing him, of course, not for that. He would have liked to have thanked him for lying: Marina hadn't asked Bruno to thank him, nor had she asked for his name. She probably didn't even know that Adrian had sent him there. Bruno had the hesitation of someone who wasn't used to deceiving others.

He wondered what Bruno could have seen in him to make him lie in that clumsy, naive way. He didn't know. Maybe the mere fact that he had tried was a sign that there was still hope for him. Then his gaze shifted to the small broken mirror that hung at an angle on the wall, and once he saw his reflection, his optimism vanished.

*Your kingdom is worthless.* How dare that ungrateful brat? What did she know of Rocavarancolia? Denestor Tul growled and tried for the thousandth time that week to get his mind off Natalia's words, but again, for the thousandth time, he failed. *You built it on a mountain of corpses . . . And what is the value of something like that?*

What made him even grumpier—if that were possible—was that another of the books that he'd sent in search of clues about Belisarius's scroll had died just before dawn. It was the third to fall in the last few days; the first two had been devoured by vermin, but in this case it had been magic that had killed it. The book was exploring the Serpent Tower when Denestor felt its death; he noticed a sudden stabbing sensation in his chest, as always happened when one of his creations died. Despite the mental link that he maintained with most of his creations, he hadn't been able to determine exactly what had occurred, so he prepared to visit the tower. Most likely the book had gotten too close to somewhere it shouldn't have been and a guardian spell had finished it off, but he also couldn't rule out the remote possibility that such a spell might be protecting something related to the vanished parchment. To be certain, he had no choice but to investigate in person. He couldn't risk sending another of his creations and having it suffer the same fate.

He descended the rope stairway that hung from the north face of the tower with a tiny crystal tarantula running around his head. The spider was an efficient curse detector, and he was planning on using it to find the murderous spell. There were dozens of active enchantments on the top floor of the Serpent Tower, and any one of them could be guilty of the book's destruction.

In spite of himself, his thoughts returned to Natalia and to what she'd said in the square. *What's the value of something built on piles of dead children?* the insolent girl had dared to ask.

How dare she judge them? Especially Natalia, who should have been so grateful to him for bringing her to Rocavarancolia. What fate awaited her on Earth if he hadn't? She was already affected by magic even before he found her; she was able to see what was hidden to most others and that, without a doubt, would have been her undoing. The pills might have made her gift dormant, but it was only a matter of time before they would have stopped being effective. If Natalia had stayed on Earth, sooner or later she would have gone insane, like so many others surrounded by wonder in a world void of miracles.

Denestor set foot on the ground and walked briskly toward the gate of Highlowtower, feeling ridiculous for still being so affected by the girl's reproaches.

*You're behaving like an idiot,* he told himself. *Not only did that girl not know what she was saying, she was also upset by what had happened. What's wrong with you, you crazy old man? You've heard infinitely worse things about Rocavarancolia. Why is this bothering you so much now?*

Denestor groaned. He knew the answer to that question, but he was terribly afraid to put it into words, to give it a shape, although it was only in his mind. It was much simpler to rant and rave about the thankless little girl than to open that door and face all of his doubts, all of his fears.

No, the girl knew nothing. Not a thing.

"The Red Moon will open her eyes," Denestor pronounced. He took the restless tarantula between his fingers and placed it in one of the many pockets in his robe. "You haven't seen anything yet, little girl, wait and see. Wait and see."

The pulleys and chains that opened the enormous gate of Highlowtower were set in motion as soon as Denestor approached the exit; the two doors opened before him with their usual clatter, and the demiurge went out into the clear morning.

He encountered Ujthan and Solberinus standing immobile just yards away from the gate. The first thing he thought when he saw them was that there had been another tragedy. The tension in the two men was so obvious that it looked like they were about to take off running.

"What's going on?" he asked worriedly. "Is there a council meeting? Did something bad happen?"

"What?" Ujthan took a step back.

"No, nothing bad has happened, Demiurge," Solberinus said. His face softened. He took Ujthan by the arm and made him step forward. The gesture struck Denestor as odd; he hadn't thought there was such familiarity between them. In fact, it was the first time he could recall seeing Solberinus touch anyone. "It took us by surprise to see the gate opening just as we were about to knock on it, that's all," he explained in his coarse, roguish voice. "But we didn't come with bad news. On the contrary: we think it's good. On a ship in the bay I came across several books written in the language that you've been asking about. At least I'm almost certain that it's the same one."

"Several books?"

"That's right. Seven or eight. Although I have to say, they're not in the best condition."

"And where are they? Did you bring them with you?"

"No, no, no. I didn't dare touch them, Demiurge," the castaway answered. "It wouldn't be the first time a book has come apart in my hands, or tried to bite me as I grabbed it. Magic things, you know. And I always say, leave the magic things to those who know what they're doing."

"You're saying these are books of magic?"

Solberinus shrugged his shoulders.

"They smell like magic, anyhow. I don't know if it's them or the trunk where I found them."

Deep in thought, Denestor observed the two men. He'd overlooked the shipwrecked boats when he gave his orders to the tracking books; as was usually the case among the inhabitants of Rocavarancolia, he wasn't used to thinking of that chaos of half-sunken ships as a proper part of the city. He sent a mental command to the books closest to the bay to prepare to investigate, then he asked Ujthan and Solberinus to guard the entrance, and he went back into Highlowtower. It was good news, no doubt, although he worried about what state the books might be in. He'd already started outlining in his mind a creature capable of translating texts written in unknown languages, but to make it work he'd need to feed it as many words as possible in that language, many more than he had now.

He looked around. Highlowtower, as always, was a hive of life. At a single gesture, two large books with white covers and short fluted tubes at the top of their spines descended from above. Those books would literally drink the words from the ones they found in the trunk; they would steal them from their pages to write in their own. They wouldn't have to touch them to access their content. He took one last look at Highlowtower, his gaze passing over the chaotic artificial fauna that inhabited it. He shook his head—the spider in his pocket and the books would be enough.

He hadn't taken one step in the direction of the gate when a sudden whirlwind of dust fell upon him. As it didn't have a ceiling, Highlowtower was a place given to air currents, but this was ridiculous. It almost seemed like that dusty whirlwind had landed on him on purpose. Denestor sneezed several times, brushed himself off, and headed outside to meet the men waiting.

Sunk in the middle of her bed, Lady Dream, despite remaining in a deep sleep, opened her eyes wide. After three long months of sleep, her pupils were so small that they almost disappeared in her irises. Her cracked lips moved slowly, whispering words in a voice so soft that the servant sitting at the head of the bed, on the other side of the canopy, didn't hear them:

"Forgive us, Denestor . . . If we could have saved you, we would have. If we could have . . ."

It was a clear, bright day.

The sparkling white clouds were scattered in the sky like packs of lazy animals who'd stopped to rest in the heavens. Two birds of turquoise-colored smoke with long twisted beaks perched atop a large flat cloud.

Denestor rode on the coat rack as its wings flapped vigorously in the air flying over Rocavarancolia toward the reefs. He hung on with one hand, gripping the rack as he leaned forward. Two white books flew behind him, and a little farther behind, on a second coat rack substantially larger than the first, flew Ujthan and Solberinus. The castaway had wanted to make the journey on foot but Denestor had flatly refused. It would have been at least two long hours of walking, and he was burning with desire to get his hands on those books as soon as possible.

The city stretched out before them, a chaotic tapestry where shadows and gray tones predominated; from the sky, one could best observe the devastation the war had wrought on Rocavarancolia. Denestor could see the purplish remnants on the rock where the Dragon Towers used to be, halfway between the foothills of the mountains and Rocavaragalago. Every last one had been destroyed by the enemy. As if killing more than eighty dragons in battle and stealing almost a hundred more from Rocavarancolia to drag them into their own worlds hadn't been enough, they also had to destroy the towers where those magnificent beasts had lived. For some time, Denestor had wondered what had compelled them to do something so drastic, so brutal. If there were no dragons left in Rocavarancolia, why destroy those majestic buildings? What sense did that make? The Dragon Towers were beautiful multicolored structures over three hundred feet tall, with extraordinary bas-reliefs adorning their surfaces; those towers were among the city's wonders, and it was a crime to destroy them, a senseless crime. That was what he had thought at first, until Esmael opened his eyes.

"They destroyed them to snatch away all hope," he said. "Seeing them might make us think there could be a chance that dragons would return. That's why they did it. It was their way of telling us that everything was over, that they had defeated us completely. It was their way of telling us that dragons would never again fly over Rocavarancolia."

Therefore, in the early days after the defeat, many people tried to disenchant the only dragon that remained in Rocavarancolia: the petrified dragon from Transalarada in Banner Square. But all of their efforts had been in vain. Stone remained stone, and looked as if it would be for eternity. The magic capable of undoing the spell that Lady Basilisk cast during the last battle was out of reach for the few who'd survived the war. Denestor sighed as he remembered the witch. He was the only one who knew what had actually happened that night. Only he knew that Lady Basilisk hadn't been just another casualty in battle.

"You won't be the ones who put an end to Rocavarancolia!" the sorceress had howled from the sky, riding on Cefal, her winged shark. Most of the shark's armor was missing, and the animal bled from a brutal injury on its side. The witch herself showed signs of fatigue. "You're no more than rats! Do you hear me?! Cowardly, traitorous rats! Rats that attack from the refuge of darkness!"

They had been fighting for over forty hours. Denestor was next to her, riding on his exhausted bronze dragon. It was one of the few moments of rest the battle had granted them; the skirmishes in the southern part of the city had dispersed, and they found themselves in a momentary break. Lady Basilisk tightly grasped the edge of the armor that protected Cefal's head and looked around her, unhinged. Columns of fire, smoke, and uncontrolled magic rose up throughout all of Rocavarancolia. Glimmers of pure energy sparkled in the twilight like fireworks. The shadows of dragons and chimeras fell over the buildings and the clashing armies. It didn't matter how many they killed; the enemy kept pouring through the open vortices. War and horror raged throughout the city. A building exploded into fragments in the east. Denestor recognized the Daybreak Tower, the tower where he'd lived during his first months in Rocavarancolia, when he was no more than a recently harvested child. He felt faint.

"No, we're not going to fall like this . . ." insisted Lady Basilisk. "But even rats can kill a dragon if they attack by treachery and in sufficient numbers." The witch was one of the most powerful sorcerers in the kingdom and one of the first to realize that all was lost. "We don't deserve this ending, Denestor. Rocavarancolia will not be destroyed by these savages, I swear to you upon my black soul." She gave him a look that was equal parts desperation and rage. "They want a massacre?! That's what they came for? Fine! I'll give them a massacre!" she exclaimed as she straightened up on her shark. "May death and destruction overtake us all! Do you hear me, damn it? Can you hear me?!" The mystical energy that suddenly surrounded the woman was so great that her hair burst into flames. "No one will survive to say that Rocavarancolia fell! No one!"

And to the demiurge's surprise, she began to launch one of the most powerful and destructive spells ever known: the Song of the Rock. Every being alive in Rocavarancolia would be transformed to stone—not just in the city, but on the entire planet. Everything would be rock and desolation. The first to be petrified were those battling in Banner Square, just beneath Lady Basilisk and Denestor. The spell did not discriminate between enemies and friends. All that was flesh was turned to stone; all life was to be destroyed. And it was then, seeing how the waves of magic began to cross the boundaries of the square, that the demiurge understood the true reach of the woman's plans: the Song of the Rock would make its way through each and every one of the open vortices in the city, extending to the linked worlds and destroying them too—those that had been involved in the battle, but also those that didn't even know Rocavarancolia existed. And Denestor couldn't allow that to happen. He couldn't let their deaths drag so many innocent lives with them.

He had no time to be subtle, not with that spell threatening to turn him to stone at any moment. He ordered one of his creations to launch onto the witch, who, with her arms raised and eyes blank, continued with the spell. The demiurge's creation, a bristly creature in the form of a pterodactyl made from arrows and hooks, dropped upon Lady Basilisk and her mount. It destroyed them in two blows before crashing into the void and turning into stone. For a long time, Denestor wondered if Lady Basilisk had been aware of his treason at any point. He hoped she hadn't.

And so Rocavarancolia fell, but it fell alone.

*Your kingdom is worthless. You built it on a mountain of corpses . . .* Natalia had dared to say.

What would she say if she knew what Denestor Tul had prevented that day? How many worlds had he saved by assassinating someone he considered a friend?

Denestor, Solberinus, Ujthan, and the two blank books now flew over the Margalar Tower. There continued the life-or-death fight between Hector and the troll venom, and the demiurge was hardly optimistic. He had an approximate idea of Bruno's power, as well as of Hector's fortitude, and neither was equal to what ran through Hector's veins. The battle would soon tip in favor of the venom; it was strange that it hadn't already. The best thing, Denestor thought, would be to let him go. The boy would not be able to hold out for the twenty-two days that remained before the Red Moon's arrival.

The demiurge shifted his gaze from the tower and focused on his objective.

The ocean that bathed the rocky coasts of Rocavarancolia had a still blue patina, peppered with lively sparkles from the languid sun that hung in the sky. The agitation of the last few days had let up, but this new calm didn't deceive the demiurge. He knew it was only momentary and the worst was yet to come.

They left the cliff behind to fly over the cemetery of ships. From time to time, the wakes of the marine monsters that plagued the area tore through the water's surface. In one of the many clearings that opened up between boats, Denestor made out the skeleton of a beast, so enormous that it rivaled the largest vessels in the bay. A multitude of birds were scattered among the ships and reefs, perched on what was left of the masts, the destroyed keels, the shattered decks . . . Their cries were deafening.

The sea stank of blood and carrion.

Denestor Tul stopped the flight of his coat rack and turned toward the men flying behind him. Solberinus clung to his mount in desperation; his face was a sickly violet hue. The castaway took a breath and pointed to the northeast. He said something the demiurge couldn't make out, but Ujthan translated it immediately:

"The reddish schooner in the barrier of reefs to your left"—he pointed it out—"the one that's half-crushed by the warship. That's where the books are."

Denestor had no trouble locating the boat. It was a dismasted schooner that had almost been split in two by the keel of a gigantic gray ship that leaned over its stern. The prow was tilted upward, practically at a right angle, and it only remained afloat because the keel rested between the sharp edges of the line of reefs. The ship conveyed an overwhelming feeling of imminent disaster. It looked like it might break into pieces at any moment.

"We have to go in there?" Denestor asked.

"It's not as risky as it seems, Demiurge," Solberinus reassured him in a thin voice. The coat rack that carried the two men had come to a stop at his level. "The chest is in a cabin that's easily accessed from the deck of the prow." He swallowed and clung to the wood even tighter. He kept his eyes closed most of the time. "Can we get down already, for pity's sake?"

Denestor frowned. Suspicion began to stir within him, but then he saw his own books fluttering around the ship and he realized that, indeed, what they were looking for was there. He didn't give it another thought.

He made the coat racks descend, heading for the schooner and the ship. As they did, the area around the two boats and the broken line of reefs became a confusion of startled birds taking flight. Solberinus didn't wait for his coat rack to come to a stop on the wreckage; as soon as he was at a safe distance he jumped onto the hull. He squatted down, took a deep breath, and straightened up. Ujthan and Denestor soon joined him. The demiurge made no move to descend from the coat rack; the raised keel of the ship didn't inspire the slightest confidence, and he wasn't about to set foot on it if it wasn't absolutely necessary.

The warship rose up in front of them, darkening the day. At their feet, the deck of the schooner fell almost vertically into the water. Solberinus crouched down again, right at the edge of the keel, and pointed downward.

"The hatch is about thirty yards away," he said. Denestor discovered a long rope ladder tied to the railing of the schooner and hanging down the deck. "Go down on those diabolical things if you like, but I've had enough for today; I much prefer my way." And as soon as he finished speaking, Solberinus jumped onto the deck, grabbed the intertwined ropes, and began climbing down at a steady pace.

Denestor urged his coat rack on and descended parallel to the deck. The immense keel of the warship rose up behind him, covered with grime, algae, and mollusks. As the demiurge went down between the two ships, shadows overtook the clarity of day.

Solberinus stopped next to an opening in the deck and waited for them there, blanketed in the shadows that swirled around the schooner and the other ship. Denestor crossed the last few remaining yards to reach the castaway, and after approaching the open hatch, he peered inside. It was the entrance to a dismal, damp cabin. The castaway tossed the ropes aside, grabbed on to the wood, and went in.

It was almost total darkness inside. Two dozen tiny wooden fireflies emerged from the sleeves of Denestor's robe, with minuscule candles attached to their abdomens that lit up instantly. Their shifting light illuminated his surroundings. The demiurge went in slowly, squinting. It was a small room with a broken, overturned bed in one corner, a dilapidated locker, and what looked like the remains of a chair. What caught his eye the most was the chest located against the wall across from the door. It was fairly large, made of black wood, its edges reinforced with iron plates.

Solberinus waited in the middle of the cabin, watching with his head tilted and a strange, eager expression on his aquiline face. Denestor frowned. The chest was too big for the room. Maybe its owner liked it so much that he sacrificed essential space and comfort to keep it nearby, or someone had placed it there after the ship became stranded. That was the most likely explanation, given its perfect condition in comparison to the rest of the furnishings. He turned toward Ujthan. The warrior looked him straight in the eye.

"The books, Denestor," he urged. "The books."

The demiurge hesitated for an instant, then nodded and approached the chest slowly, sloshing through the puddles of water that covered the ground. Solberinus stepped aside to let him by and Denestor leaned forward, still at a safe distance from the chest, on alert. There were almost a dozen books inside, thick, enormous, leather-covered volumes. They smelled like magic, it was true. He recognized characters on their covers similar to the ones from Belisarius's scroll. Solberinus was right: it was the same language. Denestor took the crystal tarantula out of his pocket, and it jumped inside the chest, searching for guardian spells.

"That's weird . . ." the demiurge said with a furrowed brow as he contemplated the spider's progress over the books. "This place smells old, but the magic of the chest seems new . . ." From inside the chest, the tarantula spoke to him in a language that only he could understand. Denestor nodded his head. "They're recent spells, indeed, indeed . . . And I don't sense anything evil in them. The only spells I detect have been extinguished recently and only serve to hide the contents of the chest from locator spe—"

His eyes opened wide when the tarantula discovered the two books of logomancy that had vanished from the library at the bottom of the chest.

Suddenly, a sphere of silence closed in around him. The contours of the world blurred. Denestor turned toward Ujthan and came face to face with Lady Serena, emerging ethereally from the warrior's flesh. The ghost moved her hands, reinforcing the spell that surrounded them with a new layer of containment. The expression on her face was one of tremendous iciness; it looked like she wasn't really there. Ujthan raised an enormous broadsword with a green blade.

The demiurge stood paralyzed for a moment, unable to make sense of the scene.

"What's going . . . ?" But before he could finish the question he knew what the answer would be. And he knew he was going to die.

"I'm very sorry, Denestor," Ujthan said. And with a swift, precise movement he sank the sword into the demiurge's stomach.

Like an explosion, the pain shook his entire being. But what was more terrible still was the astonishing sensation of emptiness when Ujthan withdrew the weapon with one tug. Denestor, mortally wounded, stepped back and bumped into Solberinus. The castaway looked at him with a deranged smile. He was enjoying every second. The demiurge tried to call his creatures, any of them, but neither his words nor his thoughts managed to cross the barrier erected by Lady Serena. And there wasn't an ounce of magic left in his body to defend himself with. The sword had emptied him completely.

A second creature began to emerge from Ujthan's body. A brown-gray being, its ribs protruding painfully from its chest. It was Belisarius, but no, it couldn't be—Belisarius didn't have a horn on his forehead. And besides, Belisarius was dead. It was his murder that he'd been investigating, it was a scroll that he wrote which led him here . . . No, it didn't make sense. Denestor took another step back, his hands clutching the open wound in his stomach. He felt his knees give out, but he didn't fall. Solberinus kept him upright, supporting him from behind, holding him up as an offering to the creature that emerged from Ujthan. The castaway laughed long and hard. The new creature, the one that couldn't be Belisarius, stretched as it stepped out from the warrior. It wielded a crystal sword, a sword swirling inside with black smoke. Lady Serena had completely left Ujthan's body; her gaze was lost in the void. Without a single glance at Denestor, she cast spell after spell around them, as if what was happening had nothing to do with her. The other creature looked him in the face, and as he saw the bottomless darkness that dwelled in those eyes, Denestor lost his footing. The castaway thrust him forward.

"No . . ." the demiurge managed to utter.

No, he couldn't die that way, not in ignorance. Not without knowing the reason, without understanding the why. He didn't deserve that. The world couldn't be so unjust, so cruel. He thought again of Natalia's words as he looked at the somber emptiness of the eyes of the creature about to kill him. He couldn't die like that, not now, not when he wasn't sure whether his life had actually been worth it.

Belisarius lifted the sword above his head, ready to deliver the final blow. Denestor escaped Solberinus's grasp and leapt forward in a desperate attempt to animate the weapon and bend it to his will, knowing full well that no energy remained in his body for such a feat.

And in a terrible flash of ice and darkness, he was erased from the world.

# DO YOU WANT TO SEE A MIRACLE?

Esmael looked up.

It was raining death. He sensed it. He could feel it in his bones. He left the tower dome for one of the platforms outside and gazed out. Rocavarancolia was witnessing a real massacre: dozens, no, hundreds of lives coming to an end. He could almost feel them as they were snuffed out. The black angel took off in flight.

"Highlowtower . . ." he murmured, incredulous. He turned slowly in the air to face the mountains.

The sky over the demiurge's residence swarmed with activity, but not of the usual sort. The black angel squinted his eyes. Denestor Tul's inventions were falling to pieces, one after the other. Dead. The kites came down, transformed into pieces of lifeless paper and simple strings, the lead soldiers succumbed to the cold dictate of their heartless bodies, boats fell against the crags and smashed into bits . . . Esmael watched as a large butterfly made out of colored glass and diamonds broke apart and fell in fragments. In the mountains it rained dead birds, birds that never should have been alive, and spyglasses and binoculars that no one would ever look through again. Only a few creatures remained airborne: those that were the work of other demiurges and those upon which Denestor had bestowed the spell of life. The rest tumbled down the mountain, in silence, with the resignation of that which has never been truly alive. Esmael couldn't see inside

Highlowtower, but he knew a similar occurrence would be taking place over there. The miracle was vanishing. The magic was fading away. And that could only mean one thing.

Denestor Tul was dead.

The black angel looked around, deeply shaken. He focused all his attention on the sounds coming at him. The city breathed in his ears, the beating of its immense heart resounded in the streets, in the wind, in the whispers of the monsters who lurked in darkness. The buildings murmured, the shadows told dreadful stories among the ruins. Esmael heard everything, his teeth clenched, his own heart beating anxiously in his chest. Suddenly the sound of water boiling furiously came to his ears; the carnivorous frenzy of the marine beasts moving in the depths, seething; and the crashing that seemed like dozens of ships ramming into one another. The sea, Esmael understood. They had killed him at sea.

He flew in that direction. He became a projectile of angry darkness headed toward the bay of shipwrecks. Someone had dared to assassinate the demiurge of Rocavarancolia, the guardian of Highlowtower. That was what truly enraged him, not the fact that Denestor Tul was dead. Denestor was a living creature, fragile and mortal by definition, but what they had dared to destroy was something much more important than that: they had destroyed one of the fundamental pillars of the kingdom. There had always been a demiurge in Highlowtower. Always.

He reached the bay in the blink of an eye. From the sky he saw whirlpools of water that ravaged the stranded ships. One schooner sank and dragged a half dozen smaller boats and a large warship with it. The water was a chaos of spray, foam, and agitated beasts. Many of the ships were fully submerged, while others surfaced again, covered almost entirely with crustaceans and algae so that they looked more like monsters from the depths than boats. The geography of the bay of shipwrecks was changing before his eyes.

Esmael swooped down. Beyond the barrier of reefs, a dozen immense purple tentacles thrust out of the water, closed around a black galley, and began to drag it beneath the sea. Something had driven all of those creatures mad. Even when the Red Moon was in the sky they didn't exhibit such behavior. The air reeked not only of salt and blood, but of primordial magic as well.

The black angel discovered a figure clinging to the reefs near where the schooner sank. It was Ujthan. He grasped the rocks with one hand while, wielding an axe in the other, he defended himself as best he could against a swarm of sharks. The waves resulting from the sinking of the schooner and the warship threatened to tear him from the reefs, but Ujthan didn't give up the fight. He defended his life fiercely, his shouts drowned out by the constant roaring of the sea. Esmael flew toward him in the chaos of plummeting ships and riotous water. He landed on the back of one of the sharks and sliced its head into three pieces with a quick flap of his wings. Then he jumped toward the rocks, grabbed Ujthan around the waist, and dragged him without hesitation to the top of the reefs.

"What's going on?" he yelled in his face. "Where is the demiurge?"

"I don't know! I don't know! He vanished!" the warrior howled. He was drenched. He pulled away from the black angel, still with the bloody axe in his hand. "It was the chest, Esmael! A spell in the chest! Everything went to pieces when Denestor got near it!"

"What are you talking about?" Esmael rocked from one side to the other. The waves crashed into him violently. "Damn you, Ujthan! Put that damn empty head of yours to work and explain yourself! What chest are you talking about?"

"Books, it contained books . . ." Ujthan panted. "Written in that strange language that Denestor kept asking about. Solberinus found them, and we came to investigate. When Denestor approached the chest, a guardian spell took effect, and the whole world went crazy."

Esmael let go of Ujthan and turned in fury. The warrior slumped to the rocks, heaving. He refused to believe that a protection spell would have surprised the demiurge. No. Denestor never would have been that careless. And all of that destruction in the bay couldn't have been caused by a normal guardian spell. There was something more at play.

Someone called to him from up above.

"Esmael!" He looked up to see Lady Serena, flying above his head in her sphere of emerald light. "What happened?" she asked. "What is this madness?"

At the ghost's feet lay Solberinus, the castaway, on all fours, soaked to the bone, shivering with cold.

"Denestor Tul is dead," growled the black angel, and he plunged into the water.

★★★

Hurza, his eyes closed and his face raised, smiled in the darkness of the ocean depths, very far from where Esmael searched for Denestor's remains. The demiurge's power flowed through his blood like boiling magma; it was pure life injected into his veins. For the first time since he'd woken in Belisarius's decrepit body, he felt truly alive. He lifted his hands in the dark. The nerve endings in his body vibrated in harmony with the secret pulse of the universe; his heart beat in time to the movement of the stars and solar storms.

He was so intoxicated by the energy robbed from the demiurge that he'd been tempted to go looking for Esmael and end everything once and for all. But finally he gave in to prudence. Esmael was still a black angel, and he shouldn't make the mistake of underestimating him.

He would wait. The only thing he needed to guarantee his victory over the black angel was to recover the power stored in his grimoire. Yes, he needed a vampire to access it, but the Red Moon would soon solve that problem. And once he recovered what was his, no one would be able to stop him. Not even the death of the boy in the Margalar Tower would put a damper on his victory. It would delay his plans, no doubt, but once the vortices opened again, it would only be a matter of time before he found a body suitable for Harex's soul. And it didn't matter if he had to wait centuries for that to occur. However long it took, Hurza would bring his brother back.

The first Lord of Assassins smiled. He wasn't a creature given to optimism, but at that moment, savoring all of the new and magnificent power that he'd taken from Denestor, he couldn't conceive of anything going wrong.

Lady Scar couldn't believe it. She couldn't admit that the demiurge was dead. She walked along the stone path that bordered one of the small squares in the cemetery, with her hands folded at her chest and a somber expression. Even the dead were silent.

The metal bird that Denestor had given her so long ago had spent hours perched at the top of the obelisk that stood in the middle of the square, its gaze lost to the east, hunched over, barely moving, the very image of despair. It hadn't died along with its siblings because Denestor had instilled in it the spell of life. Lady Scar called it again and again, but the bird ignored her. It just turned the small cannonball it had for a head to look at her for a second, before gazing back in the direction of the sea.

"He's not coming back," Lady Scar told it. "Better that you accept it. He's dead." But not even then, not even saying it out loud, was she able to accept it herself.

A sudden current of air at her back made her turn around. Lady Serena landed next to her, silently. She hadn't heard her arrive.

"Esmael and the Lexel twins are still searching the sea for the body," she announced. She looked at Denestor's bird as well. "But none of the locator spells seem to be finding anything. Maybe there's nothing left to find," she added. Lady Scar thought she seemed colder and more distant than usual. Had the demiurge's death affected her as much as it had the guardian of the Royal Pantheon herself? Or was it that it hurt to watch so many others dying around her, while she was condemned to live the illusion of life?

"They won't find him," growled the scarred woman. "Not with all those hungry creatures underwater. Someone set a trap for him, my dear. And I'm convinced that it was the same creature who assassinated Rorcual, Enoch, and Belisarius. Only the coward didn't dare confront Denestor face to face."

"Esmael suspected the same."

"And you?"

"I don't know." She shrugged. "Maybe if we find the remains of the chest, we can confirm something. But all we have is so vague, so ethereal . . ." They wouldn't find anything. She knew it. They'd been very careful to hide every trace. They would only find residue from the primordial spell that Hurza had used to rile up all of the sea monsters, nothing more.

"I just can't believe he's gone," Lady Scar said. She rested her hands on the back of one of the black iron benches scattered throughout the tiny square. "For me, Denestor Tul was as much a part of the city as . . . I don't know, as this cemetery, as the fortress in the mountains . . . As Rocavaragalago itself." She looked up to examine the phantom.

"Or as you . . . And now he's dead, Lady Serena. Denestor Tul is gone. They killed the demiurge of Rocavarancolia."


Denestor Tul opened his eyes and wondered if the thick and total darkness that surrounded him was death.

But if it were so, and for the moment he had no reason to doubt it, there was something strange in that darkness: a fresh, vital, out-of-place smell, a breath of life, of abundance. He almost thought he sensed the fragrance of an endless number of flowers. He furrowed his brow, surprised to find that he still had a brow to furrow. He took a step forward and the astonishing miracle of movement left him dazed, about to burst into tears from the relief at feeling alive. That last, fatal moment was engraved in his memory: the merciless stare from his assassin, the trajectory of the crystal sword and the whistling of the blade as it cut through the air, his desperate, futile leap . . . He brought one hand to his throat where the weapon had pierced him, but found no injury.

A voice reached him from the shadows, a girl's voice, seized by an endless sadness.

"We couldn't save you, Demiurge." Denestor recognized the voice; it was one of the many used by the old dreamer. The relief he felt multiplied a thousandfold. He paid no attention to her words.

"A dream. It was nothing but a dream . . ." He thanked the gods. Ujthan hadn't run him through with that green sword, and that brownish creature hadn't decapitated him. He had dreamed it all. What madness, what madness . . . How could a dream be so real?

"You are dreaming now, Denestor," a second voice assured him, older than the first, but belonging to the same woman. "It's your last dream," she added. "While we talk, your remains are sinking in the black waters of the bay, among leviathans and sea serpents. Your murderers will say a guardian spell left you helpless and that the same magic made the beasts of the depths go wild." Her voice changed. Now it was Ujthan's voice, more terrible than usual: "Dozens, Esmael. Dozens of them descended on us. We couldn't do a thing. Just fight for our lives. If only I'd been more adept, if only I'd been faster . . . If only I'd died instead of Denestor . . ." Lady Dream recovered her voice once again to add: "Esmael will suspect that it was all a trap to end your life, but unfortunately he won't look in the direction that he should."

"No . . ." Denestor noticed how his voice failed him. The image of his own body falling into the abyss made him shake. It didn't make sense. None of what was happening made sense. The ancient fool couldn't have come just to tell him that everything he'd felt in the last few minutes was nothing more than an illusion, a dream, and that in reality he was dead, sinking in the sea . . . She couldn't be so cruel. No one could be so cruel.

"They will never find your corpse," said the dreamer from the darkness. "And Esmael will look for it for ages, you can be sure of it."

"No, no, no . . ." Denestor emphasized each of his nos by briskly shaking his head. He covered his ears so as not to hear her stream of insanity, but the roar of the blood in his temples enraged him. It was real. He was alive. "Stop playing with me, Lady Dream! Stop scaring me. What's going on? I'm not dead! I'm here! Talking to you! And I'm not a ghost!"

"No, you're not," said another voice, old and worn out. "You're much more than a ghost, much more. You're consciousness. You're dream. I took your thoughts and your soul in my hands, and I brought them here with me when you exhaled your last breath. It was the only thing I could do. Will you forgive me? I couldn't save you, old friend . . ."

"I couldn't save you until you were dead," added another woman's voice, the same woman's, but at another stage in her life.

"No." Denestor shook his head again. He touched his face with both hands. He felt it. He was able to notice its warmth, the deep wrinkles in his cheeks, the tears that ran down them.

"Yes," replied several voices in unison.

"You're dead, Demiurge," added Lady Dream, at his side. "Your body is, at least. The rest is here, safe within the dream."

"Dead," he whispered. He raised his hands before his eyes but he couldn't make them out. Everything was submerged in an impenetrable darkness, almost solid. He wondered if this would be his fate from now on.

He felt faint. He took a step back, almost staggering. There was ground beneath his feet, a soft, muddy ground. But the place where he found himself wasn't what worried him now. The image of a brownish creature, emerging sword in hand from the body of the tattooed warrior, returned to his mind.

"Who killed me?" he asked the darkness. "What was that hiding in Ujthan? It looked so much like Belisarius! What was it?"

"The past. The living history of Rocavarancolia made flesh once more. The creature who orchestrated your death is Hurza the Eye-Eater."

It was hard for him to accept that information.

"Hurza? That's impossible! He died centuries ago! He should be . . ."

"The soul of Hurza lived in the horn of Belisarius," said a voice.

"His most prized possession," added another.

"The old man murdered the servant and then stabbed himself with the horn so the soul of his lord could possess his body," said a third, "with no concern that his own spirit would be destroyed in the process."

Lady Dream's voices multiplied. Soon there were dozens of them, all the same, explaining in the darkness, revealing mysteries and secrets for him. They didn't just tell him how Hurza had assassinated Rorcual and left Enoch the Dusty for dead. They also told him things he already knew and many others he didn't. In unison they told him how Hurza and Harex arrived in the kingdom and from which distant, bloody world they'd come. They told him what the two brothers proposed to do and the reason behind the founding of Rocavarancolia. They told him what Hurza did with his eyes and why. When he heard that, he shuddered. Denestor stopped the pandemonium of voices. He brought his hand to his chest and discovered that the illusion of a beating heart still dwelled there.

"You knew," he accused Lady Dream. "You knew. From the beginning . . . When Belisarius died and I entered your dream . . . You knew what was happening . . . And you didn't tell me!"

"It's not one single future that is presented to me in dreams, Demiurge. There are many: all the possibilities of what may come, all the possible roads and paths, as twisted and improbable as they may be. The further I try to look, the more difficult it is to specify what will happen: the futures mix and get jumbled up. But yes, I knew, Denestor. I knew. I knew that Hurza would appear on the scene since the night of Samhein. Since you brought the boy and everything was set in motion."

"You could have stopped it," he insisted. "You just had to tell us what Belisarius was planning to do, and none of this would have happened . . . We would have stopped him."

*And I would still be alive.*

"We couldn't have done more than what we did," she said. "Believe us. It wasn't the time. No, it wasn't. The wrong move would have meant the end of Rocavarancolia . . . And I've already told you: I don't see one future, I see all the possible futures, all the alternatives . . . And before Hurza arrived, Rocavarancolia had no future. All of the paths, absolutely all of them, ended with our extinction. But now, with Hurza in play, although it seems illogical, new possibilities open up. Some are horrible, but others . . . Oh, Demiurge . . . Others are glorious."

"Forgive us, Denestor. Forgive us . . ." said another of her voices.

"No!" he shouted. "I can't forgive you, because I don't understand you! I don't understand your motives! I don't understand why you brought me here . . . What are you trying to do? What are you after? Do you want my forgiveness? Is that what you're looking for? Forgiveness for letting them kill me?"

"Do you want to know why you're here?" a girlish Lady Dream asked in her turn from close by. "We saved you because we love you. We saved you because we love Rocavarancolia. Because we love this kingdom. Despite everything."

A new voice joined the conversation. A voice that didn't belong to Lady Dream but, like that of Ujthan shortly before, surely came from her lips as well. It was Natalia's voice.

"Your kingdom is worthless. You built it on a mountain of corpses. And what can something like that be worth? What is the value of something built upon piles of dead children?"

"Tell me, Denestor." Lady Dream's voice had returned. It now seemed to come from up above. "Have you dared to answer these questions?"

"Every kingdom requires sacrifices," he answered, his voice steady. He shook his head. "But that's not what we're talking about here," he added firmly.

"You're wrong, old friend," Lady Dream replied. "That is precisely what we're talking about."

Little by little the darkness that surrounded them lightened. It happened so gradually that the demiurge's eyes weren't bothered in the least; it was a smooth, sweet transition. Denestor looked around as the shadows cleared and a new landscape came into view to take their place: a prairie with tall grass waving in the wind. In the distance he could see the humped outline of a snowy mountain range. The sky was a crystal-blue color. Denestor Tul breathed deeply, and his lungs filled with air and life. The scenery was a balm for his soul.

There were two Lady Dreams with him. One was just as he remembered her from his last visit to her bedchamber: a subdued, ancient, withered old woman as wrinkled as he was; the other was a lovely girl with silvery hair, dressed in a white nightgown, who wore flowers in the folds of her skirt. They were both the same height.

"Thirteen," said the old Lady Dream, gently caressing her replica's hair. "That was how old I was when that impish little man brought me here. They took me from my home with cunning words. They tricked me to come to this kingdom of shadows, to this savage darkness overflowing with horrors." The old woman looked up and contemplated, spellbound, the enormous, sparkling sun that presided over the scene. She smiled under its light. The little girl held out her skirt with one hand while she placed flowers in her hair with the other. "The most surprising thing of all was how I came to love this place, despite the place itself. Rocavarancolia is the land of miracles, even if—for the most part—they're quite twisted . . ." It was the first time in decades that he heard no madness in Lady Dream's voice. "I love this land, Demiurge. I love it so much that I would do anything for it: even destroy it."

"Do you think that's what we deserve? Destruction?"

Lady Dream shook her head.

"What we deserve or don't deserve doesn't matter. Not anymore." She sighed before continuing, her face still turned to the sun. "Did you know that I tried to persuade Sardaurlar to forgo his insane plans of conquest? I knew what would happen if he let himself be led by his ambition. I saw it in my dreams: all possible futures would bring us defeat. But the king didn't listen to me. He didn't have time for the silly notions of a crazy dreamer, he said." She shifted her gaze from the sun to look at the demiurge. "It was then that I learned that the only possible way of changing the future is by being subtle."

"Do you want to see a miracle?" asked the girl Lady Dream, taking a step toward him.

"I want to understand," he answered, his eyes glued to the old woman with not a glimpse at the girl with the flowers in her hair. "I want to know what you're plotting, Lady Dream. I want to know once and for all why you brought me here."

"To show you a miracle," she answered.

"Do you want to see it?" the girl repeated. She had approached him and was tugging impatiently at his robe.

Denestor finally lowered his eyes to her. In the skirt of her night-gown there were no longer flowers, only broken stems here and there. Her hair was crowned with a splendid tiara of braided flowers. The girl was radiant, and she looked so innocent and pure that the demiurge's eyes filled with tears. That was the Lady Dream of the past. The girl who arrived in Rocavarancolia so long ago.

Denestor Tul felt something give way inside him. All of his doubts suddenly vanished. *A kingdom built upon dead children is worthless. No matter what it achieves, no matter what marvels it contains . . .*

"What's your name?" he asked, once again in a broken voice. He couldn't take his eyes off the girl.

"Casandra," she replied. The smile she gave him was so radiant that Denestor Tul felt inundated with light, a light that had nothing to do with the sun hanging in the sky.

"Casandra," he repeated, and finally understood why it was so important for Mistral to remember his true name.

He took the girl's tiny outstretched hand in his own, trembling, and let her lead him to the valley below, drunk on this new light. Yes. He wanted to see a miracle. He needed it with all of his heart, with all of his wounded, tired soul. The world began to change again. First it was a subtle vibration in the air. Then, he thought he made out the silhouette of a multitude of foggy buildings that rose up in the distance. He blinked to focus his vision. He was right. With each step they took, a new landscape came into view before them: a city of mist.

He narrowed his eyes and kept walking hand in hand with the girl. A blurry form at the top of a hill became a colossal white stone arch with gold engravings at its base and the statue of a winged horse at the top. The arch was so enormous that entire armies could pass below. The valley beyond the monument was filled with ghostly silhouettes, fountains of smoke that slowly solidified and became more detailed: a window here; a skylight there; a stairway that climbed up between banisters that were half smoke, half green ironwork; lavish glass displays with uncertain frames . . . until they became buildings of an undeniable solidity. And the closer they got, the more outlines appeared, one after the other, always following the same pattern: first mist, then smoke, and then finally solid matter.

Denestor watched as the most impressive turrets he'd ever seen broke through the void, so magnificent that the Dragon Towers themselves paled in comparison. He saw exquisite palaces surge from the earth, with shifting terraces on their façades, surrounded by pools of water mixed with fire; he saw two mountains of smoke become two triple-walled black castles, with infinite twisting towers shooting up toward the heavens; he glimpsed a gigantic amphitheater around which bloomed domes of marbled glass and smoke . . .

Wherever he looked, Denestor Tul found another marvel: structures peppered with stained glass that took one's breath away; dark monoliths that floated in the air and rotated gently around white minarets; sentient bridges that crossed the streets and the channels of the twin rivers that pierced the city . . . Wherever he looked, Denestor Tul saw a miracle.

And although he'd never seen that city before, he recognized it immediately.

"Rocavarancolia," he said, breathless.

"Rocavarancolia," confirmed the Lady Dream who walked before them. "But not the Rocavarancolia of our past, the one the two brothers founded through blood and fire; nor the one we inherited from Sardaurlar, with his dreams of conquest . . . What you see before you, my good friend, is the Rocavarancolia that could be."

The girl broke out in laughter.

"But that's not all, Denestor," she warned. "Wait and see. Wait and see."

As soon as they reached the top of the hill where the gigantic triumphal arch rose, more hazy figures began to appear before their eyes.

Just like the buildings in the city, the silhouettes took shape as they approached. They were statues, statues of sparkling crystal. The first were located in the entryway to the arch itself. Denestor neared the closest one. It didn't surprise him to see that it was a statue of Ricardo, the boy who died at the hands of the troll Roallen. It was a perfect likeness, carved masterfully from a material halfway between crystal and diamond. A few yards away was the statue of Rachel, the girl immune to magic, with her arms folded across her chest and a mischievous expression peering out from her crystalline eyes. Right next to her was Alexander. The redhead leaned lazily against the wall of the arch; he had a slight smile on his lips, as if laughing at a very funny joke. Next to him, a little farther back, was the boy whom Mistral had strangled in order to take his place.

Then came all the others: all the children who'd died throughout the last thirty years in Rocavarancolia, all sculpted to perfection, down to the most minute detail. Denestor saw the kids devoured by Roallen their first night in the city; the girl who was struck down by a fatal spell in the middle of the street; three who died from pure terror when the jaws of the carnivorous house closed around them . . .

The demiurge looked at the old woman and frowned. He didn't understand.

"Statues in honor of the dead children?" he asked. "Is that why you built this Rocavarancolia? To honor their memory?"

"Look inside," she requested.

Denestor caught a sudden brilliance in the statue in front of him. He leaned forward and squinted. There was something inside the crystal. It looked like a butterfly made of light, the size of the palm of his hand. He saw it fluttering inside the hollow of the statue, causing an infinity of tiny reflections and rainbows.

"Their souls . . ." he said, astonished, as he turned again toward Lady Dream. "You've captured their souls inside the statues."

"That's right," said Lady Dream. "I must declare myself guilty of such an atrocity. But allow me to say in my defense, that no one is here against their own free will." She then flashed him a smile of satisfaction. "I took their consciousnesses and their souls at the exact moment in which they died, exactly as I've done with you, Demiurge, and I brought them with me into the deepest reaches of sleep."

JOSÉ ANTONIO COTRINA

Denestor touched the statue of Ricardo and had to take his hand away instantly. The crystal burned.

"These statues are the only way I can cheat death once it's occurred," the old woman explained. "The souls remain suspended within the replicas of the bodies they inhabited. They're bubbles of time slowed down within sleep."

"They're beautiful," Denestor said. Ricardo's soul was an incandescent butterfly, graced with multiple wings of light of various sizes and colors. It was marvelous to watch its movements inside the crystal. They were so perfect that the rest of the universe seemed to have remained immobile since creation by comparison. He looked at Rachel's statue and saw the reflection of the girl's soul, now traveling through the statue's crystal arm. "But why did you do it? Why do you keep the souls of the children here?"

The old woman turned to him and smiled again.

"It's not just the children's souls," she said.

She pointed beyond the arch where they stood. In the cobblestone plaza to the east, a veritable sea of mist was moving. There were hundreds of silhouettes gathered there, all foggy and indistinct in the distance, but clear enough to tell that the majority were too big to be children. The young Lady Dream took him by the hand again and led him through the statues of the dead, with the old woman ahead of them.

The air in the plaza filled with the flashes of hundreds of souls trapped in crystal. Then, little by little, the statues themselves appeared before his eyes. The first ones that Denestor recognized were the two Broken brothers, both depicted with the same armor they were wearing when they died in the battle of Rocavarancolia; then Lady Sapience appeared, the witch who ruled over the course of rivers, wrapped in her ragged cape, with a water creature coiled around her left arm.

"By all the heavens and all the hells . . ." muttered the demiurge. With each second more familiar faces peered out from the mist.

"I began collecting souls during the battle, when our people were dying by the hundreds," the old woman explained, amused by his bewilderment. "So I began my own harvest. I knew it was necessary. I knew that one day, sooner or later, I would need them to try to change the course of destiny." The hands of the old woman began to wave in the air, as if she directed an orchestra that only she could see.

"How difficult it all was! You can't even imagine! I didn't have a moment's rest during the entire battle, not a single one . . . So much death everywhere, so many souls being set free . . . And I needed to act swiftly, quick as lightning. I found the soul of Annais Greenpearl when the arrows of the Aval goblins knocked her from her falcon. I took all of the souls of the Madariago family when their house was destroyed by the automaton from Arfes. I extracted Lady Essence's soul from her broken body at the very instant that white tiger spat her into the sea . . ."

The dead inhabitants of Rocavarancolia appeared before Denestor. First they materialized as Lady Dream named them, but soon it became impossible to contain them. Here were souls imprisoned in dreaming crystal, thousands of them. Among the multitude, the demiurge distinguished two that he had called friends, two of the people that he esteemed most in all of Rocavarancolia: Duke Desidia, with his double-bladed axe on his back, and, very close to him, Lady Corma, wearing her robe sprinkled with dust from the Red Moon, with her spectacular hair that reached down to the ground. Further away he saw Balearic Bal, a demiurge like himself, and his rival for many years for the position of guardian of Highlowtower. They emerged by the dozens: sorcerers and witches, warriors and noblemen, trolls and werewolves . . .

"You brought them all?" he asked.

"No. Only the souls that were worth being saved. Only those who still remembered the light."

"But why? What were you . . . ?" Denestor became silent. The answer to his question was before his very eyes, displayed in the square and in the surrounding streets, and it was so obvious that it had been hard for him to see it. "An army . . ." he whispered and took a step back, feeling the heart that he no longer had quicken in his chest. "You're readying an army."

"That's right, Denestor. An army. It's been encamped in my dreams for thirty years, and the time has come to set it in motion. The enemy is already in position and soon will summon its own troops. The battle is coming, Demiurge. The battle of our lives." The old dreamer approached him, took him by the hands, and looked him in the eye. "I can't promise you redemption or restore your life to you, but I can make sure that your death has meaning . . . Stay with me and you can leave this world as you truly deserve: fighting for Rocavarancolia, but for a Rocavarancolia that's worth dying for. Stay with me. We may not achieve victory, but I promise you that, whatever happens, we will attain glory."

# DREAMING AND WAKING

Hector felt nothing, thought nothing, was nothing.

The world had ceased to exist. Reality had disintegrated and become a nebulous void in which there was no scale, no point of reference. Space and time were suspended, replaced by a tranquil sensation of warmth and absence. Hector floated, distant from everything, even from himself. He was happy. He had no identity, no being, no place. In that motionless limbo, all was peaceful.

Then came the pain. It was a brutal thrust that split him in two, jolting him into awareness of his own existence. Agony gave him form, like the hands of a potter would mold clay. And with the arrival of pain, the comfortable warmth that had been instilled in him gave way to an insufferable heat. The nothingness was filled with fire.

It was impossible to measure time in that hell. Every instant was an eternity, every second a vast ocean of slow time. There were periods when the pain lessened, although it never vanished completely. In those interludes, now and again he was able to make out distant whisperings. They came from the other side of the darkness and, although he was unable to decipher their meaning, it was comforting to hear them: they spoke of a world where everything was not pain and fire.

"He's burning up, but it's not a normal fever . . . My father once reached a temperature of a hundred and four degrees, and he wasn't like this."

"You can't even put your hand on him. It's scorching."

"It's the troll's venom. It's consuming him."

When the pain let up he paid all his attention to the sounds that came from beyond the darkness, eager to hear those strange voices. He clung to them in desperation, though he didn't understand anything they said. They were his only salvation, a kind of oasis in the inferno.

"It's Maddie, kid. That's enough lounging around. We need you, okay? It's been a week since we've seen Adrian, and Natalia makes me more nervous by the day." Her voice trembled, losing its resolve. "Wake up, wake up already, please . . ."

And in that period without time, in that interminable night without dreams, Hector continued to exist, lanced with pain and scorched by fire, unable to do anything but writhe in the dark and wait for the voices to come when he got a break from his suffering.

"Don't worry, Hector, you're safe from harm. My shadows are watching you night and day. Rest easy, okay? Everything's fine here. Everything's under control . . . They obey me, you know? They're afraid of me."

For an eternity, nothing changed. Until another voice came from beyond the barrier that separated him from consciousness. It wasn't the first time he'd heard it, but on that occasion it had a different tone: it sounded closer, more intense.

"Don't die, don't die . . . Please, Hector, don't die . . . You promised you'd be by my side when the Red Moon came out. You promised."

He tried to remember who that voice belonged to, but it was impossible. He was unable to place it, and that was almost as distressing as the burning agony. There was something in that voice, something that . . . He suddenly felt a soft caress on his lips, as subtle as a butterfly's wings. The sweetness of the contact was so great that he remembered the voice's owner instantly: Marina. And with that name came relief. A powerful current of fresh air ran through the burning shadows of his unconscious; the spiderwebs that had shrouded him vanished and finally, after so long, Hector was able to think clearly. The pain and fire still persisted, but they were far away. The voice had disappeared, but he no longer needed it. His salvation was now different: the memory of the girl he loved. He thought about her, her dark hair, her blue eyes, those lips that had just kissed his own. With every detail he remembered, he felt himself reviving. Marina was on the other side of the darkness. And that was more than enough reason to return.

He made a supreme effort to wake up, tried to open his eyes, but his attempts were useless; his eyelids felt fused to his eyeballs. He tried to talk and couldn't find a mouth to open, nor a tongue that he could use. And the same thing happened when he tried to move. He could feel his flesh, and even so something kept him from controlling it.

A new voice reached him, a voice that came from the misty, painful world in which he still lived.

"Love is marvelous," it said. "Irrational and senseless, of course, but marvelous. I was in love once. Or maybe I dreamt that I was. What does it matter, dreams are real while you're dreaming."

There was someone with him in his lethargy. A woman. He tried to find her in the quagmire that was his conscience, but he couldn't. The world was nothing more than an infinite number of layers of darkness and pain placed one atop the other.

"Dazed. Lost. The boy spins on a carousel of shadows. Look at him, look . . . The violin turns and turns . . . But it doesn't know that it's turning or even that it's a violin."

"Lady Scar?" he asked, doubtful. The name had suddenly appeared in his head, linked to the blurry image of a flabby white creature, covered with pustules and marks.

"Not Lady Scar or Lady Serena." The voice faded in and out; each word was pronounced at a different distance. It seemed to whisper in his ear as quickly as it came from the horizon of his unconscious. "I am Lady Dream. I had another name, decades ago. You can use it if you like: they called me Casandra. I don't really mind one way or the other."

The curtains of darkness that had surrounded him opened at once and allowed a luminous silhouette to enter. It was a girl dressed in a white silk nightgown. She didn't look older than twelve. Her fair hair was gathered in an elaborate braid that hung to one side, held in place by tiny crystal hairpins in the shape of butterflies. She looked at him without blinking through her striking blue eyes. She carried a violet-colored ceramic cup with a mermaid pattern around the edge in her hands.

"Drink," she ordered, handing the cup to him.

"This is a dream," Hector realized.

"Everything is a dream. Always. Now drink or you will die. The venom is burning you from the inside. Your friends are doing everything they can to keep you alive, but they will need help. Drink, or I'll take your soul and keep it in a crystal statue."

Hector took the cup between hands that until then he wasn't aware he had. He looked carefully at his right hand; for some reason it caught his attention, despite being identical to the other. He shook his head. He didn't want to think about that. The important thing right now was the cup. It was filled with a cloudy golden liquid. He squinted. On the surface of the concoction, tiny typhoons and whirlpools churned. There was life underneath that liquid, a vast realm of submerged wonders: he glimpsed aquatic cities half-hidden among coral jungles, underwater temples covered with algae, mermaids reclining on reefs . . .

He looked at the girl, impressed. The cup that she'd held in her hands contained entire worlds.

"I can't drink it; if I do, I'll kill them."

"They're not alive. They're the last dreams of drowned sailors. And it's the only thing that can save you." The little girl said it with such confidence that he had no choice but to believe her.

He gave her a resolute nod. He closed his eyes and downed the cup in a single gulp. He almost thought he heard the screaming of a terrorized multitude when the liquid passed from the cup to his mouth and then down his throat. The effect was immediate. As soon as he drank it, the pain disappeared. And he remembered everything. Everything that happened over the last few months, down to the smallest detail. A rapid succession of images swept him from Halloween, when his odyssey had begun, to the present moment.

He waited a few seconds, his eyes still closed. He was trying to get accustomed to his new reality, without knowing whether to shout with rage or burst into tears. He hadn't thought it possible, but he missed the absence and the nothing. He preferred the pain a thousand times to remembering everything he'd lost. He breathed deeply, counted to ten, and finally opened his eyes.

A new world revealed itself before his gaze. Everything was light and turmoil. Above his head stretched a clear blue sky, in a strangely open perspective, as if he himself were suspended at a great height. He found himself on a tower rooftop with yellowing flagstones, bordered by a battlement that reached chest high. He could see for miles. The horizon curved in the distance, besieged by mountains in flames.

Hector only had a second to orient himself. In front of him, a dragon roared. The beast's breath enveloped him. It smelled like dust and death, of boiling blood and recently chewed flesh.

The dragon, whose scales were black and golden, measured over a hundred feet long, and its enormous head was covered in tiny dark horns. It beat its wings with such force that every shake seemed like a small explosion. On its back were several ape-like creatures of a dirty green color, all wearing rusty armor. They waved their weapons cease-lessly and grimaced in Hector's direction.

The dragon roared again. Its eyes, two black suns, stared directly at him. The boy saw a double row of curved fangs and the glow from the flames that were about to arise from its throat. He prepared to die in the following second. No one could witness such a scene and survive.

Suddenly, something immense crashed into the dragon and sent it flying over two hundred yards away. Several of the creatures on its back fell into the void, screaming desperately. Hector retreated, over-whelmed. Before his eyes now arose a rock giant, almost as big as the dragon it had just pounded. Its surface was a confusing amalgam of blocks of cracked stone, twisted doors and windows, banisters, bars, and stairwells. It was as if someone had molded a huge building into an almost human form. It flapped the wings that sprouted from its upper back, forged from twisted pipes and gutters. The breathing of that creature sounded like a constant avalanche, as if inside its throat the world was collapsing.

The dragon contorted in the air, biting furiously. The enormous beast vigorously flapped its wings and, after letting out a sobering roar, charged at its adversary. When it was only a few yards away, it thrust its head forward, opened its jaws as wide as it could, and spit a torrent of fire at the giant. The doors and windows that peppered its stone flesh were covered in flames; the rock itself began to burn. The stone colos-sus ignored the blaze and leapt upon the dragon. The crash between them resounded in the air with a devastating potency. A blast of hot, sticky air pushed Hector so violently that he almost fell backward.

For a few moments he watched the chaos of stone claws, fangs, and rock extremities as they swung and bit, enveloped in tongues of fire. Then, both combatants left his field of vision, one dragging the other. The vista that opened before him allowed him to see the true scale of what was happening all around. His legs gave way. The dragon and the rock giant weren't the only contenders: the sky brimmed with fighting wonders. There were countless outbreaks of battle scattered in the heavens: in some it was one-on-one combat; in others actual hordes confronted one another. Hector saw about twenty creatures, similar to the one who decapitated Roallen, closing in on four stone giants. Dozens of black dragons fought among clouds torn to shreds. Hector's gaze jumped from one spot to the other, with barely enough time to take in what he was seeing. Flashes of light exploded everywhere. A winged shark, split in two, fell from the sky, followed by some other indescribable being, a confusion of talons and horns; further beyond their bloody wake, two men flew facing each other, exchanging sword blows at demonic speed among whirlwinds of brilliance and darkness so tall they were like columns holding up the sky itself.

The fighting didn't just take place in the sky. The land was a hive of activity as well. A battlefield extended for miles around, with the tower where Hector stood at its center. Wherever he looked, he saw only violence and destruction. A herd of animals that looked like elephants, mounted by hairy giants, charged the hosts of armed men who protected the building. The air was full of explosions and cries of pain.

"Isn't it a shame? So much beauty torn to pieces! What a waste! Don't you agree?"

Next to Hector was the girl who'd offered him the cup. Only she was no longer a girl—she'd grown into a beautiful adult woman, with the same braid overflowing with butterflies, the same wide-open eyes. She now wore a sleeveless dress embellished with black and green spirals.

"It's a dream," Hector stammered. "It has to be a dream."

"Oh. Yes. Of course it's a dream. But it's also history. Those who are obsessed with giving everything a name baptized this battle as the End of Varago. I reconstructed it for you using the dreams of those who fought in it."

"Why? Why do you want me to see this? What does it have to do with me?"

The woman's only response was to turn her head to look past them. Hector did the same.

A tall individual, covered from head to toe in a blood-colored robe, ran from one end of the tower's terraced rooftop to the other. He held a staff of black wood adorned with precious stones, topped with an irregular polyhedron of sparkling crystal. There were other creatures on the rooftop, stone beings similar to the one who'd tangled with the dragon, although of a much smaller size. Hector saw one with a metal bench on its back, in between cracked bricks and what looked like pieces of lawn. There were also men of flesh and bone, the majority of them armed with bows. It was clear that the man in red was their leader.

"We're in Ataxia, an ancient linked world," explained Lady Dream, as she fanned herself with a peacock feather that appeared out of nowhere. "The hooded man that you see running is Varago Tay, guardian of Highlowtower and one of the most powerful demiurges to ever have existed. You're watching his finale, Hector. You should feel privileged. He gave life to the city that occupied this hill so they could confront the Rocavarancolia troops."

"They're attacking their own?" he asked.

"Does that surprise you? Treason is fairly common in our kingdom."

The man in red came running toward them, leaned against the battlement, and watched the fight unfold. Hector couldn't see his face underneath the hood, but his body language showed great tension. He strode quickly to a group of archers and ordered them to protect that side of the tower. When the man reached them, Hector realized that they weren't loading arrows onto their bows, but rather bony, eyeless serpents, their mouths disproportionately large for their tiny heads. The archers shot the reptiles in the direction of a large group of dragons that was approaching from the east. Hector watched the snakes fly toward them, straight as arrows. The dragons that were hit turned on members of their own group, leaping upon them, seemingly controlled by the strange creatures.

"Ataxia was just one more linked world, a small planet inhabited by beings similar to humans," explained the woman, completely oblivious to the chaos of the battle. "They didn't know any magic and lived in a time similar to your Earth's Middle Ages. It was a poor world, of no interest to Rocavarancolia. They didn't have riches of any kind, and the essence of their people was too weak to serve Rocavaragalago. I imagine that whoever made the decision to link that world was thinking of the future; maybe with the hope that after several centuries Ataxia or its inhabitants would be worth the trouble, I don't know. As it happened, two hundred years went by before they found a use for this insipid land.

"At the time, Rocavarancolia was immersed in the conquest of another linked world, a planet called Masquerade, and things weren't going too well. The inhabitants of Masquerade proved to be much tougher than they'd initially expected; they were magnificent in battle, they knew no fear, and they never retreated. Their magic was rudimentary, but there was something that tipped the balance in their favor: their technology, so advanced and strange that it completely defied Rocavarancolia's comprehension. It wasn't the first time the kingdom had bitten off more than it could chew. Other worlds had successfully resisted our attack. When that happened, when it remained clear that there was no chance of victory, our armies simply retreated, returned to Rocavarancolia, and closed all vortices that linked us to that land. But on this occasion, it wasn't so simple. The inhabitants of Masquerade had unraveled the mystery of the vortices and had invented a contraption capable of opening portals between worlds. And that put Rocavarancolia with its back to the wall for the first time in its history. Masquerade wasn't content with expelling the invaders, no. It wasn't that kind of civilization. They wouldn't stop until they completely destroyed those who had dared to attack them."

Something suddenly exploded in the sky behind them. Hector spun around with the echo of the racket resounding in his ears. Although he couldn't tell what had happened, he could see a brutal streak of blood against the blazing blue sky and trails of smoke hurtling down to the ground.

When he turned around again, another flash in the sky made him look up. For a second he thought it was the Ataxian sun that he was looking at, but it was too big and vague for that to be so. His heart skipped a beat as he recognized what was floating above their heads: a projection of the clock from the façade of the Margalar Tower, so enormous that it took up half of the sky. In that ghostly image, the ten-pointed star had almost completed its course and was about to reach the Red Moon at the top of the sphere. Hector turned toward Lady Dream. The woman smiled to see the dismay on his face.

"There's not much time left, it's true. But we still have more than enough to finish the story." She was silent for several moments, with her eyes closed, a smile still on her lips. "Where was I?· Ah! Masquerade, Ataxia . . . The war. Yes. The situation, as I said, was desperate," the woman continued. "The legions of Masquerade would soon attack Rocavarancolia, and after what had occurred in their world, we knew the possibility of defeating them was practically nil. So drastic measures were taken; no compassion, no mercy. Rocavarancolia would use one of the cruelest, most destructive spells known at that time against the enemy: they would use the Blackout. An ominous name, fitting for the spell in question. The Blackout is a curse that instantly and completely destroys the world it's cast upon. Nothing remains, absolutely nothing. Not even ashes. But for a spell of such magnitude to work, it requires not only the collective power of a large number of sorcerers; it also needs an initial sacrifice as brutal as the spell itself. To make the Blackout work, they must offer the soul of a planet as a sacrifice. To terminate Masquerade, Rocavarancolia had to first destroy another world."

"The soul of a planet . . ." Hector repeated. The concept was over-whelming, almost as overwhelming as the notion of destroying whole planets.

"Yes, child. Planets have a soul. Everything that is alive has one, small or large souls, tiny sparks of light or blinding flashes. It's all the same, in the end they're all identical in essence. Generally, the soul of a world is not located in one single place: it's divided in several parts and scattered throughout the surface. Reuniting the parts is arduous work and achieving it, in the best cases, can take months. And Rocavarancolia didn't have that kind of time. But there was Ataxia. The only known world whose soul was concentrated in a single point: a gigantic forest in the planet's tropics. They had only to send an expedition and take hold of it. Nothing more. A simple mission in a harmless world. They would snatch the soul, thereby condemning the planet to a slow death. Ataxia would die over decades until it became a sterile rock floating in the abyss. A terrible end, no doubt; if you want my opinion, even more atrocious than the instantaneous death they had in store for Masquerade.

"A small garrison set off toward the forest, headed by the man you see here: Varago Tay, demiurge of Rocavarancolia and guardian of Highlowtower. Not many accompanied him. Ataxia was a harmless world and they could expect little opposition to their plans. But some-thing went wrong, something completely unexpected: Varago wasn't capable of wrenching the soul from the planet. He didn't have the courage. Because it would have meant destroying the forest that sheltered it, and he couldn't do that."

"Was it an enchanted forest?"

"No. It was just beautiful, the most beautiful place that the monsters from Rocavarancolia had ever seen. Varago and his men couldn't believe what they saw. The mere vision of it changed their existence, do you understand? The soul of Ataxia, in some way, changed their own. They decided to preserve the forest from destruction, even though that meant confronting their own, even though it meant the end of Rocavarancolia. The king tried to make them see reason, but it was all in vain. Varago refused to listen; the forest had driven him mad. He swore to defend it with his life. Rocavarancolia had no choice but to pull troops from the first line of defense to defeat the rebel demiurge and retrieve the planet's soul. And this is the battle you're watching now. Varago and his men allied with the primitive people of Ataxia, confronting the troops of the kingdom commanded by the king of Rocavarancolia himself."

"Did the forest not affect them?"

Lady Dream shook her head.

"The king knew what they were up against. That's why he personally chose those who went with him to Ataxia: cohorts of the undead, goblins and trolls, demons . . . The worst of the worst. Creatures that wouldn't be affected in the slightest by the beauty of the place."

"And what happened?"

"The demiurge was defeated, of course. As powerful as he was, he faced a far superior force. Varago fell."

Something howled in pain from a close proximity. Hector leaned through a gap in the battlement and looked down. A creature climbed up the façade, some kind of wingless dragon.

Its back bristled with lances and arrows, and dozens of rock creatures grabbed at its scales and beat it furiously to stop its advance. What affected Hector most was the beast's expression: the pain and agony reflected in its face were so unbearable that for a second he thought he felt them in his own flesh. The dragon roared and jumped from the tower, with no strength left to go on, and fell to its death, dragging with it the stone beings who kept beating it, blind with rage.

Hector looked away, disgusted, and turned back toward Lady Dream.

"I don't want to see any more," he said. "Make it stop. Make it stop now."

"All right, timid little boy. We'll jump to the end."

The world surrounding them sped up; the combatants in the air and on land became vague blurs. Hector looked up at the sky. The ten-pointed star and the Red Moon were still there, intact amid the chaos of hazy and shining figures, closer to one another by the minute. When time stopped and returned to its normal flow, everything had changed. The tower was blackened and most of its battlements had come crumbling down. At one end of the rooftop was Varago Tay, on his knees, surrounded by a mob of ape-like creatures and several pale, emaciated beings that could only be the living dead. There were cadavers and pieces of stone creatures scattered everywhere.

An immaculate white dragon approached from the north. It had four wings; the top pair were enormous and wide, while those that sprouted from its back were long and narrow. It didn't take long to reach them. It had a slender head covered by an engraved silver helmet from which protruded a sharpened horn. Its eyes, two narrow horizontal slits, were of a blinding red. After tracing a perfect circle in the air, it landed in the middle of the tower. The gust of wind caused by its four wings disheveled Hector's hair and uprooted a pair of crystal butterflies from Lady Dream's braid. The majority of the creatures present knelt on the ground as soon as the gigantic beast landed; only a few remained standing, but their heads bowed in reverence. The dragon bowed as well, not to those around, but to allow its rider to descend. Hector watched as an enormous troll jumped off the dragon's back onto the rooftop.

"His Majesty Castel, the eighth troll king of Rocavarancolia," announced Lady Dream. "The Destroyer of Worlds."

Hector couldn't help but be in awe. He looked even more ferocious than Roallen. He was all muscle and vigor; nothing at all like the famished troll who'd attacked them. His eyes were tiny, two small dark points that were almost hard to see behind his snub nose. A fine gold crown sat atop his forehead, and he wore white silver armor with a red cape edged in black and gold.

Varago Tay sighed as he saw the troll approach. One of his guardians pulled back the hood from his robe, revealing a shriveled gray face with black eyes and a hooked nose. He immediately reminded Hector of Denestor Tul. It jumped out at him that this Varago was the same species as the impish old man.

The troll stopped before the kneeling demiurge. His presence dwarfed all of those in attendance, and not just because he was over nine feet tall: he emanated a staggering grandeur.

"Varago," grunted the troll, and he made an abrupt gesture of greeting in the direction of the gray man.

"Your Majesty . . ." Varago began a bow that he couldn't finish, restrained by the creatures that held him.

He groaned in pain and raised his head to the troll king. He may have been exhausted, but he still had the strength to defy the monarch, at least with his gaze. "I regret that events have left us no alternative but to face each other on the battlefield," he said, in between gasping breaths. "Neither of us wanted this to happen."

"Don't insult me, Demiurge. If you didn't want it, it wouldn't have happened. You rebelled against me, against the kingdom. You betrayed Rocavarancolia in its time of greatest need."

"I did what I had to do."

"And I will do what I must do." He gestured to someone behind him. "Bring my sword."

One of the ape-like creatures approached the dragon quickly and took the gigantic sword attached to the saddle. It was a weapon over eight feet long, with a curved handle, sheathed in a dark scabbard. The ape placed it over his shoulder and, hunched over from the weight of the sword, returned to the monarch's side. The troll grabbed it and raised it effortlessly, still within its sheath.

"You didn't even stop to look at the forest," Varago moaned. "Before you destroy it, look at it, please. You must understand why I did this. You have to know."

"Lean him forward," ordered the troll as he removed the sheath from the sword and let it fall. The same ape that brought the sword hurried to retrieve it. The weapon's blade was black. All of the creatures gathered on the rooftop watched expectantly.

"Please . . . Listen to me, Castel. Look at the forest. Even if it's just once," Varago insisted, while his captors forced him forward. One of them pulled his robe back so that his neck was visible. "Castel!" he howled, straining his head in the king's direction. "Look at it!"

"It was the first thing I did when I arrived, Varago," he said, and wielding the weapon in both hands, he raised it over his head. "And if I'm being honest, it didn't move me in the slightest."

Hector turned away to avoid seeing what came next. The image of Roallen's decapitation was still fresh in his memory. He closed his eyes tightly. He ignored the whistle of the weapon as it sliced through the air, the unpleasant, fleshy crack that came after, and the soft thud of the head hitting the ground.

"It is done," he heard the troll say.

He didn't turn around. He just opened his eyes and watched the flight of the dragons and chimeras in the sky stained with war, exhausted from dreaming, tired of observing marvels and miracles. The whole world stank of death. Hector wondered when it would all end, when peace and calm would return . . .

"Your Majesty," he heard a slow, guttural voice behind him say after several moments, "everything is ready. The sorcerers are preparing the spell of extraction. In a few minutes the soul of Ataxia will be ours, and we can begin our return. Perhaps you'd like to see how the forest is consumed. I've been told that it will be quite a sight."

When the troll king spoke, his voice sounded different; it sounded weary, bitter.

"Stop the spell," he ordered. "Make them stop. They will leave that soul where it is."

"Your Majesty? The forest? I don't understand . . ."

"There's nothing to understand, you fool. We're finished here. We will return to Rocavarancolia. Bury Varago's head in that damned forest and carry his body on my dragon. It will be buried in the Royal Pantheon. And gather the council, I want to see them when I return. We're going to need another world whose soul we can use."

At that very moment something changed within the dream. The atmosphere suddenly softened; the air that filled their lungs was free from the stench of killing. Hector turned slowly. He was still on the tower rooftop, but only he and Lady Dream remained. The monsters and corpses had disappeared.

"They closed the vortex," the woman said. She spoke slowly, avoiding looking at the spot where they'd forced Varago to bow down. The expression on her face was indecipherable. "They unlinked Ataxia and searched for another world whose soul they could take. After much difficulty they found one and Rocavarancolia triumphed: Masquerade was destroyed. And Varago got what he wanted: the forest survived."

Hector looked at the woman for a long while. Suddenly, a premonition made him look up. Above their heads, the moon and the star finally coincided. The moment he so feared had arrived. The Red Moon had come out in Rocavarancolia. And this delirious dream state wasn't where he should be. He should be awake, with his friends, on the other side of sleep, in the nightmare, facing whatever it was that was happening in the city in ruins. He was about to ask Lady Dream to send him back, but he realized that to do so would be useless; he had no voice or vote in the matter. He couldn't choose when the dream came to an end, in the same way that he had nothing to do with its beginning.

"Why did you show me this bloodbath?"

Lady Dream didn't answer; she just turned and walked slowly toward the battlements, with her arms folded across her chest, caressing her shoulders with her hands. Hector went after her.

"Am I supposed to have learned something from all this?" he asked. "Let me think: that even monsters can have a noble side? Is that it? That nothing is as terrible as it seems? Something like that? Is that what I'm supposed to learn?"

Lady Dream gave him a stern look. Hector was aware for the first time of the extraordinary power the woman before him possessed. But that didn't scare him. He held her gaze without even blinking.

"It's not me you should be asking what you learned," responded Lady Dream. "You have to ask yourself." She smiled so suddenly that Hector, taken by surprise, stepped backward. "And as I'm of a curious nature, please, humor me and respond out loud. So that I can hear you."

Hector sighed. Then he shrugged. If he had no other choice, he would keep playing that woman's game. It was all the same to him.

"All I saw was death and destruction," he said. "That's it. People cutting each other to pieces without mercy. You showed me war, Lady Dream. You showed me how horrible the world can become and how cruel those who live in it can be. No, I didn't learn anything, because you showed me nothing I didn't already know."

"So silly of me!" she exclaimed, and she slapped her forehead. "You already knew? Forgive me, Hector. And here I am, wasting your time . . ." She seemed genuinely surprised. "We dreamers aren't right in the head, you know? We lose our way easily." She smiled again, and something in her smile made Hector realize she wasn't done. "But there is something that . . ." she began. "I don't know, maybe it's nothing, but it definitely got my attention . . . It probably isn't very important, of course. The thing is, we've been here, at the top of this tower, for quite a while, and in all that time . . ." She sighed, and Hector frowned. "How to explain it? When you weren't looking at me— while I was boring you with my story—your gaze was lost on the moon and the star in the sky, or on the battalions of horrors massacring each other around us. And do you know something, Hector?" From the sparkle of her eyes it was clear that she was relishing the moment. "In all that time, you never even glanced at the forest."

And she pointed to her right.

Hector looked over the battlement. And he saw it. Lady Dream was right. It had always been there, but he hadn't stopped to look at it once; he was more focused on the chaos surrounding him than the scenery. And as soon as he laid eyes on it, he understood why Varago Tay betrayed Rocavarancolia. No one with a heart could resist the absolute, unequivocal beauty of that landscape and remain unmoved. Hector was only able to look at the forest for a moment; as his eager gaze tried to encompass that marvel in its entirety, he attempted to memorize every last detail of what he saw. And suddenly, the forest disappeared, enveloped in a whirlwind of darkness.

"No!" he screamed, horrified, as he watched it disappear. The tower and the world around him vanished as well. "No! Not now! Damn it! Don't take it away! Let me see it!"

"Maybe that is what I wanted to teach you," said Lady Dream, already lost in the shadows. "That the forest is what's truly important, not what happens around it. But it's so easy to get lost in what's obvious, in the noise . . . Or who knows, maybe these are just the lunatic ravings of an old woman." She was silent. Hector could still feel the battlement where he'd been leaning, but even that had vanished. "There's no time for more," Lady Dream said. "The hour has come. The time for you to abandon my dream and return to your own, so that you can wake up."

"Wait!" he shouted.

"Goodbye, my dear violin." He heard her voice growing distant. It wasn't just the darkness that separated him from Lady Dream; there were entire universes between them. "Hopefully we won't see each other again."

And then there was silence. A silence so great it was like sound had never existed. For a second, Hector was alone in the dark. Only for a second. Then came the light.


He woke up so abruptly that his heart turned over in his chest; he felt it stirring as if it were poorly attached to the internal architecture of his body and might come loose at any moment. He arose to a sitting position in bed. It was cold, bitingly cold. His skin felt tight, cracked . . . Everything was dim. He heard a whistle nearby, a strange noise that he couldn't locate but could identify: the sound of Natalia's shadows as they moved. He looked around. The world was nothing but a confusing mix of vague silhouettes and muted colors.

He blinked several times and as he did so, he felt something break loose from his eyelids. It wasn't sleep in his eyes: it was ice. He couldn't stop shivering. He tried to calm down. He'd been unconscious for a long time, and disorientation was normal. He had to adjust to reality, to the mere fact of being awake. He shook his head, and the world slowly cleared before him. Shapes began to take form. The first thing he saw in the watery darkness was the bandaged stump at the end of his right arm. A shudder ran down his spine. From the lopped-off hand came a rapid pulsation, a kind of frenzied drumbeat. It wasn't pain—it was something else. Something different.

He clenched his teeth and looked again from side to side, trying not to think of what was missing in his own body. His vision became clearer by the minute. He found himself in a room in the Margalar Tower, the room they'd used before as an infirmary. The bed—as well as the walls and ceiling—was covered with ice. Hundreds of red stars floated in the air, an infinity of luminous embers that swirled everywhere, slowly, melancholically. There were no shadows to be seen. Everything was illuminated by the soft red glow that filtered in through the embrasures. Outside the storm howled, but the sound that got his attention came from inside the room: it was a constant crying, a soft, almost inaudible, sobbing.

Hector looked in that direction and saw someone sitting in a chair next to the door, half-hidden in the crimson darkness; they were leaning forward with their hands in their lap. In that light it was very hard to tell who it was.

"Hello?" he said, with no small effort. His own voice sounded strange, distant.

The seated figure showed no sign of having heard him. It remained hunched over, crying very softly.

Hector pulled off the sheet that covered him and got down from the bed, dressed only in a pair of black shorts. He'd been unconscious for days, but his body showed no evidence of weakness. On the contrary: as soon as he started walking, he felt a disconcerting strength.

The frozen stone ground felt new beneath his bare feet; the whole tower, bathed in the pulsating red light, gave the impression of being recently constructed; even the air itself seemed renewed. The world wasn't what he remembered. Or maybe it wasn't that—maybe it was he who had changed. The red embers continued their slow dance in the room, with the delicate lack of urgency of the first falling snowflakes in winter. One of the particles swirled toward Hector and landed on his cheek. He brushed it away. He shifted his gaze to the embrasure, but didn't dare approach it. The bloody glow that filtered in was the light of the Red Moon, and he wasn't ready to confront it yet. Instead, he took a step toward the crying figure.

He didn't recognize Bruno right away, despite the fact that he wore his usual overcoat and held the emerald top hat in his hands. His curly hair fell in disheveled ringlets, covering most of his face. Tears ran down his cheeks.

"Bruno?" he called, uncertainly.

The Italian looked up slowly, saw Hector next to him, and smiled. "Hector," he whispered. "Hector!" He wiped the tears away with the back of his hand. His eyes were moist, but the radiant smile that he flashed quickly dispelled all of the sadness on his face. "I am sorry, I'm so sorry . . . I didn't even know you woke up."

He let his top hat fall as he got up from the chair. Without another word, he went toward him and embraced him with a fierce hug. "I am so glad to see you awake . . ."

Hector was unable to react. He remained stunned in the Italian's arms. Bruno must have noticed his bewilderment, because he drew back quickly. He seemed embarrassed.

"I'm sorry . . . I don't know how to behave. I guess it will take me a while to learn." He watched him with vivid interest, as if he wanted to confirm that his features were still the same. "I am glad to see that you're well, and I wanted to show it. Was a hug not appropriate?" he asked.

For a moment, Hector didn't know how to respond. That Bruno hugged him was one of the most unbelievable things that had happened to him in Rocavarancolia. He shook his head.

"Don't worry about it. I didn't expect it, that's all. What's going on?" he asked.

"The Red Moon came out, and now everything is . . . Everything is . . ." It looked like he was unable to put his thoughts into words and that fact, far from frustrating him, fascinated him. He sucked air in through his nose and looked him in the eye. "Everything is different, you know?" He crouched down to pick up his hat, put it on, and strode over to the nearest embrasure. "And everything is magnificent at the same time . . ." He stopped talking, blinded by a sudden attack of tears. The embers of fire rustled around him, unsettled by his presence.

"The Red Moon . . ." Hector whispered. It was there, outside. He only had to get closer to see it. He didn't do it. He remained where he was, motionless.

The Italian nodded. He calmed himself, and took a deep breath.

"Rocavaragalago has finally been set in motion. Oh." He brought his hand to his mouth, as if he'd just remembered something extremely important. "Oh," he repeated, turning toward Hector. Once again, tears streamed down his cheeks, so fast that they looked like two rivers over-flowing. "Can you feel it? The boiling in your blood? The life around you? The beating. Here and now. Do you feel it?" He turned to look outside. He smiled and extended his arms. "The heartbeat of the world."

At that point, the Margalar Tower shuddered. It was a brief quake that made them both stagger. In the distance they heard the rumbling of what might have been a building crumbling. Then more sounds of collapse echoed throughout the city. All of Rocavarancolia trembled. The tremor lasted barely a few seconds but Hector felt its reverberations linger in his body, as if the same seismic wave that just ran through the city now preyed on him. The itching in his stump worsened, the palpitations quickened. In spite of himself he gritted his teeth and approached his friend, who was still looking through the embrasure, spellbound. He grabbed him by the shoulder and made Bruno turn to look at him, while avoiding the red curve that he sensed in the sky beyond the window.

"Where are the girls?" he asked, in a hoarse voice. The itching in his arm had spread to other parts of his body. He now also felt it in his stomach and back, just below his shoulder blades. They were quick shudders, electric currents that bit at his skin at increasingly shorter intervals.

"They went downstairs just after nightfall. I stayed with you. I didn't want to leave you alone with Natalia's shadows . . . I don't trust them." He stroked his neck in a listless manner, still crying, then he stopped and looked at his fingertips as if they were the most marvelous things in the world. He smiled. "And the moon came out, the immense moon . . . And the sky above Rocavaragalago filled with stars . . ." It almost seemed like he was singing. "And the whole world changed. And I went down and . . ." He looked at the palms of his hands, serious all of a sudden. "If this lasts long, I'll go crazy . . . I have to control myself. I have to control it. How do you do it? How do you resist this flood of feelings every second of every day? This is insane!"

Hector shook his head. He had to get out of there.

"I'm going to look for them."

Bruno nodded distractedly and turned once again toward the window. He closed his eyes as the red light bathed his face. The tranquil smile on his face contrasted with the flood of tears that streamed from beneath his eyelids. Hector walked backward for a few moments, keeping his eyes on the Italian, still affected by his transformation. He left in a hurry.

He quickly went down the stairs. When he reached the last flight, another tremor, stronger than the last, shook the tower. Hector lost his balance midstep and rolled down the stairs, stumbling violently. His head struck the floor with a deep impact, but he didn't feel any pain. He stayed there on the ground, holding his breath, while the world shuddered around him. Fine threads of dust rained down from the cracks in the ceiling. A shelf came crashing down and littered the floor with broken plates and glasses.

Hector clenched his teeth. The pounding in his wrist and back beat once again in sync with the earthquake. He curled into a ball on the floor, clutching his stump with his left hand. It burned as if it was covered in lava. Suddenly the quake ceased, as abruptly as it began, but he remained at the mercy of the savage electric currents that ran through his being: from his back to his wrist, then starting over again, frenzied and brutal. Around him swirled actual clouds of reddish sparks; some of them stuck to his hair and skin, but he no longer attempted to remove them. The courtyard door was open, and the warm red light from outside streamed in, stretching across the floor like a wave of glistening blood.

*What you're feeling is the Red Moon—the Red Moon and Rocavaragalago transforming your body,* he heard in his mind. Hector opened his eyes wide. It was the same voice that awoke him his first day in Rocavarancolia: the voice of Lady Serena. He tried to stand, but the most he could do was kneel on the ground, holding the stump against his chest.

On the back of a chair perched the metallic bird that had guided him to the cemetery, with the eye of Lady Scar held firmly in its beak.

"Lady Scar," he murmured in a weak voice. Hector bit his lower lip. The images wavered in his mind. It wasn't Lady Serena who'd been talking to him in his mind during the welcome speech, he realized; it wasn't her who'd bewitched him and made him aware of the dangers of Rocavarancolia. It had been Lady Scar, the monster, the horror from the cemetery, not the ghost.

*Lady Scar, yes. That's right . . . Commander of the kingdom's armies and guardian of the Royal Pantheon to some, and simply a despicable monster to others. Lady Scar. That's me. I don't possess the beauty or elegance that Lady Serena does, nor do I inspire the same confidence, of course . . . Who's going to trust a creature as hideous as me? Not you, naturally.*

Hector closed his eyes and choked back a scream; the throbbing in his stump had become unbearable. It was as if someone was savagely stabbing him with thousands of needles of ice and fire, and refused to stop even for a second. Something began to move beneath the bandages on his arm, something that struggled to break through, biting his flesh with ruthless cruelty. He fell backward. He retreated on the ground, holding his arm out in front of him in a futile attempt to get away from the sinister seething of the bandages, from that inhuman pain that tore at him.

*It's time, child,* said the woman in his mind, brimming with sorrow. *There's no going back. There's no way home. Not for you, or anyone.*

The bandages fell to pieces. Hector screamed and tried to back away from the agony of his amputated limb. Something exploded in his stump. Hector howled as he watched, eyes bulging, as a new hand emerged from his wounded flesh. It was an intensely black hand with short pointed nails, and a strange glimmer on the back. A hand that was his, undoubtedly his. Through the chaos of stripped fabric that was his wrist he was able to tell where the pink flesh gave way to that new skin. He fell back again, holding his hand up, as far as possible from himself. The pain had stopped, but he couldn't overcome the astonishment of seeing the thing at the end of his arm.

Outside, on the clock affixed to the building's façade, the ten-pointed star and the symbol of the Red Moon finally met at the top of the sphere, occupying the same space, one atop the other, the star finally having reached the moon. He suddenly heard a creaking inside the mechanism, several gears were set in motion, and, with a slight tremor, the Red Moon began to move while the star remained motionless in the spot where its companion had long awaited it.

Inside his head, the voice of Lady Scar spoke once again:

*Welcome to Rocavarancolia, Hector,* she said. *Welcome to the city of monsters. Finally. You are one of us now.*

# THE RED MOON

The immense Red Moon rose above the city, surrounded by a bloody halo that made it look even bigger. The storm clouds that covered Rocavarancolia couldn't eclipse it; the moon peeked through them, dark and somber, but as magnificent as on a clear night. It floated in the sky with the haughtiness of gods who know they are worshiped, with the forcefulness of prophecies certain to be fulfilled. The Red Moon was everything, and Rocavarancolia prostrated itself at its feet. The city trembled.

The storm's rage intensified. Lightning bolts fell in such quick succession that the ground floor of the Margalar Tower was permanently illuminated by a pulsating red light.

Hector, still lying on the floor, tried to calm down, oblivious to the storm, the metallic bird and its eye, and the pain in his back . . . Oblivious to everything that wasn't the dark hand that sprouted from his wrist. He opened and closed it slowly, perplexed to confirm that the thing yielded just like that to his will. It was his hand. It was. It felt like it was his, and at the same time it was so alien, so aberrant to look at, like the emptiness that he'd seen there just moments before. He sat up with the hand held out in front of him. It was such a shiny black that he could almost see the reflection of his face in his palm. He turned it to look at the back. The center was studded with crystals encrusted in his flesh, more numerous around his knuckles. They were

JOSÉ ANTONIO COTRINA

like minuscule diamonds. He felt their consistency with his left hand and found them cold and hard to the touch. And sharp.

*Soon your whole body will be like this,* Lady Scar announced in his mind. Hector spun around to face the bird. *Whether I like it or not, you will be a black angel. Those demons' regenerative ability is as legendary as their madness. Not only did it save you from Roallen's venom; it also made you grow a new hand.*

"I'm not a demon," he whispered.

He got up and looked around. The ground was a mess of shattered junk and overturned furniture, but aside from the disorder it didn't look like the earthquake had caused serious damage to the tower. There was no trace of his friends. He was alone there with the bird holding Lady Scar's revolting eye in its beak, and those red embers swirling everywhere. The tower's main gate remained half-open, but he doubted that the girls would have gone outside. He looked at the stairs he'd just rolled down. The dungeons. That's where they were. He imagined the three of them locked up next to Lizbeth, already transformed into horrendous monsters, into creatures even more unpleasant than Lady Scar. He remembered the story of the castaway and the lighthouse keeper, and for a second he saw himself and Marina as its protagonists. He put that image out of his head and started walking toward the stairs.

He hadn't gone two steps when a gust of wind blew the courtyard door wide open. The storm came crashing into the Margalar Tower. It didn't just bring water; spiders fell among the dark, dense drops of rain, hundreds of them. Small spiders, with long red legs and black bodies, that entered the tower at a dizzying speed. Hector shielded his face with an arm and turned around so as not to receive the brunt of that sinister wave head on. The spiders hit him so forcefully that most of them burst on impact. Soon the ground was swarming with them; they scurried maniacally from one side to the other, searching for cracks to take refuge in before the wind carried them off again. The courtyard door pounded incessantly, never managing to close, and with each blow more waves of water and half-drowned spiders flooded into the tower. Hector ran to the door, battling the wind and what it carried. The spiders crunched beneath his bare feet. He grabbed the door with both hands and closed it with a loud crash. He stepped back, soaked to the skin, dozens of dying spiders on top of him. He slapped them away. He was bewildered, dizzy. The unreality of everything that was happening threatened to drive him crazy. He took off again in the direction of the stairs.

"Marina . . ." he whispered.

He needed to see her. He needed support in this madness, an anchor that would keep him sane. The bird had abandoned the back of the chair to perch on the seat, and it watched from there as he stumbled over to the stairway. Hector glared at it. Lady Scar was one of those responsible for what was happening to them. She and the other residents of Rocavarancolia had condemned them to this nightmare.

He went slowly down the stairs, with his new hand drawn in against his stomach. His back burned. The pain beneath his shoulder blades was tremendous; with each step he took, with each heartbeat, he felt something being torn open inside of him. He found the door to the dungeons closed. Two spiders ran along the wood, one after the other. He took a deep breath. He didn't want to open it. He didn't want to know what awaited him on the other side, but he had no choice. He bit his lower lip, took the latch in his left hand, and slowly opened the door.

Lizbeth was out of her cell.

The surprise at seeing her free was so great that he couldn't focus on anything else, only on the huge wolf. Lizbeth raised her head and looked at him with her cracked eyes open like windows into hell. She bared her fangs and took a step forward. Hector hadn't yet crossed the spell of silence and he couldn't hear her growl, but that didn't diminish the threat and ferocity one bit. He was about to close the door to keep Lizbeth imprisoned when he saw Marina, and his world collapsed. The young girl lay completely still on the ground behind the wolf. She was dead. Hector knew it at once. Her arm outstretched, palm up, fingers flexed and pointing toward the exit. There was no pulse in that wrist, nor beating in her heart. Marina was dead. Lizbeth had killed her. Hector screamed, threw the door open, and leapt into the dungeon, possessed with a rage that made what he felt when he confronted Roallen seem insignificant.

The wolf jumped at him as soon as he set foot in the dungeon. Hector confronted her without hesitating. And just as his new fist was flying at Lizbeth's head, someone pulled her back violently. His blow met with empty space, as did the wolf's furious bite. Lizbeth went limp, composed herself with a shake, and charged again, but again someone pulled her back before she could reach him.

"Lizbeth! No! Stop!" he heard.

For a fraction of a second he didn't recognize Madeleine. She sat behind Marina, with the chain from Lizbeth's collar wrapped around her left wrist. And it was Madeleine, without a doubt it was Madeleine, but at the same time it wasn't. It wasn't the Maddie he remembered, in any case. His friend was halfway through her metamorphosis. A labyrinth of copper-colored veins was beginning to clearly show in the whites of her eyes and the green of her pupils; her ears, once perfect, were now pointy and elongated, the exteriors covered with a reddish fur that continued on her cheeks down to her chin; her cheekbones were sunken and her lower jaw had thrust several inches forward, completely altering her appearance. A beast was emerging from that once beautiful face, and looking at her at that moment, midchange, made it all the more terrible.

"Stop! Damn it! Stop it!" she shouted again, as she tried to contain Lizbeth's frenzied lurching. She pulled on the chain with both hands, using her feet on the ground as leverage, but the wolf was still set on pouncing on Hector. "Lizbeth, stop! Damn it! I told you to stop!" Madeleine growled. It was an actual animal growl, a bloodcurdling sound.

The wolf finally shrank back, still biting and growling. Madeleine retreated to make sure of her footing. She slipped as she did so and unintentionally hit Marina. As he saw the body move, Hector crumbled; it was as if a black hole erupted in his insides. He forgot Lizbeth and Madeleine; he forgot his own pain. His legs couldn't hold him up any longer and he fell to his knees.

"I don't know what happened to her," Madeleine said. "She was fine, and then suddenly she fell and didn't get back up."

Marina had no visible injuries, not a single scratch, even a small one. It wasn't Lizbeth that killed her, Hector realized. It took him a few moments to notice the voice that spoke up again in his mind.

*It may look like it, but she's not dead. Or alive, to tell the truth. She's in an intermediate state. Latent. Sometimes the Red Moon causes this type of reaction. It needs to suspend the body so that the change can take place.*

"She's not dead . . ." he murmured, stunned. What he felt next was beyond relief. It was a new feeling entirely, and giving it a name would only have put a limit on it. He looked at Maddie, without knowing whether to laugh or cry. "She's not dead," he announced. "It's the moon, the Red Moon. It put her to sleep in order to transform her."

"Thank heavens," she said. Even her voice sounded different. It was deeper, more hoarse, more like a growl than a human voice. "Thank heavens," she repeated. She threw her head back and let out a deep sigh. Then she looked straight at him. "And you've finally woken up," she said. "You're alive."

"I hope so."

He sat down on the ground as well, with his legs crossed. He remained face to face with the wolf girl, separated by Marina's inert body, with Lizbeth growling a few feet away. Everything was happening too quickly. The feeling of unreality and nightmare that seized him grew more and more oppressive. He brought his hands to his head and rubbed his temples vigorously, as if with that simple gesture he was able to stop the passing of time, to end that dizzying plunge into the future.

"You have a new hand," Maddie said. There wasn't a trace of surprise in her voice. Hector, naturally, didn't mention the changes that were occurring in her.

"And you let Lizbeth out of her cell," he said instead.

Madeleine nodded.

"I'm leaving the tower and I'm taking her with me," she explained in her new raspy voice. "It's for the best. If you lock me up, sooner or later I'll find a way to escape, and when that happens I'll try to kill you," she said. "I know I will. Don't ask me how, but I know. The safest thing for everyone is for me to be as far away as possible."

"Can you control her?" He nodded his head toward the wolf, who kept watching him, growling softly all the while.

"You saw it: only with difficulty. But I don't think she'll give me too much trouble. As long as we don't run into Bruno, of course. Then things could get complicated. She hates him. Is he still upstairs?"

"He's still upstairs," he answered, shivering as he remembered the state he'd left him in. "And Natalia? Where is she?"

"Outside. She left when the moon came out. She said that her shadows were calling her."

"Her shadows . . ."

"She always has some hanging around her. They don't even bother to hide anymore." She leaned forward and lowered her voice. "She's not well, Hector. Natalia's not well at all. Be careful with her." *And with you*, he thought as he glimpsed her sharpened fangs for the first time. "It's as if those shadows were finding a way inside of her. Turning her darker and darker . . . More . . ." She suddenly closed her eyes. A grimace of pain crossed her face. "It hurts," she whispered in a thin voice. "The change hurts."

"I know, I know," he said. It felt like someone was skinning his back with a red-hot knife.

They were quiet for a few moments. Maddie looked at the ground, while Hector looked at Marina. She looked like a broken doll, an abandoned plaything. It was hard to accept that she wasn't actually dead. Hector wondered what change was occurring in her that warranted the Red Moon submerging her in that lethargy. Whatever it was, right now it wasn't visible to the naked eye, not like what they'd been suffering. Was it something even more radical? Had the Red Moon put her in suspended animation because she wouldn't have endured the agony of her metamorphosis? Once again he recalled the story of the lighthouse keeper and the castaway. He shivered. With every passing second, his thoughts grew more dismal.

"I'm glad to see you," the wolf girl told him, her voice still affected by the pain. She tried to smile, but what she offered was more a grimace than a smile. "I'm very glad to see you. These last few weeks . . . God . . . They've been horrible. The waiting has been horrible. I was almost hoping that this day would come, and it would all be over."

"Don't say that . . ."

"It's true. For better or for worse: it's all over. Everything will be different from now on. It can't be any other way." She sat upright on the ground. Hector watched as her nostrils flared furiously. She'd smelled something, he realized. Madeleine stood up to look behind him. "Hector . . . Oh my God, your back . . . It's in shreds," she said.

Hector sighed. It was time to face it. It didn't make sense to put it off any longer. He reached his hands back and felt where the pain was the most intense. Two long vertical wounds had opened up in his flesh, pooled with blood, right beneath each shoulder blade. The two tears ran parallel until just above his waist.

"It's nothing," he said, his voice devoid of all emotion. He was falling downward, his mind and his body distancing themselves from one another with each passing moment. He was no longer Hector. He was something else, like Maddie, like Bruno. Something halfway between what he had been up until then and what he was destined to become. "I'm growing wings," he finally admitted. And saying it out loud had a strangely calming effect on him.

*I'm growing wings*, he repeated to himself.


Esmael looked at the Red Moon. He was huddled at the top of his dome, the rain darkening his skin even more. The glow from the moon tinted the clouds red. Even the lightning was stained by its bloody radiance. To the west, Rocavaragalago welcomed its mother; the building shone with a blinding light, enveloped in an intense whirlwind of reddish embers that rose so high it seemed like it wanted to touch the moon itself. All of Rocavarancolia smelled of pure magic, primordial magic. It smelled of change. The flashes of the dead vortices glimmered in the midst of the storm, like fragments of aurora encrusted in the sky, like streaks of lightning frozen in time and space.

"Where are you?" Esmael asked between his teeth, straightening up in the dome and looking around him. "Where are you hiding, you bastard?"

Somewhere lurked the creature who had murdered four members of the Royal Council, the demiurge of Rocavarancolia among them. Esmael had the absurd hope that the Red Moon would make him come out of hiding, but so far there had been no indication that would happen. The Lord of Assassins bared his teeth to the red night. The longing to kill consumed him. Blood boiled in his veins. To the north, the marble tower of Isaiah, the blind clairvoyant, came crashing down, unable to resist for another year the strain of the Red Moon. The building, a dazzling white structure, split in two: the top half collapsed into the Scar of Arax, while the bottom half fell on one of Lady Spasm's brothels. Esmael yelled into the storm and punched at the air, out of his mind.

"Where are you?!" he howled.

He took flight and shot out into the night, flying aimlessly, immersed in his sinister thoughts. The rain was so intense that at times it felt like moving through a sea of tar. High in the sky, the Red Moon seemed to be aflame, besieged by lightning bolts and storm clouds.

The demiurge was dead, and his body wasn't even resting in the Royal Pantheon as tradition decreed. The remains of Denestor Tul had become fish food. As if his traitorous murder weren't enough, that insult, that humiliation, had to be added on top of it. Who was behind it all? And what did they want? Esmael had no answers, only questions and the absolute certainty that something lay in wait in the shadows, something as intangible as the wind. And what could he do? There was no trail whatsoever to follow, no way to find the assassin. Magic had proved completely useless in the matter, and his attempts to find some clue regarding the language of Belisarius's scroll had also led to nothing.

He closed his eyes to the world around him, to open them inside the vigilance spell that he'd cast in the underground passageway where Mistral was hiding. The shapeshifter appeared in his mind, sitting on the ground of the filthy cavern, with his knees folded up and his head hung between them, rocking slowly, oblivious to the tremors that threatened to bring the ceiling down on top of him. This wasn't the only spell that watched over members of the council: there was another in Lady Dream's room, keeping an eye on the sleeping old woman. Esmael hadn't cast the spells to protect them, of course: Lady Dream and Mistral, two members of the Royal Council who were practically helpless, were no more than bait to tempt the assassin. But for the moment, his prey had refused to fall for it. He felt stupid and more furious by the minute for having set such a clumsy, obvious trap.

He looked at Mistral. He'd lost count of the times that he'd entered into that spell in the last few hours to spy on the shapeshifter. The pathetic creature who claimed not to have a name had become the focus of his obsessions, the key piece to a destiny that he was dying to claim.

All he had to do was grab him by the neck and bring him before Huryel. It would be easy to make him confess. He, Esmael, would be regent: the next-to-last step in his glorious destiny. And what did the fate of Denestor's harvest matter to him? In keeping with the sacred laws of the kingdom, Huryel would order the teenagers to be executed, and both he and Esmael would be aware that this would be his last task as Lord of Assassins. Of all of them, only Dario would survive, and with the Red Moon already in the sky it made no sense whatsoever to question whether placing the fate of the kingdom on the shoulders of a single child was worth the risk. At that very moment, Dario was becoming a troll, and although his transformation wouldn't be complete for several weeks, it was clear that he would survive. If Esmael had no other choice, he would personally take charge of overseeing Dario's safety day and night. And he could do it openly, without hiding, because the coming of the Red Moon had put an end to the time of sifting. What the heck— if he wanted to, he could even lock Dario in one of the castle dungeons until the first vortices opened in Rocavarancolia.

So why did he hesitate? What kept him from taking the step that would make him regent?

"Show yourself!" he yelled to the night. Was it that dark presence that made him waver? Was the murderous sorcerer the reason why he didn't take that final step, once and for all?

*This is absurd,* he told himself. *My time has come. Why do I insist on delaying it?* He answered his own question, with the same malicious, mocking tone that he'd directed at Enoch the Dusty so many times before. *How are you going to rule, you poor wretch, when you can't even stop the creature who's massacring the council? He left Rocavarancolia without a demiurge and Highlowtower without a guardian, and the only thing you do is whine in the rain. You're as useless as Lady Scar. It's hard to admit, isn't it? Now is the time for you to accept it: you're not worthy of being regent. Much less king. Stick with what you are: an assassin.*

He flew toward Rocavaragalago. The whirlwind of embers that surged from its walls momentarily blinded him. Those ashes would float throughout Rocavarancolia for days; they were called moon pollen, and they worked to accelerate the change in the harvest. Esmael grabbed the tip of the highest pinnacle of the cathedral and climbed to its spiny point. There he crouched. The stone that Harex had wrenched from the Red Moon burned beneath his body, but no fire could compare to Esmael's rage. He clenched his teeth. From where he was, he had a privileged view of Rocavarancolia. The city looked like it was on fire. The storm clouds inundated everything, some so low that the buildings scraped their bellies as they passed over. Lightning bolts tattooed the night with their constant strikes, splitting it open from top to bottom like stab wounds.

Esmael looked at Rocavarancolia.

"I've served you for decades," he muttered. "I helped make you great, although later I was unable to prevent your fall. I ended thousands of lives in your honor . . . And I would destroy a thousand worlds if you could just return, even for a second, to your former grandeur. I'm your servant, Rocavarancolia. I live to serve you." He bowed his head, attentive to the slightest sound, to the faintest movement. "Give me a sign," he begged. "Any sign. Give me a sign so I know which path to follow. Show me your will, and I will comply at once."

Right then, a curtain of clarity opened at ground level, within the whirlwind of reddish embers that surrounded Rocavaragalago. A small silhouette staggered down below, amid the sudden clearing. He had no trouble recognizing who it was. It was Adrian, the boy who'd stabbed to death those who'd been trapped in the motionless fire. He walked with long strides, glancing around with the look of someone searching for something important.

Esmael saw him approach the lava moat that surrounded the cathedral. He shifted on the pinnacle in order to watch him more closely, wondering if that child was the sign sent by the city. He didn't notice the slightest physical change in him; he was still human, at least in appearance, but the black angel knew that the most profound changes sometimes don't show on the outside. Adrian crossed the last few yards before the moat and walked, even less steadily, over the blackened paving stones that bordered it. He gazed at the bubbling red river that surrounded Rocavaragalago. Suddenly he fell to his knees, bowing in the direction of the moat. The glow from the lava on his body prevailed over the moon's brightness. For an instant, Adrian looked incandescent.

Then, very slowly, he put his right hand into the moat.

Hector left the dungeon with Marina in his arms. Madeleine and Lizbeth walked before them. The wolf had completely forgotten about him and tugged frantically at the chain, eager to finally leave the tower. The redhead followed, hunched over in a grotesque manner. It was clear that the mere act of walking was agony for her. There was something abnormal in her posture, and it was hard for Hector to acknowledge what it was: quite simply, Maddie's anatomy was no longer made to stand on two feet. She was already more wolf than human. The girl was longing to abandon that bipedal posture so she could walk on four legs.

Hector looked at Marina's pallid face as they climbed the stairs. He saw no sign of life in her. It was impossible not to recall the night he brought Rachel's body to the cemetery. And if the body of his friend had seemed pale then, Marina's was even more so now. He felt like he could spend his whole life with her in his arms without ever tiring.

*She's empty*, the monstrous spider from the ballroom had told him, referring to his dead friend. *What matters is no longer there. She's gone.*

*But not this time*, Hector said to himself. *This time what matters is still here. It doesn't matter what she becomes. She'll still be her. I'm sure of it.*

Maddie did her best to manage as Lizbeth pulled on her chain. The wolf was impatient to leave. Since they'd left the spell of silence behind, her restlessness had increased. It was hardly surprising; after being locked up in that tiny dungeon for weeks, she wanted to smell and see everything, but she also wanted to reach the gate as soon as possible. Madeleine was in a hurry to leave too. Her hands grew larger and rougher by the second, and soon they wouldn't be able to accomplish fine tasks—like, for example, removing Lizbeth's chain.

They walked through the mayhem of the ground floor. The dead spiders crunched as they passed. Outside, the storm raged on.

"Where are you going to go?" Hector asked.

"I don't know. I guess to the mountains, but I'm still not sure. I'll let my instinct guide me. I think that's what I have to do . . ."

"Bruno will find a way to bring you back. I'm sure of it."

Maddie was quiet for a few seconds. She tugged at Lizbeth's chain. The wolf growled menacingly in the direction of the stairs. She must have picked up the Italian's smell. The redhead sighed. But it didn't sound like a sigh; it was an animal-like yelp.

"Do you know what scares me the most?" she asked, staring off into space. "That if the time comes and Bruno finds a way to help us, I might not want to return." She shook her head. "It's hard to understand, I know. And even harder to explain. But it's just that . . . everything is more intense now. Everything. Smells, life. Even you . . ."

She crouched to pat Lizbeth's back. Hector saw how her vertebrae stood out sharply against her shirt; two of them had already torn through the fabric. The wolf tugged on the chain toward the gate, then growled questioningly, and Madeleine nodded.

"We're going, dear, we're going." She looked back at Hector. She smiled, but if there was the slightest hint of joy in that smile, he couldn't see it. "It's true, Hector. Everything is more real. Fuller. And . . . I love this feeling . . . God, I love it . . . Despite the pain, despite the fact that right now my bones hurt so much I want to tear them out . . . Despite everything . . . I feel good. I feel complete. And I know that when the pain is over, when the change is complete, it will be even better. That's why I'm afraid . . . What if later I don't want to become human again?"

"Of course you will."

"You don't know that. You can't be sure, because even I'm not sure." She gestured toward the gate. "We have to . . . we have to go now."

Then she gave Lizbeth a hearty pat on her side and started walking, determined, without looking back.

"If you see me again, be careful, please," she warned, when they'd already entered the hallway that led outside. "I don't know how dangerous I might become. And, well . . . I don't have to say anything about Lizbeth, right?"

"No," he answered. "We already know how dangerous she can be."

Maddie nodded. She looked like she was about to add something, but she just shook her head and closed the gate behind her. For a few instants, Hector listened to them as they walked through the hallway, then he heard only the wind and the storm. He was alone among the toppled furniture and the dead spiders, with Marina in his arms. He hadn't felt so lonely and helpless in all his life. It was like he was the only person alive in the world. He headed for the stairs after one last glance toward the gate through which Madeleine and Lizbeth had just left.

*Don't worry about your friends*, he heard in his mind. *The pack takes care of its own. They will be fine.*

"They'll be fine?!" Hector asked furiously. He searched for the metallic bird. He saw it perched on one of the few wardrobes still standing. "None of us will ever be fine again! Look at what you've turned us into! Look at what you've done to us!"

*You can spew all the venom you like through that little mouth of yours, dear, but try not to say anything that would betray that we've had contact before today. If you at all value your life and the lives of your friends, of course.*

Hector groaned.

"Get out of here. Leave me alone. Tell your bird to take your eye to hell."

*I'm not your enemy. Don't treat me like I am. I'm just here to warn you. The hour of the sifting has come to an end, but that doesn't mean that you're no longer in danger. Far from it. While your bodies are changing, you'll grow more confident. It's inevitable. It always happens, and it will happen to you. And you already know what happens in Rocavarancolia to those who are overconfident.*

Hector didn't answer. He kept walking toward the stairs, never looking at the bird.

*And another warning,* continued Lady Scar, *the danger won't only come from the city, it can come from anywhere, from the most unexpected places. Listen to me carefully: it can even come from your own companions. Prepare for the worst, because you may have to make some very tough decisions over the coming days.*

He stopped suddenly. He couldn't ignore what those words implied.

"What are you talking about? What are you trying to tell me?!"

*What I'm trying to tell you, Hector, is that you may have no choice but to kill one of your friends. You should be ready for that. If you truly want to survive, that is.*

"Kill them?! I'll never be ready for that!" He spun toward the bird. "That's crazy! I will never hurt them, do you hear me? I wouldn't dream of anything like that!"

*Hopefully you don't have to.*

Hector shook his head. He remembered how he'd pounced on Lizbeth, how he'd hit her that fateful night in the ballroom. Once again he felt his knees tremble. He leaned on the wall to keep from falling, ignoring the pain in his back and all that boiled inside of him.

"We were kids, just kids . . ." he said, in a weak voice, gazing at Marina's pallid face. "How could you have done this to us?"

*You said it. You were kids. But you've grown up. For better or for worse, it happens to all of us.*

It didn't matter what part of the castle she was in; Hurza always knew how to find her. Lady Serena looked away from the Red Moon as the trapdoor to the tower opened to let Ujthan through. The storm instantly soaked the warrior, but he didn't seem to mind. He straightened up, water streaming from him, his eyes set on the Red Moon. He blinked several times and looked around, as if he suddenly remembered what had brought him there. It took him a moment to realize that Lady Serena wasn't in the tower, but floating above the battlements, between the flashes of lightning and the swirling embers of Rocavaragalago. There was no need for words between them. Ujthan's appearance could only mean one thing: Hurza required her presence.

The castle looked more of an abandoned ruin than ever. The small earthquakes caused by the coming of the Red Moon had knocked over furniture; scattered suits of armor, candelabras, and decorations; and filled hallways and rooms with dust. Ujthan and Lady Serena walked through the fortress in silence, without even looking at each other; it was clear that they each felt uncomfortable in the other's presence. It was no wonder. They had assassinated Denestor Tul, demiurge of Rocavarancolia and guardian of Highlowtower. They were traitors, and, although they were far from repentant, they at least had the dignity to feel embarrassed. It was little consolation to know that the kingdom was a hive of conspirators.

It was hard for Lady Serena to accept that Mistral, Lady Scar, and Denestor himself had broken the sacred laws to help the harvest. She didn't know Mistral well enough to know if something like that was within his nature, but she never would have expected it from the demiurge or the guardian of the Royal Pantheon. Even so, the memories that Hurza had stolen from Denestor left no room for doubt.

"Let's turn him in to the regent!" Lady Venom pleaded when she found out. The news made her mad with joy. "Huryel will exile them, and their bones will rot in the desert! Yes! Their skulls will become nests for my little ones! To the desert with them!"

"What a great idea," Lady Serena said scornfully. The witch's foolishness was tiresome. "That would really pave the way for Esmael to become regent of Rocavarancolia. If there's one thing we don't need right now, it's the black angel becoming more powerful than he already is. For the good of our own plans, we must keep it a secret."

Denestor Tul's death had completely unnerved Esmael. Lady Serena hadn't seen him so out of sorts since the end of the war, and she didn't even want to imagine what he might be capable of if he lay hands on the Jewels of the Iguana—the enchanted relics inherited by all those who occupied the role of king, whether they were actually kings or just regents acting in their absence.

Denestor Tul's murder had affected her as well. Not his death itself, per se, but the extraordinary circumstances surrounding it. Hurza had not only taken his life; he'd robbed him of all his power, his very essence, and every last one of his memories. There couldn't be a crueler way of killing someone. As if that weren't enough, Hurza kept Denestor's soul confined within the sword that he'd used to kill him. Lady Serena shuddered to think of the dozens of spirits that howled desperately within that weapon. The agony they suffered, locked for all eternity in that crystal prison, was too much like her own to not want to intercede on their behalf.

"You may be sure that I will free them as soon as Esmael no longer poses any risk," Hurza insisted after listening to her. "And I trust that you won't take it as a personal favor. It was something I'd thought of doing since the beginning. I spent centuries inside a horn, and although I have no concrete memories from that period of time, my soul did not emerge unharmed from such a long confinement."

Perpetual torches illuminated the path of the phantom and the warrior through the castle with their weak light. They met neither servants nor guards. Ujthan walked in front with large strides, gloomy and taciturn. Sometimes, as he passed by a window, he stopped for a moment to look outside. Lady Serena took advantage of these instances to contemplate the Red Moon. She'd been admiring it for hours, ever since its glow had appeared on the horizon. That moon possessed a savage beauty.

"There's something different in the air," Ujthan murmured, peering out a window. It was the first time he'd spoken. "It's like it's not the same moon."

"The city is changing. It always happens with the Red Moon. You know that."

"It's not just that. It's not just that," he insisted. He moved away from the window, his eyes half-closed and an indecipherable expression on his face. "This time there's something else."

Lady Serena looked at the immense moon through the window. Ujthan was right: there was a new vibration in the air, a confluence of forces like she hadn't felt in decades. New winds blew in Rocavarancolia, and what they might bring with them was about to be revealed.

It didn't take them long to arrive at the torn curtain that hid the entrance to the paradox room. Ujthan stretched out his tattooed hand toward the curtain, and as soon as he touched it, it transformed into the bronze door that they were familiar with. The warrior opened it and stepped aside to let the phantom go in first.

Lady Serena had thought that Hurza traveled inside of Ujthan, but the necromancer was in the room, seated at the head of the table. He leaned over a yellowed scroll, on which he wrote rapidly with an enormous quill. He didn't look up as he heard them come in. The room was saturated with black magic; the energies gathered there were chilling. Lady Serena could see them, most of them concentrated around Hurza himself: they were tentacles of unparalleled darkness, whirlwinds of black light with the Eye-Eater at their center.

The change that had come about in him since taking on Denestor's essence was impressive. It was hard to tell that body had once belonged to Old Belisarius. Hurza had gained not only volume and muscle mass but, above all, presence: the sorcerer now exuded a strength that had little or nothing to do with physical fortitude. His features had sharpened even more, his eyes, disproportionately large, now gave off an evil glow that seemed to pierce everything he looked at. The horn on his forehead had grown and was now identical in every detail to the one Belisarius had used to liberate the soul of the first Lord of Assassins. What Hurza hadn't managed to free himself from was the unpleasant brown-gray color of his skin. At least, the phantom thought, Rorcual had managed to leave his mark on the creature who had killed him, although she highly doubted that would have satisfied the alchemist in the least.

The son of Belgadus was also in the room, standing in silence. By his posture he appeared to have been looking at the chest that contained the horn of Harex, although right then his head was turned toward the door. They did not greet one another. Lady Serena watched the creature with disgust. He wore the skin of his creator, and as usual, he hadn't bothered to put it on very well. The effect caused by the skeleton dressed in the flayed skin of Belgadus was disturbing. The openings for the eyes and mouth didn't match up with his corresponding empty sockets and mandible, and the hollows that had once been the necromancer's ears were placed over his temple on one side and to the side of his chin on the other. At least the horror had the decency to wear a black cape to hide the rest of his body.

For Lady Serena it was enough to see what kind of creatures Hurza had called into his service to understand the grave mistake she'd committed by joining him. At least at that moment Solberinus and Lady Venom weren't present. She still shuddered to recall how the castaway had laughed as they assassinated Denestor. Until now she hadn't been aware of the true extent of Solberinus's madness. The man hated the city, hated it with an excessive passion that defied logic; if in his early days in Rocavarancolia he'd survived thanks to the love he felt for the creature in the lighthouse, it was now hatred that kept him alive. Regarding Lady Venom, she'd already demonstrated that her stupidity knew no bounds. Shortly after Denestor's death, they ran into each other in a hallway at the fortress, and the witch began to ask for details about what had happened, not seeming to care if someone might be listening. *Was there a lot of blood when Hurza cut his head off?* she'd dared to ask. Lady Serena had been tempted to kill her right then and there.

Yes, it had been madness to join Hurza. But there was no going back now. The demiurge's murder had been the point of no return for all of them. The only option left was to keep moving forward.

"This can only end in a bloodbath," she whispered at one of the meetings held in the paradox room, the first one that the son of Belgadus attended. Ujthan was the only one to hear her and he looked at her, taken aback—not by her words, but by the sorrow that accompanied them. She was even more astonished when the warrior leaned toward her and replied with a conclusive "Of course."

Lady Serena frowned. The concentration of magic in the paradox room was growing. She'd taken for granted that this was an effect of the coming of the Red Moon, but now she realized her error. She looked away from the son of Belgadus and focused on Hurza. The sorcerer was still hunched over the table, writing with such energy that he seemed about to tear the paper apart. The phantom trembled as she saw the cloudy phosphorescence that emanated from the scroll. Hurza was preparing a spell, and not just any spell, she realized: new magic was being born before her, something only within the reach of the highest sorcerers. It wasn't surprising that Hurza would choose this moment to enact it. The arrival of the Red Moon was when the power of all the residents of Rocavarancolia reached its peak, its critical point.

The quill gave off sparks as it flew over the paper. Hurza continued to mumble to himself, and the few words that she managed to hear made no sense whatsoever; they seemed like mere syllables joined at random. Suddenly, the quill became incandescent. Hurza grabbed the edge of the table with his left hand as he continued to write with the other, even more rapidly than before. His forehead was beaded with sweat, and a grimace of true suffering deformed his face. The light—both from the quill and from the scroll—became brighter and brighter. Hurza's tone of voice went up a notch. His words were just as unintelligible as before, but now they awoke strange and unpleasant sensations in Lady Serena's mind. She seemed to be listening to a language that not only could she not understand, but should never have been put into words. It was the language of darkness and the forbidden, of sadness and emptiness.

The quill began to melt in the necromancer's hand. Lady Serena saw it flow between his fingers and immediately be absorbed by the paper. The dark tentacles that had surrounded Hurza began to retreat as well. Suddenly, with a loud suctioning sound, the gloom surrounding the sorcerer disappeared, along with the remains of the quill, swallowed up by the parchment. Hurza leaned back in his chair.

"It's done." His tone made it clear that the task he'd just undertaken greatly displeased him. "It's all over." He finally looked at Lady Serena. He tried to smile, but the only thing that showed on his face was a grimace of exhaustion. "I allowed myself the liberty of preparing a gift for you, my good friend. The end is near, and now more than ever we must be ready. You never know when a last-minute surprise might ruin the best-laid plans. And I won't let that happen. This spell will be one of our safeguards against the unexpected." With a hand gesture, the scroll flew toward Lady Serena, turning slowly to face her. "I would have preferred to cast it myself, but I couldn't find a way to do it," he said. "Given the peculiar nature of the spell, I need a ghost to be the one to perform it. I'm counting on you."

Lady Serena studied the parchment with narrowed eyes. The power contained in that piece of paper was overwhelming. It emitted a faint silver glow, and if one listened closely a whispering could be heard coming from inside, as if someone were having a heated argument with themselves in the fibers of the parchment.

She only saw two lines of text written at the top part of the sheet, and they pertained to an absorption spell. When cast, the spell that Hurza had just prepared would be transmitted directly from the parchment into her mind. It was an abrupt way to learn magic, but effective. Lady Serena hesitated. She didn't like the idea of something being placed inside her head without knowing exactly what it was.

Before she could make up her mind, Ujthan cleared his throat and took a step toward the table.

"Hurza," he began, "if my presence here isn't necessary, I'd like to leave. I have to . . ." He pointed to the door with evident urgency. "I have to go."

Without taking his eyes off Lady Serena, Hurza nodded and gestured toward the door. The son of Belgadus extended this invitation to exit the room to himself, and as soon as Ujthan opened the door he took off after him. Lady Serena also felt the call of Rocavarancolia, and if it hadn't been for the document floating in front of her—and Hurza's expectant glare—she would have followed them out. Something was about to happen in the ruined city. It wasn't a premonition—it was an absolute certainty.

"You hesitate," said the Eye-Eater once the son of Belgadus closed the door behind him.

"I'd like to know what kind of spell it is before I absorb it. That's all."

"Your suspicion is tiring," he replied. "Memorizing the spell will not have the slightest side effect on you, I assure you. Except for, of course, the tiny transfer of power that I've included in it so that you can successfully perform it."

*I helped kill Denestor Tul*, Lady Serena said to herself, looking at the spell of absorption out of the corner of her eye. *There's no turning back now.*

It took her less than a second to cast the spell. As soon as she did, the scroll in front of her began to vibrate. Hurza's true spell finally appeared on its surface. She tried to decipher the words as they filled the blank sheet, but they didn't make any sense. Suddenly, those strange words detached from the paper and floated in the air like twisted insects between her and the scroll. The page shone once more and a moment later a powerful stream of black light passed through the parchment to the phantom, dragging the floating words with it. Lady Serena felt the spell penetrate her. A shiver ran down her spine. It was as if, for the first time in centuries, something had achieved the impossible: it touched her. The feeling delighted her. For a couple of seconds, the time it took for the spell to pass completely through her, she felt alive again. That alone made killing Denestor Tul worth it.

She still hadn't recovered from the absorption of the spell when its true nature and purpose were revealed to her. It was a Dominion spell, the most powerful that she'd ever come in contact with, in all of her years as a human and as a ghost. But it wasn't just its power that amazed her; it was the way in which it was conceived. She'd never seen one crafted in such a masterful way, so harmonious, so perfect and precise in design and form. It was pure and beautiful, of a sublime simplicity. It was a magic that was nothing like the magic that had been practiced for centuries—not just in Rocavarancolia, but in all the known worlds.

She immediately turned to Hurza, astonished.

"What in the world are you?" she asked.

Lady Serena hadn't expected Hurza to answer, but by the Machiavellian way in which he smiled, she realized that he was going to.

"Have you ever wondered how magic became reality?" asked the Eye-Eater. "What it was that made that turbulence suddenly slip through into the order of the universe? Have you ever been curious to know how it all began?"

"Magic has always been around. Everyone knows that. Order contains chaos within it. When reality was born with its rules and laws, it already contained within itself a way to subvert them . . ."

"That's just armchair philosophy, drunken chitchat . . . What I'm talking about is indisputable fact. Proven facts. Believe me when I tell you there was a time when magic didn't exist, Lady Serena. And I know because I was present when magic burst through into reality. I was there."

Lady Serena took a minute to respond.

"No, it can't be . . ." she said. That was impossible. It was absurd. "You can't be that ancient . . . No one can . . ." She didn't know whether to laugh or be furious over such foolishness. She had expected answers, and Hurza only offered fairy tales. "If you think I'm going to believe that, even for a . . ." Hurza's expression made her hesitate. She looked at his horn and then glanced over toward the chest where Harex's was kept. The ghost wondered how many times they had died and been reborn. How many times had they come back to life before that schooner shipwrecked on the coast of Rocavarancolia? "You?" she dared to ask. "You're telling me that you are the ones who brought magic?"

"No. We annihilated the nauseating creatures who dared to do so."


The metallic bird left the Margalar Tower with Lady Scar's eye firmly secured in its beak. An enormous bolt of lightning lit up most of the sky right as it spread its wings to ride an ascending air current. The thunder that followed was deafening.

The commander of the armies of the kingdom remained silent, seated on one of the marble benches in the main vestibule of the Royal Pantheon, alert to all that occurred in the city. She'd left the mausoleum gates open, and neither the wind nor the occasional deluges of water that came flooding in bothered her. She didn't even pay attention to the spiders who'd taken shelter within her scars.

The storm would not let up. Lady Scar knew the risk she ran allowing Denestor's bird to fly among so many electrical discharges, but at that time the safety of her eye and the demiurge's creation mattered little. She had to see what was happening in the city. For thirty years, Red Moon nights had been nothing more than sad reminders of lost glory and of the desolate future that lay before them, but this time was different. Finally, there were kids alive in the city, and that changed everything. Absolutely everything.

She'd just left Hector and Bruno next to the bed where they'd laid Marina, watching over that slumber that wasn't really sleep. The boy with the top hat was a bundle of nerves. He was the one most affected by the change, and it was no wonder; the barriers that he'd constructed between himself and his feelings throughout his life had come crashing down as soon as the Red Moon appeared. And that, together with the changes that were occurring in his body and his mind, had unhinged him. She hoped he wouldn't lose his head entirely. It would be a shame for the kingdom if that happened.

*If I were you, I'd seriously consider slapping him to get him to focus,* she'd advised Hector when Bruno broke out in tears for the thousandth time. The ungrateful little boy had let out a growl as his only answer—a reaction typical of a black angel, she had to admit. Hector's change had surprised her greatly; the others' metamorphoses had been obvious long before the Red Moon came out, but his had been a mystery to them all until that very night.

The bird took flight, and Rocavarancolia came into view for Lady Scar, amid the quick rainfall and the bolts of lightning.

She discovered Natalia surrounded by a multitude of deformed dark onyxes near the Margalar Tower. Lady Scar still hadn't gotten used to seeing those aloof creatures show themselves so openly. Until a few weeks ago, she'd been able to count on the fingers of one hand how many times she'd been able to see them, but since Roallen's attack their behavior had changed substantially. She watched the girl with some concern. At that moment, dozens of shadows surrounded her, and there were many more scattered throughout the city. Hundreds, possibly thousands. Although they were beings of a fragile consistency, they could cause serious damage if Natalia ordered them to attack Rocavarancolia. The young witch was squatting on the ground, talking to one of the larger shadows. The onyx's head, a shell shape covered with stems and tendrils, was only a few inches from Natalia's face.

To the west ran the two wolves, one still halfway through transformation and the other trapped in a body that would never reach its prime. They headed toward the mountains. There, in the castle courtyard, howled the pack, eager to accept them among their ranks. Madeleine had finally gotten rid of her clothing and exposed her new body, covered with red fur, to the storm. There was barely anything human left in her.

Lady Scar watched from the sky as the wolf stopped on top of a rock to wait for her companion, who was unable to keep pace with her. Even halfway transformed and with her fur matted from the deluge, it was clear that Madeleine was going to become a magnificent specimen. She was already larger than Lizbeth, who looked more hunched and deformed by her side than she actually was.

The two wolves passed near Rocavaragalago on their way to the mountains. They both glanced at it at the same time. Lizbeth bared her fangs and growled, frightened by the gigantic construction. The colossal red cathedral glowed in the midst of the storm's onslaught, surrounded by an enormous whirlwind of incandescent embers. The wind dissolved into desperate howls around its towers.

A silhouette walked back to the city through the plain that surrounded Rocavaragalago, made smaller by the enormous hulking building at its back. It was Adrian. He seemed distracted, submerged in a kind of deep trance. He looked up at the clouds at the very moment a bolt of lightning touched down just yards from where he stood. The boy staggered from the impact, but didn't stop.

*We did it*, Lady Scar said to herself. Detritus and black pus flowed from her eyes, the closest thing to tears that she'd spilled in decades. *We did it, Denestor. We did the impossible: we saved Rocavarancolia . . . May the gods protect us now . . .*

Outside the Royal Pantheon, the dead kept talking.

"Can someone get these heavy slabs off," murmured one of the entombed at the top of a hill surrounded by seated statues. "Let someone put eyes in our empty sockets. So we can see what's happening, so we can see what's going on."

"Did you feel it?" one asked. "Can you feel it? Even my worms are trembling tonight. Is it the Red Moon?"

"Everything is different now. Everything. I feel it in my bones."

"It's always different. The moon changes the world."

"But it's never the same moon or the same world."

★★★

"Do you want to get your name back? Is that what you want?"

The shapeshifter opened his eyes, surprised by an unexpected voice. He looked around, but there was no one in the cave. It had been a dream, he realized. He'd fallen into another one of those heavy slumbers that had become so frequent recently. It was no surprise. He was growing weaker with each passing day. He'd lost track of the time that he'd spent in darkness. But that was his place. That was where he should be. In the darkness. Away from everything and everyone.

The world shook again. He almost thought he heard the clattering of skeletons in the Scar of Arax as they rattled against one another. A peal of thunder resounded in the distance, and in his head it sounded like the bellowing of a mortally wounded animal. Another building collapsed. It was as if the world were ending out there. Maybe that was exactly what was happening. Maybe the end was here.

He wondered if all the children had died yet. The last he knew was that Roallen had killed Ricardo and that Hector was dying in the Margalar Tower, poisoned by the troll's bite. He'd had no other news for some time, since Lady Scar had come to announce that Denestor Tul had died and that, for the first time in centuries, there was no demiurge in Highlowtower.

"It's the end, Lady Scar," he told her. The news hadn't affected him much. Why would it? He was waiting for the end of the world, and Denestor's death was nothing more than another sign that it was approaching. "This is what we deserve. This is what we earned for ourselves."

"You don't know what you're saying, Mistral. You're insane and you're going to die here, in this damned darkness. You're going to die alone and insane."

"I'm not Mistral. I don't know who Mistral is."

The shapeshifter closed his eyes while the world trembled around him. He sighed. Not more than a few minutes had passed when he heard the voice again.

"I can tell you your name. I can."

He opened his eyes again, but this time they didn't rest on the familiar dim shadows of the passageway; this time they came face to face with the rough stone of Rocavaragalago. He was in front of the red cathedral, barely a few yards from the lava moat that surrounded the building. Rocavaragalago stretched straight up before him, immense, forceful, and terrible; its turrets and buttresses shot out into the night like spouts of blood that had solidified. The Red Moon shone high in the sky, but by its position and size it must have been about to finish its cycle. It was cold, a terrible cold that not even the heat from the lava moat could dispel. He looked at his hands. They were small: the hands of a child. It took him a minute to recognize them. They were his. His hands, the hands of the child he had been. He began to tremble. What was happening? Had he finally gone crazy?

"It's easy to forget your true name, much easier than anyone can imagine. Don't torture yourself," said someone behind him. A woman, judging by her voice. Mistral did not turn toward her. Those shaking hands had him bewitched. He brought them up to his face. The face that he felt was also his. The woman moved by his side. "I still remember the day that the four of us came here and got rid of our names." She paused for a long moment before continuing. "How naive we were. How easily we tossed aside everything that we had been, with what haste we rejected our past to rush headlong into the future."

"Lady Breeze," he whispered. He was dreaming. But it was a sweet dream, a million times more preferable than the nightmares that accosted him every time he closed his eyes.

He finally looked at her. The shapeshifter revealed her appearance, that of a poorly made doll. The chaos of strings that gave her form didn't even try to simulate a feminine body; she looked like a crude scarecrow. Lady Breeze watched him out of the gloomy orifices that she had for eyes. The knots that formed her lips curved upward in a sorrowful smile. Then she began to change. Every string around her body began to twist and tense. They fused with one another at dizzying speed. The knots came loose to tie themselves again in different spots on her anatomy. What before looked like dead string transformed into live flesh. Soon, standing before him was a dark-haired girl in a dark blue dress that was actually her own skin, stretched and colored. She was much more beautiful than he remembered.

The girl smiled.

"Lady Breeze, yes," she said. "That was the name I chose. Just as you chose Mistral. It was here. Right here. At the bank of the moat at Rocavaragalago. I remember it like it was yesterday."

"And my name?" he hurried to ask her. "Do you remember it too?"

"I remember it," she told him. "And I can tell you, if that's what you want."

"There's nothing in this world that I want more!"

Lady Breeze looked at him with deep sadness.

"Although I can't give it to you for nothing," she stated. "I would like to, believe me, but I can't do it. In exchange for your name I must demand a promise from you. There's something that I need you to do. Not now. Not immediately, but in the near future. It's something horrible, but at the same time, completely necessary."

"Whatever it is. I'll do whatever it is. Tell me my name, please."

"Reconsider. Think carefully before you accept."

"There's nothing to think about. Tell me what you want me to do and I'll do it. Ask me to tear my heart out, and I'll open my chest with my own hands to give it to you."

Lady Breeze shook her head.

"I can't tell you yet. It's risky for you to know before it's time. Very risky. But you must promise me that the next time someone visits you in a dream and asks you to do something, you will do it, no matter the cost, no matter what it is. As horrible and unpleasant as it may seem. Promise me, and I will return your name to you."

The shapeshifter nodded vigorously.

"I promise. I promise. I promise."

Lady Breeze smiled. He remembered how he'd brought her body to the Scar of Arax and thrown it in, without ceremony, on top of the piles of the dead that flooded the crack. But here she was again, alive in his dreams.

She approached him, rested her hand softly on his shoulder, and finally whispered his name into his ear.

Adrian looked with astonished delight at the unmoving flames that surrounded the building that marked the entrance of the torched neighborhood. He was mere inches away from the three large tongues of fire that raged in front of the house's gate. Those flames had been there for thirty years, burning without ever burning out, as much a part of the city as the stones that upheld it. The red embers of Rocavaragalago floated in the air, and their movement around the fire made it look alive.

Esmael spied on him from the shadows of a nearby alleyway; his eyes had become two alert slits. The storm hissed around him. The world was made of motionless shadow and light.

Suddenly, Adrian plunged his right hand into the fire. It was a brusque movement that didn't seem premeditated, but rather the result of an impulse. For a split second nothing happened, but then the red color of the flames grew more intense around the exact spot where he'd thrust his fist. Adrian shouted and, at the same time, with a deafening explosion, the fire erupted back to life. It began to roar feverishly, rapidly, as if in just a few seconds it wished to compensate for all that it hadn't consumed in thirty years of stillness. That quick resurrection began to stretch to the nearest flames and climbed up the house's façade, ran along the ground, leapt in the air . . .

Adrian stepped back. He withdrew his hand from the inferno and extended it again at once, this time without touching it. The flames went erratic at his gesture. The whole fire turned into one blazing wave that whipped in the storm and licked toward Adrian's hands. Euphoric, he began to scream at the top of his lungs. Fiery whirlwinds flew through the burned windows and doors, through the cracks in the walls and the floor, to join the one immense scorching tongue that rushed over the boy. The night erupted in flames, and the same hands which had returned them to life absorbed them at dizzying speed. In a few seconds, the only trace that remained of the fire were the flames that surrounded Adrian's hands. The young man shone as brightly as the lightning in the sky.

He staggered, his arms burning. From his nose and mouth flowed threads of black fumes. Adrian raised his hands in front of his face. The flares that licked his skin were an intense red. He smiled, and his smile—sharp, animal, smoldering—filled with smoke. Then he broke out in laughter. His skin glowed as if all of the fire from the underworld had taken refuge inside him.

Esmael studied the boy carefully. Adrian had become a pyromancer, a warlock capable of mastering fire. The flames not only doubled at his will; they were a part of his essence and, at the same time, the nucleus of his power. Although it was hard to tell the extent of his abilities at this point, from what he'd just seen he suspected that he would be no ordinary pyromancer.

Arador Sala, the most powerful of the three pyromancers that participated in the battle of Rocavarancolia, had set that part of the city on fire. The warlock had cast his scorching spell on the vanguard of the rival army as they made their way through the labyrinth of alleyways toward Rocavaragalago. His plan was to block their path so that they had no choice but to go through the most heavily defended parts of the city, but he hadn't been able to finish it. By one of those most unfortunate coincidences that happened so often in battle, the spell that Lady Basilisk had used to petrify the warriors in the square nearby also reached Arador, so suddenly that the warlock was unable to avoid it.

Arador Sala was turned to stone twenty yards in the air, and he crashed into pieces as he hit the ground. The inferno should have died with him, but somehow Lady Basilisk's spell interfered with his own, and the flames, instead of extinguishing, remained suspended, trapping their victims inside. Esmael remembered the enemy sorcerers' vain attempts to rescue them, once the battle came to an end. Only a pyromancer could put out a fire started by one of their own, and all of the pyromancers of Rocavarancolia—the only faction that had them among their ranks—had died in battle. Esmael recalled that during the years that followed he'd derived a sinister pleasure from hearing the cries of those unfortunate wretches. Until that boy, that same boy who'd just put out one of the hundreds of fires that scorched that part of the city, had killed them all.

Adrian didn't flinch when the building whose flames he'd absorbed collapsed. He remained still, watching spellbound as the fire cut off the other side of the street. Meanwhile, to his left the ruins came crashing down, as they should have done thirty years ago, among clouds of ash and smoke. Then the boy looked beyond, toward the streets aflame in the heart of that inferno. Esmael frowned. He hoped he didn't have the genius idea of extinguishing all of Arador Sala's creation. The very act of attempting it would finish him off. Although

Adrian was already able to work wonders, his body wasn't yet ready to handle such a flood of power. Esmael had seen many die their first night of the Red Moon, when, drunk with power, they tried to achieve feats that they weren't ready for.

But Adrian quickly made it known that he had something else in mind. He diverted his eyes from the fire and looked to the east. Then he began walking toward a nearby alley that led in that direction, his arms still enveloped in flames and his gait unsteady. Esmael retreated into the shadows as he passed by, scarcely a yard away.

The black angel smiled in the darkness. He knew where the boy was headed.


Bruno collapsed as soon as he saw Hector enter the room with Marina in his arms. The Italian burst into tears, hysterical, distraught, blaming himself and shouting that everyone around him would end up dead. Hector couldn't manage to make him understand that she wasn't really dead. Bruno was so out of his mind that he barely heard him. Finally, when Hector was about to give in and resort to slapping him like Lady Scar advised, Bruno seemed to perceive something in Marina that he'd overlooked until then. He calmed down at once, in the same abrupt, disconcerting way, switching from one emotional state to another.

"Wait," he said as he leaned toward the girl, "there's something about her . . . A fragment of life that's not life, I feel it, I sense it. A breath of withered flowers and dust . . . Of watercolors and silk . . ."

Hector was now able to explain that she wasn't dead, but immersed in something like a deep coma. Bruno didn't ask him how he knew, nor did it seem to bother him that the metallic bird watched them from an embrasure nearby.

After putting Marina to bed and carefully examining his new hand for some time, Bruno offered to cure the carnage that was his back, but Hector refused. It wouldn't have done any good. What was hidden beneath his flesh would just break through again. He didn't even let him cast a spell that would lessen the pain. The pain had diminished enough that it was tolerable, or perhaps he'd simply gotten used to it.

Hector left Marina in Bruno's care and went downstairs once again. He opened and closed his new hand repeatedly; he noticed its strength, its vigor. As he watched it, he suddenly felt an absurd outburst of euphoria and was about to test its strength by punching the walls. Instead, he looked at his left hand. There hadn't been the slightest change in it; not in his hand, nor in his arm, nor in any other visible part of his body. He shook his head and headed toward the gate. The idea of leaving the tower was still unpleasant, but it had to be done. Natalia was out there and he had to see her, to know that she was okay. Just when he was about to open the door, a furtive movement next to some toppled barrels made him look in that direction. For a second he thought it was another spider, but he soon realized his mistake: it was Bruno's watch, running stealthily across the ground—the one that his grandfather had given him. It moved jerkily using its hands and lid as if they were paws and sweeping its chain like a tail. It was alive—Bruno's pocket watch was alive. Hector watched it disappear under a pile of broken plates and reappear from the other side.

"And what happened to you?" he asked.

The watch, of course, didn't answer.

Hector shrugged his shoulders and opened the door. The storm and the wind waited on the other side of the passageway. The whole world was waiting. And the Red Moon.

He took a breath and went into the hallway. The floor was full of puddles and covered with dead spiders and rocks carried in by the current. He continued on, barefoot, dressed only in the black shorts he was wearing when he woke up. The idea of getting dressed or putting on boots hadn't even entered his mind. He wondered what he would do with his shirts once his wings finally came out. Wondering about something so mundane at that moment made him smile. His back barely hurt anymore, but the tightness, especially beneath his shoulder blades, still grew. He could feel the wings moving under his skin, as if they were a new pair of arms eager to see the light of day and stretch. He brought one hand to his back and when he withdrew it, it was covered in blood.

He finally left the Margalar Tower. The rain poured down on him, and a sudden gust of wind made him stagger to the left. At least it wasn't raining spiders or anything of the sort; only water fell from the sky, warm and fast, which soon left him drenched. And it wasn't an unpleasant sensation. There was something primitive about walking half-naked in the storm, something primordial. He looked up at the sky. There, between the clouds and the flickering dance of lightning bolts, he saw the Red Moon for the first time.

He was ready for anything, except for the revelation that it would be so beautiful. Seeing it left him breathless for some time. It seemed twenty times bigger than Earth's moon and twice as bright. Hector felt weightless in its presence, as if at any moment he might break loose from the ground and float toward it. It didn't surprise him in the least that Rocavarancolia welcomed it with earthquakes and tempests. If Earth's moon could cause tides and influence human behavior, what couldn't that immense celestial being that floated up above do?

On the surface of the Red Moon he could see with perfect clarity all the craters, mountains, and valleys that made up its geography. There was a large mountain range in the eastern zone that wrapped around itself like a gigantic serpent, and very close to it, a perfectly spherical high plateau, pocked with hollows. But what most caught his eye on the surface was, of course, the infinite number of intersecting canyons and crevices that crossed most of its equator. According to the scrolls that Ricardo had translated, that's where Harex had extracted the rocks that he used to build Rocavaragalago, although Hector doubted that the sorcerer was the only cause of those marks.

It took a great effort on his part to tear his eyes from the Red Moon. He looked around in search of any sign of Natalia or her creatures, and although his eyes went back to the sky time and time again, it wasn't hard to find her. Toward the south, very close to the tower, a multitude of shadows moved about. It looked like a fire of quivering darkness had broken out in that part of the city. Hector furrowed his brow as he saw them. They were the same beings that had filled the square of the three towers when Roallen attacked, the same ones who'd urged the troll to kill them. He crossed the drawbridge and headed that way. The wind changed direction constantly; as suddenly as it pushed him down the hill, it forced him to move back up again. The light from the Red Moon and flashes of lightning illuminated his path.

The shadows were gathered in a small rectangular square enclosed by buildings in ruins. There were dozens of them, in the air as well as crouching on the ground. Their hazy pseudopods and raggedy bodies shook in the wind so violently that they seemed on the verge of tearing apart. The first line of these horrors turned toward him while he was still some distance away; soon the others imitated them, both those flying over the square and those that moved on land.

Their savage dark heads watched him in a vacuous silence. As soon as he reached the bottom of the hill that led to the square, they all moved at once, at an explosive speed; most of them disappearing from his sight so quickly it was as if they'd never been there. They didn't go far. Hector could hear them whispering behind him.

Natalia was in the center of the square, crouched next to the only shadow still on the ground. They both stood on one of the many empty pedestals—free of statues or monuments—that were scattered throughout the city. Hector approached slowly. More than a dozen shadows still twisted around, like dirty bandoleers carried by the wind. One opened its multiple mouths wide and hissed his name, but Hector didn't respond, not even with a glance. Natalia didn't seem to be aware of his presence. She talked with the sinister creature in front of her and, although Hector couldn't hear what she said, by her tense posture and the expression on her face he guessed she was angry.

Suddenly, the monster rose up on an endless number of murky extremities and looked at Hector from the top of the grotesque formation of bubbles that was its head. It was the largest of the shadows that Hector had seen by far. The tentacles that emerged from its back slowly joined together with one another to form a pair of enormous wings. The creature unfurled them, shook its head from right to left, and then took off in flight. Natalia watched it until it was lost from sight between the storm clouds, and then she turned toward him. They looked at each other in the rain. The girl's hair had darkened to an impossible shade of black.

"Hector," she said.

"Natalia," he answered.

"I'm glad to see you're awake and alive." Even her voice had changed: it now gave off a passion and strength that it had lacked before. "What do you think?" she asked him as she turned halfway to look at the Red Moon. "Have you ever seen anything so beautiful?"

"Once, not too long ago. In a dream. But it was only for a second. Then I woke up."

He sat next to her. Natalia cast a fleeting glance at his back but didn't say anything. The girl wore a black sleeveless shirt and a skirt of the same color with tattered hems. The clothes looked good on her; Hector thought they oddly matched with the storm and her shadows. One of them, a dark cloud that propelled itself through the rain with over ten pairs of wings, flew above their heads.

"You said the first thing you'd do would be to get rid of them," he reminded her.

"I changed my mind," Natalia answered with a teasing smile. "They have no choice but to obey me, like it or not, so it would be silly to get rid of them, don't you think?" Now that he was facing the girl, Hector could see that her features had darkened as well. It was as if someone had gone over them methodically with a black paintbrush. He'd never seen her looking so beautiful. On that first night of the Red Moon, Natalia seemed more real than ever. "They want me to kill you, you know?" she said suddenly. "They say that you hurt me and you should pay for it."

"Did I hurt you?"

"No. I did that to myself. But it's in the past. Don't worry. I won't let them kill you, at least not for now. Try not to make me change my mind."

"I'll do what I can."

The girl smiled. She stretched out her arm and caressed his human hand.

"The Red Moon finally came, Hector. And the world didn't end, not even close. Why were we so afraid?"

"Because it's normal to be afraid. And I still am. Afraid of what awaits us. Afraid of what we're going to become." He raised his dark hand in front of her. The tiny crystals encrusted in his skin sparkled in the flash of a lightning bolt. "Afraid of everything."

"Well, you don't seem afraid."

"I am. I promise you. That you don't see it is another matter. You're not?"

Natalia shook her head.

"No. I'm excited. Exhilarated. But not afraid. I feel good for the first time in my entire life. It's as if everything suddenly fits. Like for the first time, everything is as it should be."

"Maddie said something like that before she left with Lizbeth. She said she was afraid of not wanting to go back to being human again."

"I can understand that. I understand that very well." She let out a chuckle. "They both passed nearby. Well, the truth is that they made a detour to avoid me. I make her nervous, you know? My shadows and I make the little wolf girl nervous."

"She was worried about you. She said that you've gone dark."

"And you came to see if it's true?"

"No. I came to see how you were. And if you say you're okay, I'll believe you."

"Thank you for your concern." She ran her hands through her wet hair and tucked it behind her ears. Then she looked to the west. From the square she managed to make out the prison walls where they'd woken up after the night of Samhein. "I gave you a good thump the day we met each other, remember?"

"How could I forget? My forehead hurt for hours."

"You deserved it. You didn't know it then, but you deserved it. You were an insufferable whiner. Did I apologize for hitting you?"

Hector thought back.

"I think so," he said, without being sure. "I don't remember it that well. It's been a long time since then."

"Just over seven months. It's not that long, if you think about it."

"Seven months can be a lifetime."

"Who would have thought? That one day you and I would be here, sitting in the storm, on the way to transforming into who knows what . . . You with your new hand and me with my army of shadows." The whispering, which had remained in the background because of the rain, suddenly got louder. Natalia brought her hands to her head and massaged her temples. "Enough already . . . You hear me? That's enough of your nonsense, no more of this silliness." She looked up and watched angrily as the shadows fluttered around the square. "Enough, I said!" she exclaimed. "I'm not going to kill him! So shut up already! Just shut up!" They went silent. Natalia huffed, annoyed, and turned to look at Hector. "I'm sorry. I'm very sorry."

"Well, it looks like they've got it in for me."

"For you? Oh! No, no, no . . . They're not talking about you now. They want me to kill Adrian, or at least let them kill him. All night it was the same thing . . . They say it's our last chance, that if we leave it it'll be too late. I'm sick of it."

Hector remembered what Lady Scar had said about the difficult decisions in store for them. He wondered if Adrian would be one of those. Or if it would be the girl sitting next to him.

"Why do they want to kill him?"

"They don't like him. They don't like what he is or what he's going to become. He's going to be a warlock, a witch like me. Adrian will be a pyromancer. His Dominion will be fire."

The image of Adrian walking into the neighborhood in flames, sword in hand, killing all those trapped there, came to Hector's mind. Then he remembered him shortly after they arrived in Rocavarancolia, fleeing terrified from the flaming bats or paling at the very mention of fire. For a second he was tempted to ask Natalia to listen to her shadows and kill him.

The girl sighed. Her face was still blurred from the downpour.

"Maddie is right," she said, "I'm turning dark, whatever that means. I think it's part of my metamorphosis . . . The Red Moon changed Madeleine from the outside, but it's changing me from within." She looked at him out of the corner of her eye. "Did you realize that a while ago it was raining spiders?" He nodded. "I was dying to make myself a necklace with them. Who would think of such a thing?"

A *witch*, Hector thought, but he had enough sense not to say it out loud.

"And what if I turn evil?" Natalia asked. She suddenly moved in closer to him. "What if I lose control and do things I might regret?"

"That's a danger that we all face. In Rocavarancolia, on Earth, or in any other place. It's something we have to learn to live with."

She smiled and got even closer, almost springing upon him. They stayed there, one next to the other, with their bodies so near even the rain couldn't fit between them. Hector was aware of how close Natalia's lips were to his own. He felt her breath on his face, and it was warm and sweet.

"But you still don't know what I'm capable of," Natalia whispered, looking him in the eye. "You can't even imagine what kind of thoughts run through my mind. You don't know anything about the

darkness that moves inside of me, or the forces that writhe in my guts."
Natalia's lips glistened, bathed by the storm. They formed a diabolical
smile, covered in rain. "It's closing in on me, Hector. If I get lost in it,
will you come looking for me?"

"I'd go to the underworld for you," he said in a faltering voice.

"How thoughtful," she answered. She let out a laugh and moved
away from him as abruptly as she'd approached him. "Maybe that's the
destiny that awaits us. Going to hell. All of us. From the first to the
last. And maybe it's not as bad as it seems."

A shadow chose that moment to land next to her. It was small, the
size of a German shepherd, with dozens of feet and a head that resembled a dolphin's. It whispered something into Natalia's ear. The girl
wrinkled her brow and groaned softly. She sat in the rain for a
moment, lost in thought, and then looked at Hector.

"I have to go," she announced reluctantly. "They insist that there's
something I must see and it has to be now. Something regarding
Adrian. They won't leave me alone until I go with them."

She got up from the ground and Hector, after a brief pause, did the
same. As he changed position he felt two brutal pangs in his back. He
clenched his teeth. The pain returned, stronger than ever. He could no
longer tell up from down; they became blurred before his eyes, and he
was about to pass out. Natalia kept talking, but he couldn't hear her. In
his head war drums were beating.

"Hector?"

The pain was insufferable. What was hidden beneath his skin was
fighting to break free, and in its battle it seemed like it wanted to split
him in two. The world became a distortion of shapes and colors. He
stretched out his hand for support, and Natalia grabbed him by the arm.

"Hector!"

He looked at her, dazed. He blinked to focus his vision and then
took a few steps back, almost falling off the pedestal. The pain was still
terrible, but now, at least, he was able to think clearly. He thought he
heard some shadows laugh behind him, although it easily could have
been a figment of his imagination.

"Are you okay?" she asked.

"It's my back," he managed to whisper. "It's like it's bursting from
the inside . . ."

"Do you want me to stay with you?" she asked, worried. "For all I care they can take a hike, both them and whatever they want to show me."

"That's not necessary. Go. I'm better, seriously. I'm better now . . ." he lied. It was hard for him to breathe. His back felt dense, soaked, and he knew it wasn't just water running down it. He didn't want to even think about what it might look like. "It's time. And it hurts. It hurts a lot."

He sat down carefully on the pedestal. The pain intensified as he bent down. He closed his eyes and clenched his teeth. Why wouldn't it stop once and for all?

"I'm staying, I can't leave you like this," Natalia said, and attempted to sit next to him.

"Yes, you can . . ." He cut her off with a brisk hand motion waving her away. "I'll be fine," he assured her. "Go with them. Go, please. I . . ." He moaned, huffed, and looked her in the eye. He had to take a breath before he spoke again. "I know what's going to happen now, and to tell you the truth, I prefer to be alone when it does."

"Are you sure?"

"I'm sure. Very sure. Please go." He bit his lips to keep from screaming. "Go . . ."

Natalia looked at him, puzzled. She seemed hurt by his refusal, but Hector didn't have the strength to keep explaining himself. The girl nodded slowly, turned away, and looked up at the sky. When she spoke, it was in the same incomprehensible language that her creatures used, and it sounded even more horrible on her lips.

Just then several shadows came out of the clouds to land in front of her. Hector, despite the pain, couldn't help looking up. The shadows joined with one another in front of his friend and with their bodies formed the beginning of a hazy stairway that soon rose taller than the pedestal. After one last glance at Hector, Natalia began climbing it. Her feet sank in the steps, as if they weren't entirely solid, but she moved with the same confidence with which she'd gone up and down the stairway at the Margalar Tower a thousand times. Behind her the steps stayed in the air for several moments before the shadows that molded them dispersed, hissing in their dark language; some of them vanished into the night and others flew up to the evolving head of the stairway. Natalia always found a new section to step onto, even though a tenth of a second before there was nothing but a void in front of her.

The whirlwind of shadows began moving toward the south, always with her at the apex, climbing higher and higher.

Hector watched her disappear into the crimson darkness of the night as he panted in pure agony; it took everything he had to contain his desire to scream and writhe. Then, when the girl was nothing more than a shadow among shadows, slowly, very slowly, he lay down on his side on the pedestal and hugged himself in the storm.

Esmael landed on the flat rooftop of the Temple of the Selfless Suicides and crouched between the endless ash-gray gargoyles that occupied its overhang, each with a noose around its neck. From there he had a privileged view of the dragon of Transalarada. The beast had been turned to stone in the middle of an attack, its jaws open wide, its claw thrust toward the riders who tried to take it down with their lances. The stone gleamed under the intense rain.

Adrian wasn't long in arriving. Esmael watched him approach between the warriors and stone monsters, heading in the direction of the dragon. The boy rested one hand on the back of a horse that was reared up, and instantly the stone turned black beneath his touch. He left the mark of his smoldering hand on the rock and approached the dragon; he walked slowly, as if he had all the time in the world, as if, in fact, his whole prior existence had just been a preamble to what was coming and he wanted to calmly savor those last instants of a trivial, insignificant life.

Esmael couldn't resist the impulse of peeping in on the surveillance spell that Mistral was under. He wanted to check on the shapeshifter one more time, and make sure that the door leading to the regency was still open, no matter what might happen in the square. The black angel frowned to see that Mistral had abandoned his original form. What was now rocking in the shadows of the grotto wasn't a crude doll made of string, but a boy, thirteen years old, with bronze skin and green eyes. Esmael wondered what the point of that change might be, if there even was one and it wasn't just another plot twist in Mistral's madness. He didn't have time to reflect on it: Adrian had reached the dragon.

The teen stopped a yard away from the creature. They made a curious picture there in the rain: both totally still, although the dragon's stillness was charged with violence and the boy's with an unearthly calm. With his hands enveloped in flames and his head half-raised, Adrian looked into the monster's eyes, as if he meant to bring it back to life by sheer force of will alone.

It had been in that same square where Rocavarancolia had lived its last moment of glory, barely a week before the vortices in the north began to spit out enemy armies and everything came to an end. Esmael remembered that afternoon very well. Banner Square looked very different then: the fourth tower, which had been constructed from magic ice from Arfes, rose solemnly next to its sisters, all perfect, without a single crack marring their surfaces. High up in the air floated the fifth tower, the one built from weightless stone. The ground of the square was paved with multicolored tiles, and, in the very center, two silver minotaurs stood on either side of one of the largest vortices in Rocavarancolia. The portal led to Livingsoul, a fierce world populated with fierce creatures, hybrid reptiles and humanoids who rode on dragons that breathed ice. In addition, Livingsoul surpassed Rocavarancolia in sorcery as well as science, and in the more than ten centuries that it had been linked to the kingdom, not a single king had been mad enough to try to conquer it. But Sardaurlar had sworn not to stop until the very last of the linked worlds was under his command, and when it was Livingsoul's turn, that was where his armies went. The war against the ice dragons lasted over two years, and for that duration victory always seemed an impossible utopia. Until the last battle, the one that was, without a doubt, the most savage and bloody of all that had been waged during Sardaurlar's reign. Against all odds, Rocavarancolia won.

The return was glorious. Esmael would never forget the moment that Sardaurlar emerged from the portal, mounted on his giant falcon and bathed in the amber light from the vortex. The king, as exhausted as all of them, unsheathed his sword under the Rocavarancolian sky— the same weapon that he would soon use to dig the tomb of those who'd battled that day at his side—and let out a cry of victory and jubilation. The square roared in response. The name of Sardaurlar echoed from thousands of throats at once. Esmael was next to him, ecstatic after the battle, and for once he gave in and added his voice to the deafening cheer of the crowd overflowing the square. Never had they been so close to defeat, therefore the taste of victory was even sweeter. The sky was overrun with dragons, sorcerers, and chimeras. The trolls and the necromancers' living dead danced feverishly; the pack howled among true lycanthropes and scorpion men; the giants cheered on Sardaurlar by clashing their lances over the backs of their armored mammoths; the warriors raised their bloody weapons in his honor; even the vampires smiled in the thick swathes of shadow that protected them from the sun.

Esmael wondered how many times he'd relived that moment, how many times he'd tortured himself with the thought that most of those celebrating victory that day would be dead soon after, piled atop one another in the common grave that split the city in two. In Livingsoul they almost suffered defeat; how ignorant, how naive they'd been to believe that after that triumph nothing would be able to stop them. While they acclaimed Sardaurlar, the enemy armies were preparing for battle. It had all been a huge lie, an illusion that reached its peak in that very square, where, after seeing death and destruction so close, every last one of them thought they were immortal.

Without changing his position in the least, Adrian began to levitate until he was face to face with the stone dragon. In all the time that he'd stayed still, not a single lightning bolt had flashed in the sky. It was as if the storm had stopped to watch as well.

Esmael straightened up between the suicidal gargoyles. He wasn't the only one watching the square. He saw the witch girl, very high in the sky, atop a wave of dark onyxes that looked like another storm cloud. The shadows hissed endlessly at their mistress, but she paid them no heed: she only had eyes for Adrian and the dragon. The Lexel brothers floated in the air, one above the north tower and the other above the south tower. Their postures were identical: arms crossed over their chests, heads tilted, one to the left, the other to the right; even the flapping of their capes seemed symmetrical. Lady Spider watched from a ruined corner of the ice tower, looking even more pathetic than usual with her soaked frock coat and matted fur; very close by was Denestor Tul's metallic bird, holding Lady Scar's eye. The son of Belgadus was also there, just a few yards away from the dragon, as motionless as the petrified combatants. He saw Ujthan, crouched in the middle of the square, in the exact spot where the vortex to Livingsoul had opened; the warrior expectantly rested one hand on the wet ground while he rubbed a tattoo located on his back with the other, as if he wanted to erase it by scrubbing it away. He also saw the witch Lady Moreda perched in a window on the north tower with her vulture wings folded at her back; in the hollow of her right arm she held the head of Alastor, the traitor, the miserly immortal rat that Esmael himself had decapitated. He made out Lady Venom, covered in vipers and chuckling next to one of the stone trees; Derende, the sorcerer sucked dry of his black magic—with no hope of ever regaining it—by a remora on Livingsoul, who had lived as a hermit underground since the end of the war; Solberinus, half-hidden in the shadows; and Laertes and Medea, the two cursed witches . . . Half of Rocavarancolia was there.

Adrian raised his arms and began the restoration spell before the monster's open jaws. He'd repeated the spell so many times that he didn't need the book to perform it. His voice went from a normal voice to an unpleasant crackling, in a sizzle of words that arose scorched from his throat; Adrian's voice was the voice of ash, the flame was his word, and the smoke his diction. Many sorcerers had attempted that same spell before, and most of them had been more powerful than that boy would probably ever be, but none had been a fire warlock, and that made all the difference. The magic and essence of pyromancers were connected with dragons. The fire united them. Ultimately it didn't matter what spell Adrian used to bring back the dragon; what mattered was that the fire that ran through his veins was powerful enough to make the dragon respond.

As he watched Adrian, he remembered the words that Sardaurlar had used to honor the victors of Livingsoul, ignorant of what was brewing in the worlds they believed to be harmless, unaware that the end of the empire was soon to arrive.

"Look at you!" Sardaurlar howled from the back of his falcon as he pointed to them with Arax. His voice echoed throughout the square and asserted its authority over the multitudes who chanted his name. "Look at one another! You're larger than life! You're so huge that not even history can contain you! Look at yourselves, sons of the inferno! Now you are legend!"

The black angel huffed impatiently, without taking his eyes off Adrian and the stone dragon.

"Do it, child, do it," he urged him from up above. "Let fire call to fire. Let the curse of the frozen stone be lifted. Get us out of here. Free us from this darkness, from this sad oblivion . . . Bring us back to glory, return us to legend."

*Wake the dragon.*


The pain stopped. It happened suddenly, without warning. At one moment Hector found himself in the purest agony, and in the very next everything was calm.

He stayed still for a long time in the rain, panting like an exhausted beast. He awaited the pain's return. He didn't by any means expect the respite to be permanent. But minutes passed, one after another, slow, tense, and nothing happened.

He finally decided that the time had come to try his luck and move. First he uncurled slowly on the ground and then, slower still, he turned halfway and sat up. For the first time since he'd woken up, he felt no pain whatsoever, just a slight discomfort in his back and a vague, elusive prickling sensation. Even so, he needed a few more minutes to calm down and gather enough courage to stand. As soon as he was vertical once again he staggered backward, off balance. It was as if the weight of his body had been redistributed in an entirely new way. He tried to compensate by leaning forward and almost slipped on the wet stone. That was when he felt them moving. He covered his mouth with both hands, the dark hand covering the human one, as if he were afraid he might start screaming at any moment. He could feel them. He could feel his wings. He felt them folded at his back, hanging heavy, devastatingly real, as much a part of him as the bloody flesh from which they emerged. He wondered if he was able to move them, but the very idea of trying it made him press his hands more tightly over his mouth.

He had wings.

He looked up at the sky. It no longer seemed so distant, so unreach-able. He took his hands away from his mouth, his eyes set on the broken dance of the lightning and the solemn quietude of the Red Moon. The dimensions of the world had changed. Boundaries that he thought were unmovable before had just been blown to pieces. He took a step forward, and his wings went with him.

For the first time in his life, he was aware of the forces that anchored him to the surface. But now this restraint, this grip, was nothing more than an illusion. He had wings. He could mock the force of gravity whenever he wanted. He took two steps forward, his gaze still fixed on the chaotic images drawn by lightning in the sky. He thought he noticed a pattern, as if it weren't just chance that shaped them among the clouds. It was as if each bolt of lightning were a sign in a secret lan-guage, a letter of the alphabet unknown to him until then.

*Fly*, the storm urged him.

Everything was movement. Action and reaction. Everything was con-nected. Just like the bones, muscles, and tendons in his wings were connected to his back. He set them in motion. It was what he had to do.

*Fly*, the Red Moon demanded.

Hector took another step forward to the edge of the pedestal. He spread his wings with a crack and the sound, forceful and vibrant, pre-vailed in his ears over the rumbling of the storm, the howling of the wind, and the distant roar of a dragon awakening.

Then he jumped.

# BONUS CHAPTER: MOONS AND WATERFALLS

Lady Fiera sat cross-legged at the top of an obelisk that overlooked the Square of Yesterday. From there she watched the city with an absent air, oblivious to a storm so brutal that it seemed like it wanted to erase the world; oblivious to the Red Moon that brought the sky to a standstill above her head.

From a nearby temple came the chant of the worshipers of the Immaculate Heresy, an insane accelerating melody; after their song they would slit the throats of two dozen slaves to celebrate the coming of the blessed moon. The whole city was a chaos of celebrations.

Esmael approached his fellow black angel with a few quick flaps of his wings. He tried to get close to her silently, but when he was within a few yards' distance Lady Fiera stood up and looked at him sidelong with a sneering smile on her lips.

"You still have a lot to learn to catch me off guard," she warned.

"I thought you would be at Count Ortan's party," he said. Esmael was young; he was a long way from the moment when he'd be sworn in as Lord of Assassins of Rocavarancolia.

The black angel shook her head.

"I'm not in the mood for a party," she grumbled. "Damn nostalgia and damn melancholy. Visiting my homeland was not the best decision."

Esmael landed next to her and studied her carefully. The woman's savage beauty was obscured by an elusive shadow, a kind of vague sadness. He was greatly surprised to see Lady Fiera show signs of vulnerability.

"Ah . . ." she whispered, and let out a vibrant laugh that dispelled all trace of turmoil from her expression. "I couldn't help it, I allowed myself a moment of weakness. I had to see the diamond waterfall again. It's been a while since I've visited. Years." She looked back at him. "I must have told you about it," she said, and Esmael responded by shaking his head. "It's one of the wonders of my world: a waterfall that falls from a cliff made of diamond and crystal," she explained. "It's a wondrous cascade of water, it plummets more than eighty yards to the ground, but it's not the height that makes it so incredible. At twilight the water is tinted by all colors of the spectrum, it's filled with lights that dance and sparkle. It's majestic, words cannot do it justice. I haven't found anything like it on any of the planets I've been to." She looked Esmael in the eyes. "You don't visit your world anymore, do you?"

The black angel shook his head again.

"There's nothing there for me," he answered with scorn.

Esmael renounced the land where he was born. In fact, he was embarrassed by it. His home planet was called Nubla, and it was a world of meek cowards, a harmless land. Its landscape was a succession of pastures and seas that were always calm, and its inhabitants mirrored the countryside: they were a gentle and weak people, a bunch of simpletons with no ambition. When Rocavarancolia conquered it, they turned it into a breeding planet. The potential of its people was tremendous, despite their placid and servile nature. The harvests of Nubla were magnificent. Besides, the people thought of the inhabitants of Rocavarancolia as godlike. They idolized them, worshiped them . . . there was no greater honor for them than serving the kingdom. It didn't matter if they were enslaved or used as cannon fodder in the wars waged with other worlds. The night of Samhein was the most anticipated night of the year because it gave them a chance to become a real part of Rocavarancolia: to become gods themselves.

In the first few years after his transformation, Esmael had visited his world on several occasions, and each time he felt more disgusted. Everyone adored him in the same exaggerated way that they adored anything related to Rocavarancolia. His parents even went to the extreme of building a small altar in his honor in the dump that had been his bedroom. That servility had ended up nauseating him. After six visits he decided it didn't make sense to return. He'd broken all ties with his world.

"There's nothing about it that you miss?" Lady Fiera asked him, curious, as if she were trying to find a reflection of her own weakness.

The black angel scowled. For a second, he remembered the moons of Nubla. There were twelve that orbited the planet, and the nights that they all coincided in the sky were amazing . . . as if a gigantic bead necklace had broken apart in the heavens. When Esmael was young, he could spend hours watching the slow movement of those moons in the sky, mesmerized, lost in the resounding majesty of that spectacle that left him breathless. He frowned. That child had been dead for a long time.

Nubla was a cesspool. It was a cesspool back then and it always would be, with or without moons in the sky.

"Nothing," he answered, with a fierce smile. "Nubla stopped being my world when the Red Moon transformed me. I belong to Rocavarancolia," he asserted. "In body and soul."

# DELETED SCENE

The heartbeat of Rocavarancolia sped up. Even the clouds themselves, stretched gray threads beneath gigantic white cumulonimbus, seemed to move faster than usual, as if they were in a hurry to get out of the city, as if they knew what was about to happen and refused to be present. The contrast between the speedy movement of those masses of suspended water and the majestic stillness of the castle floating in the air was overwhelming.

"I'll never get tired of looking at it," Ricardo said. "It's amazing."

Hector agreed. The castle was a shocking spectacle, even unfinished as it was. It floated solemn and powerful in the sky, a hundred yards above the winding streets of Rocavarancolia: a chaos of towers and turrets that emerged from three sturdy rectangular buildings joined by curving bridges.

It had started to appear a week ago. First there were the pointed rooftops of the towers, like upside-down ice-cream cones in the air. The next day, the top floors of the towers appeared beneath the conical rooftops. They were made of walls of tiny irregular stones, dotted with small windows that appeared to be scattered randomly throughout. Little by little, day by day, the castle grew more detailed as the outlines of arcades, buttresses, terraces, battlements, flags, and banners all came into view . . .

Bruno flew toward it on the third day, when twenty completed towers now floated in the void, so close to one another that they looked like absurd bouquets of stone hanging in midair. From below, they watched him pass through the walls, and at first they thought that he'd used some spell to do it. When he rejoined them on the ground, he told them that it hadn't been necessary.

"The castle is intangible. An ethereal presence that floats in the sky," he explained.

"A ghost castle?"

The Italian shrugged his shoulders.

"Perhaps . . . Or maybe it will gain solidity once it is complete. Or perhaps it's not really there, but rather on its way between this world and another. I do not know. And another thing: it is occupied. I ran into people as I was exploring. They are human, at least the majority are."

"Did they see you?" Hector asked, worried about the possibility that the castle could pose a threat to them.

Bruno looked up and his top hat wobbled dangerously on his head.

"They saw me, yes, but they did not pay any attention to me. I suspect that they might be accustomed to strange presences in their castle."

Hector and Ricardo sat atop a rock promontory located in the southeast of the city, watching the unfinished fortress. An enormous pedestal of gray marble was behind them, with no trace of the statue or monument that it once supported. From that particular spot in the city they had an exceptional view of the floating castle. Two pale guards passed behind the battlements, with long lances slung over their shoulders; both had long white hair and were dressed in the same light armor, the color of bone.

The two boys were silent for a long time, leaning with their backs against the rock. Ricardo gave Hector a pat on his shoulder to get his attention.

"Look at the sentinels," he said as he stood up.

The two pale watchmen had stopped around a bend in the battlement and pointed toward the west, in the exact direction of Rocavaragalago. Today, its red walls seemed to exude a restless scarlet mist.

"Do you think they're pointing to Rocavaragalago?" Hector asked.

"Of course! Of course that's where they're pointing!" Ricardo turned to him, smiling from ear to ear. "It's not just them slowly appearing before us—we're also appearing to them!"

Then he got up and climbed onto the pedestal behind them. He began jumping on it and gesturing wildly while he shouted in the direction of the castle.

"Hey! Over here!" he shouted. "Can you see us? You in the castle! Do you see us?"

"Do you think that's a good idea?" Hector asked.

"What if they can help us get out of Rocavarancolia?" he said.

Hector doubted it. He stood up and climbed onto the pedestal too, although he didn't shout. He looked at his friend with a furrowed brow, wondering if he should stop him or let him continue with his crazy stunt.

As he looked at the castle he saw that Ricardo's cries had gotten the attention of the two guards. One of them took off running inside one of the towers while the other stayed on the battlement, looking at them on the alert, gripping the lance in his hands.

Soon there was a huge commotion on the rampart. Almost twenty people emerged from the castle. Most of them, to Hector's dismay, were soldiers armed with bows, harquebuses, and rifles.

Some of them aimed in their direction. He looked at Ricardo out of the corner of his eye. His friend still waited excitedly. Of the newcomers, two were dressed entirely in black, and by their posture and the behavior of those around them it was clear that they were the ones in charge. One was a muscular man about fifty years old, with harsh, weather-beaten features; the other was a young man of barely twenty. Hector realized that they were related, perhaps father and son.

The younger man looked directly at him from above. His gaze was somber, his demeanor dangerous. They looked at each other for a long while, one in the air, from the battlement of the unfinished castle, the other atop the empty pedestal in the city of ruins. Hector wondered what the young man's story was and what had brought him there, what twisted magic or science was responsible for them both coinciding at that precise moment, in that very place.

# Character Glossary

## The Harvest of Samhein

The name given to the group of twelve teenagers that Denestor Tul brought to Rocavarancolia from Earth.

HECTOR: A shy kid, kind of clumsy, who always tries to stay in the background and not attract attention.

NATALIA: A surly teenager, very active and quick to anger. She sees shadows that are not visible to anyone else.

RICARDO: A natural leader, who soon takes charge of the group. He's athletic and noble minded.

BRUNO: A strange boy, cold and distant. He spent most of his life on Earth in seclusion. He is said to bring bad luck.

ADRIAN: The youngest. A goofy kid, as quick to show enthusiasm as he is to panic. He's afraid of fire. He was gravely wounded shortly after the harvest arrived at Rocavarancolia.

MARCO: Not what he seems. He is Mistral, the shapeshifter.

MARINA: A pretty girl with blue eyes. Hector is attracted to her. On Earth she wrote stories that were later discovered to be about Rocavarancolia.

ALEX: An extroverted boy with a very peculiar sense of humor. He felt guilty for getting his sister to accompany him to Rocavarancolia. He died from a fatal spell at one of the city's enchanted towers.

MADELEINE: Alex's sister. A red-haired beauty, at first glance frivolous and superficial.

LIZBETH: A girl with extraordinary leadership qualities and maternal instincts.

RACHEL: A girl with a joyful, optimistic personality. She is immune to all nonprimordial magic.

DARIO: A boy who did not join the rest of the group. In a chance encounter with the others, he ended up gravely wounding Adrian.

# THE ROYAL COUNCIL

DENESTOR TUL: Demiurge of Rocavarancolia and guardian of Highlowtower. He has the ability to give life to inanimate objects.

LADY SERENA: A ghost whose greatest desire is to die.

LADY SCAR: A pale woman covered with scars. She's the commander of the kingdom's armies and the guardian of the Royal Pantheon. She vies with Esmael for the position of regent.

ESMAEL: A black angel. The Lord of Assassins, a creature as beautiful as he is cruel. His greatest desire is to become king of Rocavarancolia.

UJTHAN: A warrior whose body is covered with tattoos.

BELISARIUS: An ancient sorcerer wrapped in endless bandages. He was found dead shortly after the arrival of the harvest.

ENOCH THE DUSTY: A vampire. He's been thirsty and desperate for over thirty years. He almost killed Adrian, but ultimately spared him.

RORCUAL: The kingdom's alchemist. Years ago he became invisible from a spell gone wrong, and since then he's been unable to reverse the process.

LADY DREAM: A sorceress with extraordinary powers. She sees the past, present, and future. She has predicted that the end of Rocavarancolia is near.

MISTRAL, THE SHAPESHIFTER: He infiltrated the harvest after killing Marco. He promised Alexander that he would look after his sister.

THE LEXEL BROTHERS: Two unusual beings who hate each other with a passion and are perpetually in conflict.

HURYEL: The kingdom's regent. He has been on his deathbed for some time. Lady Scar and Esmael aspire to take his place once he passes away.

LADY SPIDER: Not a member of the council. She's an enormous arachnid who acts as a servant to the others.

# ACKNOWLEDGMENTS

To the same people listed in the first volume, for the same reasons and with the same desire: that they stay with me on this journey; without them, it wouldn't be worth it.

Also, to all of the places that in one way or another have inspired Rocavarancolia: the places that actually exist, as well as those that are the products of others' imaginations. To Vitoria, which once again lent me its cemetery; to Santander, which lent me its lighthouse; to Granada, which in a matter of hours bewitched me for a lifetime; to Barcelona, where it's always a pleasure to return; to Madrid, because—despite the chaos—it agrees with me more and more; and to Gijón, which, once a year during its "Semana Negra," becomes a truly enchanted city.

And to the fictional places, not just cities, that have accompanied me throughout all these years and that, in one way or another, also appear in Rocavarancolia. To Middle-earth, because honestly, that's where everything began; to Gormenghast; to the asteroid B612; to the loony Discworld; to Fantastica, where the stories are Neverending; to the bloody lands of Westeros; to Hyperion; to Melniboné; to Unknown Kadath; to the cities of Calvino; and to the many, many other worlds and lands that made me dream.

# ABOUT THE AUTHOR

José Antonio Cotrina was born in Vitoria, Spain, in 1972. He started publishing short stories and novelettes at the beginning of the nineties, and his first full-length novel, *Las fuentes perdidas* (The Lost Sources), appeared in 2003. *Las fuentes*, a dark fantasy piece with a road movie premise, showed his inclination toward stories that mix the fantastic with the macabre.

Since then he's published fantasy, horror, and science fiction for all ages. The *Cycle of the Red Moon* trilogy is his best-known YA work, as well as the later *La canción secreta del mundo* (The Secret Song of the World). Among his many accolades he holds a Kelvin (one of Spain's biggest fantasy awards) for *Las puertas del infinito* (The Gates of Infinity), which Cotrina cowrote with Víctor Conde. He also writes and publishes with Gabriella Campbell. *Crónicas del fin* (Chronicles of the End) is one of their joint works.